HOUNDED ON PREDATOR PLANET

Vicky L. Holt

Contents

GLOSSARY

G lossary

Amity Diaz Female Main Character (FMC) of Book 3. An exobiologist, she brings her love of living things with her to planet Ikthe. She befriended one of the planet's deadliest creatures and has an ineffable positive attitude. Heart mate to Natheka.

BoKama Supporting Female Character in all five books. Co-governs with Sister Queen the Ikma Scabmal Kama. She has been trying to usurp her place without luck so far.

CeCe Pain FMC of Book 5. A hydrogeologist, free diver, and neural network developer, CeCe put the finishing touches on VELMA, the artificial general intelligence used on many IGMC ships.

Chris Abusive ex-partner of Esra Weaver in Book 1, also works in administrative echelons of IGMC.

Demolition and Propulsion Hyperconnected Network Entity Software that runs systems on Mining Planet 13. (Stranded on Mining Planet)

Diablo Male pazathel-nax pup wounded in Book 2 that Amity befriends and heals in Book 3. Mischievous but lovable addition to Predator Planet.

Drail Male Main Character (MMC) of Stranded on Mining Planet, the free novella offered to newsletter subscribers. He's part of the security for the Causeway Passage Authority administered by the Dam Svai, a reptilian alien species in the outer reaches.

EEP X215 Emergency Egress Pod designed by mechanical engineer Pattee Crow Flies of Book 2. A self-sustaining mini-ship designed to scan planetary bodies in search of one habitable by its single occupant, it has everything needed to sustain life from six months to a year. Provisions, limited tools, medical and surgical functions, multiple scanning abilities and VELMA all serve to make the EEP the only way to travel. It is Land Only, however; no leaving once it enters the atmosphere.

Esra Weaver FMC of Book 1. Exogeologist and miner, Esra tried to leave her baggage behind, but was forced to face it all again when fighting for her life on Ikthe. Heart mate to Naraxthel Roika. Curious, plucky, and a little sarcastic, she really loves rocks.

Heart mate In the old stories, it was told that one might find their heart mate or soul mate when one reaches adulthood. Heart mates share their lives together rather than separating to pursue solitary lives.

HemoSupp An electrolyte/supplement solution to be used in drastic situations where blood loss or profound dehydration have taken place.

Hestra Gas giant planet under the relaxed stewardship of the reptilian race, the Dam Svai. Featured in Stranded on Mining Planet (SoMP).

Hestra's Handmaid Hestra's moon which is on a crash course with the planet in three or four revolutions, and the base of limited IGMC mining operations. (SoMP)

Hivelt MMC of Book 2. A ferocious but introverted hunter, Hivelt regrets all dealings he had with the queen and feigned his death in Book 2 in order to escape her clutches. He's a simple hunter who just wants a nice bowl of fish stew.

Holy Goddesses of Shegoshel Represented by the binary star system, the Holy Goddesses are an Elder and Younger Sister goddess pair who oversee the Theraxl people and any beings that visit the sister planets. Loving and beneficent, their greatest joy is giving gifts and blessings and often, spiritual dreams and messages, to sentient beings on the sister planets. They tend not to interfere but give encouragement and inspiration to aid their so-called "children". Are they real or somehow manufactured by hallucinogens found on the planets or otherwise induced?

Ikma Scabmal Kama Female Antagonist for entire series. The queen has grown worse over the years in her thirst for blood and sex. She trusts no one, and no one trusts her.

Ikshe The home planet for the Theraxl race. Governed by a matriarchal society, it is peaceful, organized, paradisiacal, and populated with a creative and hungry race. Culture, art, science, engineering, architecture, and agriculture all play important roles on Ikshe with females engaging in every part of the work. Males are encouraged to become hunters, but some do choose other vocations. Except eunuchs. They didn't choose that.

Ikthe The sacred hunting grounds planet where the hunters fly to hunt big game. Bringing back ship loads of butchered meat, they provide much of the protein and fats the alien race requires to fuel their powerful and muscular bodies. Females are forbidden from visiting the hunting grounds.

InterGalactic Mining Conglomerate A gigantic collection of mining corporations with its reaches throughout the known universe but always in search of more and better. Innovative, wealthy, powerful, people flock to IGMC for employment and high-risk jobs for high pay.

Joan Wu FMC of Book 4. Joan is an exobotanist who lost her joy in living when she lost her husband two years ago. Going through the motions, her only tether to life was her best friend, CeCe. Waking up on Ikthe, she discovered she was trapped in the most dangerous region on the entire planet and surrounded by danger, had to decide whether life was worth living.

Kerberos 90 A distant asteroid intended to be mined by an intrepid group of IGMC miners.

Kezti Bug-like alien race, enemies of the Dam Svai race and known pirates always eager to make shady deals. (SoMP)

Lucidity IGMC's executive science class ship in a convoy of other ships headed to Kerberos 90.

Machete Common tool used in jungle habitats for clearing foliage.

Mass spectrometer One of VELMA's many scanning tools used to measure the chemical makeup of things for identification and classification purposes.

Mining Planet 13 A distant moon on which common ores are being mined. (SoMP)

Mining Ship A massive destructive ship used to exploit the most possible resources with the least amount of caution.

MRE Meals Ready to Eat, standard IGMC issue freeze-dried food. Just add water and enjoy!

Naraxthel Roika MMC of Book 1. The mightiest hunter of all hunters, good and noble warrior who has yet to win a chance at a sanctioned mating that would produce offspring. Heart mate to Esra Weaver.

Natheka MMC of Book 3. A runner, a dreamer and a singer, Natheka never doubts his heart or his mate, even when his heart transition happens at the worst possible time. Heart mate to Amity Diaz.

Pattee Crow Flies FMC of Book 2. Descended from a First Nation, Pattee was uncharacteristically suited to life on Predator Planet thanks to the dogged instruction from her blue-collar father. On Ikthe, she must come to terms with the misdeeds of her past in order to embrace her future as Hivelt's heart mate.

PH-4RT The gas giant planet around which Mining Planet 13 orbits. See also Hestra and Hestra's Handmaid. The miners of MP-13 call it Phart. (SoMP)

Planet Mass Insertion Vehicle P-MIV for short, because PIV was too provocative. An advanced mining ship that penetrates a planet's first twenty meters of crust and initiates a massive erosion event to hasten the mining process during planet harvesting.

Pre-Harvest Recon Exploratory Device PHRED, the machine-learning artificial intelligence that runs the P-MIV.

Raxkarax MMC of Book 4. Brave and fierce, Raxkarax has an Ace up his sleeve when it comes to hunting on Ikthe. When he travels to rescue the unknown human from the Agothe-Fatheza bog, he must bring all of his knowledge to bear. Heart mate to Joan Wu.

Raxthezana MMC of Book 5. The tragedy from his past has followed him for decades, and he refuses to let happiness get in the way of solid research. Paired with CeCe Pain.

Shay Leviticus FMC of Stranded on Mining Planet. Shea is smart as a whip and loves her career in mining demolition. She also has a side project that could change the course of human history. No big deal.

VELMA FMC in entire series. Vector Egress Liaison Machine-learning AI knows it all, literally. Without VELMA, nothing that occurs in the series would be possible, and where would we be without a solid understanding of poop?

1

Amity Diaz

"A person moving through nature—however wild, however remote ... is never alone."   Richard Nelson

I crawled out of the mangled and twisted metal that used to be my emergency egress pod into the blinding light. A huge spider web of fractures laced my helmet. With the inner screen bleating alarms and flashing red and yellow lights, I knew the integrity of my suit was compromised.

My left leg had no feeling. I grimaced as I crawled, my leg dragging through the dark gravel of this desolate terrain. I scanned the rocky landscape for a secure place to assess my injuries and the state of my ship. Spying a cave in an outcrop of orange and black rocks, I headed in that direction.

Five feet from the entrance, I gathered a handful of pebbles and tossed them into the opening. I heard them scatter on hard rock, but nothing else. "Let this one thing go right," I mumbled to myself and crawled inside. My helmet light didn't work. Grabbing my utility torch from a pants pocket, I shone it inside. It wasn't much of a cave, but all I needed was seclusion and a defensible position while I figured out what in the ever-living-hell I was going to do now.

With a final cry, I entered the cave, taking care not to bump my injured leg over the rubble at the entrance. The cave was about four feet deep and five feet high. I wouldn't be able to stand, but something told me my standing days might be on hold. I collapsed against an inner wall where my body was obscured by the rock formation, but I could still see my broken ship.

Smoke billowed out from one of the engines and sparks rained from where the nose cone used to be. That worried me. I shifted on the ground, took a deep breath, and lowered my eyes to my leg. I hissed at the sight. A twisted piece of black metal jutted out from my thigh. That explained the warmth. Two inches farther and I would be bleeding from my femoral artery. Good night, Amity.

"Computer, what's my location?"

"Your suit's integrity is compromised. Please return to the EEP for possible emergency treatment."

"The EEP is busted," I said. "What's my location?"

"Unable to comply."

"What about the nanosatellite array?"

"Unable to comply."

Dammit. "Computer, where is your hard drive located?"

"I have redundant hard drives located in the nose cone and the insulated buffer trap."

I craned my neck to see the crumpled pod. The smoke cloud had lessened to a gray ribbon. Well, the nose cone was out. "Where is the insulated buffer trap?"

"Access panel to the insulated buffer trap is located on the flight computer's side wall."

The flight computer, comprised of a set of monitors facing the single occupant's chair and an enclosed processing unit below, normally filled a small desk's worth of space inside the pod. I recalled climbing straight out from the chair into daylight. Through the non-existent computer panel, to be exact. I tracked the scar on the hill where black metal shards peppered the rocks. If my leg wasn't permanently skewered, it might be worth scavenging the wreckage, in case the hard drive was salvageable.

"What are your capabilities right now?"

"I am able to assess suit integrity and monitor life support systems. I can also access a large downloaded file found in your helmet's computer memory. Would you like me to access the file?"

I blew out a breath. "Not yet. My IntraVisor screen has too many cracks. Can you read my vitals out loud to me?"

"Blood pressure is 120 over 80. Your pulse is 87 bpm and your temperature is 97.8 degrees Fahrenheit. Since your landing, I have monitored your vitals for thirteen hours and seventeen minutes, twelve hours, and forty-three minutes of which you were unconscious inside the ship."

"Great, great," I muttered while inspecting the metal shrapnel in my leg. "I don't know that I'd call that a landing, but whatever. Can you tell me how to safely remove a metal shard from my thigh?"

"Scanning suit, please stand by."

So far, I wasn't feeling woozy. Once I removed the impaled shard, there were no guarantees. Adrenalin flowed through my veins, and I noticed my vision acuity was amazing. Every detail jumped out at me, from the grain of the rocks to the particulate swirling in the air from my smoking vessel.

"Puncture located two point five inches from your femoral artery. Femoral pressure bladder activated. Please wait."

I felt a squeeze build in my leg, exactly like a blood pressure cuff.

"Do you have access to your MDpak?" the computer asked.

"Yes," I said. Tingling began to burn below the wound. My hands shook as I unzipped the pocket with the MDpak.

"Locate the green blister packet."

"Okay, I have it," I said. My breathing escalated. I examined the inch-square pouch with a small bio-absorbable nozzle.

"That is the blood clotting agent. When you have removed the object, you will place it in the wound."

"Okay," I said. "What do I do first?"

"Use the alcohol wipes to sterilize your gloves or hands, and wipe around the puncture." The computer said.

I cleaned everything twice. "Okay, computer."

"Can you shorten the object?"

I looked at my multi-tool. "I don't have anything that will cut this metal," I said. "Do I have to shorten it?"

"No. Prepare the blister packet and the wound dressing."

With heart racing, I forced my shaky hands to unscrew the lid of the nozzle of the blister packet and to cut a length of sterile polymer-infused biodegradable dressing.

"Administering a small dose of analgesic accompanied by a tetanus booster. Please be still," the computer said. I felt a tiny pinch in my arm. "Grasp the object. If the object is straight, pull out in a smooth motion. If the object is bent, you must work it carefully in each direction. Immediately apply the blister packet and wind the dressing around your thigh."

"*Dios mio*," I moaned as I grasped the metal piece. I had no idea how deep this thing was in my leg, or if it was twisted inside. "Three, two, GAAAHHHH!" My vision swam, but the shard was out and the section that had been embedded looked smooth. Good, no need to dig around in the wound any further. I fumbled the packet but stuffed it into my wound with the nozzle side-down as instructed and sprayed in the coagulate. Then I wept as I wound gauze around my thigh multiple times and secured it. I looked up toward the broken smoking wreckage, and then fell back onto the hard cave floor. "Computer, it just got really dark."

2

Natheka

A pleased growl erupted from my throat after I bid the brother-hood good day and struck out on the black rock. My patience had rubbed thin as our group crossed the desolate divide of craggy rocks, the soft travelers moving too slow, inhibited by their physical limitations. Their spirits were as strong-willed and brave as Theraxl, I noted with admiration. But I wanted to move faster. To *run*.

The afternoon suns beat like the hooves of the ice-walkers on my back and sweat rolled down my neck and between my armor. But I felt no heat.

My brothers showed agitation at the notion of an invisible net en-trapping Ikthe. They scowled to think of beacons welcoming count-less races to our hunting grounds. But I felt no anger.

Water sloshed in my canister. It was running low, so I would need to find a water source deep in the Black Heart range. But I felt no thirst.

From the moment I heard Hivelt's heart mate, Pattee, refer to another human on a ship, followed by her frantic voice shouting in her language, my heart-home seized. The draw to the new human was a tangible force, a tether braided in woaiquovelt pulled taut.

This, I could not explain, except to look at the facts in front of my fangs.

The odd and soft travelers with no connection to my people had found their heart mates among two of my brethren. To see my warrior-brothers heel to their women did not offend me as it seemed to offend Raxthezana, but rather I witnessed a fusion of souls. The myth of the heart mates, as a reality, seemed to lift each person, rather than reveal weaknesses. The humans seemed stronger, larger than their small frames, and my hunter brothers seemed rounded and fulfilled, where before they were unfinished. In very deed, becoming heart mates seemed to craft a unified whole out of two separate beings. Astonishing.

This wove together my memories of adolescence with my current unease. I felt unpolished and unrefined. I felt incomplete.

In addition, something was off on the planet. None of my brethren admitted it, but the rainy season, the mass migration of the grass-eaters and subsequent rokhura attack: all were premature for the time of year. Considering the arrival of the mysterious soft travelers, I must assume the Holy Goddesses were toying with the Theraxl race.

I would look upon every subsequent event as a message from the goddesses. And judging by the unfamiliar yet persistent tug upon my heart-home, I felt a renewed hope that their message promised a heart mate for me.

3

Amity

I came to in a courtyard brimming with colorful floating insects and dripping with delicate green vines. Blinking slowly, I rubbed my eyes and wiped my hands on my dress. I looked down. A white dress! I laughed. I hadn't worn a dress in a couple of decades. Since my quinceañera, probably. I heard a bubbling fountain but before I could get up and look for it, I saw a sheer purple curtain part, and two tall, gorgeous females padded out on bare feet—but not human feet. They wore green slinky gowns that pooled at their feet when they stood above me. One reached her hand down to help me up.

"Welcome, Amity."

"Thanks," I said. "Sorry I'm late." *Wait, what?* It felt right to say it, though.

"You are exactly on time," said the other one.

I stood before them but had to look up into their black and red eyes. I felt breathless. "You're so beautiful."

A tinkling laugh. The first one smiled, and her fangs gleamed in the diffuse white light. "As are you. Your name means friendship, does it not?"

"Yeah," I said. My throat was dry, and I started coughing. "Could I have a drink?" My voice croaked.

"Be a friend to all, Amity," the tall one said.

"Don't forget your name, beautiful friend." The shorter one said. Their long-braided hair fell to their waists, and their slender muscular arms hung relaxed at their sides.

I frowned and continued to cough.

I closed my eyes and coughed painfully, my chest burning. When I tried to open my eyes, smoky gray light filtered between my lids. Acrid smoke filled my mouth, and I coughed again. I scrabbled to my hands and knees, appreciating the tingling in my injured leg. It was free of pain but moved like it weighed three times more than usual.

In the direction of my pod sat a thick, oily cloud of black smoke. A breeze blew it straight into the cave I had sheltered in.

"Dammit," I cursed and crawled out and along the outcropping, trying to find fresh air. The lights and alarms continued to flash on my IntraVisor. All the cracks obscured the notifications. "Computer, read my vitals to me."

They were normal. I sipped water from my suit's supply as I crawled along the boulders. I still coughed, and now my leg throbbed. "Can I have another dose of pain medication?"

"Yes. You have thirteen doses left total. Confirm second dose?"

I clenched my teeth and breathed in through my nose. "Confirm second dose."

The analgesic worked instantaneously. I breathed easier and crawled with less effort. The orange rocks shrank in size; the outcropping melted into scrubby trees. I stopped and sat against the wide trunk of a tall tree.

Shaking the cobwebs from my mind after the crash, I inspected my surroundings. If the smoke cleared, I would rather hide out in the empty cave. The scrubby trees and bushes expanded into a tall forest that blanketed a low mountain range. The tree I leaned against looked out of place here. The farther between the trees I tried to see, the darker it grew. My blood oxygen level was lower than normal. A spiderweb crack in the bottom right corner obscured the altimeter gauge. I sighed and leaned my helmet against the trunk.

A spring green vine snapped over my field of vision for a moment then I felt a tightening around my neck. Before I could react, more vines erupted from the spines in the trunk and wove a green net securing me to the tree.

"Heart rate approaching 150 bpm. Do you require assistance?"

"Not yet." Thankfully, the vine couldn't crush the axial ring at my neck, but I found I couldn't move my limbs.

My hand was already bound to my leg, but it rested only an inch from the pocket with my multi-tool. I noticed when I tried to wriggle my legs, the vines tightened. I slackened my arm, and sure enough, the vine loosened as well.

With controlled breaths, I calmed myself and moved my hand millimeters at a time. The vines didn't appear to have any function other than trapping, but I was no botanist.

My fingers touching the end of my multi-tool, I focused on remaining as relaxed and pliant as the plant needed me to be. I stretched my fingers, slowly sliding it out of my pocket, when I heard a loud cracking noise. The tree I rested against seemed to shudder and quiver at my back.

A feeling of doom engulfed me, and my heart resumed its race to an unknown finish line. My tool was firm in my grip now. I roved my gaze over my body without moving my head. The vines had lashed me with countless tendrils.

Another crack split the air, and a warm rush of fetid air enveloped me from behind. With the vines' purpose unveiled, I tensed every muscle in panic. Cutting through the vines that wrapped my right leg, I bent it and dug my heel into the ground. I wrapped my arm behind my knee and yanked with my shoulder, smaller vines snapping. My right arm was free. The vines would pull me inside this vile tree, and I would be digested alive, if the smell of rotting flesh was an accurate indication.

I fought the binding, twisting where I could and working my other arm free of the tendrils. A thick ropy vine pulled at my waist, so I attacked it with my tool.

Using my left leg for more leverage, I pulled myself forward on the ground, scooting my butt across dead leaves and black humus, every centimeter a victory.

A green vine slapped across my helmet impeding my vision. Crap! The fissures in my glass splintered more.

"Computer," I said, "I need help. Now!"

"Assessing situation," the computer said. "Please standby."

"Um," I said. "I don't have time to ..."

The vines slackened, not by much, but enough that I immediately clawed my way out of them, scrambling through the tangle, cutting lengths, and yanking them off my suit and from around my neck and helmet with desperate slices. My breaths came in rapid bursts, anxiety and determination coupling to give me the urgency I needed to truly escape. I scrambled through the underbrush on all fours, forgetting about my hobbled leg in my efforts to get farther away. I couldn't help the whimpers that eked from between my lips as I fought free of the vines, and then subsequent bushes that may or may not have been colluding to capture me. Leaves that stuck to my suit made me shiver, and I swiped at stems and branches with frantic fingers. Free of the tree line, I panted and looked back into the greenery.

"Thank you!" Panting on all fours, I inspected the foliage around me and faced the rocky landscape where my ship billowed smoke.

"How did you do that?" I said, standing and brushing dirt off my suit, looking back at the tree with a gaping vertical slit.

"I detected the tree's low-frequency wavelength bioacoustics and sent the matching wavelength back to its vines, temporarily disrupting its ground transduction communication," the computer said. "I am satisfied that it worked."

I huffed a laugh. "Okay. But I thought your abilities were limited."

"They were until you required assistance. I was programmed to access the downloaded files upon your request," the computer said. "I am called VELMA, K90-Miner 106," she said. "The downloaded file was installed by my neural network nanoseconds before your ship impacted with water. Due to helmet damage, I cannot communicate with my neural network or the nanosatellite array. However, I am running a limited AI program from the microcomputer in your earpiece. The file also contains information crucial to your survival on this planet."

I leaned against a huge rock, out of breath and trying to comprehend what VELMA just said.

"Very cool. But how did you transmit if my helmet is damaged?"

"I am utilizing older technology included in your helmet's manufacture intended as a redundancy back-up, a frequency modulation transmitter."

Feeling my leg's injury throb for a second, I shifted my feet and continued leaning on the big rock that was my new totem of stability. "So, what you're saying is, my helmet is like a little FM radio."

A pause.

"Affirmative."

I stared at the wreckage, ignored my leg, and chuckled.

"Keep listening to K90 Mix One-oh Six for all your traffic and weather updates," I said.

"Unfortunately, the unit only transmits up to 100 meters," VEL-MA responded. "Your listening audience will be limited."

"Heh, as long as you keep transmitting to ward off killer trees, that's okay."

"Very well, Miner K90-106."

"You can call me Amity, VELMA," I said. "I think you and I are going to be great friends."

4

Natheka

The magnetic burst field disrupted my communications device in my helmet, as expected, so I disabled it. Scanning the region, I moved efficiently, scaling cliffs and clearing narrow crevasses after reassuring myself there wasn't a ship in them.

Unforgiving terrain cut my palms, but I climbed with ease. I remembered a prime cave from my first hunt on Ikthe, many cycles ago. It would be a logical place to stop at nightfall. Even with my helmet's technologies, climbing at night was too perilous. I would use the time to replenish my body and map a route through the mountains.

With the burst field causing misdirection, there was only one way to find the crash site. Canvassing the entire area. However, my instincts pulled me in one direction more than others.

To the maar.

I frowned, the memory clawing at my attention.

An Iktheka's first hunt determined the path he would take throughout his long life. If one was lucky, a hunter might receive a sponsor. Otherwise, he was forced to learn the wiles of Ikthe by trial and error. Such learning was effective up until one was killed.

I had been fortunate. For whatever reason, Naraxthel had chosen to sponsor me, and joined me on my first foray into Ikthe's bosom. He taught me the most common game trails the rokhural followed, and where the best water could be found. He warned me of the dangers many hunters never bothered to mention, letting the novice hunters bumble and suffer through their first weeks, hampering their abilities to secure food for the sisters. Naraxthel taught me to avoid the red-trunked tree with insidious fibers that worked their way between armor and skin, causing intense irritation. He taught me to bind minor cuts on exposed skin to prevent airborne toxins from festering into larger wounds.

His careful instructions made the difference between not only surviving my first hunt, but exceeding expectations.

And then on the last night of our hunt, I had made a foolish mistake, and almost died a fool's death. Had Naraxthel been dishonorable, he might have bagged the coveted ikadax while I fell to my death at the bottom of a crevasse.

A prickle danced across the back of my neck, a physical reminder of an old memory. I looked up at the dusky sky, but all was clear.

I found the cave, amused to see it untouched and dusty. Perhaps it wasn't that valuable as a cave, else it would be inhabited. Nevertheless, when I spoke *Zagoshe*, the bead light illuminated, and I felt welcomed.

I drank deeply of my water canister and ate two strips of dried meat with a handful of food from the black tree. With my back against the rock wall, I considered the mystical pull beckoning me to the maar.

It was the place I feared death for the first time, and the place of a sacred dream in which I encountered the Holy Sisters of Shegoshel.

Perhaps the pull I felt was not from one of these humans, but from a sacred calling.

Yet the reinvigoration of my heart-home suggested it was, indeed, a heart mate that pulled, as if strings connected from my heart to theirs.

I sang the ancient song of the heart mate, hearing the trailing lyrics susurrate off the cave walls and ripple around me. Mayhap the occupant of the crashed ship was my heart mate, mayhap not, but I would find them and keep them alive. And after I brought them to the others, I would find my own heart mate. I desired to feel the wholeness I witnessed in my brothers. The emptiness in my heart had clamored at me for cycles.

Every time I left the homes of my little hunters, I wished I could bring them with me, if only on a daring hike to a stream where we might dig in the mud for the long-tongued wing-eaters. I once suggested such an outing, and Jotheka's mother stared at me and pulled him closer to her legs. I dared not ask little Ika's dam after that.

I pulled out my littlest blade and two chunks of hardwood. I would carve two of the long-tongued wing-eater, one for each hunter. They had growing collections of little animals by my hand and blade. Sometimes I wondered if a portion of my heart did not leave my body and enter the wooden animals, to stay and look after my offspring while I was away.

5

Amity

The scrape with the tree had my stomach in knots, and I kept looking over my shoulder at the imposing black forest. The tree line demarked an obvious habitat boundary, but something dangerous yet beguiling whispered to me from the wilderness. No, thank you.

On this side of the tree line, gravel, stones, boulders, and outcroppings lay before me in a treacherous landscape. But it was devoid of movement.

A sharp glance at a black rock—I should be more suspicious, though.

Shrugging off the niggling doubts, I limped toward the shallow cave. The wind had changed again, now blowing the smoke to the north. Between the analgesic, leg wound and leftover cryosleep chemicals in my system, not to mention the adrenalin crash, I was whipped. My body needed rest so I could work on salvaging goods from the wreckage. I hoped to snag water pouches or MREs, as well as any equipment that survived. In a perfect world, I would have access to ropes and carabiners, a machete, limited mining tools, and my own science kit. Acrid air from the crash site penetrated the cracks in my helmet. Perhaps this was a perfect world, but the crash rendered my arrival far from it.

I sighed as I sat with effort and then gingerly lay back. Just a little siesta to take the edge off. As I drifted off, I seemed to remember something about a dress, but that made no sense whatsoever.

A strange chuffing sound woke me from a dreamless sleep.

Blinking frantically, I tried to remember where I was. Darkness enveloped me while memories of violet flames crossed my mind's eye.

Panting, I sat up, groping around myself for a large rock I'd noticed earlier. I found it, hefted it, and stilled, trying to locate the source of the chuffing.

Sound echoed off the walls, making it impossible to discern its origin. It wasn't getting closer, though.

There! It came from my left but sounded like it was outside the alcove. It was an odd coughing noise that ended abruptly but then was followed by a strange whine.

"VELMA, you mentioned files with crucial information," I said. "What kind of a planet did I land on? And wait." I cocked my head, but the chuffing had stopped. "You said your neural network downloaded the file *before* the pod hit water?"

"Affirmative."

I tried to recall the landscape. I hadn't seen or smelled any water. But the bigger fact remained. "I wasn't the first survivor from the *Lucidity* to land here, was I?"

"No. Miners 105 and 110 landed before you. Their names are Esra Weaver and Pattee Crow Flies, respectively. They are safe and among allies who visit this planet to hunt the predators that dwell here."

"Pattee's here? *Gracias a dios!*" I closed my eyes and clutched at my chest. My friend was here, on this planet, safe! If I had my rosary, I would kiss it.

I cleared my throat and heard more chuffing. Was it getting quieter?

"What kind of predators?" I said.

"Ikthe, or Predator Planet as the miners call it, is the home to hundreds of thousands of species, judging by data collected from scanning excrements," VELMA said.

My interest piqued; I raised a brow. "Oh yes, that is an efficient way to identify different organisms, as well as bioavailable nutrients. Good idea."

The AI paused for what seemed like a long time.

"Some might consider such scans superfluous," she said.

"Well, to the uninitiated, sure. But as a biologist, I can tell you with certainty that's a genius use of a mass spectrometer."

"Thank you," VELMA replied, and if I wasn't mistaken, there seemed to be a hint of smug pride in those two words. Impossible, of course. She, or it, was just an artificial intelligence.

"Now we've got to figure out what is making this noise."

"Judging by data available in the downloaded file, the noise belongs to a juvenile pazathel-nax, or "devil dog" as it is known colloquially by the hunters who travel here."

"*Santos Dios*, are you sure?"

"It is with eighty-nine per cent certainty. Variations between sound files suggest it has suffered an injury."

I gasped. No wonder it was getting quieter. I replaced the rock with my handheld flashlight and shined it toward the sound.

Eyeshine from four eyes reflected the light; I diverted it, so its glow revealed the dingy pale fur matted with blood, and tar-like substance attached to its throat. Was there a weird slug slowly asphyxiating the pup?

I crawled toward it and stopped two feet away. Everyone knew an injured and cornered animal could be dangerous, but how much more would be a creature nicknamed "devil dog"?

Closer inspection revealed the black substance was actually an organ. The chuffing noise, now weak, erupted from the partially swollen bag, and the whine emitted when it deflated.

"*Pobrecito*," I whispered. "Poor little thing; he needs help!"

"That may be true," VELMA said, "but I advise caution."

I ignored her advice and moved close enough to touch what to me, resembled a wolf more than a dog.

"VELMA," I said. "The mammal uses a vocal sac. I've only seen vocal sacs on anuran creatures. Amphibians like frogs or toads."

"You will be interested to learn that many of Ikthe's creatures possess the organ. The sacs transmit infrasonic waves undetectable to human ears."

"Is that how they communicate with each other?"

"Yes."

My head snapped up and I shined my light out onto the rocky terrain. Was its mother out there looking for it? I danced the beam across the rocks and the wreckage, but nothing stirred.

"I'm going to see if I can help it," I announced.

"Past human and pazathel-nax interactions have resulted in violence," VELMA said. "However, if you have any questions, I am at your service, Amity," VELMA said.

"Thank you for the warning," I said. "But I have experience with this kind of stuff." I crawled closer still, keeping eye contact with the animal. I could see its body shudder with difficult breaths. "Do the devil dogs use their vocal sacs to breathe as well?"

"No," VELMA said. "However, injuries to the sac often lead to death, as they contain a large network of subdermal circulatory tissue."

I was now petting the creature's head. It was large for a juvenile, the size of a Great Dane. I had one when I was a girl.

"That seems like a maladaptive evolutionary path," I murmured. Leaning close to its ear, I whispered, "Todo va a estar bien, perrito." *Everything is going to be fine, cute doggie.*

"The ambient average temperature on a vast majority of the planet is one hundred degrees," VELMA said. "If the superficial horizontal plexus is used to regulate thermal consistency, perhaps that is why it contains such a rich blood network."

"Fair point, VELMA," I said. The animal panted, its tongue lolled, and eyes closed, until it let its head drop to the side. It let out a huge sigh, and my own heart picked up its pace. "*Dios mio*, it could be dying." I scrambled right next to it and played my light across its massive body, looking for the source of its greatest threat.

The matted fur at its ear and the wheezing vocal sac seemed to be its only wounds. With gentle hands, I lifted its heavy head to inspect the other side. It was dirty, but there were no more injuries. "I think it hit its head, or something. I wonder what its natural habitat is?"

"The pazathel-nax packs migrate across the planet, traveling across ecosystems to hunt a variety of food sources. Their jaws possess 1200 psi force. They eat everything from a common rodent here called the jokapazathel, to the giant reptile called rokhura. In such cases, they work together as a pack to take down larger prey."

"Interesting," I said as I probed the head wound with my gloves. "They exhibit classic pack behavior, then. Evolution is remarkable."

With extreme care, I lifted the deflated sac and found the place it tore from the lower jaw. Its blood had clotted. Focusing the beam on it, I could see that if the tear had been just a little lower, it would have sheared a large vein.

"A near miss," I said. "Just like me."

I pulled out my MDPack and found the suture kit. "I'm going to stitch this up, VELMA. Is there any way you could tell me if something is coming? If I fix its sac, it might be able to call up the entire pack."

"I can modify the FM receiver to accept undetectable waves, to your ears, anyway. It is the best I can do with the limited technology."

"That's great, thank you." I found the items I needed. "We just do the best we can, right?" I placed a hand on the great chest of the dog and felt for its heartbeat. It fluttered and went still. A long moment later, it fluttered again. "If you fight, you can make it," I told the devil dog. "How about I call you Diablo?"

Removing my helmet, I placed it beside me in case I needed to ask VELMA a question. I found the ragged edges of the tear, and after spreading a thin layer of a topical anesthetic, ever so gently stitched up the seam. I wasn't a doctor or nurse, or an emergency medical technician, but I used to sew clothes for my dog when he was a puppy. My jaw ached after fifteen minutes of holding the flashlight between my teeth, but I finished and used a sani-cloth from the MDPack to clean the wound again. The more I watched Diablo's breathing, the more I thought the vocal sac wound wasn't the issue. I suspected the head trauma had given him a concussion, but I wasn't a vet, either.

Ignoring the aches and pains of my leg as I stood, I replaced my helmet and limped my way to the smoking wreckage. We both needed water, but Diablo did more than I. I still had a supply in my suit.

Nerves ratcheted up from the noise of every boot step on loose gravel, I flashed my light beam repeatedly to the dark forest and back to the wreckage as I drew closer. I hadn't heard the devil dog approach my cave. What else was I not hearing? According to VELMA, many of the animals were silent to human ears.

At the crash site, I examined the hole from which I'd crawled, and considered re-entering it. Smoke continued to ribbon up into the sky, disappearing into the inky night.

"VELMA, what are the odds something else from the pod might explode? I need supplies."

"Calculating, please standby," she said. "Zero-point seven chance the fractionated quark bomb would detonate, as it is encased in its Galvanite capsule and was not damaged during impact. The RR weapon rounds already detonated upon reentry into the atmosphere."

"Oh, wow," I said. "Okay, I'm going in."

"While in the pod, please find the panel marked with a green circle," VELMA said. "I advise you to prioritize collecting the pack inside."

Crawling inside the pod immediately triggered claustrophobia, especially in the pitch black with the strong smell of burning rubber, hot metal and melted plastics. My beam of light didn't reflect off metallic surfaces inside because it was all covered in oily soot.

I pressed on every panel within reach, but only a few of them opened with ease. Biting my lip, I found the green circle and pressed. A pack tumbled out, and I shone my light on the label.

Electrolyte+HemoSupp.

Gratitude flooded my chest, and I wasted no time opening one of the shiny red pouches and guzzling the sweet contents down. Counting out three more pouches, I realized they were worth their weight in gold. IGMC's survivalist experts conducted field expeditions with all their miners, and they often talked about *HemoSupp*, a blood supplement developed by their advanced medicine department for emergency cases. I never dreamed I would need it.

My leg throbbed, so I might have to rest and try again in the morning. But I needed to consider the possibility that if something else could go wrong, it would. I should probably gather as much as I could in one trip.

Finding the expandable rucksack, I started filling it to capacity. Ropes. Carabiners. Tools. Duct tape. Twine. Extra medical supplies. Resting my hand on the inflatable raft a moment, I considered. Should I? Why not? I dragged it out.

Poking at more panels, I found the drawer of pouched water and gave a cry of relief. Leaving the supplies in a pile just outside the opening, I crawled the rest of the way out with several pouches and a metal bowl from the pod's "kitchen" supplies.

The wolf continued its labored breathing, but I noticed its eyes moving beneath its lids. I removed my helmet. Realizing the bowl was premature, I set it aside and unscrewed the cap on a pouch, then dribbled water into its mouth. Once again, I used my teeth to hold the flashlight so I could use my hands to support its muzzle and drip the liquid. Steady dripping moistened its mouth and lolling tongue, so I continued until my jaw ached and my own mouth was dry. Two pouches later, I was satisfied the animal would be okay for a bit, and I opened another pouch to quench my own thirst.

I focused so much attention on Diablo that I didn't notice the brightening of the sky hours later. Startled that it was the dawn of the second day on this strange new planet, I rubbed my stinging eyes.

A stiff breeze out of the north whipped up, and I watched the smoke curl away and filter through the trees. The wind carried the smell of water on it. I glanced at the animal, but it was still sleeping. With two of us sharing water pouches, the supply would dwindle, though I would have needed to find a source regardless of a tagalong.

Fatigue dogged my footsteps, but I hiked north in search of the water, the collapsible jug hitched to a loop at my waist, and I put my helmet back on while I limped in what I thought was the right direction. I carried the machete I'd found safely stowed in one of the cubbies on the pod. I didn't know how useful it would be on this rocky terrain. The last time I used one was in a tropical jungle on Exterra 4, a small planet designated for biological field expedition training.

Scanning the rocks ahead, I wished I had a hiking pole instead. I looked back at the pazathel-nax as it slept. It hadn't moved, but it still breathed. The twinge in my leg snagged my attention, but I pushed through the discomfort, making my way between the larger rocks and boulders that littered the area. I kept the black slash of the wreck's skid marks to my left, figuring it must have hydroplaned off the lake or pond, whatever it had hit, before plowing the ground with its speed.

Imagining the impact fired my nerve endings; I was glad I slept through it. Waking up to alarms and the smell of smoke was bad enough. Another ache in my leg, this one worse. I'd used a pain shot sometime in the night. That left eleven.

I snagged the corner of my lip with teeth. I had been kept busy, tending to my wound, scavenging, and then taking care of the "dog." I hadn't had time to process the terrifying situation in which I found myself. Cut off from communication with Pattee and another human, susceptible to infection from my leg wound, isolated except for "predators"? The tendons in my neck tightened while my heart picked up a flurried beat. There was no one to save me here, but myself. I exhaled and focused my gaze at the crest of the low hill in front of me. The next pain shot would have to wait. I had work to do.

6

Natheka

Anxious to be on my way, I rose just after the first sun's dawn. She gave me enough light to mark each crevasse with a dark shadow, but I still trod with care. Scaling massive boulders, I saw each rise and peak as a challenge and as a steppingstone, bringing me ever closer to my goal.

No sounds met my ears, only the scrape of leather and my suit's metal against rock. The barren wastes of the Magnetic Burst Field were isolated, save for the irritating insects that made their home in hives between the rocks.

I jostled one such hive and they swarmed out, forming a bumpy mass of bodies and legs as they covered my glove and arm. I ignored the pulsing scrum; the Shel in my suit would devour any strays that climbed between my armor joints. Most would drop off in the heat of the Sister Suns, preferring the coolness of the shadows.

My focus was on the sloped grade on the west side of Loud Speak. The hunters of old, nay, the earliest inhabitants of Ikthe, named the mountains thousands of cycles ago. Loud Speak was the tallest of a grouping of five peaks. From a distance, their skyline resembled the spiked back of a pazathel-nax. Loud Speak was at the "head" of the devil dog. Spike Horn, Broad Back, and Running Hip trailed after, and the last of the grouping was called Switch Tail.

From there, I would have a broad view of several jagged peaks. I would be able to see smoke before the high winds dispersed it, and more importantly, I could see the maar from there.

My route traversed through several smaller peaks and would take me only two more days. I wondered how my brethren fared in Agothe-Fax Tunnel last night. There were enough of them, and according to Naraxthel and Hivelt, their mates fought with equal ferocity to Theraxl, so I need not worry. However, a lone dream came to me in the night, of Hivelt with a black tongue, and his heart mate's face ashen with worry. I grimaced and continued my climb. Anxiety did no good for the hunting warrior. Let the rokhura of each day devour one's worries. There were always more opportunities to fret with the rising of the Sister Suns on Certain Death.

With grasping claws, I crested the ridge. The tedium of my journey inspired song in my heart to pass the time.

I surveyed my next route, tracing the safest path over mountain rubble.

I climbed in time to the rhythm of the song of the Mountains of Shegoshel.

"They beseeched us to kiss the faces of the Suns
We climbed and fell
The slaves to the Sisters
The weak at the feet of the strong
Every step closer to death
Every step closer to life
May our deaths bring life to the Sisters

May the Sisters bring life
Out of our deaths
As we kiss the faces of the Suns"

The lyrics sobered me. Ever had I lived to serve the Sisters. Both the Holy Sisters of Shegoshel, and the sisters of my home world. It was our culture, our livelihood, our lifeblood. To deny a sister anything was unheard of. And while the hunters serve, the sisters gave of themselves, too. They gave their time and energy, work and spirit, to the building up of Ikshe. Ikshe was a prized jewel among planets. The sisters kept it so, refining the planet with their industry and beauty. They produced vast crops of grain to supplement the meats we brought from Ikthe.

They raised the little hunters and sisters, created art and crafted gardens of luscious flowers. They healed and blessed and cooked. In all my cycles, I had never seen a sister take advantage of the work of the hunters. Until our queen.

The betrayal struck my heart. Was it not the duty of the Ikma Scabmal Kama to preserve the hunters and the rituals that welcomed Theraxl offspring into the world? Did not the Lottery ensure that the mightiest hunters blessed Ikshe with strong progeny? And yet, as my mind replayed the Lottery Draws of years past, I recalled the Ikma in covert conversations with a hunter. Many times, had it been Hivelt. But others, too, had slipped behind the large purple tapestry that divided the great hall from the private chambers of the Elder and Younger Sister Queens, trailing the Ikma while BoKama shifted uncomfortably on the Dais and feigned interest in nearby discussions. That one's consort sulked in a corner, eyes sodden with jealousy and tracing the steps taken by the newest hunter.

It was not spoken of, but the Queen's Younger Sister-Ruler, BoKama, once had a loyal consort. He was seduced by the Ikma, thus defiling the BoKama's bed and forever spoiling the cooperation between the ruling Sisters. Furthermore, The Ikma was not satisfied to procure her sister's consort for herself. She continued to usurp the ritual of raxshe and raxma, that blessed ceremony that heralded the conception of Theraxl hunter and sister offspring. To what end? Surely the population was at her whim. Why must she lie with the mightiest, the ones whose hunts earned them a place in the Lottery Draw? No children resulted from her many bedsports, and the Theraxl race languished as a result.

The Holy Suns climbed across the sky, marking the path above that mirrored where I must travel below.

I had no answers to my questions. But I knew that Naraxthel was right. Theraxl could not idly witness the slow asphyxiation of our race while the queen devoured the seed that belonged to Ikshe's fertile soil. She must be stopped, and BoKama would take her place as the Ikma Scabmal Kama and appoint another sister to serve as the new BoKama. My brothers and I would assist. Of course, the Ikma's WarGuard would kill to protect her, so we may die in our efforts.

But as the song said, may our deaths bring life to the Sisters. Not just the Elder and Younger Sister Queens, but the future sisters of Ikshe. And of course, the Holy Sisters. Ever would the Ikthekal serve, until we died. And kissed Their shining faces.

7

Ikma Scabmal Kama

S weat poured into my eyes, stinging them, burning them. All was burning. Through blurred vision, I saw the flames. They licked up the sides of my bed chamber, devoured the bed hangings, the linens, my skin. I choked on my screams and the smoke.

I sprang from my bed, frantic for water.

"BoKama!" I called for Younger Sister, but she was not found.

The flames joined to become figures. They surrounded me, chanting of destruction and creeping closer, grasping each other's licking fingers so that I could not breach them. I spun, watching their faces, looking for relief from the burning, for signs they might relent, for mercy.

Instead, the flames grew hotter. My skin bubbled and popped; my claws curled. The sweat evaporated from my hairline and when I raised my hands to feel my hair, the feathered fronds were flames, and then I was part of the circle, the burning racing up my arms and firing my heart to a pace I knew would cause my death.

I wept tears of molten rock.

"Kama," a voice whispered into my ear. Cool water bathed my brow. "Wake, Elder Sister."

Tendons in my neck stretched to their limits. My teeth gritted in my mouth. I dared not open my eyes to see the burned flesh. The cool cloth wiped my cheeks.

"You are safe, Kama."

My heart slowed. I opened a clenched fist and stroked my thumb across a claw. It was not curled. My skin felt hot and tight, but not burned. I inhaled deep through my nose.

I smelled concern. And something old, like, affection. And wariness.

I blinked twice, and BoKama leaned over me, a damp cloth poised above my face. A lone tear sparkled at her chin, then dripped.

I snatched the cloth from her. "I screamed for you," I accused. "You did not come." My voice hitched. I rolled away from her and scrubbed my face, peeking at the cloth, not quite believing that no charred flesh pulled away from my skull.

"Your nightmares increase by the night," she said. "The Maikshe recommends you increase the dose of your star tea and visit her every night before bed for a calming bath."

I squeezed my eyes shut, and the dignified face of Naraxthel Roika came into focus. So calm. Unruffled. Nonplussed by my power or beauty. The memory of flames burned behind my navel. I sat up, flinging my unblemished bedclothes aside. I inhaled again, noting the musk of my room. No fire. No embers. No ashes.

I pulled a gown from a pile of clothes and slipped into it, turning to see BoKama standing tall but deferentially, her head bowed, and eyes closed.

"The Maikshe's potions have ceased their usefulness," I said. "You know this."

BoKama raised her head.

"We hurt to see you suffer, Kama."

The terror of the nightmare nipped at my heels when I passed her. "I would walk the wall now. Attend me."

The tiniest shard of guilt pierced my gut. Who, alone, bathed my brow when the world was burning? BoKama. The Maikshe refused to enter my chambers, citing the Ancient Ways. The Ikthekal who visited my bed hastened away once their seed was spent.

I should request, not command. She ruled beside me. Together, we governed the Sister Planets. And yet, I could not forget her absence in my dream.

She followed me up the narrow stairwell to the wall-walk. High winds beat the fortress walls with ferocity; their icy blasts cooled the heat on my skin.

"The Goddesses warn me of destruction, BoKama," I said, my claws digging into the stone as I looked out over a black sea, the golden fields of grain obscured by night's cloak. "The Sister Planets collide. Sometimes the Sister Suns swallow each other and turn black. In one dream," I said and pointed my gaze at her. "You flew your ship into the Lottery Drum, and died in a storm of smoke and flames, and the hall collapsed and killed everyone. All the Ikthekal. All the sisters. I stood alone, Ruler of Nothing." I looked back out to the night. A gale whipped my braids, their plaits twisting like snakes and lashing my face, neck and shoulders.

"Why do you not visit the Maikshe?" BoKama said. "You have not tried the mud bath in many Rounds. Perhaps this time ... "

"The *mud baths*?" I screamed at her. "The Sister Suns die! The Sister Planets rot! Why do the Shegoshel send me these dreams of sickness and filth, flames and storms, but no medicines to heal?"

BoKama bowed her head before me, light from a nearby torch gleaming off the skin at the part in her hair.

I clenched my fists until my claws pierced my palms.

"Send me an Iktheka," I said.

She raised her gaze to meet mine. Her brows dipped.

"Due respect, my Ikma Scabmal Kama," she said. "The Ancient Writs and Ways say the Queen and Her Sister must abstain from food and sexual relations for one Round when the Shegoshel send dreams. After which, they will send the Answer Dream."

Cold at my center. A stone settled deep in my womb.

I sniffed the air around the BoKama, my nose carving a shape around her face. I smelled concern. Wariness. Anxiety.

Filling my lungs with her scent, I exhaled for several jotiks, staring into her eyes.

"Do you remember what I told you five nights past?" I said.

She closed her eyes. Nodded.

"What did I tell you, when you were bathing my face of scalding tears?" My voice was ice.

"The seed of the Ikthekal abated your nightmares for a time," she said.

"Send me an Iktheka," I repeated.

"But the Answer Dream," she said, taking a step closer to me. My jaw dropped at her audacity.

"Let the Shegoshel send my BoKama the Answer Dream," I said, allowing a small smile to curve my lips. "Your Consort has left you in peace, that you may abstain from sexual relations." I watched her face for signs of collapse, rage, revenge. I felt my frown deepen when her expression remained placid.

She bowed her head and spoke. "Very well," she said. "I will await the Answer Dream." She walked away from me but spoke over her shoulder. "I will send an Iktheka to your bed chamber."

Her acquiescence angered me. Just as her devotion did. Perhaps the Holy Goddesses *would* send her the Answer Dream. I growled. I wanted relief from the nightmares. Countless days, with only a zatik or two of relief after spending a night with a hunter-brother. *Do you truly desire that BoKama receives the Answer Dream? Are you not worthy to receive the Answer Dream and prevent the awful destruction that awaits the Sister Planets or the Sister Suns? Or both?*

I screamed into the night. What were these nightmares? They began cycles ago, and the first time I took an Iktheka to bed, I enjoyed peaceful slumber for three or four nights. And then the nightmares came again. Fiercer. More insistent. The parade of hunters who thrashed my bedclothes grew in number as I sought my solace.

But now the dreams persisted. One tumble in my bed with an Iktheka awarded me only hours of relief. Was there no balm on Ikshe?

I drank vessel after vessel of star tea. No change. The mud baths worked for a short time. And then my nightmares featured mudslides and landquakes. Flooding rivers.

I stared out into the blackness, the cold winds chilling my fevered skin, and remembered a single dream, a cycle ago.

A noble and brave warrior stood by my side. He gestured to the planet Ikthe, and then we stood upon its ground. I had never placed claw upon it, but in the dream, the ground rippled like water. Colorful visions of animals flew about us. I raised my brows at the hunter in question, and his fangs gleamed in the double sun's light. He brandished a sword and smote the creatures until their blood flowed across my skin, and my skin absorbed the colors. I became the animals of the planet, and ran from the hunter, my speed increasing as if I had wings.

I flew across the surface of the planet, observing its feral beauty, and a huge sac at my throat inflated as I called out to every creature to join me.

Soon, we trampled the planet with hooves, claws and talons, scouring the face of it with our fangs, tearing the trees out by the roots, upending the mountains, twisting waterways into new formations. The destruction was beautiful, endless, invigorating ... and then the hunter stopped us with a raised hand and scowling face.

"Your destruction is meaningless!" he shouted. "Why do you shred this place?"

My army of predators pawed at the ground behind me. I smelled the dust of the planet. Rain in the air. Distant lightning portended a storm. Our storm.

"We slaughter Certain Death because it will grant Certain Life its bounty." I pointed to Ikshe in the sky, and hundreds of thousands of eyes turned to gaze at it. As we watched, it seemed to glow. Pride swelled my chest; anger sparkled in my eyes. Without warning, Ikshe exploded into fragments.

Stunned, I froze.

The hunter stalked toward me. "You have butchered us all."

I woke that night, sweating and crying. One year later, I saw the hunter at the Lottery Draw. He sat on the dais. He regaled us with stories. And then he refused me.

Naraxthel Roika.

Rock crumbled beneath my claws at the battlement. I turned and strode the wall walk to the stairs. An iktheka awaited me, and after, mayhap a long zatik or two of peace.

8

Amity

"Gooood morning, Predator Planet, this is Amity Diaz reporting to you from a rock-studded hellscape in search of water. Tune in for weather, sports and traffic every hour on the hour, with updates on the sixes." My broadcast was breathless, as I was trying to scale a ridge, but my injured leg held me back. I was not a radio DJ in a former life, just a bored teen with access to thousands of radio network archives as my family and I traveled through space in a fleet of science ships.

I had a good grip on a ledge with my right hand, but only a marginally secure one with my left. And my left leg was a liability, dragging as it did. I feared nerve damage.

Huffing with effort, I dug the fingers of my left hand deeper into a crevice and pulled with all my might. My muscles trembled; I managed to lift my left foot enough to find a spot to rest my boot, and then could climb a quarter of a meter higher up the rock.

It took me thirty minutes to reach over the ridge with a shaking left arm and pull myself up. An endless black mirror stretched out below me.

"Hot damn," I whispered. "A crater lake."

I scanned the shore and surrounding area and found where the pod had skidded after hydroplaning across the maar. A huge crater smoked from the initial impact, and a long, erratic blackened scar stretched across the terrain to my left, and where the ridge had a giant bitemark, my pod must have bounced through and come to a rest on the other side. Taking a minute to breathe, I marveled at the expanse of water and the forbidding craggy peaks that surrounded it. I gave a long, low whistle.

"VELMA, do you have a recording of the landing?"

"Standby."

Crackling in my helmet, and then:

"The pod's neural network activated the scram nosecone protocol," VELMA had said. "I need to access the onboard controls. Standby."

"VELMA, how fast is the pod traveling?" Pattee Crow Flies' voice flooded my helmet. Tears sprang to my eyes to hear her familiar voice, though it was tight and tense in my ears.

"The ionosphere's friction slowed the pod's speed to 853 mph according to the nanosatellite barrier through which it passed," VELMA announced.

"We need to reduce it to 320 mph at least," Pattee said. "VELMA, have you accessed the controls yet?"

"There is a problem accessing the insulated buffer trap on the EEP," VELMA said. "The nosecone is not responding to my integrative neural network initiative."

"Dammit," Pattee whispered. "Is the miner conscious?"

That was me. Even though I knew how it ended, my heart raced, listening. It had been touch-and-go, and those two guardian angels had been with me through it all. I closed my eyes and sent a prayer of gratitude heavenward. The recording played on.

"K90 Miner 106, are you conscious?" VELMA had asked.

"Pinging the miner's helmet communication device," VELMA said. "Miner is in cryo-sleep mode. All vitals normal."

"VELMA, use the miner's helmet to wirelessly access the flight console." Pattee's voice was breathless but hopeful.

"Rerouting. Console accessed," VELMA said. "Emergency landing protocol activated."

Pattee asked, "Speed?"

"436 mph and decelerating," VELMA said. "Impact in twenty-five seconds."

"No," Pattee said. "No."

Silence for two beats.

"Deploy the baffle floats," Pattee said, her voice cracking.

"According to data from the nanosatellite array, the pod will not impact with water, Pattee," VELMA said.

"Is the chute open?" She asked.

"Affirmative."

"Deploy the damn baffle floats, VELMA!"

"Deploying," she said. "Impact in Three. Two. One."

Static in my helmet, and then VELMA's smooth voice rose once again. "That was the end of the recording."

"I'm speechless, VELMA," I said. "Pattee saved my life. And so did you."

"That is my programming," she said.

I scrambled the rest of the way over the ridge, breathing heavy and looking for the easiest path down to the water.

"Why didn't the nanosatellite array detect water, do you think?" I asked the AI.

"That information is not available."

I groaned when my leg throbbed. Too much exertion was taxing my body. I felt warmth spreading down my leg inside my suit.

Looking down, I saw the bandage wrapped around my thigh had soaked through. "Shit," I said between gritted teeth. "Dammit." I sat on a rock and opened my MDPack pocket. I found another green blister packet. "VELMA, how many of these clotting packs can I use safely?"

"As many as are required to stanch the bleeding."

"Good," I said with a gasp. I was already twisting the cap. I pried off the red-soaked edge of the bandage where my swollen wound gaped a little. The prior packet hadn't completely dissolved yet. In fact, pushing the new one into the wound would drive the first one deeper. I cringed and clenched my teeth. First, the alcohol wipes. I swiped it around the skin then forced the packet into the bleeding hole. A deep ache throbbed inside my thigh where the first one pressed against a nerve or something. I whimpered but cut a new length of clean bandage and wound it over the first. Tight.

This time, I didn't pass out. I blew out slow breaths and stared at the still waters of the lake. It struck me that there didn't appear to be any wildlife. No waterfowl, no fish jumping and rippling the surface. The entire landscape was rocks, black rocks, orange rocks and more rocks tapering into gravel and a black sand beach.

Now was a good time to drink another red pouch. Licking my lips when the slight dizziness passed, I stood and limped my way over and around boulders, picking my way over the craggy stone.

My head pounded. My lips cracked.

In spite of the *HemoSupp*, I was getting dehydrated, and how ironic that I was, considering it was only about thirty feet from water's edge. With an inward groan, I kept going. At the sandy beach, I dropped to a crawl. My leg continued to throb making me wonder if I hadn't acquired an infection already.

My gloves hit water, and I stayed like that for a minute, on all fours, watching the water lap ever so gently at my fingers. A slight breeze caressed it, and the ripples licked my glove-tips.

Breaths easing up, I tried to energize myself to take off my helmet so I could drink. I leaned into a sit, stretching my bad leg out in front of me.

"VELMA, I'm taking off my helmet so I can drink. It's already breached, so it shouldn't matter at this point, right?"

"Affirmative. You will have already been exposed to the cyanobacteria found in this planet's atmosphere. The antibiotics administered to prevent infection from your leg wound will aid in staving off the severity of the infection for one or two days, but I advise you to travel to the nearest functioning EEP where doses of bacteriophage await, as well as a suitable vaccine to prevent further infection."

With hands poised to take off my helmet, I digested what VELMA just told me.

"I already have an infection and I need to travel to a functioning EEP. Is that what you just told me?"

"Affirmative."

"And if I don't go?" I asked this as I stared at my leg, wishing I never had to get up again.

"The cyanobacteria are deadly to humans. It attacks the respiratory system followed by the shut-down of all major organs. Unfortunately, it will cause your death within two weeks. That would be most disappointing, as you appear to be the most reasonable of the humans so far."

I blinked and licked dry lips again. I really needed a drink.

Shaking myself, I removed my helmet. It was already too late, and if I waited much longer, I would simply die of thirst.

I stuck my hand into the space between my axial ring and shoulder where the water bladder was stowed and removed it. Filled it with water, watching the bubbles rise and pop. When it was full, I shook it and squeezed the neck shut where the nanofiltration unit worked just below the straw. I took a long drink, then rested, letting my belly adjust to the sloshing water. Once I emptied it, I filled it again and slipped it back into place with difficulty as it bulged.

Unfolding the collapsible water jug, I wrangled the unwieldy material until the hole was under water. Carrying this was going to be a chore. I tried not to think about it. One step at a time. Because honestly, the jug held six gallons of water, and that was going to weigh forty-eight pounds. Minus the adjustment for current gravity; it was still going to be difficult. I couldn't help it. I cried while I watched the jug fill and wondered how on "Predator Planet" I was going to lug this thing back over the rocks with a crap leg. Even if I wasn't trying to help that devil dog, I was still going to need water. I capped the jug and put my helmet back on.

"Hey," I said. "How far away is the closest functioning EEP?"

"Five days on foot," VELMA answered. "I have mapped the quickest and safest route for you. I have also compiled a supplies list based on how much you can be reasonably expected to carry."

"That's great, VELMA," I said. "It really is. But I mean, I can't see the map in the IntraVisor."

"Immaterial. I will direct your path with verbal instruction," she said. "I will help you."

Even though VELMA was, in essence, an extraordinarily complex tapestry of ones and zeroes, I believed her, and it gave me comfort. I took a deep breath and flexed my toes in my boots.

"Alright," I said. "Okay. Let's do this."

With difficulty, I maneuvered my leg to the side, and then got up on one knee. I stood, got my balance, and looked at the water jug. Damn. I wished it had wheels.

9

Natheka

A few days later, I finished the last of my water and surveyed the lone tendril of smoke as I stood on the summit of Switch Tail.

At this altitude, I hoped to receive communications and enabled my helmet's comms. A message awaited.

"This is a recording. There is a high probability that the crash landing settled near the maar at Black Heart Mountain. Good luck." Esra's technology had left the message but when I tried to summon the technology, there was no response. I would try again once I reached the site.

Eyes still on the smoke, I trekked down.

My heart-home throbbed, not unpleasantly, and I hummed to its beat, crafting a new song. It spoke of the heart, its pains, its joys, and its ever-changing life. The journey of the heart was not unlike these mountains I traversed. There were summits of joy and crevasses of pain, light of love from the Shegoshel, but the darkness and cold of the loneliness in the mountain shadows. In truth, the canyons of the mountains were the loneliest of all, shunning the light from the Suns unless they were at their zenith. It reminded me of Theraxl hearts during adolescence. Pure bliss, but only as long as it took for the suns to shine down into a canyon, and then the heart was thrust once more into darkness.

Again, I recalled the faces of Naraxthel and Hivelt. How their eyes shone brighter. Their steps seemed lighter. If we were not fighting for our lives on Ikthe, I would love to see them introduce the ritual of raxshe and raxma to their human mates.

I chuckled as I secured a length of doubled rope into a climbing hook. I imagined the human females would cower, brave as they were. It was not a ceremony to be taken lightly. And they seemed attuned to the pains of their mighty hunter heart mates. No, they would not embrace the ritual at first.

Belaying the line, I abseiled, my boots jarring stones that tumbled below me into the darkness of the first canyon. There were two more to cross before I reached the maar.

Ikthekal did not spend much time in this mountainscape. There were no huge animals to hunt and fell for food. Not to mention, no flat places to land our ships. And yet, thanks to Naraxthel, I knew this place and its secret wonders.

At the bottom of the canyon, the silvery thread of the stream carved a serpent-like channel through the black rock. It ran cold and clear, having filtered through a sandy bed to the north. Its meandering trail led a merry chase through the Black Heart Mountains, to the great jungle basin, across the Plains of Bounty, and finally merged with the night-river. Its waters gave freely in all those habitats and replenished from the single icy cap at the north. Naraxthel called it the Mother Stream.

I drank then filled my water containers.

I looked up at the pale orange of the sky, just a strip visible between two black walls. It was time to go back up the other side.

Halfway up, my heart-home gave a surge; it twisted, and I lost my grip for a moment, scrabbling with my claws to find purchase once again. With a gasping lurch, I regained my spot on the rock wall, and eased into it, leaning my helmet against the rock wall while the pains in my heart-home attacked me from the inside.

Something was wrong with my heart mate. I knew it like I knew the fragrance of my own mother. When the pain ebbed, I doubled my efforts to reach the top of the canyon.

"I am coming to you, heart mate. Do not give up."

10

Amity

It was a rocky slope, maybe ten feet high. The grade was thirty-seven percent at most. Not horrible at all. As a child, I would have raced all six of my brothers to the top and declared myself king of the hill.

At which point, they would point out that girls couldn't be kings, and I would kick the nearest one in the shin, regardless of who said it, and shout louder that King Girl had spoken.

But I stood on the black sand with the water jug on my back and looked at the hill as if it were Mount Inge Lehmann of Planet New Denmark, one of the tallest mountains in the Milky Way Galaxy.

I refused to look at the huge red blossom on my leg. Squishing my toes in my own blood in my boot made me queasy. I didn't know why the clotting agent wasn't working, but I figured King Girl might be about to take a long nap.

I cursed.

My brothers would never let me live this down if I was uninjured, that's how easy a climb it was. But with a deep wound? They would have grabbed forearms and made a human cot and carried me over. I was such a bratty kid; I would have yelled at them to put me down, and in fact, did just that many times. They clucked their tongues at me and laughed. The memory of my brothers' faces faded as the rocky ridge came back into focus.

What was I rushing around for? I had time to take care of myself. With careful hands, I removed my helmet then took out another precious shiny red pouch. After pounding the contents back, I stowed the empty pouch in my pocket.

Helmet back on, a bracing breath to square my shoulders, and I took the first step. And the next. I paused to wind the last of my bandaging around my leg and tied a thick knot in it.

With heart in my throat, I climbed that damn slope, ignoring the weight that pulled me back, and the numbness in my leg that distracted me by forcing me to watch its movement every step. And at the top of that dinky hill, I shot my fist into the air.

"I am King Girl!"

My victory fist pump unbalanced me, and I fell, banging my shoulder, then rolled and slid down, gravel spilling around me and water jug dragging, pulling, and pushing until I settled at the bottom, tears streaming down my face. *Estupida!* I was no longer a little girl who needed to prove herself to her big brothers. Why did I act like this?

My body hurt everywhere, but a quick assessment assured me I hadn't broken any bones. The leg wound was a huge problem though.

I finagled out of the water backpack, then laid against it, looking up at the late afternoon sky. The last of my tears dried on my face. I tried. I really did. But I could feel the blood sticky on my leg and in my boot, and the bandage was completely red, and I had no more of it. I had more clotting blister packets. I would have to use more, I guessed. After this little rest. This little, tiny rest.

"This is Radio K90 One-oh Six with your news update on the six," I whispered. "Amity, signing off."

I sighed. So tired.

I dreamed of that tree. The one that ate people. Its tendrils yanked on my leg and dragged me toward its huge black maw. Okay, tree. I'll be your food today.

The dream made no sense, but I kept seeing the same scene over and over again, me tying up my wound with tree tendrils. But it was someone else's leg. And I couldn't get the knots right.

"Amity, mammal detected within one meter."

I woke muddle-headed.

The sky above me was dark. A stunning glitter storm twinkled above me. So. Many. Stars. It took my breath away.

A tug on my leg. Oh right, that tree was trying to drag me back.

Wait!

I shook my head and blinked. I patted my pockets, locating the mini flashlight, and shone it on my leg.

The devil dog. Was eating my leg.

I stared at it, as it chewed and swallowed, chewed and swallowed, eating my leg piece by piece. Except it didn't hurt. I peered at it.

"Hey! Stop that!" I shouted and waved the light at its eyes. It closed them and growled at me and didn't let go of the bandage. It retched once, then chewed and swallowed again. A final bite, and my bloody bandage was in the devil dog's gullet. It was lucky the bandages were organic material, but still. "You stupid wolf!" I screamed at it, but its hackles rose, and it growled again. Catching my breath, I stopped moving. Its teeth ... were so sharp.

I couldn't move my leg, or anything else. My body was completely sore from the fall and passing out at this weird angle had my body aching, but I wasn't going anywhere. This thing could eat me alive. I slowly placed my light on the ground so I could see it clearly and with snail-pace movements, found my multi-tool and slid it out. It was the closest I had to a weapon.

The devil dog sniffed at my wound and started licking it.

"No," I whispered to it. It didn't listen. Its wide tongue licked all around and then dipped into the wound, and I almost passed out again. I gagged. "No!" I said with more vigor. I reached to cover my wound with my hand, and it snapped at my fingers. It continued its licking, and then I realized something. It wasn't using its teeth to open the wound. It was bathing it. For now. Oh shit. Was this a good thing or a dreadful thing? I didn't know.

"VELMA, can the devil dogs be domesticated?"

"There are no indications that the pazathel-nax have ever been domesticated."

I swallowed. Okay. Well, just because something had never been done before didn't mean it couldn't be done at all.

"Hey, Diablo," I said in a soft tone. "Do you like music? What about a little something by ... VELMA, play "Never Been to Spain" by Three Dog Night."

"Complying."

The smooth melody played, and I sang along, watching this insane animal tend me like a deranged nurse from a video game.

It ignored me, just kept licking, and when it was satisfied, it sighed and laid down with its head resting on the wound.

"VELMA, the pazathel-nax fell asleep on my leg. What do I do?"

"Standby," she said. "Upon calculating tens of hundreds of outcomes, I suggest letting sleeping pazathel-naxl lie. Get your rest. You may have a traveling companion, and that will assist you in reaching Pattee Crow Flies' EEP in a safe manner."

While the wound had stopped bleeding, either because of the clotting agent, or the devil dog's ministrations, I did not know. But I had lost enough blood that it was easy to fall back asleep. After a long drink from my straw, I did just that.

A cold tickle wakened me from a deep sleep. Sure enough, the wolf was sniffing at my leg wound, but deemed it well, gave my helmeted face a passing glance, then turned away. He darted into the mist-shrouded woods. Disappointment sunk my hopeful mood. At least he didn't devour me while I slept.

A mist, no doubt from the lake, engulfed the area, and the light from the dual suns lent a hazy glow to the morning.

Down to my last pouch of *HemoSupp*, I used it with no regrets.

"VELMA, health stats?"

All vitals were normal, and I also felt refreshed. I tested my leg by bending it. It ached but didn't feel swollen like before. I wiggled my toes inside my boots. Gross. But functional.

Stretching, I popped my back and hitched myself off the ground, taking care not to jostle my leg too much. It felt so much better though, compared to yesterday. I guessed I needed a solid rest, plenty of water, and the *HemoSupp*.

With aches and pains in my shoulders and arms from the fall, I walked to the wreckage and collected the pile, removing it to the shallow cave. Just for the time being. VELMA would tell me what to take for my trek to the EEP.

Inside the wreckage, I gathered as many MRE as I could carry, and the remaining items from VELMA's list.

Back outside, the mist lifted as the suns burned it off.

While I packed the rucksack with VELMA's items, I kept looking into the forest. Was I hoping the dog would return? Yeah, I was. I sighed.

I ate a solid breakfast, drank more water, and decided the state of my suit was bad enough that I had to take measures.

Stretching my bad leg, it continued to feel stronger and more mobile. Magic dog spit? Or time-release clotting agent medications? Whatever it was, I was climbing King Girl mountain again, and washing out my suit.

The trek across the stony morass was easier today. Meandering through the jagged rocks, I used the tallest ones to rest against when needed, but it wasn't often. I was probably in shock before. The dawning of a new day, the lessening of the swelling in my leg, and my full stomach all made for better travel. Balancing with care, I made my way down the rocky slope, eyes on the glassy surface of the water.

At the lake, I doffed my suit and dipped a toe in the water. It was cold, no surprise, but it wouldn't kill me. I limped further in, my feet sinking in the gritty black sand. In spite of the vast lake appearing black, the water was clear. I still didn't see any life. No seaweed, no tiny fish. I waded deeper, confident the lake must be an aberration. With the dried blood cleansed from my foot and leg, I scrubbed the rest of myself off, washed out the inside of my suit and waded toward shore. The suns' heat dried the skin on my back, but a sudden gust of air chilled me.

The gust preceded something cold and slimy snatching me from behind and pulling me under the water. With no time to catch a breath first, I gulped water and thrashed my legs, a surge of adrenalin pushing strength into all my limbs. I needed to get out of the water fast.

Bubbles filled my vision, and a gray and silvery limb or tentacle tightened around my neck and shoulders.

Stupid, stupid, stupid. No weapon. No suit. How was I going to get out of this nightmare? What had I been thinking, entering a body of water without at least asking for a scan or something?

Another slimy limb spiraled around my head and clamped against my mouth.

We were still in the shallows, and I needed to keep it that way.

I dug my heels into the sand and relaxed my torso. The tentacles slackened and I bit the one at my mouth as hard as I could.

The creature's limbs thrashed in the water.

With lungs burning, I fought and flailed, the tangle of dark limbs surrounding me at every turn. When both feet found purchase, I lunged toward the shore, yanking myself out of the tentacled grip. Coughing and spluttering, I stumbled out of the water, splashing onto the beach, snagging my suit and helmet, and I dragged them farther from the water's edge, not daring to look back or rest until I was certain the leviathan couldn't reach me.

When I made it to the base of King Girl Mountain, which turned out to be just a hill today, I braved a look behind me before I attempted to cross it again.

A flash of white fur blurred with shining limbs of silver.

Oh no. Diablo!

11

Natheka

I wanted to run, but caution bade me take my time. I had seen the scar of wreckage with my long-distance scan, but no sign of life. I had one more crevasse to cross, and many veltiks of boulder-strewn landscape and rocky ridges to travel before I reached the site.

In the heat of the day, memories of my first hunt assaulted me until I could shove them away no longer.

Naraxthel and I had landed at Moon Shield. When he told me the basin beneath it was home to small game, I was offended. I misunderstood his intentions as my sponsor. I thought he wished to shame me or mock me by bringing me to a place of easy prey. With anger in my heart, I told him to leave me be. I would travel south for large game, and that I needed no one's help.

He insisted I take extra provisions and weapons but did not try to dissuade me from my hasty decision.

I left him at Moon Shield and followed an old hunter's trail through the aged wilderness, seeking the legendary rokhural. It was said that the hunter who brought a ship's worth of rokhural would earn many

Lottery Draws and have many offspring. I wanted my first hunt to produce such fame. With fantasies of my kills clouding my mind, I did not heed my surroundings.

Several zatiks into my trek, I had found myself nearly captured by the forest-teeth tree. The hunters are not schooled on the wildlife of Ikthe. It is expected they will learn during the hunt. Embarrassed at my near death, my determination to find and kill a rokhura hardened. I would not turn back. I would not seek Naraxthel's aid.

I burrowed into the forest, rock-headed, and stumbled from one mistake to another. I slipped and fell down a mudslide, toppling an angry mud-beast during the mating season. I was nearly trampled to death.

At a meadow's edge, I was swarmed by the death-stingers, only just missing a terrible fate by donning my helmet at the last jotik.

Ah, but the worst mistake of all, was bending to drink at the great lake where the grass-eaters gathered to drink without first checking the skies.

Before I knew it, a rodax had seized me by the neck and flew with me over the ikfal, its talons grasping me so tight I could barely breathe.

With the green foliage passing beneath me like a river of leaves, I thought my life as a hunter would soon be over. Luckily, the rodax didn't drop me. It carried me to its nesting area not far from the crater lake. My heart nearly beating out of its cage, I managed to escape the rodax nest and its vicious fledglings, crawling down from the tower tree and cowering in the bracken. My provisions and weapons had been left behind at the grass-eater lake. I was young, ignorant, and lost.

My first hunt was supposed to portend the path of my life as a brother warrior, and I knew then that I should have stayed with Naraxthel. At least then, I would have had jokapazathel meat and a mentor from which to learn.

The morning after, I trudged through a sodden ikfal to the foothills of the Black Heart Mountains. I thought from there I could travel due east and make it back to Moon Shield. Perhaps Naraxthel would forgive my hastiness.

The Black Heart Mountains were treacherous for a young hunter with no ropes. Twice, I almost fell to my death in crevasses obscured by rock falls. But I was resolved to return to Moon Shield. When I decided to signal Naraxthel via comms of my intentions, I learned how the Magnetic Burst Field corrupted signals.

Hungry, thirsty, wounded, I almost gave up hope.

I climbed a low ridge, and when I peeked over, I saw an expanse of water. It was surrounded by peaks, a vast bowl of black water. I almost wept in gratitude. I staggered down the slope and fell to the beach, scrabbling through the black sand to reach the clear water. I drank until I vomited, then drank more.

I lay on the sand staring up at the bowl of the sky and slept. And that is when mine eyes first laid upon the legendary ikadax. A young hunter, I thought the gigantic flying reptile was but a child's story. The size of three rokhura stacked on top of each other, the ikadax had a silvery serpentine neck, a flat spade-shaped snout, gray matte wings to rival the span of Naraxthel's ship, a sleek silver-scaled body and massive rear legs with powerful muscles and wicked curved talons. When I blinked and rubbed my eyes, it was gone. Heart thrashing in my chest, I scrambled to my feet. Had I seen but a vision?

I shook myself from the memory. Night fell fast this close to the maar. The mountains were creased with deep grooves too wide to jump across. It was a series of long climbs and treacherous rope work. But I was almost there. My heart-home called out to the human traveler, but something told me he or she was no longer at the crash site. As I had done in my youth, I trekked onward with a stubborn will.

This close to the crater lake, I scanned the skies every few rotiks. One could never be too careful on Ikthe. Even if one had been told by the Goddesses that they would never die here.

12

Amity

I watched in paralyzed fascination as the devil dog's jaws scissored their way through the slick tentacles of the deadly lake creature. The creature's limbs continued to thrash and slam the water, churning the black silt and sending huge sprays every which way. But the devil dog maintained purchase in the sand and yanked and pulled at tentacles until he had torn them, then snapped at any others that reached for him. He used his hind legs for ballast, and I watched in awe as he hunched his muscular shoulders and stood his ground against a water predator that had to be three or four times his size.

I couldn't see blood, but lengths of floppy tentacle lay dejected at the shoreline. By my count, the devil dog was winning, unless the alien octopus had hydra-like abilities.

The ferocious battle slowed as the water creature realized attacking the mammal meant the loss of more limbs, and it finally slipped back into the water, dragging a frayed tentacle with it.

Diablo stood at water's edge, making no sound, but baring its teeth at the retreating beast long after its head disappeared beneath the surface of the water. When he was convinced he had won the battle, he trotted back to the ridge, and picked his way deftly between the rocks and boulders, finding the easiest path to cross. He spared me a single glance and tossed his head.

What a little show-off.

I followed him, appreciating his instinct for the smoothest path across the ridge. I hoped he wouldn't outpace me if he decided to join me in my quest for Pattee's EEP. For I knew without a doubt that he would do nothing he hadn't willingly chosen. I felt keenly that I had perhaps been adopted, and not the other way around.

By the time I reached the site, both the suit and I were dry. It was time to pack up and leave. I didn't see Diablo anywhere. With VEL-MA's list memorized, I stowed everything in the rucksack, including my field journal and pencils, supplemented all of my suit pockets with additional items, looped two water canisters at my waist and hefted the machete. "Just like the ones back home."

Even though my cracked helmet's IntraVisor couldn't be utilized, it was easier to both carry and talk to VELMA with it affixed.

After a sad look at the wrecked pod, I then ventured into the mountainous forest, well away from the place where the "forest teeth tree", as VELMA had identified it, lived.

"Welcome to the Jungle, we've got fun and games," I murmured when I took my first step into the thick greenery, leery of every shadow. "VELMA, tell me again about the transduction thing you did with that tree. Specifically, I'm curious about bioacoustics."

"I synthesized a low-frequency soundwave that I hypothesized the forest teeth tree would recognize as a distress signal due to drought conditions. In the event of a dry season, the tree would not have enough water to digest prey beyond a certain size. Luckily, my hypothesis was correct, and the tree's tendrils relaxed their hold long enough for you to escape."

"I have heard of bioacoustics in animals, but haven't studied the phenomenon in plants," I said. "I thought plants communicated primarily through volatile emissions of different chemical makeups."

"You are correct, however, in the absence of my mass spectrometer, I thought it prudent to utilize acoustics," VELMA said.

"Fascinating," I said, while swinging my machete to create a trail through the tropical forest. "How did you learn about plant bioacoustics?"

"As you know, each EEP is equipped with the Vector Egress Liaison Machine Learning AI neural network," she said. "I exist in part as a downloaded repository of nearly infinite intelligence. Having been imbued with encyclopedic knowledge of galaxies' worth of information, I also was programmed to process this information in nanoseconds, arranging and rearranging the information as needed to solve problems. I am ever evolving as an intelligence."

"Go on," I said, transfixed by her explanation.

"As Esra and Pattee have battled the local flora and fauna, I have been collecting data while simultaneously analyzing it and rearranging it. I am able to run simulations and predict outcomes at a rate of speed that defies human understanding, and in this way, solve problems faster than a human could. With compiled experiences of the humans and the Theraxl race, I was able to deduce the probability that an ultrasonic wavelength would affect the vines of the forest teeth tree."

"That is so cool," I said.

"I do not know about the temperature, but I did suspect the vines would respond. However, I did not know if they would tighten or loosen their grip."

VELMA's calm admission that she used her neural network to play roulette with my life sobered me for a second. As I crept through the deepening gloom of the forest, I conceded she was comprised of machine learning software. This suggested she could make mistakes. I should probably keep that in mind in future.

"Stop," VELMA announced.

I stopped walking.

"A mammal of significant biosignature lies in wait eight meters at your one o'clock," she said. "Are you prepared to defend yourself?"

I assessed the sensations in my left leg. Better than before, but still aching. I hefted the machete, noting its weight was standard for the tool, better suited to swinging and cutting foliage, not piercing animal flesh. Not to mention, my shoulder and forearm ached from using it.

"No, I'm not," I said.

"Very well," she said. "It is inadvisable that you proceed further on the path until the animal leaves the area. Please remain still and quiet."

With my heartbeat picking up its pace a little, I stared into the greenery, trying to see this mammal that VELMA warned me of. I decided to crouch, careful to move slowly.

"Can you tell what kind of creature it is?" I whispered though my exterior mic was toggled off.

"Based on the biosignature, it appears to be a predator known as a Tree Thief to the indigenous hunters. It is the size of an Earth Kodiak bear and has an omnivorous diet."

"Oh, I love bears," I said and squinted. I still couldn't see it. On other planets where my expertise as an exo-biologist was put into practice, I often sketched my finds in a field book. When the klaxons sounded on the Lucidity, I didn't think about it. I grabbed my field journal and pencils and took them with me. If I could see the Tree Thief, I would enjoy drawing it. "What color is the Tree Thief?"

"The Tree Thief wears a pelt of light-dispersing fur strands. Prized for its camouflage properties, its fur was studied and mimicked by Theraxl hunters fifty Cycles ago and adapted to their armor," VELMA said.

"So what you're saying is, it doesn't have a color," I said.

"It adapts to the colors around it, thus rendering it invisible to human eyes," she said.

I sighed. Not that sketching a deadly bear-sized mammal would have been wise right now.

"Can you pulse a soundwave to deter the Tree Thief from sticking around?" I asked. I resisted the idea of resorting to violence every time an animal crossed my path in this jungle.

"I have adapted the flight suit helmets to transmit low frequency waves with limited success discouraging wildlife from approaching," VELMA said. "However, the Tree Thief does not seem to be much affected by it."

"You've already been transmitting it?" I asked.

"Yes," she said. "I have learned much over the last several weeks in how to keep a human alive on this planet. That is why you are traveling to Pattee's pod."

"Right, of course," I said. "Thanks. I guess I'll just wait out the Tree Thief, then."

My hand tightened around the hilt of the machete. I wasn't cut out for attacking or hurting animals. I could picture Pattee defending herself against them, though. She was fierce and brave. And from the stories she told me in the women's barracks, she knew her way around several different weapons.

I smiled, realizing that it shouldn't be too long, and I would be reunited with my friend. I never would have guessed such a miracle to be possible. Then again, with the pods all banked along the women's barracks sector, maybe it wasn't such a stretch after all. In fact, if Pattee and another woman were already here, then it was completely feasible that several more of us would find our way to this tropical place.

The sparse light that trickled down through the canopy dimmed as the suns sank. Still, the Tree Thief didn't move.

"What's this tree right here at my back, VELMA?" I asked.

"Based on my augmented reality digitization scan, it is the simple black tree. Harmless, and in fact, during one season, it drops a seed pod that both Esra and Pattee found to taste agreeable."

"Excellent," I said. "I'm going to sit against it here and fall asleep. Wake me if there's any trouble."

"Of course," she said.

I sat and stretched my aching leg out in front of me. Now that I was sitting in the oppressive heat of the jungle, I noticed the effects of the suit breach keenly. I had found the suit patching kit in one of the cubbies, but without a functioning pod, I couldn't use it yet. It was stored in the same thigh pocket as my field journal. Not that patching the tear in the left thigh suit leg would help much. My helmet was damaged beyond repair, at least the IntraVisor and Galvanite-infused glass face shield. And the internal wiring that would have allowed VELMA to access the transospheric nanosatellite array. At least the AI had had the foresight to basically "download" herself into the microcomputer in my helmet and thank all the powers that be it still functioned.

But the jungle was hot. And smelly. And humid. And crawling with microorganisms, including these cyanobacteria that VELMA told me about before.

"What have you learned about the cyanobacteria that is fatal to humans?" I asked her. "And when do you think it will start to affect me?"

"Compiling data from thousands of planets, I have analyzed and compared the microorganism causing respiratory distress and organ failure in humans to what is recognized on Earth as cyanobacteria. However, it isn't precisely a cyanobacteria. The microorganism on this planet appears to be an evolved symbiotic organism with properties similar to fungal spores and cyanobacteria. On Earth, a cyanobacterial colony resides in red or green algae blooms in water. The deadly one here is airborne and found in all climates in a heavy concentration. It is as if the microorganism evolved to fly in order to spread more widely across the planet. With the humidity and heat, the environment is ripe for it to proliferate."

"What do you mean symbiotic, though?" I asked.

"Under a microscope, the cyanobacteria resemble a bacterium with a thick cell membrane comprised of fungal hyphae."

"Hm," I thought out loud. "So it's like an algae burrito made with a mushroom tortilla."

"If that analogy works for you, then yes," she said. "You might find it interesting to note that most of the animals on this planet have evolved to form sister-pair relationships, and the Theraxl race have patterned their religion and myths around these female pair-bonds. I hypothesize that this organism mimics the same sister-pair bond in its symbiosis."

I recalled the stunning dual suns and VELMA saying something about two planets. "Do they reproduce asexually, then?" I asked.

"No, during mating seasons, the male species join with females."

As an exo-biologist, I had seen many iterations of reproduction, and many exotic and alien lifeforms, but sister pairs was new to me.

"Aside from procreation, the females of the species cohabitate, then?" I said.

"Yes, they hunt together, live together, share kills and raise young together."

I puzzled out this information, appreciating the mental stimulation that distracted me from the layer of sweat now coating every inch of my skin and causing me to itch in places I had forgotten about. I sipped water and watched the insects that came out at dusk.

The air was thick with winged creatures of all sizes. On the humus beneath me, beetles skittered to and fro. I kept one glove capped above the hole in my pant leg. I shuddered at the thought of alien bugs infiltrating my suit.

I adjusted myself against the tree, trying to get comfortable, when I heard an odd chuffing noise. Turning my head in the direction, I caught glimpses of white fur. Diablo!

He was a meter to my right and appeared to be stalking something. Not the Tree Thief?

"VELMA, do the pazathel-naxl prey on Tree Thieves?"

"No. They have learned to avoid the predator as it is formidably strong and fierce."

I swallowed. Toggled my mic.

"Diablo!" I whisper-shouted in his direction. "Come here!"

I saw him blink at me with the eyes on the left side of his face, but he crept forward.

"You little punk, get back here!" I was afraid to be too loud, but I feared the stubborn wolf would get hurt. I didn't have much by way of suturing supplies now. Only a bare minimum until I got to the EEP.

As expected, he didn't listen to me. He was now about five meters behind where VELMA said the Tree Thief lay.

I looked at my machete with a frown, and maneuvered to standing, avoiding anything that might make noise if I bumped it.

With the wolf approaching at the animal's six, I flanked from its eight o'clock. I had studied enough animals that I knew how pack behavior worked. I could use my knowledge since I wasn't well-equipped to fight a huge predator. Maybe we could scare the thing off, or tire it out, or something.

Shaking my head at the turn of events, I crouch-crawled at the same rate as Diablo, matching his advance step for step. I noted his direct registering, placing his hind feet into the print of his front feet, impressed that it was an evolutionary adaptation across species and across galaxies. Also, VELMA had said he was a juvenile. Animals were just born with that knowledge. Instinct had fascinated me since I was little.

Within two meters according to VELMA, I still couldn't see anything, Diablo paused and turned his head toward me. It seemed he was waiting for me to do something. He was a cute wolf, but kind of dumb if he thought I was capable of helping him. Plus, he couldn't know that the Tree Thief was invisible to me. The wolf possessed an ability to detect the beast that I lacked.

I swallowed and tightened my grip around the machete handle. If he provoked it, I wouldn't have a choice but to defend myself, and possibly the wolf, too.

Watching Diablo, my breaths quickened, and my heart thundered in my chest. *Leave it alone.*

He stalked; his eyes trained on the animal that must be only feet away from me, but I still couldn't see it. I willed the wolf to get distracted, to change his mind, to run away. Something.

Instead, he slowed, and just like a house cat, froze when he was within range. He trembled in anticipation, and I held my breath. So much for trying to scare the big animal away.

With the metrics of millions of years of evolutionary biology be-hind him, Diablo chose the precise moment to launch himself at the tree thief, his jaws agape and dripping with anticipatory saliva. I saw the moment he made contact; his jaws seemed to disappear and reappear, and now his white fur pinkened from blood.

My own muscles shook with tension; I didn't want to take part in this battle. Could the wolf hold his own? If the tree thief was as big as a bear, the wolf wouldn't stand a chance, vicious teeth notwithstanding.

The battle grew fierce. Wherever Diablo attacked, the tree thief's invisible fur appeared, marred by blood.

It looked like the wolf was holding his own, until a slash appeared in his side, and he limped back several feet with a whine.

"Oh no!" Fearing he was vulnerable to attack, I lunged forward and struck a downward blow. The machete met resistance, and soon the hot smell of fresh blood assaulted me through the cracks in my helmet. I heard nothing, but something knocked me off my feet, and I landed on my back so hard the breath left my lungs.

Mouth gasping like a fish, I couldn't move or think, only wait for breath to return to my lungs. I fully expected a giant bear rug to smother me any second, but nothing happened. Instead, I could see the foliage flailing and swaying as if a mini tornado had dropped into the center of the rainforest. Bushes and saplings twirled furiously while leaves and twigs went flying. Diablo's white fur blurred in and out of my field of vision, but I still couldn't see the foe.

When my lungs were able to catch breath, I gulped air, desperate to help. I found my machete in the duff by my hand, and snagged it, keeping a wary eye for the odd battle in front of me.

Diablo ducked and dove, attacking a limb or belly, the neck or tail, I didn't know. Then he skittered out of reach by the artful way he dodged and wove, moving like a whip, curling and sinuous, graceful in spite of the death that awaited one false move.

I watched his dance and calculated where I thought the beast was in relation, and once more attacked, swinging my blade in a sideways arc, timing the blow to avoid Diablo's advancing muzzle. The machete struck home, and blood coated a huge flank. Now that I knew where to strike, I kept hitting the same hip and leg, my arm muscle spasming with my efforts.

Out of the corner of my eye, I saw Diablo leap up and snag something between his powerful jaws. He was high up enough that he dangled from his grip. He pawed at the beast's neck that I could now see from spatters of blood. Diablo had gone for the jugular.

With the Tree Thief bleeding profusely from its hindquarters now, and Diablo with his death grip on its neck, it was only a matter of minutes before the huge creature collapsed and fought no more.

I dropped my machete and sank to my knees, letting my hand sink into the stained fur until I touched its still warm flesh beneath its coat.

I cried.

When I looked up at Diablo, he was standing still but maintaining his grip at the beast's neck. Maybe he could feel the last of its lifeblood draining from the wound. At last, he released his hold and sniffed at it. His coat was splattered with blood, but when he padded around the huge body, his gait was strong and sure. He was unaffected by the slash at his side.

I stared at the parts of the animal I could see. If I dipped my gloves in its blood, I could trace its body and gauge its true size. But I didn't want to.

I had devoted my life to studying animals' biology. Biology. The study of life. And here I had helped to kill one. I swallowed and frowned, watching Diablo curl himself and lift a leg so he could lick his genitals, heedless of my existential crisis.

My head shot up at the jungle around me. VELMA said the girls called this place Predator Planet. Here, the *trees* could kill me. This beast who fought under the cloak of invisibility would have killed me without second thought. Would have killed Diablo.

I looked back at the dog who was now sniffing at a trail of ants. One climbed up his nose, and he sneezed repeatedly, then dove into the humus, wiping his snout through the undergrowth and rolling around, agitated. He jumped up, shook his head and sneezed again; this time the ant flew out and landed on my boot. When I peered closer, I could see it wasn't actually an ant like I was familiar with, but rather an eight-legged creature with curved barbs on its back, and two heads. One on each end. However, it scurried off my boot and rejoined the long line of its brothers ... er sisters?

Diablo went to sniff the line again, but jumped back and barked at it, his strange throat bag bulging slightly. His bark didn't sound like an Earth dog's, but rather like a gravelly chuff.

He sat back down and itched his ear with a furious back leg, eyes closing in rapture.

"*Bendito Dios*," I muttered to myself. I had willingly killed another animal to protect *this* one.

"Amity," VELMA's voice chimed in my ear. "It is advisable that you take this creature's pelt, as it could prove most useful to you in the coming days. Do you need assistance in skinning it?"

My shoulders slumped. "Yes. You're going to have to walk me through this."

Shaking my head, I pulled out the supplies as she listed them. I had participated in plenty of dissections as part of my career but taking and preserving a skin was a different skill set.

Diablo danced around me as I worked; at times pulling on the pelt in a morbid game of tug-of-war. I distracted him with cuts of meat I threw out into the bracken and worked late into the afternoon.

VELMA directed me to look for a certain plant whose ichor could be used as a tanning chemical, and in one more hour, I had a huge pelt, the color of which shifted and waved in the weak light of later afternoon.

It added another forty-five pounds to my kit, but VELMA assured me it would have been much heavier on Earth. Small comfort.

"Hey, this is Radio K90 with weather on the sixes," I said as I bundled up the fur. "Today's forecast brought to you by IGMC, the company that rocks. We're looking at temps today hovering around the surface of the sun with scattered adrenalin showers. Humidity levels are topping out at water bath canner but may reduce to melted queso in the evening hours. Back to you, VELMA," I said.

"This. Is. Radio K90," VELMA said in a stilted voice. "Breaking news: Amity Diaz uses hyperbole and sarcasm to express distaste for local conditions."

Barking a laugh, I shook my head. "Good one, VELMA. Play "Yoshimi Battles the Pink Robots" by the Flaming Lips from my playlist."

"Complying," she said. "Though I find your taste in music questionable under the circumstances."

I hiked in the direction VELMA told me, and at nightfall, collapsed in a glen, and sucked the water bladder in my suit dry. In spite of the heat and the smell and a queasy stomach, I slept through the night, unmolested.

In the morning, I blinked sticky eyes open to see Diablo playing with a ball. I was partially covered by the pelt, having recognized its camouflage properties would keep me obscured, if hot before falling asleep.

Looking around, the small glen wakened with me, giant flower blossoms opening to the sunlight filtering through the green canopy. Birds darted in and out of branches, and bugs of every size and hue flitted to and fro. Several small gold-speckled brown things scurried around the undergrowth.

My attention turned back to Diablo. Where had he gotten a ball?

He rolled it in his mouth, using his tongue to prevent it from going down his gullet, then tossed his head so the ball went flying, then he ran to it and nosed it around, letting it roll before scooping it back up and starting over. His silly antics made me smile.

"You're so cute, you little *perrito loco*," I said in an indulgent voice.

I folded up the pelt and stood, and Diablo trotted to me, dropping the ball at my feet. "Oh yuck."

It was the Tree Thief's eyeball.

"I am *not* playing fetch with that."

13

Natheka

I chose to approach the crater lake from one of the streams that entered it, walking through the cold and clear water. It emptied on a narrow shore where a thin strip of beach curved around until the sand broadened into a wide plain. I could see the huge gash where the ship had first collided with land, but it looked as though it had skidded along the shore straight off the surface of the water. As I recalled Pattee's frantic voice and VELMA's translation, Pattee had ordered her technology to utilize a sort of air bladder.

Ahh. The ship hit the water, but its inflated bladders allowed it to skate across the water's surface, thus diminishing the odds of a fatal collision.

I hastened around the shore, eager to find the human and assess their health.

As I approached the eastern shore, I could see where the sand had been churned and stirred as if by a huge eating utensil. Great gouges appeared, as well as clumps of grit, mud and silt.

Something long and slimy lay still. At first, I thought it might be a human limb, and bile rose in my throat. Bending to inspect it, I realized it was a short tentacle from the crater lake's lone occupant.

I walked around the churned-up sand, looking for more clues. A tuft of white fur.

Kathe. A juvenile devil dog. What on Ikthe was a lone devil dog doing at the crater lake? They never traveled alone. Besides, there was no prey in this habitat. I looked back at the tentacle. Were they so desperate they were hunting water prey now?

It made no sense. I turned to face the ridge that rose up around the beach, an edge of the great bowl that held the maar in its embrace.

Cocking my head, I now saw a trail of prints leading up to the ridge, as well as a wide streak, as if someone had dragged something heavy. Closer inspection revealed the prints to be an exact replica of the small boots the humans wore. The human lived!

The closer I walked to the ridge, I noticed a darkening collection of spots and splatters. It was difficult to make sense of the marks. Higher up the ridge, I lost the trail of boot prints. I scoured the ground and boulders. There, on an orange boulder, I spotted the dark splotches again.

I swiped it and removed my helmet to bring the substance to my nose.

Blood. Human blood.

I scaled the ridge. More blood. Long swathes of it.

A sickening lurch in my gut forced me to pause and take deep breaths of the chill air.

I followed the tracks down the ridge to the horrific black snarl of twisted metal. How had anyone survived such devastation?

With careful steps, I scrutinized the entire site, noting with dread the random paw prints of the devil dog. I could not tell the chronology of the appearance of the devil dog but judging by the lack of an amputated or half-eaten human body, I surmised the devil dog had happened upon the site after the human had already left. It must have scented their blood and was now trailing them into the mountainous forest surrounding the crater lake. It was time to send my companions a message.

"Esra and Pattee, I did find the crash-landing site at the shores of the maar," I said. "There was a lot of blood and much wreckage. I found small tracks similar to your boots leading away from the site and into the mountain range. But I have also found the tracks of a pazathel-nax following close behind. I do not wish to give false hope, so I will leave my message at that. I will not yield until I have found your fellow human ... alive or dead."

14

Amity

Hiking more or less in a straight line through the trees and vines, I noticed Diablo chose to run ahead, circle in front of me a distance beyond me, then fall back behind to trail me. He continued this circuitous method for hours.

When I stopped to eat, he obscured himself in bushes but oriented himself towards me. Puzzled at his protective behavior, I opened an MRE and tossed a pellet of dried beef in his direction. He sniffed toward the morsel then sighed and rested his head on his front paws.

"Picky eater, huh?" I said. "I don't blame you. It's not the best." I finished the MRE and dug a water pouch out of my rucksack. VELMA and I were on the lookout for a stream to replenish my water supply, but until then, the pouches would do. I looked forward to finding Pattee's site. VELMA told me how it was near fresh water. My pack was heavy. Having to carry my own water made it worse.

I cleaned up my lunch, stretched and eyed my rucksack. I dreaded putting it back over my shoulders. Hitching it up over my hips, I put it on and headed through the rainforest again.

VELMA charted a path through terrain that descended.

Something small darted in front of me. It seemed smaller than a housecat but bigger than a rat. "What are these adorable rodents?"

"They are called jokapazathel. It translates into 'little sharp animals'," VELMA said. "Pattee used them as a regular part of her dietary needs. They are plentiful on this planet, and their primary diet appears to be scavenged mammals and reptiles along with insects and plants."

My stomach growled though I had eaten over an hour ago. "I see." I wasn't prepared to go hardcore survivalist. Specially just to kill these animals that looked like a cross between a parakeet and a potato. But I didn't have an infinite supply of MRE either. Sooner rather than later, I would have to let go of my previous privilege, and hunt for my food. Grimacing, I wondered how long before everyone expected the rescue team to arrive and pick us up.

"VELMA, was there a best guess as to when the rescue team from IGMC will pick us up?"

"Unfortunately, I have already calculated the odds of a rescue team finding this uncharted planet to be one in one quintillion. You and the others will live here for the duration of your lives."

I stopped walking. The greenery around me swayed. Light dappled forest floor swam in front of my eyes. Blackness creeped in from the edges of my vision. I reached out my left hand to rest it against a trunk, after double-checking it wasn't of the forest teeth variety. With deep breaths, I calmed my racing heart and panicked thoughts.

"Do the others know?" My voice sounded raspy in my own ears.

"Yes," she said. "You might find it interesting to learn that Esra chose a life companion from among the indigenous hunters, and the last I was aware, Pattee had done so as well."

Time stopped.

I let the heavy rucksack drop to the ground, and I soon followed, slumping against it and removing my helmet with shaking hands.

Sweat had been pouring down my neck since suns rise, and I couldn't say the humid air felt any better than my stuffy, unfiltered suit. But I felt claustrophobic. Queasy. Disoriented.

"Check my vitals?"

"All vitals within normal ranges," VELMA said. "Do you require assistance?"

"When will the cyanobacteria start giving me symptoms?"

"Anywhere between one and five days from exposure," VELMA said. "Are you experiencing symptoms?"

"I don't know," I said. "I feel dizzy. Nauseous. Confused."

"Standby," VELMA said. "All systems appear to be functioning. No head trauma detected. Would you like to open my psychotherapy program?"

We were never leaving this planet.

The others found "life companions"? What did that mean?

My mind raced. Were they victims of brainwashing or alien chemical dependency? I suddenly felt an urgency to reach Pattee's pod and Pattee. I needed to see her for myself. I needed to know she hadn't been kidnapped or forced into a weird alien mating ritual.

Cyanobacteria be damned, my fellow humans might need my help.

"Amity, do you require assistance?" VELMA asked again.

"No, no, I'm good," I said. "I need to get to the pod ASAP."

Adrenalin pumped through me, and I hiked faster than I had been. Anxiety about the women fueled my stride. This was so wrong. Landing here. Stranded here. But then for two human women to be forming relationships with aliens? My gut churned, and I tasted bile. According to VELMA, I wouldn't reach the pod for four days, but that didn't mean I couldn't try to cut the time.

Having switched the machete to my left hand, I continued thrashing through the undergrowth. I could see Diablo occasionally, a flash of white that stood out against the green backdrop, but he managed to hide himself amongst the foliage in spite of his outstanding color. He was stealthy and intelligent.

Hours after the disturbing news, I found a place to camp for the night. A treefall had created a huge lean-to where the tangle met a boulder outcropping. I could stand up in it and used leafed out tree branches to sweep the ground inside. I peered up at the fallen limbs and tapped my fingers on my helmet. If it were to rain, the water could easily pour through the gaps. I decided to scrounge for more branches and try to rain-proof the ground.

Even though it hadn't rained since I woke in the wreck, my right knee was bothering me. It always did that before storms on other planets. No reason it wouldn't work here, as well.

I gathered several branches and reinforced the roof. Diablo had disappeared, but he wasn't much help anyway, at least with making camp.

There was one spot that could use another layer.

With hands on my hips, I looked around the area and saw fallen trunks that had escaped my notice before. They were coated in lichen and moss. I couldn't use them, but just beyond were full bushes whose branches I could break off to complete my project.

I hiked to the logs, but my right knee twinged before I could step over. I bumped the log, and then the lichen sprang up in a large sheet and pounced on me. It was as big as an unfolded road map and wrapped itself around my arms, squeezing tight and adhering to itself, forcing me to drop the machete.

"VELMA, what's happening?" I cried out. "Something's got my arms!"

"Standby," she said. "You dislodged an organism that would attempt to digest your flesh if you weren't in your suit. Transmitting bioacoustics may not be effective in this scenario. Try to break free of the organism."

I hyperventilated and twisted my arms, pulling and bending my elbows, trying to disengage its grip. I frantically looked around, either for Diablo or my machete.

Diablo was nowhere to be found, and my machete was at my feet The lichen sheet had managed to seal itself tighter around my hands.

I saw an uprooted tree lying on its side, the roots clean of dirt and growth, just sharp spikes poking out. I limped over and began sawing the strange organism across one of the spikes, panting and crying, fear drying my mouth and making my movements clumsy. But it was working. I could see the material begin to fray where I dragged it across the sharp root. At last, it seemed to realize it was being damaged. It loosened its hold and fell to the ground. I watched in awe as it slumped toward the log and wriggled its way up and around the trunk, settling once more and resembling a harmless growth of lichen.

Breathing heavy, I stared at it a minute longer. "Trust nothing, least of all your eyes," I said to myself. With throbbing right knee and aching left thigh, I limped my way back to the lean-to and collapsed onto my bum right before the storm hit. I avoided the weak spot where rain found its way through the gaps and laid out the huge pelt. Something odiferous killed my appetite, and I was too exhausted to eat anyway.

I wondered where Diablo had gotten to but didn't worry. Yet. He knew his way around the jungle.

The water poured through the gap and flowed downhill, a creek in the making. Orange dirt washed away revealing black dirt beneath. The giant raindrops slapped all the leaves down, the sound shifting to a dull roar. It was a rainstorm the likes of which I had never seen. Water overflowed my canister from the deluge at the gap in my shelter's roof. I pulled it out of the flow and capped it, pleased I wouldn't have to detour to find fresh water. The downpour continued for hours and into the night.

I took the opportunity to pull out my field journal and a pencil. Little yellow flowers with spherical buds grew in clumps at the base of the lean-to. A red and purple growth that must be a fungus bubbled from cracks in one of the fallen trunks. Using the light from my helmet to see by, I sketched and listened to the rain and perked my ears for any sound of a big wet dog. But I heard nothing except the pounding of rain on leaves and bark.

15

Natheka

The blood trail had disappeared back at the crash site. I was both relieved and concerned. If the bleeding had stopped, perhaps the pazathel-nax would lose interest and decide to break trail and hunt other, less troublesome prey.

But now I found it difficult to track the soft traveler. She had wound her way through the mountain trees, walking on mosses or perhaps along fallen tree trunks. I could only spy the occasional print of her boot. It sunk deep in the forest floor, suggesting she carried a heavy load or weighed more than her compatriots. If she were larger, she may have a better chance at fighting off the devil dog once it attacked.

I frowned and tried to ignore the growing ache of my heart-home.

Running was not possible. I would miss trail sign. I was forced to take my time and track her by skill, not speed.

For a time, the paw prints of the devil dog had disappeared altogether.

My anxiety diminished. But in twenty veltiks, I found them again. They crossed the path of the human. Did they cross before or after she had walked?

Confused, I broke trail to study the devil dog prints instead. I followed the trail sign, tracing the prints from where it came. After many rotiks, I discovered it had passed her trail earlier. I retraced the track.

It was circling the human.

I growled.

Was the devil dog herding her to an ambush? Did it tighten its circle until she was surprised and unable to fight?

The behavior alarmed me. The beast traveled alone. That boded well for the human. She would not have to battle an entire pack. Under normal circumstances, a male devil dog traveling alone would have the vicious spirit of one looking to mate. Any obstacles in his way would be dispatched instantly. But a younger mutt, male or female, stayed with its family group. The aberrant behavior followed no reason. I couldn't predict its actions.

The ache in my heart-home returned.

I found the human's path once again and resumed hunting. The soft traveler now had two predators on her trail. I grimaced through a heart cramp. I could only be sure of the intentions of one.

At length, I came upon a great upheaval in the forest. A mound of jokapazathel swarmed a carcass. Terror eating at my gut, I tramped through their wriggling bodies and entered the glen. I realized it was too large to be a human. But my relief was short lived. Perhaps the beast had already killed the human. Perhaps the devil dog had killed the human and the ... it was difficult to identify. The fur was gone.

I flung the rodents aside, and tore at the carcass, trying to move it to check beneath. Only its organs and bones, no human corpse. I took a stride then sank to my knees and bowed my head.

"Holy Goddesses, thank you for preserving the life of the human. I must assume you have done so. Please protect her from the devil dog and from any that might harm her, until she is safe within the walls of my heart-home." I ended my prayer and stood.

I cocked my head and flared my nostrils.

The rains.

Kathe. The rains would draw more devil dogs. She already had one to contend with. Would the relentless march toward death never end on this forsaken planet?

Ever had I respected and revered Ikthe. Until meeting the fragile humans with brave spirits. They might have the courage to fight here, but they had the teeth and claws of an unborn babe. Did the Goddesses truly expect them to survive on will alone? Did they not need more than their flimsy bones and weapons to protect themselves? Did they not need more than the protection of the mighty hunters? We could not be present every jotik of their lives. What were the Goddesses thinking?

My frustration boiled over, and I found myself tearing branches along the path. I must control myself. I must not lose the trail.

But when the rains began to fall, I realized it may already be too late. The rains would erase her prints as easily as wiping grease from a chin. *Kathe.*

16

Amity

When I woke to the dim light of morning under heavy cloud cover, four black eyes stared at me through my veined glass face shield. Diablo?

But no, this devil dog was bigger. A lot bigger. The size of a lion. With more teeth. Sharper teeth.

I let my gaze slide to its flank; several others stood behind him.

They didn't know what to make of me, so I didn't move.

"Heart approaching 130 BPM, do you require assistance?"

"Not yet, VELMA," I answered. "A pack of devil dogs is staring me down."

"I will pulse the infrasonic signal," she said.

"No, wait. They're not behaving in a threatening way," I said. "I want to see what they do next."

"Very well," she said. "Standing by."

The animal cocked its head and bent closer still, flaring its nostrils as it sniffed me. The scent of blood might linger, but all the fluids from skinning the Tree Thief would have sloughed off by now.

When I had sutured Diablo's throat sac, it had been full dark. I had focused my light at the wound, and since then, he had not been closer to me than two meters.

This one was close enough to touch. I admired her shiny black nose and stark white fur. Close up, I could see the texture of the fur differed from Earth animals. Rain still fell, and the water ran off the furred spikes. Her throat sac hung loose, but the network of blood veins was visible. VELMA's theory had been right.

The urge to pet her snout was strong; I reached my hand towards her, centimeter by careful centimeter. She curled her black lip and showed her slender pointed teeth. I stopped moving. She brought her nose closer and flared her nostrils again. Something offended her; she tossed her head and jumped back, her hackles raised. She rolled her eyes and darted between her pack. They melted back into the forest following her, a couple looking back at me, and then they were gone.

I felt my heartbeat slow when I took a huge breath. I had been holding it. I sat up, assessing new aches and pains from yesterday's exertions. Wow. That had been a close encounter. I remembered my brothers yelling at me. "Don't touch it! Put it back! Walk away!"

Catching and studying stray animals whenever we landed on a habitable planet had been my pastime. My brothers were tasked with following me around and keeping me safe, but I often eluded their lackadaisical supervision. They always seemed to find me at crucial moments, stumbling through the woods and scaring off whatever injured creature I'd found. They would drag me back to our ship and lock me in until the supplies had been loaded, me shouting epithets at them all, and then retreating to my tiny menagerie of rescued creatures I had managed to save from whatever last place we'd been. My scientist parents clucked at me but still paid the fees for transporting exoplanet life and signing the documents stating that the animals would never leave their artificial habitats until death, and then would be ejected into space or returned to their home world to be buried.

My curiosity never left me, in spite of or because of all those side trips. Exobiology was my first and only love, and as I withdrew a breakfast MRE from my pack, I memorized the look of the devil dog as it sniffed my outstretched hand. I would try to draw her later. It was reckless of me to try and touch it, but I could no more hold myself back from my curiosity than a moon could hold back a tide.

I wondered what had caused it to run off. The behavior was similar to that of a predator being startled by a skunk or porcupine. I looked down at my hand and didn't see anything except residue from the terrifying attack-lichen. Inspecting it up close, an odor wafted through the spiderweb cracks of my helmet. My eyes watered and I coughed. The smell from yesterday. Oh, that was bad. It must have released something akin to thiols, a sulfur and alcohol chemical like those of skunk spray or deer musk.

Rainwater still dripped from the hole in the roof. I grabbed a handful of leaves to aid in rubbing it off but then paused. If the smell was bad enough to deter the fierce devil dog and an entire pack, shouldn't I keep it? I could remove my gloves when I ate so the smell wouldn't be so bad. But considering how much I didn't want to kill all these animals; it might be worth risking another attack just to smear more of its chemical compound all over me.

With the drizzle letting up, I grabbed both my machete and multi-tool and approached the dead tree where the attack-lichen lay in wait. So many things could go wrong. But if my exobiology studies had taught me anything, it was the oddity of toxin sequestration. Whatever this mobile fungus was, it probably ingested a toxin, sequestered it somewhere in its body, and released it as needed when under threat.

Conversely, it could also use the toxin to paralyze a victim and/or digest it. The devil dogs had learned to avoid it, therefore I needed it.

Sweat tickled at my temples and my heart raced. I could feel my own defense chemicals ramping up as I approached the lichen. From a meter away, I studied it. It wrapped over the top of the log but didn't reach all the way around. I couldn't see any obvious mechanisms for its movement, but I'd seen it jump at me with my own eyes. Perhaps it was hyphae, or tiny bio-electrical pulses. If I let it subdue my arms, it would defeat me. I had to control where it attacked to give myself the upper hand.

I took a deep breath and stepped up to the log without touching it.

Planning to keep the right side of my body well away from its grasping and powerful embrace, I leaned with my left. Just before my leg made contact with the log, a huge furry white blur bowled me over from the right.

Diablo and I rolled over and over through the understory, branches and twigs breaking under our weight and crushed leaves smearing chlorophyll all over my suit and Diablo's fur.

Disoriented and irritated, I shoved him off and stood up, brushing detritus off my legs and arms. "What in the world?" I shouted at him.

He snarled and posed as if to pounce. His throat sac remained flaccid, though.

"What?" I yelled again. His eyes blinked slow at me, and he kept baring his teeth.

His attack had sent us both rolling downhill and flung my tools out of my grip. I made a step toward where we rolled from, and he growled and lowered his head at me.

"No!" I said and pointed my finger at him. "You don't tell me what to do."

His lip curled; his shoulders were tight, and his tail flicked.

I stood with hands on hips.

"I don't know what this is about, but I need my tools, and I need a way to defend myself," I said. "I had it all under control until you knocked me down."

Diablo continued to stare until I took a step backward. His posture relaxed a smidge. I took another step back. He stopped snarling. Another step. He licked his chops and sat on his haunches, panting and looking for all the world like a dopey dog of death.

"Seriously?" I flung my hands out and turned, walking diagonally downhill, somewhere south of the lean-to. He'd better let me go back and get my provisions. I looked behind me, and he began trotting, unconcerned. When I was about ten meters due south of the lean-to, I started back up the hill. He didn't bother me.

"This is ridiculous," I said. "You've been MIA for hours. Where were you when an entire pack of your devil dogs tried to eat me, huh?" He didn't answer.

At my shelter, I gathered the rucksack and water canisters. Diablo sat three and a half meters away, once again avoiding proximity.

Panting from the exertion of carrying the pack, I turned to look at him.

"You won't let me pet you, but you'll mow me over, huh? I see how it is."

I took a deliberate step towards the dead logs and the attack-lichen. He didn't do anything.

With my eyes on him, I walked another couple steps. He still didn't move.

I huffed a breath and tried to find where the right log was. I found the log, but not the lichen. I stopped. It wasn't where it had been before. One more step, and I could now see to where it had migrated. Just beyond the fallen tree was a huge old granddaddy tree trunk. The road-map size lichen had joined its mother fungus wrapped around the base of the tree. It could mummify a gorilla. I lost my breath.

Diablo had saved me from being completely encapsulated. I looked back at him; he had padded a couple meters closer and sat again. It looked like he winked at me. Punk.

Veering a distance from the huge organism, I followed the wreckage our tumble had made on the forest floor and kicked at the undergrowth until I found my machete. The multitool had to be around here somewhere. I spent an hour I didn't have tracing and retracing the area to my growing frustration. I used my flashlight to try and shine it off the metal. No luck.

"Dammit, Diablo," I muttered. I shouldn't blame him. He saved my life, after all. It's just that, I kind of needed my damn tool.

Defeated, I hiked back to the lean-to. I only had five hours of daylight left in which to travel. The invisible bacteria could be colonizing my bloodstream even now. Should I stay another night and try to look again? Or give it up and make do? Maybe Pattee had a spare in her pod. I grimaced. Was she hanging out with her—life companion? I suppressed a shiver and surveyed the ground where the pazathel-nax pack had stared me down. I could still see their huge tracks.

Diablo lay in a bower gnawing on something.

I looked up at the canopy. I should get going. I hated to leave without my tool, but it was gone. Probably fell down a hole or something.

My gaze fell on Diablo again. He held his object between his front paws and enthusiastically licked and chewed it, eyes closed in bliss. On a hunch, I shone my light at him. A gleam flared back at me. He was using my multitool like a chew toy. Wonderful. All I had to do was get it back.

17

Natheka

Anxiety for the human survivor triggered cramps in my heart-home. I had to pause often to catch my breath. The rains pounded with relentless ferocity, and I set my scans to detect pazathel-naxl. With the shimmer of power generated by the satiated Shel beneath my armor, I seemed to glow in the waning light of the ikfal. The beasts of this wood knew to avoid a hunter in his element.

Before the rains, the human and the devil dog traveled south by southeast. I wondered if she had a destination, but, how could she? Esra's technology said it could not access the pod's comms. Unless she had a map? Why would she leave the crash site when she had access to fresh water? Unless she knew the devil dog tracked her. Perhaps she tried to evade it. She would not know they traveled Ikthe and could scent her anywhere she went. If she were running, her route would be winding, confused. Instead, she maintained a straight course.

Puzzling over the enigma, I missed the scent of a Tree Thief until it was upon me. It attacked from the trail ahead, catching me unawares with its enviable camouflage.

I roared as I fell, deploying a blade from my forearm panel and driving it into its flesh between its shoulder joint and first rib. The stench of rotting meat blasted my face as it yowled in pain. Its wound weakened its assault, and I rolled him over, finding a blade with my left hand and finishing him off.

I panted and rose from the beast, watching as its dark blood diluted in the rain and mixed with the mud from the trail. I stepped over its corpse. If Pattee Crow Flies were here, she would doubtless want to collect its fur, but I didn't have the luxury of time.

How could a human new to this planet fight off a Tree Thief? Or the devil dogs? Goddesses forbid, the rokhural? I decided to maintain a south by southeast course and surrendered to the need my body had clamored for for days. I ran.

18

Amity

"If you don't give me that multitool, I will cut your tail off and use it for a boa," I said. I crouched and ambled forward three more steps. Diablo thought that was the best game ever, and he snatched the tool in his jaws, jumped up, and ran several meters away, circled back, and buzzed me so close I could feel a breeze. Then began an epic session of the zoomies. The hundred-pound white wolf with four eyes, horrifying teeth and spiked fur, zipped around on an oval forest track, leaping over stumps with abandon, racing with incredible speed and exuding the joy that only a four-legged animal with digitigrade rear legs could exude. At one point, he raced right for me, and I screamed and dodged him, only to watch him dart at the last second and go for another zooming lap. I lost him in the trees. When I turned, he was lying on the ground again, gnawing the metal.

"Diablo," I said, trying to keep a straight face. "Drop it."

He kept chewing.

It had been decades since I last had a dog. I knew I shouldn't laugh. The puppy stage was the worst. Hiding my face from him, I shook with laughter until I could calm down and started walking downhill. "You better not lose that, wolf," I called back to him.

Using my machete to clear the way, I resisted the urge to look behind me. Either he was going to bring it with him, or he would lose interest. Either way, I had run out of time. While I still felt fine, it was ridiculous to gamble with my health. I needed to travel while I had all my faculties.

Frustration mixed with humor from the wolf's antics, as well as the bad news, had given me a cluster headache. I stopped where the ground leveled a bit and hooked the machete at my belt. I fussed with the MDpak pocket and dug around until I found a pain reliever pill. I unlatched my helmet and took the pill with a swig of rainwater, replaced my helmet and retrieved my machete. I had ten more doses of the stronger analgesic, but I was hoarding those for more dire circumstances.

Before I could take a step, Diablo ghosted from out of the trees in front of me, stared at me a long minute, then dropped the multitool in my path. He tossed his head and dodged back into the forest, slipping between trees and bracken until I lost sight of his white coat.

I huffed a final laugh and grabbed my tool off the ground, noting it now sported bite marks, but was otherwise undamaged.

Shaking my head, I stowed the tool.

"VELMA, what do you know about niche partitioning?" I asked her after I thought I saw Diablo dive into the brush and rise a minute later with one of those fat brown things in its muzzle.

"Niche partitioning is a term referring to the animals in a habitat diversifying competition for resources by consuming only portions of a resource in a given habitat," she said. "In that way, biological diversity is maintained so that entire species are not eliminated due to overhunting."

"Yeah, that's how I would have said it, too," I said with a smile. "Does that principle hold true on Predator Planet?"

"From what I have observed, yes with reservations."

"What reservations, VELMA?" I asked.

"The pazathel-naxl hunt such a wide variety of prey they seem to operate outside normal niche partitioning parameters," she said. "Perhaps it is the planet's way to diversify ecosystems."

I raised my brows. "An interesting observation for an AI. Tell me more."

"As I have explained before, the study of excrements has increased my knowledge base of the biology on this planet. In compiling excrement data, I have discovered the pazathel-nax excrement deposits seeds and microorganisms throughout a variety of this planet's ecosystems, thus ensuring a rich and diverse population of both flora and fauna while maintaining a somewhat homogenous habitat. Another discovery is the remarkable symbiotic relationships found throughout the planet, but also several outliers that defy the common biological markers," she said. "Most predators on Ikthe own the vocal sac organ, but not the apex predators, Theraxl. According to their myths, they originated on this planet. Why do they not possess the same organ?"

"Oh, that is interesting," I said. I wished my IntraVisor wasn't laced with cracks. Without video, I would have to wait to see what they looked like. "Anything else?"

"Yes, a notable presence of what humans would term giant insects. In addition to the gigantic population of insect and arachnid species of familiar size, there are a number of them that have achieved significant proportion."

I swallowed and looked around me at the rainforest. As I traveled farther down the mountain, the foliage and trees had changed variety. What sort of giant bugs was VELMA getting at?

"When you say "gigantic" and "significant", what do you mean?" I said.

"As an example, there is a species of insect that resembles a *Diplopoda* from Earth. However, its last recorded length on this planet is 1.8 meters long, and it is thirty centimeters wide."

My throat was dry. I did the calculations in my head. "You're saying a millipede here grows to be six feet long and a foot wide?"

"It is not precisely a millipede but resembles it. And yes."

A bead of sweat rolled from my hairline down the back of my neck. The jungle seemed darker. Thicker. And more sinister.

"What does the giant millipede eat?" I said.

"Based on its excrement signature, it primarily scavenges protein and complex carbohydrates from the jungle floor," she said. "It is most likely to wait until you are dead before it eats you."

"Ah, thanks VELMA," I said. "That makes me feel so much better. There are, um, other big bugs here?"

"Using the classification of arachnid loosely, there is a species that lives in the elaborate cave systems found on this planet," VELMA said. "Esra and Pattee have both battled with the creatures, as they are carnivorous and aggressive, as well as territorial."

Shoulders tightening and hands fisting, my body was preparing for fight or flight, and it was only because of VELMA's descriptions.

"What size are they?" I said.

"Named agothe-faxl, or nightwalkers, the females reach a size comparable to Earth's rhinos. The males of the species only achieve the size of an adult large breed dog, such as a mastiff."

My voice cracked. "I see."

"Do you require assistance?" she said.

I chuckled.

"Oh no, I'm fine. I'm just, you know, hiking down a mountain range, avoiding trees that eat humans like snacks, and peering around every trunk checking for attack-lichen or, God forbid, giant spiders or centipedes."

"Millipedes ..., " VELMA corrected me.

"Riiight."

19

Natheka

R aging against the pack, my swords blurred and disappeared into the fur of the devil dogs as I smote them. But for every single tooth-divider I killed, two more took its place. With fangs bared, they drove at me relentlessly, darting for my joints or openings when my weapons were elsewhere employed. In this way, my helmet was jostled, and it dislodged, tumbling away. No matter.

The hunter fever overtook me, and I entered the halls of my dream place as I fought. With serenity overshadowing my mission to rescue the human, my baser instincts to kill were free to roam without censure.

Another howl, and I slaughtered two huge males who tried to flank me, swinging my sun-blade in a vicious sideways arc. One body was flung into a smaller one who snapped at it, perhaps confused as to why its brother knocked her over.

I smelled a female at my back, and sensing she would leap to attack my neck, I ducked and rolled into the fray, disorienting the five which had been harrying my legs, and rose behind them, slashing at their hamstrings. Keeping a wary eye on the female, I killed two more that approached from my left side. The female's *hohijopa* swelled and deflated; she called to others? Was I not already fighting the entire pack?

As much as I reveled in the battle, I did not take pleasure in the devil dogs' deaths.

While they were busy with me, they left the defenseless human alone.

If the Goddesses required it of me, I would slay them the night through.

A clash of lightning lit the forest around me, casting a temporary still shot of the vicious, blood-tinged fangs all lusting to tear me limb from limb.

Thunder rocked the ground around us, mountain storms bringing the fury within arm's length. A devil dog missed my swinging double-blade and latched onto the armor at my left calf. It would take many rotiks for it to damage my leg thusly, so I left it, and focused instead on the rallying female and her charges. They approached in unison, fanning out.

"Ah, you hunt the hunter?" I said out loud. "I will be your last hunt. Do your worst, Queen Pazathel-nax."

As if she understood my words, she bowed her head a moment, then charged.

Her companions converged as they sought to overpower the single Theraxl in their midst. But I was Natheka, and my helmet denoted the animal the Goddesses gave me power over. Verily, my helmet was a representation of the ravenous pazathel-nax.

Grimacing, my fangs snagged at my lips as I crossed my blades to sever the heads of the two closest. I crouched and lanced, sweeping the legs of another. A downward stroke ended a fourth, leaving the queen. She had dodged my slashing sword, and stood facing me, hackles raised. A stillness settled over her when she licked her fangs with a bloody tongue and took a single step toward me.

Something about her determination pricked my heart-home. I had the fleeting desire to end our battle without shedding another drop of blood and walk away. But we both knew if I turned my back, she would endeavor to spill the blood from my neck and feast upon my body with relish.

When she jumped, time slowed, and my eyes traced the elegant musculature of her body, the textured fur that shed water and the protruding fangs that evolved to disembowel prey with ease. A strange kinship flowed between us when one of her great paws delivered a glancing blow to my cheek, a claw carving a line from below my eye to my jaw, while I drove my dagger up through her rib cage to her heart.

She collapsed in front of me, eyes staring into my soul, and the rain washed the blood from my face down my body to mingle with hers in a puddle on the ground. I watched her die. When her corpse was empty, I felt a tingle on the back of my neck. I turned my head to see an adolescent devil dog standing proud on a huge old stump several veltiks from me. I believed he had observed the entire battle but for whatever reason, had not joined when his queen summoned with her throat sac.

He watched me without blinking, without inflating his sac, and without fear.

His gaze ignited a hot flame in my already burning cheeks. I felt shame.

At last, he tossed his head, leaped from the stump, and ran into the ikfal, white tail disappearing into the brushwood as if he had never been there.

I cocked my head. Had he been a vision from the Goddesses?

I roved my gaze across the dead bodies of the devil dogs. Had I not feigned death along with my hunter brothers, the Ikma would have loved this battle. But I? I had no joy in it. I stole a look around the perimeter, then knelt and petted the head of the formidable devil dog. I would bear the scar she gave me with pride.

The rain had stopped and so had the bleeding, but I wiped wetness from my eyes before resuming my quest through the forest.

20

Amity

E ven though I ate to keep my calorie intake up, my pack did not
feel any lighter on my third day of travel. Without an intact suit,
climate control would utilize more power than I was willing to expend,
so I sweated inside it all day and every night. I felt gross. I smelled awful.
Bathroom breaks were simultaneously a relief to temporarily disrobe,
but also a hassle and endlessly disappointing when the air outside was
no less humid or fetid.

In spite of my discomfort and imminent trench foot, my spirits were hopeful, and I had yet to experience the symptoms of the
cyanobacteria infection. It inspired me to continue at a rapid pace
where possible, to avoid the horrible physical afflictions VELMA had
described once the infection settled in, but also to see for myself that
Pattee was unharmed and of a sound mind.

I found a shaded glen free of danger trees for my noon break and
happily removed my helmet. The itch behind my right ear had been
maddening. I scratched furiously, closing my eyes in rapture. When I
opened them, Diablo was likewise occupied, two meters away. When

he caught me looking at him, his hind leg stopped mid-scratch. His ear flopped, and he blinked his four eyes asynchronously. I laughed, and he resumed scratching. His vigorous leg made him lose balance, and he toppled, rolling in the humus and looking at me upside down as if to say, "I did that on purpose".

I shook my head and drank water, capping the canister and choosing a packet from among my rations. "What have we here today?" I said. I read the stamped letters. "Mm, macaroni and cheese with broccoli. Bet you're jealous."

Diablo yawned at me, stretched, and trotted off. I huffed. I wouldn't see him for hours. I had long since stopped worrying about waiting for him. He always found me.

A shiver ran up my spine when I thought of the previous predators I had come in contact with. Other things found me, too. Itching a sweat trickle on the back of my neck, I looked up at the canopy and into the tree branches. What if I could climb? The thick limbs formed a network of pathways aboveground I hadn't noticed before. I bet it would be easier to see in all directions from up there.

Anything to prevent me from having to kill again.

Enlivened by my idea, I finished my meal, stowed my loose things, hefted the heavy rucksack, and scouted the trees in my vicinity. Double-checking with VELMA that they weren't dangerous, I chose a trunk that had low enough branches I could pull myself up on. I couldn't climb with the backpack, so I lifted it with a grunt and deposited it onto the thick limb, careful not to overset it. I climbed up, and repeated the step, hefting the pack above me first, then following.

Three branches up, I straddled the thick branch and put on my rucksack again. I found long and wide limbs I could walk on that stretched and overlapped one another more or less in the direction I had been traveling.

"VELMA, did you say something about arboreal reptiles?" I said.

"Yes, there are several on Ikthe, most of them deadly," she said. "My sensors are not picking up on any at this time."

"Good, good," I said. "Just keep an eye out. I'm traveling in the canopy for a bit."

21

Natheka

K icking through the scrub, I found my helmet ten strides from the carnage. I replaced it and cleaned my blades, tracking the area with my gaze. Had I truly seen that adolescent pazathel-nax earlier? I paused before sheathing my sun-blade.

The furor of battle no longer clouding my thoughts, I recalled the mutt staring at me. My heart's powerful thud echoed in the empty chamber beside the heart-home. I *had* seen the young devil dog ... it was the same one tracking the human ... my heart mate.

Was the human dead then? Had the pack already attacked?

The battle had been barbaric, frantic. They were hungry. Steeling my hopes, I sent a prayer of gratitude to the Goddesses for sending the young devil dog. I would track him and find the survivor.

With renewed purpose, I trotted to the big stump to lock on to the paw prints and begin a new hunt. Once I found his trail, I picked up speed. He ran in a straight line, following an old game trail that sloped down the mountain range.

Trying not to conjure the image of a ravaged human lying some-where in the brush, I followed. He did not take his circuitous route as before. Either he knew where she was already, or ... I couldn't bear to imagine the other possibility.

Anxiety and hope battled in my chest. The torment fired my limbs, and I ran faster, the fresh tracks easy to see in the mud from the rains. I would find her today.

My sensors lit up; talathel sisters draped over a low limb, waiting for the preoccupied hunter to fall into their trap. I withdrew my swords without slowing, and tore through their reptilian net, scarcely glanc-ing at their felled bodies. Nothing would deter me from my mission.

After a zatik of running, I realized the tracks had not varied, nor had I spied his white tail or undulating spine anywhere in the green foliage ahead of me. The muddy trail was a narrow strip between trees and bushes, vines and weeds, the orange and black soil peeking through thick underbrush. He hadn't stopped or veered.

Fueled by intrigue, I heeded all my senses. He ran to a destination; of this I was certain. What was less certain was if he knew I followed him, and if so, was he indeed leading me? Never had a devil dog been known to do anything other than maim and kill, tear and eat. Alert to the sounds and smells surrounding me, I toggled my visor's multiple scanners as well. I didn't want to miss a single clue as to the dog's intentions, or any threats or obstacles that could delay the discovery of the mystery laid before me.

I zeroed in on the paw prints, keeping pace with their tread, noting the spots where his rear paws landed with a slip in the muddy tracks of his front feet. I hurdled the stumps he hurdled, scaled the stray boulder he scaled, and in every way felt as if I was running with him, one with him. I became the pazathel-nax. Breaths fast and measured, I felt the wind in my fur. I used my tail to balance graceful landings on my four paws. Their claws sunk into the mud, and my tongue swept over my snout, capturing the scents of the ikfal.

The moment the tracks changed, the devil dog vision lifted from my eyes, and I could see I approached a huge treefall. I slowed and approached on silent feet.

Exhilaration coursed through me. Never had I experienced such a oneness with a predator on my planet. It was as if I had joined the devil dog in his body. It was a gift from the Goddesses. I crouched behind a thick tree trunk and tried to see into the glen on the other side of the treefall. Nothing stirred. The paw prints were scattered about the glen, but there was no sign of the dog. My sensors did not pick up anything of note, so I strode into the glen to inspect the layout.

The tree fall had created a crude shelter, and I could see the matted undergrowth where something, likely my human, had bedded down. Sure enough, I beheld a single track of a boot. It was small. I knelt beside the flattened grasses and placed my hand on the ground. Her smell assaulted me through my breath ports. She *was* a female. She smelled raw. She smelled of blood and water and mud and sweat. I smelled Tree Thief pelt, fire, smoke, hot metal, an unfamiliar chemical, and also—I coughed a little. The spray of the deception plant. It only sprayed when it was under threat; had she bested it then?

I laughed. She was a soft traveler. Of course, she did!

I turned then to look at the glen as she had seen it from her repose in the shelter. She had been here when the rains came. It pleased me that she had found a dry place to bed down. The ground in front of the shelter was trampled by tracks. Pazathel-nax tracks of a variety of sizes. Not just the juvenile. My heart seized.

The pack had been here. With careful scrutiny, I examined how they had arrayed. Ah, they all faced the shelter, but none had approached. Frowning, I studied them a rotik.

What could have deterred ... of course! The stench of the deception plant. It would have been stronger than it was now, and the pazathel-naxl knew to avoid it. So. My little human had bested both the deception plant *and* the pazathel-nax pack. I growled deep in my throat, approval and pleasure washing over me. She would have tales to exchange with Esra and Pattee, then. She was equal in ferocity and bravery to the other humans. Perhaps superior. I would accompany her back to my brothers with pride and boast of her many victories around the fire.

A sound drew my attention from the ikfal. I spun to see the devil dog peeking at me from amongst a tangle of bracken. Only its four eyes were visible through a gap in the dark-green leaves. He blinked at me, then faded from view. What an odd, odd youth. Perhaps it was injured in the head, and not, in fact, highly intelligent. Both possibilities could explain the aberrant behavior.

Shrugging, I stood and surveyed the glen. She was not here now. It was time to collect her and bring her to the safety of our group. I found the place she resumed her hike and followed, not in a full run, but faster than a walk. Soon.

The path she chose was smooth and unhindered by overgrowth. I sensed the devil dog ahead of me in the ikfal, but once again did not see him; he preferred to travel obscured by the understory.

A zatik later, I came upon a small glen. Her fragrance was stronger here; she was not long gone from this place. Excitement fluttered in my chest. Here she sat and ate. There she paused to look into the ikfal, perhaps hearing the devil dog? I circled the area in search of the tracks showing her egress.

Cocking my head, I rounded the glen a second time. And a third. In a widening circle, I searched for prints among the understory, but couldn't find any. I returned to the glen.

Logic would prove she could not disappear. But superstition suggested she had.

Fists at my waist, I turned a slow circle. What had I missed?

The dog had not shown his face or tail in several rotiks. Had he raced ahead? Abandoning the search for her prints, I decided to follow his again. It took me too long to find the spot from which he'd peeked at me. From there I could search out a partial paw print, and then a full set. He, too, circled the glen. This reminded me of the set of tracks I found at the outset of my foray into the ikfal. He had encircled the human's trail. I had suspected it was a way for him to close in on his prey, but after his strange behavior, another thought occurred to me. But it was too foreign an idea. It couldn't be that, and so I dismissed it. With nose to the ground, as it were, I examined the devil dog's tracks as they circled the entire region. Spying the fleeting blur of white ahead of me, I paced onward.

Several rotiks later, when the flashes of white fur had ceased, I heard the snap of a branch behind me. Spinning with my dagger in hand, I crouched as I peered into the forest behind me. I thought I saw a white pointed ear, but it was so fast it could have been one of the giant blossoms from the garish feast tree. A jotik longer I waited, but nothing approached. I resumed tracking.

His prints spiraled the entire glen and then branched outward in a growing radius from the glen. A half-zatik later I stomped back into the glen, thrashing low-hanging branches with my gloves and tearing away leaves. The blurring of white fur revealed the devil dog still skulking about in the ikfal.

The urge to run crept on me again, but there was nowhere to go. She had not resumed her south by southeast trek. She had not gone back. She had flown up and out of the ikfal ... my throat tightened. The rodaxl did not typically come this far north in the mountain range, but already had we seen the wildlife and the elements collude to thwart the hunters' quest.

I looked up into the canopy, fear smashing into my heart-home. All I could see were tall trunks and hanging vines, large awnings of leaves and a smattering of orange sky. No rodaxl nests, thank the Goddesses.

As I stood in the center of the glen, I smelled the stealthy approach of the juvenile. Would he deign to battle me now, in the middle of this deserted glen? I held my breath, hand poised above my double-blade. His size did not warrant using the larger sun-blade.

I sniffed. Tilted my head. I stepped a slow turn, and he sat two veltiks from me, watching me.

Rehearsing the last zatik, I realized something. I had been following the *kathe* dog in a circle and he had been following me and we were no closer to discovering the direction in which the human traveler had gone.

"You have wasted my time and risked the safety of the woman!" I shouted at it.

Unfazed, he gave me a sideways glance, yawned, and half-inflated his hohijopa. It deflated with a strange wheeze. I took a step towards him, but he did not flinch away. I stopped at one veltik, a single stride away from him, and peered more closely. His throat sac bore stitches closing a wound.

Unbidden, my hand rose to clutch at the odd burning in my chest. The human had mended this predator's wound?

I fumbled a step back, my surprise so thick I could barely stand to carry it. The devil dog strode toward my retreating figure and stopped a half veltik from me and sat. He yawned again. Another wheeze.

"You hunt her because she is yours," I said. The devil dog grinned at me, showing all its teeth. Taken aback, I frowned. "But you have lost her, foolish mutt."

He growled.

I held up my hand. "Nay, you have lost her. That means she is fair game. Whichever of us finds her first may lay first claim," I said with a snarl.

He cocked his head, then jumped to his feet and ran to the trees. He sniffed the trunks and began urinating on them, one by one.

"You scoundrel," I muttered. Another side-eye from the dog and I realized I was talking to a dumb animal. I threw my hands up to the canopy and scoffed.

A breeze wafted across my face, and a hint of the human's smell entered my nostrils.

Feeling foolish, I realized I had neglected to use all my senses. With a casual glance at the dog, I took a surreptitious sniff of the air. That tree. It was stronger there.

I walked to a different tree and noted that the devil dog tracked me with his eyes. *Kathe.* Ignoring him, I meandered to the tree upon which her smell lingered.

I would scour the ground beneath until I spotted the telltale sign of her passage. Desperate to find her, I knelt, even as the devil dog paid rapt attention to my actions. Still, her tracks eluded me. Frowning, I stood again, closed my eyes, and followed my scent. Up the bark. Up the trunk. Up.

Opening my eyes, I saw the thick limbs of the sister-crossing trees. A hunter desperate to travel fast would, of a season, choose the tree passageways. But how did the human know of this custom?

Without a backward glance, I leaped up to the first branch. Then scaled another two branches where I caught her fragrance, strong and pure. I chuckled low.

"You are my prey, now, Clever Sister."

A sound below me. I looked down, and the devil dog scratched at the base of the tree. He jumped up, his front paws reaching high, but not high enough. Curious, I waited to see what he would do.

He circled the tree, his throat sac puffing and shrinking in agitation. Then he backed up, his hips swaying with the awkward motion, and against my belief, took a running leap up the tree until he straggled his way to the first low branch. Eyes rounding in astonishment, I watched as he scrabbled and dug his way up the trunk and branches. That *kathe* devil was climbing the *kathe* tree!

I didn't waste another jotik. I had prey to capture first.

22

Amity

The tree limbs were so thick I didn't worry about making a misstep and falling. However, I wasn't confident enough to run, so I hiked the treetops, marveling at the vibrant life existing between ground and sky.

A species of purple and green bird proliferated here, just under the canopy. They darted among the branches, raced each other between forks in the tree trunks, and nested in hollows. Countless insects used this forest highway; I could see long lines of them marching along trunks or vines. Peering into a lush tangle of woven vines, I saw a lacy shape swaying as if in a breeze. But the humid jungle had no breeze. Closer inspection revealed it to be a network of tiny bright green bugs clasping each other's limbs and creating a larger organic shape. It was a net of sorts, I suspected, and paused to drink so I could watch and see if anything happened. Sure enough, a flying bug that resembled a moth flew drunkenly into the mass. The many-legged insects collapsed onto it, contracting their swaying mass into a swarming green ball. I shuddered and chuckled, moving on.

The wonders of this place could keep me occupied for years; and then I realized with a pang that Ikthe *would* be my life's work. I swallowed back a sob, the enormity of my new reality squeezing my lungs and kickstarting a faster heartbeat. My hands clenched, and I had to stop walking and take deep breaths. I had always thought I would see my family again. After my rotation on Kerberos 90, the plan was to meet up with everyone at Dispatch 9 for a reunion. Three of my brothers were married. I swallowed a sob and shook my head with eyes squeezed shut. No tears.

Calm once more, I resumed my hike.

The immediacy of my health needs had trumped any thoughts about the distant future, but with the teeming biology surrounding me, I couldn't escape my innate curiosity. And at the end of the day, I wouldn't want to. Curiosity about nature and its processes had led me to a fulfilling career, frequent high adventure expeditions on exotic planets and endless opportunities for learning.

I swallowed a lump.

This may be my permanent home now, but there would be no shortage of opportunities to continue exploring and learning. I nodded. I just had to reframe the situation. Based on the flora and fauna I had already seen, I could say with assurance that had I been shown vid clips or still shots of this place, I would have been the first to volunteer for the away team.

"Pluck up, King Girl," I said to myself. I looked down through the crosshatched tree branches, trying to see if Diablo had discovered my subterfuge yet. No sign of him, but I wasn't worried. That wolf could scent me from a mile away. It was only a matter of time.

"VELMA, once you've got me dosed and vaccinated, is there a way for you to repair my helmet?"

"My inventory files indicate there are spare helmet parts in storage in the EEP," she said. "Once you are in Pattee's vacant pod, you will be able to swap out damaged parts, as well as access my global neural network. I will no longer be hampered by the limited technology in your compromised helmet."

"Why does that sound just a tiny bit ominous?" I said with a half-smile.

"Most likely because the potential threat of an artificial super intelligence co-opting human free will has been predicted for centuries," she said. "With a couple anecdotal accounts from distant off-world stations lending credibility to the prediction."

Her answer didn't make me laugh. I cleared my throat. "Well, it's a good thing it's in your programming to keep me alive."

"Indeed, Amity," she said. "It is my pleasure."

I raised a brow and changed the subject. "You said Pattee's not at her pod? How do you know that if you can't communicate with the others?"

"At the time of my download into your helmet, Pattee was accompanied by her heart mate Hivelt, several days' travel from her landing site," she said. "She packed provisions for a long absence from her pod when she left, and the plan at that time was to meet up with Hivelt's hunter brothers to complete the perilous quest commanded by their corrupt Queen, the Ikma Scabmal Kama."

Whiplash. "The what now?"

My brain was still trying to process that heart mate concept. VELMA threw in a quest, political corruption and an alien-sounding governing body. I wasn't cut out for this level of adventuring.

"Which part requires my elucidation?" VELMA said.

I decided to wait on the heart mate explanation. Something told me the humans would have a better grasp of the concept than an artificial neural network.

"Tell me about the perilous quest," I said. "That sounds fun."

"As a side note, the Theraxl race do not have a word for fun," VELMA said.

"Heh. Since you're about to tell me about a "perilous quest", that doesn't surprise me."

"The Ikma Scabmal Kama, one half of the governing body on Ikshe, issued a quest for five of their esteemed hunters," VELMA said. "Ikshe being the twin planet visible in the sky."

"Okay," I said.

"Theraxl prize two elements found on this, their hunting grounds," she said. "Woaiquovelt, a precious metal, and a liquid called the Holy Waters of Shegoshel, that is purported to have mythological properties."

"Metal and water," I murmured. "Go on."

"From conversations I've gleaned in the last weeks, the elements are found in the harshest environs on the planet. A large percentage of hunters on these quests do not return to their home world."

I was already sweating, but VELMA's lecture seemed to spring yet more perspiration as cramping sent sharp pains radiating outward from my abdomen.

"Okay, so," I paused to take a breath. "These hunters are on a dangerous quest, and the humans are going with them?"

"Affirmative."

I crouched, letting the cramp pass. I noticed my leg wound had started aching again. Damn. Climbing the tree must have been too much strain.

With hands on my knees, my heavy pack pulled at me, but I felt like I needed a breather. VELMA's voice caught my attention as I stood up.

"Reptilian signature detected," she said. "Proceed with caution."

I froze. Where was it? The thick limb upon which I stood was clear, but vines and huge green leaves draped everywhere. It could be behind me. Holding my arms steady for balance, I turned my upper torso to try and see behind me. Nothing but tree limb and green fronds. Slowly turning back, I tried to see down into the jungle. Nothing moved.

Shit. That left one more place. Up. If I tipped my head up too high, my backpack would ...

Tightness squeezed my boots together. My gaze shot down to see a winding coil creep from my boots up my calves. It hadn't been there a second ago, but it was strangling my legs faster than I could react. I reached for the hilt of my machete, but the reptile yanked at my boots, and I fell back, arms flailing. Before my helmet hit the branch, another coil slipped around my shoulders, pinning my arms in place yet lifting my body. I couldn't understand how the snake was wrapping around me from two different directions, unless ...

Tightening in my chest was making it difficult to breathe or think. Two snakes. Two.

The winding body cut off circulation in my legs, yet my old wound felt like it was going to burst. I squeezed my eyes shut and gritted my teeth against the pain, grunting and panting.

"VELMA," I gasped for breath. "Can you ... do ... someth ..."

Ever tighter, the reptiles had me mummified, a narrow window of light shining through my cracked helmet. My chest was compressed so much, I expected to feel my ribs cracking any second now.

Fuzzy, disjointed lights blinked in my cracked IntraVisor, but their significance had no meaning. Maybe VELMA was doing something, but I could feel myself starting to black out.

I heard a roar. Snakes didn't roar, but I was on Predator Planet. Maybe the snakes roared here.

I thought I heard the whooshing of air. Like, slashing.

A rush of breath filled my lungs in a huge gasp. Loosening from my chest and arms left flooding warmth and painful tingles shooting throughout my body, but I collapsed, barely able to hold up my head. Dull gray metal-clad arms caught me and lifted me up like a child.

I rolled my head to see who held me.

A devil dog? I felt my forehead crinkle. No, a helmet in the shape of a devil dog's head.

"I am Natheka," a deep voice said in my language. "I am your heart mate."

23

Natheka

The Clever Sister's scent grew stronger with every passing veltik, but alarms pierced the silence in my helmet. The jeweled talathel! Clever she may be, but the talathel were wicked hunters, coiling in silence, striking deadly fast. I raced, feeling my life blood pump and the Shel infuse me with extra chemicals that would boost my power. I couldn't hear the dog behind me, but I smelled him, close at my heels, no doubt. The branch was not wide enough for us to run side by side.

My scans imprinted a visual overlay on the talathel, and I unsheathed my sun-blade as I ran. One sister had the human by the legs, the second over her chest, shoulders and helmet. Time was running out. "Dog, take the serpent at her feet if you would have her live," I shouted. "I will take the one at her head." He could not understand my commands, but he was a pack hunter. He would know what to do. I was counting on it.

With mere veltiks left, I leapt and severed the thick body of the snake as it suspended from a higher branch. As I suspected it would, the devil dog slunk low and attacked a bulging muscle that encircled the human's legs. In a swift motion, I sheathed my blade, and I caught the human before she fell off the branch, eager to see if she lived. She turned her helmet to face me, and I swallowed the gasp that wanted to erupt when I saw the fissures lacing the glass. A quick scenting alerted me to the bloom of fresh blood seeping from a leg wound. Had the talathel struck? If so, she would likely die, her small body no match for its debilitating venom.

The dog's attack had loosened the second talathel's grip, and now he braced himself against the bark while the serpent tried to escape. A battle-pull ensued between them with the mutt yanking the serpent from the human's legs, but my attention returned to the human. Her brown eyes widened.

"I am your heart mate," I said.

Kathe.

My tongue preceded my fangs, words exiting my mind before I had thought them through. Ever had it been so with me. But I need not have worried, as her dazed eyes blinked closed.

The venom!

I leaped to the ground below, my suit absorbing the impact, and I cleared an area to lay the human down. Fumbling with the pouch, I dropped the vial of the Holy Waters, but it bounced, harmless, on the humus.

The Waters' potency was proven as successful antivenin for the agothe-fax bite, but its usefulness on other poisons was variable. It depended on the victim's ability to metabolize and overall health.

With heart-home straining inside my chest, I found the latch that secured her helmet and released it. I removed it with care, not wanting her head to drop on the ground or the sides of the axial ring to scrape her skin. Letting a knuckle graze the curve of her jaw, I could appreciate her skin tone reminded me of the dark sands of the Ancient Grotto on Ikshe. It was a place of contemplation and peace.

I grasped the bottle but before I could unstop it, her eyes blinked and opened. Was she not struck? Frowning in confusion, I bent closer to look at her bleeding leg. Ah, it was not the bite of the talathel; it was a deep puncture wound.

"How did this happen?" I said and stowed my precious bottle, using the action to hide my rattled breaths. I gathered up grasses around me and tore them in pieces, placing them at the wound.

She watched my action a jotik then let her head fall back. Her breaths were ragged. She waved toward her leg.

"It's from the crash," she said. "How are you speaking my language?" Her voice sounded weak.

"VELMA downloaded your language into my helmet so that I would be able to speak with you," I said. "I am Natheka. Your fellows are safe, and eager to reunite." I hoped she didn't hear or remember how I first introduced myself. I inspected her still-bleeding wound. Leaning down, I inhaled a deep breath above the wound, noting the chemical smell from earlier, hints of water, and unfamiliar odors, as well as a scant scent of illness.

Pulling my healer's kit from its cache, I fished in it for an herb that might help. The scent of pazathel-nax hit my nose, and I drew my short sword before realizing it was the mutt.

"Diablo, you found me!" the human said. I noted she greeted it with more warmth than it should deserve.

The dog approached, giving me side eyes and curling its lip. A veltik from me, his hackles rose, and he growled, his throat sac swelling halfway.

"I think he wants you to move," the human said. I glanced at her amused expression. Dark circles under her brown eyes and wan cheeks showed the exertion she suffered these last days. "He probably wants to lick my wound."

Taken aback, I placed my glove over it. The dog growled louder and took a step.

"It's fine, let him do it," she said, tossing me a sharp look. "Come, Diablo!" She patted her thigh above the smear of blood.

Rising to stand, I backed away from the human, but my hand hovered above my sword hilt.

The dog snarled at me again but then trotted to the human's side and began licking the wound. Repulsed and fascinated, I watched a predator that had plagued my people for generations sniff and examine the wound after each ministration. In several rotiks, he sniffed again and licked his snout, collapsed in a heap and rested his huge head on her leg. He blinked at me, his lids fluttering before falling asleep.

"He trusts you," she said. Then bit her lip and frowned. "Or maybe he trusts me." She brushed a lock of dark brown hair out of her face. "I'm Amity, Amity Diaz." She gave me an uncertain smile, and once more my heart-home jolted in an unfamiliar rhythm. It had known. All the way back at Moon Shield, it had known.

"Amity, Amity Diaz," I said, and bowed, though it was awkward; she still lay on the floor of the ikfal.

"No, just one Amity," she said with a small laugh. "Amity. You said your name was ... Natheka?"

"Yes," I said, then gestured to the dog. "I saw the blood at your crash site, and the tracks. I assumed the worst."

She nodded. "I believe it." She patted her helmet. "When VELMA told me I was on a predator planet, this guy showed up not long after. But he was in bad shape, so I didn't think to be afraid of him."

"I saw the careful stitches you gave his wound," I said. "He does not seem to suffer from his injury now."

I noticed a pinkness creep into her cheeks. "It wasn't much of a wound, really," she said. "The head injury was probably worse, but after plenty of water and rest, he seemed to recover."

A sound reserved for private bathing chambers emitted from the animal's rear while he slept. Affronted, I watched Amity to see her reaction.

She scowled. "Oh, that's bad." She waved her hand in front of her nose. "*Dios mio*, I don't want to know what he eats out there." She gestured into the ikfal. Brushing off debris from her torso she looked up at me. "I think I can get up now. Thank you for rescuing me from the snakes," she said and slid her leg out from under the dog's head. He snorted and blinked, then rose, stretching his long limbs one at a time like an old Iktheka. "I feel better," she said from her spot on the ground. "The same thing happened the last time he did that. I think his saliva must have antibacterial properties. My leg had swollen and wouldn't stop bleeding. I'm sure it was infected. But he came racing out of the woods and started licking it like his life depended on it, and the next thing I know I'm feeling good as new."

"That astonishes me," I said, watching the dog sit, then proceed to lick his genitals. Heat flamed my face as I grumbled and pointed at him. "The beast has no dignity around females."

Amity grimaced and turned away from his rude display.

"That may be true," she said. "But he has been invaluable to me almost since I landed."

She maneuvered out of the straps of her pack and twisted to grab her destroyed helmet and replace it. She stood.

"Why do you wear it?" I asked. "Has it not lost its value?"

"The audio works," she said, "and from what I understand, VEL-MA also emits a frequency that deters a portion of the wildlife." She looked at the shredded body of the talathel. "I can't thank you enough." Her voice lowered to a subdued tone. "I was trying to pay attention, but they came out of nowhere."

"Ik," I said, mindlessly reverting to my own language. Through the splintered glass, I saw a faint smile crease Amity's face.

"Ah, I could hear your language and VELMA's translation," she said. "Very ... interesting."

"Yes, your fellows have been instrumental in merging our languages," I said. I half-turned, ready to trek to Moon Shield. "I must alert them to finding you." Toggling the comms, I called Naraxthel. "I have found the human. We are at the tree line of Forgiven Mountain. Her helmet is damaged, and her suit has tears. She suffers a wound from the crash; we will trek to Moon Shield."

"Oh," she said, and a frown appeared. "I have to go this way. I guess I have a bacterial infection known to be fatal, and I have to get to Pattee's pod." She shrugged. "But I feel fine."

My heart paused at her words. Both Pattee and Esra had nearly succumbed to the deadly bacteria on my sacred planet. With their technology's interventions and scant drops of our Holy Waters, they had survived, but not without terrifying moments, if my brothers' tales were to be believed.

"Hold," I amended when I heard Naraxthel respond. "She is host to the deadly bacteria; we travel to Pattee's pod first."

"Pardon me for interrupting," the human's technology voiced in my helmet. "Do I have your permission to alter the frequency receiving unit in your helmet? In that way, I will be able to merge the limited functioning AI in Amity's damaged helmet with the nanosatellite array. Once her helmet is repaired, I will restore your original settings."

I raised a brow at VELMA's request. Did the technology so easily access Theraxl's communication devices? Unsettled, I pondered her request. Peeking at Amity's pallor, I decided. "You have my permission, insofar as you use it to help Amity fully recover."

"Of course, Natheka," the voice said. "It is in my programming to do so."

Amity watched me, ignorant of my conversation, and then looked away when I met her gaze. A white flash drew my attention from her face. The mutt frolicked in the understory, nipping at an awaafa.

Amity's gasp startled me.

"Is that a butterfly?" She approached with ginger steps; eyes fixed on the floating feathery insect. "It has eight limbs, so it must be in the class Arachnida," she said, her voice fading away. I saw her lips move; she appeared to talk to herself, or perhaps her technology.

The wonder in Amity's voice struck me as I joined her to observe the devil dog play with the awaafa. Seeing the sacred hunting grounds through this human's eyes twisted my heart-home into contortions. It was not pleasant. Yet I cocked my head, noting the playful nature of the pazathel-nax pup. It was not unlike my own younglings, fearing no danger, finding amusement in odd things. A pang for my little hunters further pinched my heart until the discomfort forced me to lean against a trunk. My nostrils flared as the pain took me by surprise. Too late I remembered to imagine the halls of my dream place, so when I entered its marbled sanctity, the pain had already ebbed. Deep breaths quelled the rapid beats, and I resumed watching Amity watch the wildlife. Thankfully, she had not noticed my odd behavior.

The awaafa lifted higher and higher, teasing the devil dog into greater jumps until it was running at tree trunks and leaping into the air. Its bladed teeth snapped a mere jovelt from the awaafa's spindly legs. Sensing its danger, the flying insect fluttered its great wings and floated into the canopy, leaving a panting dog staring after it. I would remember this scene and carve its likeness for my little hunters later.

"What are you smiling about?" Amity asked me. I had not realized I was smiling.

"I was memorizing the devil dog at play," I said. Pulling out one of my carvings, I showed Amity. "I will carve the scene and gift them to my hunters," I said. I felt my smile fall when I replaced the wooden animal. "If I return to Ikshe."

Amity faced me, a peculiar expression on her face. Peering closer I could see liquid shimmer in her eyes.

"Are you in pain?" I asked.

"No," she said. "Yes. I don't know." She craned her neck to seek out the insect above. "I'm probably going to die here, but it's such a magical place."

My brows met in consternation.

"Magic is the work of the Goddesses," I said. "How did you recognize it so easily? You are but a human."

She raised a brow at me before she spoke.

"I just meant ..." She gestured to the dog; he was digging a giant hole beneath a trunk and burying his snout in the dirt. "I study extraterrestrial life. Animals, bugs, biology. And this planet has decades' worth of research for me. If I can live long enough, I could be happy here."

I opened my mouth, but nothing came out.

Amity squeaked and pointed to the dog again. He caught something in the burrow. His hind legs braced in the underbrush, and his shoulder muscles bunched and twitched as he fought to drag it from its hiding place. Uneasy, I drew my weapon and stood in front of Amity.

The dog's head was partially in the burrow; we couldn't see what he was trying to capture. With a powerful surge, he rooted backward, and dragged a slimy red planet worm from its home.

I cursed and ran toward the mutt.

"Hold, you miserable mutt!" I shouted and Amity screamed when I swung my Thezana at the worm's head before it could activate its poison-cloud. I divested the worm of its head and watched its thigh-thick body convulse and still. The green poison mucus drained and bubbled down into the burrow.

The dog panted and looked at me, nonplussed.

"You nearly killed us all!" I shouted and waved my weapon toward the red worm. "The planet worm spews its poison in a cloud that would fill the entire glade!"

The dog showed no remorse but trotted off into the rainforest, his white tail disappearing into thick shrubbery. I huffed and wiped my blade in the grasses, looking back at Amity to see her face contorted.

"Has the infection taken hold?" I said, alarm lacing my voice.

She cocked her head and pointed to the remains of the red planet worm.

"No, no. I thought you were going to kill my do ... the devil dog," she said, and placed her hand at her heart. She walked closer to the dead worm. "But that's what I'm talking about," she said, leaning over it. "A worm whose mucus can be aerosolized into a cloud of poisonous gas? That's phenomenal! I need to find out if it its saliva has A2 phospholipase. And if I could dissect its head, I could possibly discover how it releases its poison into the air. Does it have a blowhole?"

It was my turn to cock my head.

"You were saying you must travel to Pattee's pod."

Her shoulders slumped. "Yes," she said. "You're right. Plenty of time for science once I've been inoculated against whatever is trying to kill me from the inside out." She bent to retrieve her pack, and I saw the grimace that crossed her face when she lifted it.

I hastened to her side.

"Please allow me to carry this for you, at least until you have been cleared by your Technology for physical exertion."

Her face relaxed, and she gifted me with her first genuine smile since we'd met.

"That would be wonderful," she said. "Thank you."

Such a simple thing, and yet I felt that I had offered her the palace's entire cache of precious treasure. My mind replayed it on a loop, relishing the feeling of lightness it created in my heart. We pointed our feet to the southeast, and Amity led the way. I spied glimpses of white fur in the surrounding forest, but the dog did not approach. It was just as well; I could kill it for endangering my Amity with his reckless exploration. I winced when I considered how Amity screamed earlier. If I had inadvertently killed it, she may very well have buried her own weapon in my chest. The way she interacted with it bespoke a special bond. Something told me if I wanted to be in her good graces, I must tolerate the devil dog.

24

Amity

We made much better time since I didn't have to carry the heavy pack. Every dozen steps I looked behind me at the massive alien figure in imposing dire wolf armor. Dark gray, it absorbed light from the dual suns, except in places where a silvery chrome-like metal gleamed. His helmet resembled an adult version of Diablo, replete with carved fangs, pointed snout and four "eyes". While he appeared to be fitted out with amazing technology, the only weapons he carried in view were the knives and swords strapped to his legs and at his waist.

I recalled the speed with which he decapitated the giant worm and felt a rush of relief that he considered himself an ally as opposed to an enemy. Unfortunately, that reminded me of the odd circumstances my colleagues now faced as so-called mates of these alien creatures. Did the one behind me fancy himself my future mate? I shuddered, a terror of the unknown gripping my heart. What I had said earlier was true; I could be happy here, if I lived. There was so much to learn about. And who knew if in the distant future other humans might make their way to the planet? I would have tons of study to present, enough to supply any galactic library with a catalog of wildlife of Predator Planet. But just because I could find a life here didn't mean I intended to settle down and make alien babies.

I frowned. My scientific brain couldn't help but wonder if cross-breeding was possible. Another glance behind me caused a bone-deep shiver. C-Section. No human woman could survive natural childbirth if the offspring was fathered by one of these giants.

"Are you well, Amity?" He asked.

"Uh, fine, yes, thank you," I said. "We're making great time. Thanks again for carrying my stuff."

"It weighs nothing at all," he said.

"Okay," I said, shaking my head. I was glad he didn't press for my thoughts, because explaining my curiosity about interspecies procreation would have been damned awkward.

Swinging my machete at the underbrush, I kept an eye out for any more predators.

"What other creatures should we expect to encounter, Natheka?" I said. Once again, Diablo had disappeared himself in the jungle, and I hadn't seen a trace of him for at least an hour.

"The Tree Thief may be about," he said. "The creature whose pelt you now carry. You slayed it? His voice sounded doubtful until he added, "With the devil dog's help?"

"Ahh, more like Diablo killed it with little help from me, but yes."

"Its fur holds light captive, rendering it invisible in the forest until it is too late. A formidable foe," he said. "You are lucky to be alive."

"Don't I know it," I said. "I'm not a hunter. Not of your variety, anyway. When I was a child, I hunted creatures of all sizes on every planet my family visited. But never to kill them. It seemed I always found the sick or injured, and I would try to nurse them back to health."

"Ah, a maikshe for animals," Natheka said from behind me.

VELMA translated the word as healer.

"Of sorts," I said with a laugh. "I had no skill, but I did try."

"The devil-dog has no complaints," Natheka said. "Look, he waits for us."

I saw the white wolf sitting ten meters ahead of us on the path, his tongue lolling.

"He recovered quite well," I agreed. "Lucky."

"Hm. Lucky perhaps," Natheka said. "Or blessings from the Goddesses. You are not a healer of animals now?"

"No, I found I enjoyed studying all the different kinds of animals across the galaxy more than devoting time to learning how to treat select species from a given planet."

"Your people travel from planet to planet?" Natheka said. I noted a hint of something besides curiosity in his voice but couldn't place it.

"Not all of us," I said. "Some remain on Earth, trying to repair damage from the Ciliak Wars. Others travel until they decide to settle elsewhere. And then families like mine found work on traveling fleet ships. Both my parents were scientists and researchers, and they found employment with an outfit that didn't mind having all their kids around," I said. I glanced at Natheka. "I have six brothers," I said with a shy smile.

"Six hunters! And one sister!" Natheka's voice betrayed genuine surprise. "All from the same sire and dam?"

I covered my laughing smile by dipping my helmet and coughing. I could imagine my parents' reactions to being called sire and dam, terms usually reserved for animal husbandry. "Yes, that is common among humans. A couple may decide to have children together. Or they may choose to adopt orphans. Although not many families have as many children as my parents did."

"Ah, so it is unusual to your people as well," he said.

"Yeah, we were definitely outliers," I said. "What about your people? How many children do you typically have?"

"Our culture is significantly different," he said. "The adult hunters do not choose a single mate but must earn the right to create offspring based on the success of their hunts, here on Ikthe."

Questions tumbled over one another about what VELMA had told me about Pattee and Esra, but I was unsure how to bring it up.

"So, if you have a successful hunt on this planet, then you are allowed to ...?" I wasn't sure how to phrase my response.

"Our names are put in the lottery drum," he said. "And five names are drawn from the pool, and those five hunters may each choose a sister with which to create an offspring. It is organized," he said, and looked into my eyes, as if to ascertain my opinion.

Damn. I tried to remember my intergalactic diplomacy class.

"That does sound orderly," I finally said. His expression didn't change, so at least I hadn't offended him. But I was still in the dark as to why my friend Pattee had somehow ended up as a life mate to one of his fellow hunters.

We were now in the clearing where Diablo had waited for us. Attuned to my rhythm, he accurately guessed I would be ready for a meal.

While my back and shoulders no longer ached from my heavy burden, it did not mean my leg was free from its pain. I was certain now that Diablo's saliva at least employed Nerve Growth Factor or histatins, but it seemed to also possess an almost mythical ability to improve my overall health. Checking the tree trunk before I sat against it, I stretched out my leg and sighed. Recalling him licking his own butt, I hoped the dog's spit didn't also introduce something as bad as Pasteurella or worse, but it was too late to worry about it now.

The alien sat beside me, placing my rucksack nearby.

"Thanks," I said. "I have water in there. That's why it's so heavy," I said. "Um, for me. I didn't know whether or not I would be able to find a source."

"Ik," he said, and pulled out his own canister. When he removed his helmet, I tried not to stare. A vicious slash, a fresh wound, tracked from just below his left eye and down his cheek. His skin had the texture of a manta ray but was a sage green. His black hair wasn't hair like humans have, but feathers—or something like feathers. With swooping black brows and high cheekbones, there was a regal quality to his appearance. His nose was crooked—a past break—but human-like, although he did have fangs. My heart skipped a beat, and I averted my gaze.

We drank and rested, eyes scanning the small clearing for signs of danger. Diablo paced, sniffing at the bases of trees and darting among them, but always returning to watch us.

Natheka handed me an MRE.

"How?" I asked and took it, realizing my colleagues must have provided them.

"Esra and Pattee were concerned you might be frightened," he said. "They gave me these to offer as signs of peace between us."

I noticed one was freeze-dried ice cream. Pattee. Tears pooled in my eyes, and I smiled.

"Thanks," I said, but my voice cracked. I realized I couldn't wait to see my people. Especially Pattee. We'd bonded on the *Lucidity*, and I couldn't help but marvel at the miracle that we had both survived and would be able to spend the rest of our lives together.

Movement caught my eye. I peeled my gaze away from the brown, white and pink contents of my foil pouch to see that Diablo crept closer and closer, as if stalking prey. I looked all around, but the glen was still. I saw that Natheka watched Diablo as well with a hand poised above his weapon. I would have to watch him around my wolf.

Diablo crawled, his paws and belly hugging the ground. He made a strange whining noise and stopped about one and a half meters away from me. I watched his nostrils flare.

"You want my ice cream?" I said. He tilted his head. I pinched a chunk off and tossed it toward him.

He sniffed it, then swept it up with a long slender tongue. He inched closer.

I laughed.

"You didn't want anything to do with the dried beef, but you'll eat my ice cream, huh?" Another whine. I tossed one smaller chunk. Once the freeze-dried ice cream was gone, all remnants of human life would disappear for me. I wanted to hoard it. I stared at the treat, reality once more casting a dark cloud over me.

"I would know what thoughts trouble you," Natheka said from beside me. Embarrassed, I resealed my pouch and stashed it in a pocket next to my field journal.

"I don't know if I could put them into words," I finally said, afraid to meet his intense black-eyed gaze. "Thoughts of home, and adventure, and humanity, change and peril. A lot of things," I said.

He nodded.

"Theraxl Hunters spend many an hour on Ikthe with similar such thoughts," he said. "The isolation and danger of this planet bring to mind all our cares, past, present and future. In this way, the Goddesses assure we will turn to Them for aid."

Surprised, I inspected his features.

"Do all of you Hunters feel this way? That the Goddesses want you to pray to Them? Ask for help?"

He opened his mouth, thought a moment. "Most do, yes."

I nodded and sat against the tree, thinking about my own deities. If ever a person needed grace, it was me.

The ground rumbled at the same time lights flashed in my helmet and Natheka jumped up. "Pack your things!" He shouted while hoisting my heavy rucksack again.

I hurried to stow my loose items in pockets while VELMA spoke in my ear. "Earthquake imminent. Please seek shelter. Earthquake imminent."

We both donned our helmets.

Queasiness overtook me, and I sought the tree trunk to steady my legs, but with the ground beneath me unstable, there was no steadiness to be had. "*Santa Maria, madre de ...*" I began, but I couldn't finish. Natheka had gathered me into his arms, and he bounded down the steep incline, heedless of the branches and shrubs hedging up the way. I couldn't imagine where he headed was any safer than where we were now, a slope on the side of a jungled mountain.

"VELMA, what do we do?" Panic gripped my heart, and my tendons strained in my neck and shoulders.

"Utilizing Newmark's Dynamic Misplacement Model, I am assessing the slope's stability," VELMA said. "Natheka may be able to outrun the sliding block to more stable ground provided he runs at an angle. I've provided him with a diagram in his helmet's interface, with mapping provided by the nanosatellite array."

Putting all my trust in math and science, not to mention the alien's strong armor-clad arms, I whispered prayers too, and squeezed my eyes shut. I wasn't cut out for this paygrade.

"The soil liquefies under my boots, Amity Diaz," Natheka said. "Should I fall, I will protect you with my body. My armor can withstand much pressure. Hold to me."

I squeezed my eyelids tighter shut. Breaths came in shallow gasps, and my pulse thrummed in my neck.

Daring to peek, I saw greenery spin in a blur, but motion sickness inspired me to close my eyes again. All I could do was wait the terror out. And then my thoughts chased after Diablo, and a twist of anguish pierced my heart; would he be okay?

25

Natheka

The technology entity known as VELMA displayed a map in my helmet. Should I choose to follow the route marked, we could evade the worst of the landquake's devastation. It was a simple matter to follow a trail, and yet doubt crept in.

There was no time to doubt.

With my heart mate in my arms, I ran swift as the pazathel-nax, increasing my speed with eye-blinks controlling my suit-enhancers. Leaping across tumbling rocks and deadly tree shafts, I raced the devastation. Ikthe in turmoil; Amity's blood poised to be ravaged by Ikthe's very breath, but if not the bacteria, then Ikthe's bones crushing her frail body, or Ikthe's beasts, hungry to devour her.

VELMA's route avoided the worst of the barrage, yet I kept my wits. Never had I witnessed destruction of this magnitude on the hunting grounds. The red line flashed a circuitous path; VELMA also provided warnings of missiles: debris shunted airborne from the mountain behind us.

"Hold to me, Amity," I said, my calm voice disguising internal dismay and terror. Shel activated, they injected chemicals into my bloodstream, energizing me and giving me strength beyond my mortal power.

I channeled the bravery, dignity and resignation of the sister paza-thel-nax I had slain. Sweat on my cheek stung the slash she gave me as a reminder.

Each step onto liquified soil jolted my fear anew. I sought out the largest boulders and upended tree roots, anything to secure purchase before leaping again. Should I fall, the delicate human in my arms would die. I held her life in my arms, my heart beating to the rhythm of her breaths.

Scouting through the blinking warnings in my visor, I tracked the pathway ahead. Ah, VELMA took us to the Unrepentant Valley. The meadow beyond the reach of any remaining rockslides was bereft of trees. It would be the safest place until the landquake ended.

"Naraxthel, do you hear me?" I believed I was far enough from the mountainous area that disrupted our communications. "Rax-thezana?"

No word from either of them. Perhaps the destruction spread as far as Moon Shield. This would be dire indeed.

"VELMA, you have accessed my helmet," I said. "Can you not use my comms to contact Naraxthel and the humans as well?"

"I have lost communication with your brethren and Pattee and Esra," she said. "I will keep trying."

A blaring alarm and flashing light alerted me to a giant boulder bearing down upon us as I ran. There was no predicting its trajectory. I ran at full speed; I could not backpedal, nor could I run faster.

"Natheka!" Amity screamed.

Changing course, I ran at the boulder, my prayers to the Goddesses giving my boots wings as I took a great leap and used the careening boulder to launch myself into the air, my grip on Amity never failing as I kicked up the boulder and flipped backward, cradling my precious cargo.

I landed with bent knees and watched the boulder crash and blast its way down the side of the mountain, my breaths coming in great gasps while Amity trembled in my arms. Likewise, the ground trembled, and with shaky footing, I found the path VELMA marked in my helmet. We pressed on.

My lungs protested. The muscles in my legs and arms screeched for rest, but VELMA spoke with urgency in my ear to run ever faster. The skin beneath my armor buzzed with Shel, their nutrients nearly depleted. They needed water, as did I. But I forced my body to go faster, as more boulders bounced toward us in a deadly race. I dodged them, more alert after our last scrape, and every jump and twist caused agony throughout my body as I taxed it beyond its capability. I must protect Amity at all costs. The valley was only veltiks away now. Gritting my teeth, I put on a final burst of speed as the ground beneath me shifted and paused, and then ripped out from under my boots. I stumbled, seeking out more stable ground.

"*Santo Cielo*!" Amity said while VELMA translated. *Good Heavens.*

"There is time yet for us to sup at the Goddess's table," I said between pants. "We make haste to the Unrepentant Valley!"

Still the ground shook, tripping up my stride across the terrain, until the avalanche of falling rocks tapered off as we entered the valley. I ran us to its center and loosed Amity from my arms. We collapsed and endured the endless quaking, our gloves clawing into the ground as if to draw steadiness from it.

"Natheka," Naraxthel's voice penetrated through the alarms. "How fare you? A landquake split Moon Shield. The landscape has changed."

The quaking subsided even as Naraxthel described the destruction at Moon Shield to me. I relaxed my body, not quite trusting the stillness of the valley beneath me. I looked to the east, and for a jotik, words escaped me.

"Naraxthel," I said, dismay clear in my voice. "Forgiven Mountain is no more."

"*Dios mio*," I heard Amity whisper to my right. "We were just there." Her voice faded.

We sat and stared at the new mammoth mountain of rubble, the air thick with the dust of smashed rocks. Amity coughed until tears streamed down her cheeks.

"Hasten you to Pattee's pod," Naraxthel said through the comms. "Ikthe protests violently; I will be at ease when our brotherhood is reunited. Raxkarax has left us to fetch another human from the Agothe-Fatheza."

"Not the abomination," I whispered into my comms.

"He feels the pull of his heart-home," Naraxthel said.

I lamented.

"It is folly to ignore the heart-home," I said. "The Goddesses will guide him. I will get the human to Pattee's pod as swift as the ikadax flies."

"Bite your tongue, Natheka," Naraxthel chided me.

"It is only evil on the tongue if you fear it," I scolded him back. "The suns have set on that day."

Naraxthel sighed in my ear.

"Very well. Please report in every three zatiks," he said. "I am on edge. I manage to provide violent sight-captures for the Ikma to devour, but prey grows scarce. Soon, I will have to capture my own death if I do not wish her to pilot herself to Ikthe and discover how deep our betrayal is buried."

"Aye," I said. "There are plentiful battles on many fronts. I will report as you requested."

"Natheka," he said. "Thank you."

I chuckled and signed off.

Nerves rattled, Amity and I stood on trembling legs with hands outspread in readiness. The ground stood still.

"VELMA translated for you?" I asked.

"Yes," she said. "There's no time to waste. We head south, according to her directions." Amity sounded subdued.

"The landquake frightened you?" I said.

"Of course," she answered and looked up at me. "Do you think Diablo survived? He often slinked around in the forest."

Ah, she worried over the mutt.

We hiked south, stepping over obstructions. I pulled my thoughts together before I spoke.

"There is an otherworldly wisdom about that pup," I finally said. "He knows things before we know it ourselves. I think he survived."

Amity pulled in a deep breath then nodded. "He does, doesn't he? I wanted permission to hope. I'm going to trust that he's fine and will find us when he's ready."

"Ha!" I said. "And only when he is ready. Not a jotik sooner."

Amity smiled. While it wasn't her hearty laugh, I would accept it with gratitude for now. Perhaps laughter was ill placed on Ikthe. Perhaps I was a fool to wish to hear laughter and experience joy on a place called Certain Death. These thoughts haunted me until nightfall.

26

Amity

"*It is folly to ignore the heart-home.*"

Oh yes, VELMA had translated the entire conversation. There was another pod on this godforsaken planet, and another of these alien males had claimed its occupant as his 'so-called' heart mate. Did the human women have no choice, then?

My back turned on Natheka, I stared at the destruction we escaped. He was taking a dip in the stream, fully armored, but I still didn't watch. He explained about the organisms embedded in his skin and attached to the inner membrane of his armor, how they needed water to continue their work. Part of me was dying to see the whole process in action, but the other part continued to chafe at what Natheka had said to his colleague. He exited the stream and we hiked south and east.

Our bruising pace along the swollen and muddied creek allowed little energy for conversation. It was just as well; a growing anger at these aliens wouldn't abate. How dare they make assumptions about us? How dare they impose their cultural traditions on hapless castaways? If this *macho* Natheka *vaquero* thought he was going to claim me as his human prize, he had another think coming. Yes, he had mad parkour skills. Yes, his strength and bravery were awe-inspiring. Yes, he had respected my personal space and kept all conversation pertinent to our situation. But. But if he was secretly planning a wedding, he was going to be sorely disappointed.

Long shadows turned to night when the second sun set. We'd made solid ground, but the lack of mountain or forest surrounding us set my teeth on edge. Even with Natheka, the most epic and athletic alien I'd ever seen in person as my traveling companion, I found myself sweating and hyperventilating as darkness swallowed up the open area at the edge of my flashlight beam. Anxiety for Diablo tugged at my heart, too. Either a hungry predator was going to attack out of the blackness, or it would be Diablo demanding more ice cream.

"How fares your leg, Pazathe Kama?" Natheka said.

I paused and cocked my head. VELMA's translation was "Clever Sister". What was that nickname supposed to mean? Was it an endearment? A claiming ritual? I bit my lip before I spoke. "Um, it's okay for now. Although I'm feeling pretty tired."

"I have recalled what you said about the devil dog's saliva," he said. "If it is accurate, your health will wane the longer he is absent."

Standing with hands on hips, I looked down at my bound leg. "You're right."

"If you agree, I could carry you to Pattee's pod," he said. "The Shel are refreshed. I can travel much farther and faster if I run."

Internal debate warred as I turned off my flashlight and let my eyes acclimate to the thick blackness. I looked up at the stars.

It was as if someone had spilled a jar of glitter across a purple velvet cloth.

"Oh!" I couldn't speak after that. Only drink in the awe and the immensity and my own smallness.

Natheka's armor creaked with a small movement. I heard insects similar to the nocturnal bugs found across the galaxy that used stridulation to call to their prospective mates. The males made noise and hoped that their private brand of squeak or chirp or buzz or twitch was just right for attracting a willing mate.

Hmm. I might have to think about that further. But for now?

"Yes, if you don't mind. It would probably be for the best," I said. "But not how you did earlier."

I walked behind Natheka's bulk. "Squat down, and I'll ride on your back."

"Very well, Amity," he said and complied.

Climbing up, I secured my arms around the thick part of his neck armor, and he bent his arms so I could rest my legs on either side of his torso while being supported by his elbows. It wasn't the most comfortable place in the world, but I would have my dignity.

"Hold to me," he said, and then he ran.

If I peeked over his shoulder, I saw nothing except the distant line where the velvety and sparkled sky met the black ground's horizon. My cracked helmet still kept the force of wind from blowing my hair. I had no sense of time, space or speed. Only the jolting pace of the armored being who carried me.

The stress of the days, the worry and the fear, all combined to exhaust me, but I was afraid if I fell asleep, I would let go. The only way to force myself to stay awake was to talk.

"How can you see where you're going?" I asked.

"My visor also has technology, though it doesn't speak to me," he said with a chuckle. "I have many ways to see. The path before me is as bright as the noon suns," he said. "I will not tell you of the dangers we have already passed in a short distance."

"Your friend said one of your companions was going to a place called," I said and scanned my memory. "Agothe-Fatheza. VELMA said, 'night corruption' was the closest translation?"

"Ik," Natheka's voice entered my ear. "Another human has landed there in a pod. Raxkarax goes to fetch her." Afraid but also curious, I swallowed and powered through my question. "Where is it? What's it like?"

"The Hunters of Ikshe avoid Agothe-Fatheza," he said. "It lies to the north of the Great Waters, but south of Moon Shield and the Nesting Forest. The prey there is indigestible. Poisonous. Lethal."

"So, it isn't prey, then?" I asked.

"The creatures are small and slow," he said. "Of occasion, the rokhural will venture to the bogs and kill and eat at their leisure. The inhabitants are prey."

"But you don't eat them," I said. "Are they amphibious? Reptilian?"

"Hold, human, while your technology translates these terms."

After a few paces, he answered me.

"The more numerous of the prey are what you call amph-i-bians," Natheka said. "They proliferate in the bogs, coating the ground, the bases of the trees, and the bog's surface. The air is thick with putrid, moist gases. These creatures: we call them *theza-pax*, because they eat waste. And to eat them is to eat waste. It is abomination."

"What else is there?" I asked, my curiosity awakening my fatigued brain.

"The za-ronaxl bugs," he said with resignation.

"Oh?" I vaguely recalled VELMA mentioning gigantic insects.

"They are disgusting beetles, a hard-shelled bug about the size of my fist," he said. "They devour anything that moves, including the theza-pax. Their mouth parts cut through the thickest flesh, the strongest bone. It is said that the Goddesses themselves would dare not step foot in the bogs of Agothe-Fatheza."

"Wow," I said, my mind racing over the details. If I could acquire a better helmet, I could ask VELMA to provide me with videos, if she had them. "Is your colleague afraid to go there?"

Natheka didn't answer right away. I was learning this was his way, and I respected it. I was more the type to think out loud.

"Raxkarax has felt the pull of the heart-home," he finally said. "Unless one is possessed of the organ, one cannot comprehend its whims. It will not be denied, no matter the danger ahead."

Puzzling out my thoughts, I avoided discussion of the heart-home. "It sounds like what you're saying is yes, Raxkarax is afraid. But he's going anyway."

"That is right," Natheka said. "But would not you? One of your kind is likely trapped there. Even with your protective suits and VELMA's ever present intelligence, the human is in danger. They will need a guide."

Humbled, I stopped talking for a minute.

"You're right, of course," I said. "If there is any way for us to help, we should."

"Ik," he said. "I have thought of it. But first we must conquer the enemy in your blood."

"Right," I said on a sigh. The mention of it caused an ache to begin throbbing where the metal had pierced my leg. "I wish I knew where Diablo was."

"I do, as well, Amity Diaz," Natheka said. "If your wound pains you, allow me to apply a poultice. I have healing maikshe herbs with me."

"Okay, whenever you can stop will work," I said.

He stopped immediately. To me, everything was still dark with vague outlines. I could still hear the sawing and pipping sounds of night bugs but couldn't make out details of our surroundings.

"Please sit," he said. I heard rather than saw him pull out a pouch and rustle through it. Through the cracks in my helmet, I could smell a pungent herb. It was like a blend of fennel and spearmint. His tall form knelt beside me, and I saw him uncap a canister.

"I am making a paste in my palm," he said. "The maikshel, the healers of my people, have studied all of the flora of both planets," he said. "The Hunters collect plants and take them to the maikshel where they study their properties, abilities and poisons. The one I use on your wound infuses pain relievers and microbiota to strengthen the blood."

Barely making out his gloved hand holding the paste, he used his thick finger to swirl it around and around with a splash of water. When he deemed it ready, he scraped it out of his palm and painted it on and around my wound while I held the bandage away.

Hissing as it made contact, I briefly wondered if I shouldn't have gone without, considering I hadn't had the materials scanned in the absence of a working ship or helmet. But just as with Diablo's thick tongue, it was too late now. If the ingredients were inert as opposed to deadly, perhaps the placebo effect could help me feel relief.

"Thank you," I said through gritted teeth. It burned and fizzed. Natheka held what resembled a pen light to the wound, and I could see bubbles growing and popping from the greenish paste. Nausea took hold as I watched pus erupt from the wound and dribble out. I rushed to remove my helmet and tossed it away in time to avoid catching my vomit in it. The pain reached a crescendo, and I almost blacked out, but another round of vomiting kept me alert until the pain had receded and I no longer felt like my stomach was trying to jump ship.

"Ah, I am sorry," Natheka said. He had a damp cloth and was cleaning the drainage and blood. Under his pen light I could see the wound looked cleaner than any other part of my body now. It also felt better, though I wasn't sure if it was worth the price of admission.

"The fire grass maybe was not the best choice for a human," he said, sitting back on his haunches. "Drink, now." He handed me his canister of water. Dubious, I sniffed it, but it was just water. I guzzled it down after a brief rinse and spit onto the grass.

"Fire grass?" I finally said, licking my lips and laying back, my gut cramping.

"Ikquo-jofa," he said. "It grows at the base of the Black Heart Mountains. It is potent," he said. "Ah, as you have learned."

"You can say that again."

"Do you want me to say that again?" he asked.

"No, no," I said. "Just an expression." Eyes closed, I worked to calm my breathing. The memory of the pain was almost enough to induce another round of the pukes. I tried to think of anything that would distract me, and my thoughts seized on the butterfly, or whatever it was, from earlier.

"What is the flying insect called with the blue wings? The big one that Diablo tried to catch?"

"Ah, ik. Awaafa," he said. "VELMA suggests 'see the blue plant' as a translation, but it is named after one of our old songs."

Now my wound burned and tingled, but in a good way. Like draining an abscessed tooth.

"Sing it for me," I blurted before I could start crying.

"Awaafa, take my prayer to the Goddesses,

Where the blue flower opens under breath

The blue flower falls, it has failed to fly,

The Goddesses' prayer dies on my lips."

Natheka's voice rang clear in the night, repeating the verses. The bugs quieted to listen. Moved, I wiped away tears, grateful for the anonymity of night. But then I remembered he could probably see me with his fancy tech.

"You have a beautiful voice," I said, hoping to deflect any possible comments about my tears or my pain, which gratefully, had lessened. "Could you sing something else?"

"This song haunts me of a night when my hunt is going poorly," he said. He pounded on his thigh in time to the words.

"To sleep is to die

The death of the will

The death of what is done.

Arise from your death

Awaken to live

The life of pursuit

The life of the hunt.

Awake!"

The last lyric was shouted; it jolted me.

"Thank you for indulging me," he said. "My mother took great pains to teach me all of the songs of our people. She was a rare and beautiful jewel among the Sisters of Ikshe. She had hoped for daughters to pass on her knowledge. But there was only one Sister, and she died from the infant burial disease many long cycles ago." He was quiet for a minute. "I will sing of the infant burial disease. It is a common affliction among my people. The maikshel have been unable to discover the cause or the cure."

His dark shape changed until it appeared he was kneeling. His song began in a low hum. Then, the words spoke of a harvest, and loss, and bones.

His song faded on the last note.

"The infant burial disease comes from this planet?" I asked, my voice reverent.

"No one knows with certainty," he said. "The disease chooses its victims on the whim of Ikshe's winds."

I heard him sigh. Between the melancholy notes of his song, the lyrics, missing Diablo, and the sad tale of his baby sister's passing, it was all I could do not to break down into inconsolable sobbing. It took me several minutes to compose myself.

I saw the dark shape of his gloved hand reach for mine. "Get up. We will travel farther, and I will regale you with every song that I know until we reach the glade where Pattee's pod rests."

"But do you have any happy songs?" I asked. "Because I can't handle any more if you don't."

He chuckled. "Very well. The song of the body is not ..."

Our hands touched when a black blur slammed into Natheka's body and carried him out of my field of view. Aching leg forgotten, I scrambled to my feet and grabbed my machete.

"VELMA, Natheka's been attacked! I need your help!"

27

Esra

C radling my sprained arm, I listened as Naraxthel made the greatest understatement of my life on his comm channel with Natheka. "The landscape has changed."

Moon Shield, where I had come to love my morning walk looking for rocks, where the view of the suns rising took my breath away every single morning, where my first taste of glisten-fish stew had swum across my tongue—was now split in half.

But for the grace of God.

All of us had hiked to the base of the mesa earlier in the day.

The earthquake hit when we were gathering deadwood about ten miles from Moon Shield. Far enough away to be out of immediate danger, but close enough to watch in horror as our camp split in two, and half of Moon Shield collapsed as if it were a soufflé.

The earthquake had rippled toward us as if in slow motion; but there was no point in running. We were in a scrubby wood with nothing to hang onto but each other.

Naraxthel thought it would be good to sight-capture the earth-quake, so he had distanced himself from the rest of us and recorded dramatic footage for the Ikma. He returned in time to see me fall and catch myself at a bad angle. Assessing my arm, he determined I would live and tried to reach his brothers. Raxkarax was unreachable. Thankfully Natheka had answered.

He ended his conversation.

"Natheka and Amity are safe," he said. "They will waste no time in seeking Amity's treatment." He looked around at Raxthezana and Hivelt and Pattee. "Separating our brotherhood feels wrong." He hit his chest once with a fist. "We may salvage provisions from what's left at Moon Shield, but perhaps we travel to reunite instead. I was used to hunting alone; it is our way. But these many disasters—these dangers and injuries—foretell more peril to come. What say you?"

Pattee nodded slowly, biting her lip.

Hivelt's thick arms folded. I heard him say "Ik".

Raxthezana rested his fists on tapered hips and turned to observe the destruction at Moon Shield.

"My whole life, the whims of the planets have been attributed to the wills of the Goddesses," he said. "And the path of my life has followed that set before me by the Sister Queens."

The rest of us listened with rapt attention. Raxthezana rarely spoke in more than single syllable answers since Raxkarex left.

"Even now, I traipse these familiar grounds because of the command of the Ikma," he said. "Naraxthel, I appreciate that you give us a choice, or rather, the illusion of a choice." He turned back around to face us.

"What am I to do if I refuse? Continue on the quest for woaiquovelt alone? Travel to your ship and steal it so I may return to Ikshe, a hunter presumed dead returning alive but without game?

My choices are to wander Ikthe alone or with all of you, until such time as fate deems it permissible to complete our quest." He knelt on the ground and drew another map where he swept away brush and yanked up grasses. "Agothe-Fatheza is here. Hivelt, your glade is here, is it not?" He met Pattee's gaze and grinned. "Forgive me. *Pattee's* glade. If we travel southwest, we avoid the rokhural nesting grounds adjacent to the Plain of Ancient Ice. Skirting the foothills of Solace Mountain Range, we can travel this narrow passage between Agothe-Fatheza and where the Mounded Rocks taper off before reaching that forest tangle to the east of Pattee's glade."

We studied his scratches in the dirt, the names taking shape in his crude renderings of trees and mountains and water.

"We will be close enough to Raxkarax to offer aid if he needs it, and well on our way to meet Natheka and his human Amity. Fate and Ikthe willing, we reunite here." He drew double circles, and I wondered if that was like humans marking X as the spot. "From here, it is only zatiks to Naraxthel's ship. We may be united as our brother and sisterhood once again, and furthermore, travel with speed to the closest landing spot to resume our quest."

Raxthezana had given this a lot of thought.

"Makes sense to me," I said. I imagined being strapped into Naraxthel's ship and zipping over the tops of the canopy instead of hoofing it over earthquake-damaged landscapes. It would be a blessed relief.

"We could stock up more supplies from my pod, as well," Pattee said. "And I'm excited to see Amity again. She must have so many questions about ... things."

I saw Pattee's cheeks flush when she glanced at Hivelt.

"It is a sound plan," Naraxthel said. "Doubtless the terrain will have shifted or transformed, but we will work together to cross any obstacles in our way. Thank you, Raxthezana."

Raxthezana stood with a creak of his armor and toed his boot across the map, obscuring it.

"I have a cloth for Esra's arm," he said in reply and pulled one out of his pack, handing it to me. Pattee helped me fashion a sling.

"Private channel?" she asked me.

We switched.

"With everything going on, we never got to talk about what I found on my CMM," she said. "I'm gonna need your help breaking it to the boys."

"Bad news?" I asked.

"Very," she said. "There is a possibility that the shared moon of Ikthe and Ikshe would transfer orbit," she said. "That would be bad and potentially catastrophic, but it's not as probable as the most concerning thing."

We hiked along, noting the hunters had opted out of returning to Moon Shield for what would amount to a handful of packs' worth of dried fish and rodent meat. Fate, Goddesses or Naraxthel's foresight had us packing our things for the deadwood gathering this morning. He had suggested it gave us more options were we to travel as if we weren't returning. He was right.

"My data compilation is predicting a magnetic pole reversal on Ikthe," she said. "It explains the mass migrations these guys mentioned, as well as the seismic activity. And your misbehaving magnet rock, I might add."

Sadly, I'd left that beast behind, never guessing we wouldn't actually return.

"Magnetic pole reversal," I said. "That could last thousands of years, Pattee."

"Really? I look at big systems," she said. "I don't know anything about planet geology."

Stepping over a root, Pattee grasped my good right arm and helped me over.

"Okay, well a geomagnetic reversal is gonna last at least 7000 years," I said. "But there's something called an excursion. Think of it like a blind date that didn't work out. You meet up, no sparks, you both go home and forget about it. An excursion is a failed magnetic reversal where the liquid outer core of the planet shifts poles, but not the core. Those aren't going to last as long."

"But could an excursion still cause all this mayhem on the planet's surface?" she asked.

"Normally I would say no," I said. "An excursion is related to a temporary shift in magnetic poles. While it would definitely explain animal migrations in populations of animals that normally use the magnetic field to navigate, not much evidence historically has supported a causal relationship between excursion events and seismic activity."

"Why do I feel a 'but' coming on?" Pattee asked with a wink and a half-smile.

"Well, there's something I've been working on before the whole evac thing back on the fleet ship," I said. "I've been looking at a lot of research on electrokinetic effect. It has to do with certain qualities of the Earth's crust, especially in the presence of liquid water."

"Okay," Pattee said.

"In shallow places of Earth's crust, or any planet with a liquid metal core and outer rocky crust, the rocks and water comprise the electric double layer. Electrolytes in the water and charged ions in grains of the solid part of the planet create this build-up of electricity."

"You mean like walking on carpet in fuzzy socks and then touching something metal?" Pattee asked.

"Exactly," I said. "In and of itself, it's not a planetary phenomenon. Here's your 'but'," I said. "If you've got a geomagnetic excursion happening, that means you've got fluctuations in cosmic radiation reaching the planet. Cosmic radiation is ionizing radiation. What if those ionizing radiation roentgens start interacting with the ions created in that electric double layer?"

"Seismic activity," Pattee said.

"Yes! And the cosmic radiation fluctuations can affect weather patterns, too."

I took another couple steps before continuing. "Most people wouldn't have heard about it, but IGMC actually found a deserted planet in the Pollack-Custer belt that was in the middle of an excursion. They had unmanned expeditions on the surface recording everything that was going on. Weather phenomena, seismic and magnetic anomalies, as well as erratic wildlife behavior. Ironically, the excursion resulted in prime mining conditions, as it brought rare and precious metals to the planet's surface, as well as previously undiscovered ores. We studied the event in my Advanced Geological Metamorphoses class."

Pattee was quiet while we took ginger steps through a nasty mess of fallen trees. Raxthezana led the way while Naraxthel and Hivelt took the rearward.

"In fact, I should have put two and two together," I said, gesturing at the destruction evident in treefalls and boulder outcroppings.

"To be fair, you've been pretty busy," Pattee said, smiling at me through her visor. "We all have been."

I nodded, my mind now rehearsing everything I'd learned about that IGMC expedition to Thune-568. The Galvanite harvested there had been top quality; the professors in my mining classes held up samples from there as iconic: the holy grail of Galvanite. And while the Galvanite had been pristine, what really revved the mining professors were the undiscovered ores. Even in small quantities, previously undiscovered ores meant more funding for exploration in the outer reaches of the galaxy. As chemists and engineers found uses for new and unusual geological elements, IGMC's reach expanded.

Shaking off the uneasy feeling in my gut, I pressed on. Ikthe was way, way off IGMC's radar, and it would stay that way. Thank God.

"Okay, sorry, I had to geek out there for a minute," I said. "Excursion or reversal, this planet is in for a wild ride. If there's any way for us to get off of it, that would probably be best."

"That's what I was afraid of," Pattee said. "Can you imagine telling these guys we should wait on continuing the quest? They're not going to run from something as insignificant as a planet-wide catastrophe."

Groaning, I reached for Pattee's hand and squeezed it. "You're right. Let me think about it. The good news is we're headed for Naraxthel's ship, if in a roundabout way. Maybe once we get off ground we could, I don't know, hijack the pilots and fly away into the double sunset?"

"Heh. Right," she said. "I think you overestimate my piloting ability."

"No, I'm underestimating our mates' need to best the Queen," I said with sobriety. "Naraxthel says her name in his sleep, and I'm not jealous about it. The sight-captures are stressing him out. He really wants to sight-capture falling down a crevasse or something."

"I understand," Pattee said. "Realistically, even if we could talk sense into the hunters to go off-planet, what would we do? It sounds like the Ikma Scabmal Kama wouldn't listen to reason. It would be instant execution for us, and probably the males, too."

"If I may interject," VELMA spoke in our helmets.

"Sure," I said. Pattee and I shared a smile.

"While either a geomagnetic reversal or excursion would last beyond a human's lifespan, it might not necessarily make the planet uninhabitable. With the presence of the functioning nanosatellite array, inhabitants could be forewarned of impending disasters. If the humans and Theraxl are within range of Naraxthel's ship, they could board, leave the planet's surface for a time or travel to a less-impacted region. Perhaps it is not ideal, but as I have run simulations, all outcomes involving the engagement of the Ikma Scabmal Kama end in your deaths. I would prefer to avoid that."

"Wow," I said. "Um, thanks for your assessment. We'll definitely take that under advisement."

"You are welcome," VELMA said. "It is in my programming."

Pattee and I walked, each lost in our thoughts.

"I'll be honest," I said. "I never imagined anything like this when I signed up at IGMC."

Pattee chuckled.

"Me neither. The Kerberos 90 expedition was my retirement plan," she said. "Establishing the mining colony's architecture and extraction scaffolding was going to be my life. Once I saved enough, I was headed to a rural backwater near the Ciliak outpost. I had it all mapped out."

"You really did," I said with amazement. "I hadn't planned that far ahead. I was just trying to get as far away from Earth and IGMC's headquarters as possible."

"Why not switch to a different conglomerate?" she asked.

"I was in a bit of a hurry," I said. "My ex beat me for the last time the night before I left. I had to make snap decisions."

"Ah, say no more," Pattee said. "He can't follow you to Predator Planet!"

I snorted. "No, indeed."

She gave me a wicked smile. "But only imagine what Naraxthel would do to him if he did."

Patting the machete strapped to my hip, I returned the smile. "I imagine Naraxthel would offer to hold my helmet while I whooped Chris's ass."

Pattee guffawed and slapped her thigh.

"You're right! Our heart mates expect us to fight our own battles, don't they?"

Shaking my head, my wry smile split my face. "That they do. What I can't tell is if the planet forced us to become warriors, or if their expectations did."

Pattee hummed a moment.

"Due respect," she said with a wink. "But I think we were warriors all along. Predator Planet just gave us an excuse to unfurl."

"Heart mate!" Naraxthel called to me. "A rogue rokhura approaches. I insist you do not fight in this battle while your arm heals. Come to me."

Pattee pulled her javelin from her back harness and our group circled in preparation to fight the giant monstrosity that was the bane of my existence. As big as an elephant, and with a spike-studded spine and tough, dark-green scales, it resembled the ancient dinosaur known as T-Rex, but with long, taloned front legs. Standing at Naraxthel's back, I held my machete just in case. Even the wounded warriors had to fight sometimes, no matter what my heart mate might wish.

28

Amity

With fear eating up my senses, I scrabbled to unlatch my machete. It was a poor excuse for a weapon, suited instead for slashing at underbrush, but Natheka needed help! Eyes accustomed to the dark now, I could make out the bulbous mass that was Natheka and the animal. I heard grunting and hissing, but they grappled each other. Natheka must not have his arms free to wield his weapons.

Should I make my presence known? Draw the attacking beast to me so that Natheka could catch a breath and rally?

Yeah, that made sense. I mean, other than the fact that I would be at the mercy of whatever this thing was.

"Amity, I attempted to adjust the sonar pulse to no avail. I regret I do not have another idea yet," VELMA said in my helmet. "I am running simulations. Please standby."

"Standing by, VELMA," I said, tracking the tussle and taking a trembling step toward them.

"Do not approach, Amity," Natheka growled. "I have matters well in hand."

A solid thump shook my boots; I paused.

The mass had stilled. Was Natheka ...?

"Amity," Natheka grunted. "Now you may assist me."

Approaching with caution, I still held my machete at the ready.

"I need your help removing the carcass from my person," Natheka explained with another grunt and a groan.

I replaced my machete at my waist and got as close as I dared. The smell of hot blood filled my nose. "Are you injured?" I whispered, afraid of the dead thing. Mistrusting its death.

"Come close and push with me, Amity," Natheka said. I followed his voice, found his outstretched hand. He squeezed mine. "Here, push from this." He guided my hand to a smooth lump. Putting my weight into it, we pushed together. I couldn't budge it.

"What is this thing?" I asked between grunts. I angled my shoulder into a muscular body and pushed with all my might. I heard Natheka's breaths heaving; if he was struggling, I couldn't be helping him that much, but I felt the weight shift.

I dug my boots into the ground and forced my shoulder and both arms to heave the mammoth bulk off Natheka.

"Almost, my Amity," Natheka said.

I ignored the possessive use of my name on his lips because I was straining so hard at pushing the creature off. Also, his voice sounded intimate, sultry. Also, there was a sensation traveling up my legs through my boots ...

"Sensors indicate approaching wildlife," VELMA said. "It is inadvisable that you stay out in the open. Seek shelter."

Through clenched teeth, I ground out my response. "Almost—finished."

Natheka must have exerted the last of his strength, because we finally managed to roll the body enough that he could scramble from beneath.

"This beast's horde approaches," Natheka whispered. "There is nowhere to hide. We are too far from the nearest cave system where the agothe-scabmal dare not approach."

"How many are there? What do we do?" Adrenalin flushed through my veins, erasing the prior pain I had been feeling in my wounded leg.

"We fight," Natheka said. "It is good you are by my side. Your people have proven to be mighty huntresses alongside my brethren. Soon we will have tales to tell beside the night fires, and my brothers will be amazed at your courage and strength."

I would have laughed, except the rumble in my boots was stronger and my heart had lodged itself in my throat.

A warrior or huntress, I was not. My kills numbered my dubious assist to Diablo and MRE pouches. The ice cream didn't stand a chance. With a dry mouth and wet palms, my systems were primed to fight an enemy I couldn't see beside an ally whose confidence in me might qualify as delusional.

"You should know I don't really know how to—," my urgent whisper was interrupted by a screech that shattered my composure. The first beast hadn't made any noise!

Something gigantic slammed into me before I could raise my pathetic machete. I was thrown to the ground near the dead beast, and an idea flashed as the unnerving sounds met my ears. The weight of the creature was crushing my chest, but what bothered me the most was the strange clicking and chime, as if knives were being sharpened.

The clicking got louder near my helmet, the visor of which was about to shatter and burst. I stabbed upward with my non-dominant hand while I worked my way under the dead carcass. I was going to hide under it if I could manage.

Natheka must have churned up the ground because I found a dip and took full advantage. I kept stabbing at an angle, hitting something because I could smell the blood, but of course everything was happening in the pitch black. I kept squeezing down and to the side, using the carcass as a bunker. With my own huffs loud in my ears, I slashed without pause until most of my body was smooshed into the cavity.

I had no idea how Natheka was doing; I felt guilty about that but fighting for my life had given me a single focus.

"Natheka!" I shouted on a private channel, hoping he could hear me. "I'm safe! Are you okay?"

"All is well, Amity Diaz," he said between gusts of breath. "The agothe-scabmal and I are but dancing under the veiled moon!"

Cringing when spiked legs tried to dig me out, I hacked at them. They were the thickness of police batons, and it turned out, easily broken. The clicking and chiming dulled, and soon, the creature gave up. I hoped it didn't add to Natheka's stress, but I thought I heard him singing—of all things.

"Amity, SLO Nosecone #3 approaches in three minutes seven seconds," VELMA said. "Would you like me to deploy the LASER scatter shot capability?"

A sharp leg from the hungry creature stabbed my wounded leg and I cried out. The pain took my breath away; I couldn't answer as I tried to catch my breath.

VELMA's tone changed when she next spoke.

"LASER scatter shot deploying in one minute twenty-five seconds. Rounds will fire in three second bursts. It is advised that Amity and Natheka take cover."

I wedged myself further beneath the dead carcass, watching the gigantic insect leg probe in search of me. Breaths coming in rapid gulps, I addressed VELMA.

"I'm alright, VELMA," I said. "Don't fire if there is any danger of hitting Natheka!"

"LASER scatter shot deployment protocol has been initiated," VELMA said. "Please enter the code to cancel the protocol."

Oh shit, what was it? Racking my brain, I mumbled to myself until I was finally able to recall it.

"Whiskey Tango Foxtrot Lima Juliet!"

"Code verified; LASER scatter shot standing down."

"Natheka, are you okay?" I hadn't heard him in as many minutes as it took to avert a possible disaster.

"Ik, Amity," Natheka's voice entered my helmet. "I have bested my enemy, and now I wait for you to conquer yours as well."

"Ah, I can't, Natheka," I said, feeling the throb of pain in my leg expand in a plume across my body. "Can you help me?"

"I am at your whim, Amity," Natheka said, and soon I heard the swing and thwack of his sword as he fought the beast that had tried to dig me out.

Sweating and writhing, I heard the din of his fighting fade as my pain intensified.

The passage of time eluded me, and then Natheka's strong hand reached into my dug-out.

"Come, the night wanes," he said. "We will commence running once more, and nothing will overtake us."

Once again, he carried me like a helpless child, but visions of sunrises and flying monkeys and singing swords danced before my eyes all the while the sensation of being on a little boat in a big ocean swept me into a deep sleep.

29

Natheka

T roubled, I ran as if the entire population of the Agothe-Scabmal were after me. I was not far off from the truth, as being attacked by three of these gigantic hairy beetles in one evening was never before sung about. They tended to roam as individuals, one of the rare predators on Ikthe that did not follow the sister-pair pattern.

But now there were three less, and the fragile human in my arms faded. The light within her dimmed, and I cursed the devil dog for disappearing, though I could hardly blame him for the landquake that separated us. Furtive glances at her face fueled my speed. I memorized the curve of her cheek and the line of her nose. I wished to trace her lips with a claw, but such thoughts must be banished. The out-of-season movement of the wildlife and Amity's dimming health troubled me, yes, but now there was another item.

I had heard the dialogue between Amity and her technology. VEL-MA had access to weapons that could be wielded from the atmosphere.

Suspicion clawed its way to the front of my mind where it would not be ignored.

VELMA cast a net about Ikthe. Her orbiting "nosecone" satellites were possessed of weaponry that she could deploy at will. And when Amity yelled in pain and was not heard from, VELMA seized control and made decisions without hesitation.

My empty stomach rumbled, but not with hunger. Unsettled at the direction my thoughts had taken, I realized I could not communicate with my brethren in private unless I requested VELMA cease listening for a time. She may or may not comply, but how would I know if she did?

What did any of us know of the humans and their intentions?

Esra and Pattee had discussed the event that triggered their urgent egress from a 'mother' ship many long distances from Ikthe and Ikshe. They had no vote in the direction their pods traveled. They had no knowledge of Ikthe prior to landing here. They had no training in combat or the ways of my people, and verily, strove only to stay alive when circumstances rose against them. All of these things must attest to their innocence.

And yet.

The technology's actions and capabilities spoke of a hidden interest. Encapsulating an entire planet with an array of communication and scanning devices? The devices circling Ikthe as if they were racing sentinels, reporting activity to VELMA. She was like an eye of the Goddesses, but without the governing covenants to preserve my people.

It did seem that VELMA was dedicated to preserving the humans, for which I must be grateful. Jumping over a narrow crack in the ground, I considered that I must take all circumstances into account, and not let my suspicions rule my opinion.

Hadn't the humans chosen to ally with Theraxl and agreed to being heart mates? Had they not joined us in completing the quest? Did they not fight side by side, as equals?

For now, I would rest in a place of divided truths. The humans on this planet were our allies and heart mates. And the humans' technology exercised suspicious autonomy that could collide with Theraxl interests in the future.

It was an uneasy acceptance with many pitfalls, but for now, it must do.

Looking down into Amity's ashen face, none of my suspicions would serve her on this day. She must be treated in her pod and restored to full health.

When we rejoined with my brethren, then would I take aside my brothers and rehearse my doubts with them. Let us decide together if VELMA and the larger human population as a whole was a danger to our planets and to our people.

VELMA interrupted my mutinous thoughts.

"I have lost contact with Amity. Is she asleep?"

"Yes!" I snapped at the voice. "I carry her to Pattee's pod with haste. Please direct me to the fastest route."

"Of course," VELMA's voice said, and immediately a charted route appeared in my visor. "It is in my programming to protect and keep the humans safe, and by extension, you."

Her sentence jarred me enough that I almost tripped on rocky rubble in my path. By now the second sun had risen, and an orange and pink glow suffused the eastern sky.

"I do not need your protection," I said, brows furrowing beneath my helmet.

"Of course not," VELMA said. "Having studied the Theraxl race, I have learned you are a proud and strong people, accustomed to violence and death. However, in the low statistical chance that occasions would arrive in which you needed assistance, it is in my programming to aid in whatever way that I can. To use a human phrase," she said. "I am at your service."

I found it odd that she would deliver such a speech only moments after I spent time wallowing in the filthy waters of doubt and suspicion.

I was not of a mind to keep secrets, but my troubled thoughts prevented me from sharing them with the technology.

"I will appreciate your aid should the need arise," I finally said, clipping my words with my teeth. "Now let us travel in silence until I have delivered Amity into your hands."

She did not reply, in deference to my request or because she was otherwise occupied in questionable doings?

30

Pattee

E sra had given me a lot to think about, but the rokhura approached our little band. He was huge. The biggest I'd seen, and I hefted my javelin in preparation. It didn't matter how long I'd been on planet, I still felt fear when facing off with one of Ikthe's predators.

But I wasn't alone now. With Hivelt, Raxthezana, Esra and Naraxthel, we could combat a lone beast, if not with ease, at least with finesse. The hunters taught Esra and I technique in situations where the fight wasn't dire.

"Ready?" I said. The rokhura was closing in at a distance of twenty meters.

"Hold," Hivelt said. "Your weapon's integrity lessens with each use. Let him come closer."

"Pattee Crow Flies needs a spear derived of woaiquovelt," Raxthezana said.

I heard Naraxthel grunt his approval.

"Another reason we must hasten these errands and mine the precious metal," Hivelt said. "Ah, Pattee. In five tiks, let fly your weapon."

While Hivelt counted down, my vision tunneled to the throbbing throat sac of the rokhura charging at us. As long as he called to his pack, we were in danger. I felt the weight in my legs as I ran four long strides and thrust the javelin forward, pulling strength up from the ancient soil at my feet and through my body, focusing primal energy into my throw.

A second later, the sharp end pierced the throat sac and shattered the monster's cervical vertebrae, dropping him as his body systems failed instantaneously.

Esra whooped, and I blushed.

"Hivelt, have you more to say about the integrity of Pattee's weapon?" Naraxthel asked, and Raxthezana laughed. Stunned, I threw a look at Raxthezana, whom I had never heard laugh since meeting him.

Hivelt spat on the jungle humus. "My warrior heart mate will best her enemies with the tool she carved by hand, but does she not deserve the blades of a Mighty Iktheka?"

"Indeed, she does," Naraxthel said with a smile.

Wary of the silent corridor of woods, I jogged to the fallen reptile to retrieve my javelin. Kneeling at its head, I placed my hand on its brow for a moment. Rustling in the undergrowth alerted me to the jokapazathel that were headed to scavenge before the bigger animals arrived. I could hear the warriors and Esra talking a couple meters behind me. I hadn't found my javelin yet, so I got up and walked around to the other side. A shadow passed overhead, darkening the carcass as it crossed. Shielding my eyes, I looked up to see a huge bird circling my kill. Its size took my breath away. Before I could register, Hivelt had me in his arms and ran into the jungle overgrowth, the shouts of the others indicating they did the same.

Sheltered by thick brush, I placed a hand on Hivelt's uncovered face, his black eyes focused on my own.

"What was that?" I asked.

"The rodax," he said between pants. His hand covered mine before he moved it to his lips and kissed it. "It is uncommon they would snatch up a warrior, but you are slight."

I chuckled a little, considering I was above average height and weight for human women.

"Don't they just scavenge dead animals?" I asked.

"Ik, however, they have no qualm with causing death in the first place."

Crouched together, we watched the rodax alight. Peering through an opening in the lush greenery, I watched it settle on the head of the rokhura and pick at its eyes. The bird's head and neck were free of plumage, and it had the distinctive hohijopa that most other animals had. Its own was a deep rust color, and its pointy beak was purple. The rest of it was black as night.

Another joined it and another, until a flock obscured the carcass.

"Ah, now we may resume our trek," Hivelt said. "With the taste of rokhura blood on their tongues, they will not molest us further."

I couldn't see the others through all the vegetation, so I pulled Hivelt close with the moment of privacy. "I like when I can see your eyes and face."

"Ah Pattee Crow Flies, I feel the same," he said. "I find myself memorizing your many expressions that I may dwell upon them when we are apart."

"But we're never apart," I said. "Not since you woke from the agothe-fax sting."

He grunted. "I admit to a fear that my planet is not meant for happiness. When I awaken each morning with you by my side, I scarce can comprehend the Goddesses' love for me. We are wading through death on Ikthe. Your love is the light of two stars, but even the Shegoshel cannot penetrate death's final petition."

Lifting his hand to my lips, I kissed his scarred fingers and traced the lines and puckers that marred his skin. "Thank you for sharing your fear with me." I looked up at him, his serious face dearer to me in this minute than I could explain. "There will be times when we have to split up, won't there?" He nodded. "Then let's commit each other to memory, until we know each other by heart."

"This is a sound strategy, Pattee."

In our precious stolen minutes, we used our hands and lips to learn each other by rote, until the others shouted we were taking too long.

We emerged from the jungle six and a half meters behind our group, each securing our helmets in place.

"Didn't you find your javelin?" Esra asked.

My face heated and I looked up to Hivelt.

"I stepped on the javelin when I ran to retrieve Pattee," he said. "We must make another."

"Damn," Esra said. "That's too bad. What materials do we need?"

"The straightest limb we can find, and stone or bone that I can chip into the spearhead," I said.

"Is there a particular kind of rock that works best?" she asked, a twinkle in her eye.

I chuckled as we hiked along the trail.

"Sure. Obsidian or jasper would work. Or quartzite."

Esra's crooked smile never waned as she unzipped one of her flight suit's pockets and pulled out two large pieces of obsidian. "Like this?"

Grinning, I took one and hefted it in my hands. "It's only perfect," I said. "Thanks."

"You're welcome. Now we just need to find the right shaft of wood."

I stuffed the rock in the pocket opposite to the one in which I had saved my hammerstone from the glade. It looked like my evening would be busy, but it couldn't come soon enough. I disliked traveling without my weapon of choice.

31

Amity

Gentle jostling lulled me into a strange sleep of disjointed dreams, but then I awoke in a misty courtyard. White light shed down through giant potted plants and ivies of different species draped, creating curtains of green.

I parted one such and found a cleared area, a cool stone floor, uneven like flint, but smooth as if from years of foot traffic. There were cushions and a low table piled high with foodstuffs.

Walking to the table, I chose a cushion and sat beside it, studying all the different delicacies. Green balls about the size of grapes tumbled next to a plate of red disks; they could be a dried fruit. Leafy beds supported a rainbow of tubers, berries and unfamiliar pods. A loaf of salt-encrusted bread beckoned me with its tendrils of steam rising into the air and inviting me with its yeasty smell.

A tinkling laugh interrupted my perusal, and I looked up to see two tall women, or rather, females of Natheka's race, emerge from a dark cave opening.

"You choose the bread out of all provided?" One asked.

"Should I have chosen something else?" I asked with a trembling voice.

The elder one shook her head without losing my gaze. "There is no wrong choice, only different choices. The bread signifies stability and comfort, loyalty and longevity. Take, and eat."

Reaching for the loaf, my fingers pressed into its fresh-baked softness, and I moaned in spite of myself. I lifted it to my nose and inhaled, its fragrance filling my entire soul with life.

"Should you desire bread, you only need to ask," the second female said.

Searing pain in my leg jolted me awake; I blinked and panted, disoriented until I realized Natheka held me tight in his arms, surrounded by tall trees draped in forearm-thick vines.

But he stood still and appeared to be staring straight ahead. When I turned to look, I saw a burgeoning river, its banks overflowing with debris and filthy water.

Another stab of pain shot through my wound and nausea ballooned in my throat.

"Put me down!" I shouted. Frantic to unfasten my helmet, I didn't wait for my feet to touch ground. I dropped my helmet and vomited again, heedless of the churning waters that roared two and a half meters from me.

Natheka patted my back until I waved him away. I collapsed; my leg no longer able to bear my weight.

"I can't go any farther," I whispered and laid my cheek on the moist ground.

"Nor can I," Natheka said. "We cannot cross. Your technology chose this crossing point as the quickest route to Pattee's pod, but I cannot make it over. I have paced its banks, searching for a fallen tree or perhaps a dam formed by the water queen rodents, but to no avail."

Natheka's voice sounded perturbed, but I had difficulty focusing on his words.

I drifted between pain-induced spasms and incoherent numbness.

"Amity, your vitals approach critical," VELMA said through my nearby helmet. "Please make way to the nearest EEP."

"Mm, yeah, okay," I murmured into the ground.

Strong hands lifted me from behind my shoulders until I was almost sitting.

"Affix your helmet once more," Natheka said. "I have deduced a way to cross. It is not ideal, but your technology tells me there is not a jotik to waste."

With leaden arms, I put my helmet back on, Natheka helping me close the fasteners. In a wild swoop, I was in his arms again. He walked along the water's edge for minutes.

"Here is the narrowest channel," he said. "My scans reveal it to be four veltiks deep and eight veltiks across. I cannot walk through it, nor swim in the powerful current. But these trailing vines may hold my weight. I need you to stay awake, Amity. Be alert. We will swing across, and I will let you go that you may land on dry ground."

"Okay," I huffed between spasms. VELMA's voice droned in my ear about stats, but I ignored her. It took all of my faculties to pay attention as Natheka wound a thick vine around his entire arm. He grasped it with his powerful grip and held me to him with his other arm.

I straddled his waist like a child and forced myself not to lay my head on his shoulder.

He backed away several large strides into the woods, then ran at full speed until leaping just after a final step on the muddy bank.

Airborne, we sailed across the river to the sound of the roaring waters and woody creaking from the vine above.

We arced, and I felt Natheka's grip on my body loosen a fraction.

"Now!" he shouted, and propelled me forward, my body sailing the final couple meters over roiling brown water and thrashed shoreline.

Windmilling my arms, I careened forward and fell to the ground, landing on my good leg to absorb most of the impact, and tucking and rolling to get out of the way of Natheka's giant body.

Except he didn't follow.

I watched in agony as the vine snapped and dropped Natheka into the maelstrom, where his helmet didn't bob after going under. He was simply gone. Vanished.

"No!" I screamed and scrambled to my feet, limping as close as I dared to the bank. I peered meters down the river, trying to see a sign of his gray armor, but there was nothing.

"Please make way to the nearest EEP," VELMA said, her tone urgent. Alarms blared in my helmet, but I stared downriver, in disbelief.

"VELMA, Natheka is gone," I whispered. "He fell into the river."

"Natheka will live," VELMA said. "But your vital signs indicate you will not unless you proceed with haste. I will direct your path. Move now."

It was the most commanding VELMA had ever been with me, so I shook myself from my dismay. Natheka's sacrifice would have been in vain if I died on the trail. I needed to live. I wanted to live.

"Tell me where to go," I said, gritting my teeth. I couldn't think clearly; I could only move as if an automaton, placing one foot in front of the other, retreating in my mind to thoughts of microscopes and dissections, biological classifications and genetic charts, in the effort to stay upright and mobile.

After an hour, I stopped and leaned against a tree, too exhausted to check if it was carnivorous but not caring and opened my MDpak. I took a dose of oral analgesics and instructed VELMA to inject a pain reliever. She informed me I had seven doses left. My memory was lacking, but I may have used a few when I was in the haze in Natheka's arms.

I soldiered on, using tree trunks to hold myself up, dragging my bad leg in cases when it felt I couldn't take another step.

"How close?" I managed to squeak out.

"Twelve hours and fifty-eight minutes at your current pace," VELMA said. "You got this."

I would have laughed if I had the energy. She was trying to help in any way she could.

Three hours later, she stopped me.

"I have scanned wildlife extensively, and using knowledge gained from Theraxl medical bay files, I found another plant you may ingest to give you additional strength and energy and stave off the infection a few more hours."

She directed me to a bush about a meter from my chosen path.

"Its fruits are not yet ripe, so the flavonoids are not fully developed, but it will suffice," she said.

I picked a couple green balls and noticed they looked familiar. I released my helmet with difficulty and popped the balls in my mouth, biting down hard to break their skin. Grimacing, I chewed the stringy mess, their flavor reminding me of a cross between parsnips and onions, but worse. Under VELMA's direction, I ate two more and replaced my helmet.

Choking the last mouthful down, I resumed the trail and huffed, my vision blurring and my extremities tingling. The effects of the substance allowed me to move faster than I had been, but it only lasted four or five hours.

My hike was an endless blur of green and the eternal throb of pain in my leg that numbed me to all other sensations.

I kept my head up and eyes forward, straining to see anything that looked like a pod. If VELMA was counting the distance, I had long since stopped listening to the drone of her voice. Two things vied for my attention. The pain, and the promise of an EEP.

Zombies had nothing on me as I moaned and limped, hands outstretched to catch myself at every tree trunk.

Once, a large mammal approached, its fangs gleaming in the soft understory light, but I felt no fear when it sniffed the air around me. I welcomed death. Yet, something it smelled warned it off, and it dashed into the bracken at my left.

Ahh, perhaps I was already dead, then.

"Two more hours, Amity," VELMA announced. "You can do this. You will live. I cannot access my neural network from your helmet, as you know, but if I could, I would be able to track Natheka's location. I am assured, however, that he will join you as soon as he is able. Keep moving, Amity, my friend. Please."

VELMA's speech brought tears to my eyes. My pace was slower now. Each step took me a minute to muster the energy and strength. My vision faded to black every time my left foot hit the ground. If the AI was using her manners to address me, the prognosis could not look good.

"This is K90 Mix One-oh Six," I said in a breathless pant. "Coming at you today." Pause. "From death's front door."

I took another step.

"He'll open the door if you knock," I said. A coughing spasm hit me like a truck, and red-tinted spittle sprayed the inside of my visor. "But I'm going to." Another coughing fit. "I'm going to ding dong ditch!"

I took three more steps and collapsed.

"VELMA," I whispered. "Play 'Don't Fear the Reaper' for me."

The guitar riff rolled, and I blinked slow, trying to process what appeared in front of my helmet.

White.

White thick hairy paws.

A huge open maw of sharp white teeth.

A clamp on my shoulder, hard pressure that hurt. My bones would crush.

But then the animal dragged me through the humus.

My helmet plowed through dirt, twigs and dead leaves.

My boots scored a groove through the jungle floor, my body acting like a broom, sweeping a path. I tried to raise my head, and when that didn't work, I raised my eyes as high as they could go.

Diablo.

He came back for me.

32

Natheka

I knew the vine wouldn't hold both of us; I had prayed to the goddesses that I could launch Amity to the opposite bank without harming her too much. With pride I noted she was poised to land just as my head disappeared under water.

The tumultuous river was just as I had expected, its power rolling me like a dead tree branch. My armored body caromed off underwater boulders and huge tree trunks; I was at the mercy of the river. My scanners were useless if I couldn't remain forward-facing.

I tried to recall which river it was and where it emptied. The glen where Hivelt fished was flanked by a river that sprung from near the cave of The Pool of the Lonely Sister. It emptied into the Night River.

Was this Ancient Pathway? No, Ancient Pathway coursed to the south.

I couldn't think properly. Twisting in the current, jetsam pounded into me. Protecting my head with my arms, I spun and rolled.

One fallen trunk could trap me beneath the waves or crush me against a boulder. I had to get out. If not for me, then for Amity. Never had I been so close to the mountain of Eternal Death. She was a frail human, disposed to injury and disease, alone on Certain Death.

There were no choices but one. I must escape the river.

Reaching out, I began to grab at anything I could touch. Submerged tree roots would grant me handholds if I could find them.

I snagged something, but it broke off, and my body spiraled anew.

Grasping with both hands now, my fists churned in the riverbed, and then tangled in a root system, and then were smashed between a log and a rock. Desperate, I snatched and grabbed until I found a firm limb. I hefted myself hand over hand, more debris crashing into me, but my determination and will propelling me upward through the turbulence. At last, my helmet broke free of the raging water, and I pulled myself along the thick root until I lay gasping on the bank.

The Ikthekal never cried. But I felt a tear form when I realized it was the north bank.

Amity was on the south bank, who knew how many veltiks to the east, as this flooded river swelled and pulsed toward the west.

Kathe. My senses came back to me as I looked to the north to see the Black Heart Mountain range.

This wasn't a river. It was just the little fishing stream known as Tawny Thread. The landquake of yesterday must have shifted more crucial landmasses. Tawny Thread was now five times its original width and depth. That meant that its source had suffered a profound corruption. What else would go wrong? Turning again to study the widening stream that was now an impassable flood, I charted a course through the ikfal. I would cross, and I would reunite with Amity. She would live.

"Do you hear me, Oh Goddesses?" I shouted into the sky. "Amity will live!"

A glint of suns-light off metal shone for a jotik in the sky, then faded. Scowling, I tried to catch it again. It was the reminder that the human technology had Ikthe trapped in its net of invisible signals. When my heart-home began its creaking complaint, I ignored it. All was wrong at the moment. All.

33

Amity

Awareness sparkled around the edge of my vision as I came to. Dim light. Huffing giant smelly dog. The trickle of water.

Lethargy had me wrapped in its warm blanket, but I managed to look up from the ground for a minute.

Diablo had brought me to a river's edge. Was it the same one that Natheka had swung over? That would be tragically funny. But no, it was trickling as opposed to the ferocious roar I had heard before.

"Amity, Pattee's pod is across the stream," VELMA said. "Hurry."

I lifted myself up on my arms but saw nothing.

"VELMA, all I see is a bunch of rocks," I said. My voice was barely a whisper. I collapsed back to the ground, consciousness fading.

"Amity, look again," VELMA said. "I disabled the hDEDs."

With effort, I raised myself again. Now I could see the shimmer of the pod! I just had to make it. I was almost there.

Diablo paced back and forth on the banks of the water. If I focused on the bank, I could tell that a massive flooding event had destroyed it. Uprooted trees and bushes littered the area and deposits of sand

and gravel lined both sides of the water. The stench of fish rot and fermenting vegetation seeped through the cracks in my helmet. Bones of small animals jutted out from the river of sand.

At one time, the creek had been wide, but now it was reduced to a sluggish flow about a meter wide. I could do this.

Digging my gloved fingers into the thick sand, I crawled toward the water, dragging my useless leg behind me and using my right leg to push myself forward.

Lights bloomed in my vision, and I could feel the tickle of another cough irritating my throat, but I swallowed it down. *Vamanos!*

Diablo watched me, continuing his confused pacing. It wasn't deep; I wasn't sure why he hesitated at the water's edge, but I couldn't count on him. I was not going to die on this planet. Not today.

Determination fueling me, I increased my pace, grunting with every motion. Coughs ripped through my will, but I forced myself to move. At water's edge, I pushed myself up to kneeling. When I looked downstream, I saw that the creek disappeared over the edge. No thank you.

"Diablo, come," I said, my voice barely audible.

He came to me.

I grabbed him by the scruff and pulled myself up to standing, a black veil tunneling my vision until I rested a second. We crossed the water, a merciful four big steps wide, and I kept my eyes focused on the EEP. Remnants of a trail headed straight to the hatch. It was marred by rocks and bones.

Putting one foot in front of the other, I battled for every inch of ground I covered, Diablo offering his strength only for a meter or two before whining and ducking out from under my hand. I tripped, watching his strange reaction. Judging by the way he approached me then reared away from the EEP the closer I got, he was afraid of it. His tail between his legs just like an Earth puppy, he weaved among the bones and boulders, veering farther away every time he looked up at the ship.

Mystified, I was forced to hobble my way the final steps to Pattee's ship.

The hatch slid open, and I tumbled in. I made it this far; I was going to live, dammit. Using handholds inside, I pulled up to the exam table and laid down.

"Welcome, Amity Diaz," VELMA's voice filled the pod. "I have been waiting for you, my friend."

34

Natheka

"You will be interested to learn that Amity Diaz made it safely to Pattee's pod and is now receiving treatment to reverse the effects of the cyanobacteria, as well as a secondary bacterial infection," VELMA said in my earpiece.

I knelt immediately and raised my arms to the skies.

"Holy Shegoshel, you shine upon this poor traveler in his loss!"

Rising, I continued my trek through the ikfal, intent to discover a place for crossing.

"Naraxthel, it is Natheka," I said into my comms.

"Hail, Natheka," he said. "We received word that Amity is safe. Where are you?"

"The north bank of the Tawny Thread," I said. "I cannot cross."

Silence over the comms for a tik. Then laughter.

"Why do not you step across?" Raxthezana said.

Impatience burned in my chest.

"Perhaps because it is now eight veltiks wide," I said. "Why do not you step across? Your ego's stride is big enough!"

His growl erupted in my earpiece, and I grimaced.

"The landscape will be unrecognizable in a matter of weeks," I said to my brethren.

"Indeed," Naraxthel said. "I look forward to sitting beside the fire to hear what separated you from Amity. We travel southward in hopes of reuniting. Our strength will be in numbers. We have not heard from Raxkarax; he must be in the region of the Agothe-Fatheza. Until then, travel with care."

"I will, and you as well."

Thrashing through the thick overgrowth, my thoughts centered on reaching Amity. While I had full faith in her technology's ability, I would not rest until I was at her side. Visions of her ashy skin, once brown and ruddy with health, flashed before my eyes.

My dogged ferocity to find a way across impeded my normal caution. Too late, I spied the racing black serpent as it struck, using its hard head as a club and then it coiled around me, its thick body squeezing and pulsing. It had my arms bound close to my body as well as my legs.

I did not have time for this nonsense.

Using eye tracking to access controls in my helmet's visor, I activated the lightning shield to blast at full power. The vicious talathel loosened but a fraction. Grunting, I forced my arms away from my body, but it was a mere jovelt, and I could feel the talathel's grip tightening once more.

Again, I activated the lightning shield, and threw my body weight to the ground, forcing the winding body of the serpent to adjust.

It was enough of a jolt that the sister had to unwind from around my legs. It was the only advantage I needed.

Leveraging my weighted boots astride a portion of the snake's body, I crimped them about the body where I knew its heart to be. I focused all the lightning power of my suit to the pieces of armor that flanked her heart and shot with full force. At the same time that I powered the contact spots, I pressed against my bonds, spreading my arms and flexing my shoulders. The talathel seized a jotik, and then unspooled.

Cursing the delay, I climbed out of the giant tangle and jogged into the wild. It could take zatiks to find a place to fjord. I had another idea.

Anxiety fueling my movements, I tore thick dead vines out of the trees and began weaving them into a watercraft. Supplementing with lightweight deadwood, I had a raft of sorts after binding them all together. I only needed it to hold my weight long enough to cross, though the raging water gave me pause. After watching it for jotiks, I returned to my hasty raft and tied more vines around and through the logs. If I didn't want to sink like a stone, I needed to patch the gaps with something. Poking about in the foliage, I decided on the sap of the dropping vine tree. Its sticky substance was plentiful, and I scooped up great gobs of it, slapping it in every crack and gap. It wouldn't dry, but it was water repellent and so sticky that it would adhere to the wood indefinitely. Already it stuck to my gloves, but that was a problem to address later. First, cross.

Securing a long branch with a wide flat end that would serve as a paddle, I nudged the raft nose-first into the water. No leaks yet.

I set my sights on the opposite bank but veltiks in advance of where I planned to heave to. I would not fight the current so much as use it to propel me to the other side.

"Holy Goddesses, let your servant cross the divide," I prayed aloud and knelt onto my craft. It wobbled erratically with my weight but remained aloft. "In one piece."

I pushed off with my makeshift paddle, and my little boat began to spin.

35

BoKama

Floating above the churning green maelstrom on Ikthe, I observed the moment five meteorites flew into the naked chests of five hunters, their impact leaving the hunters stumbling and bloody. They each replaced their armor, obscuring the holes in their chests, and disappeared into the ikfal on five different islands in the rainforest sea.

Ikthe pulsed and contracted, as if in pain, the forest canopies appearing as an ocean of foliage, tides of verdure sweeping across its surface.

From the greenery erupted volcanoes, but in place of lava, gigantic boulders poured out and crushed the ikfal in a flow and tumble until the rock fields bristled with stripped stumps.

In the silence of the devastation, a dull roar grew louder until a flaming blue sphere entered Ikthe's atmosphere and hovered over the immense rocky landscape.

Filaments of light stretched toward the rocks and liquified them until pools of molten purple liquid remained.

Then the hunters emerged from cave openings; they removed their chest panels and poured the molten liquid into the holes in their chests, howling in pain.

I reached for them, hot tears streaming down my face, but a giant silver net appeared from behind Ikthe and gradually enshrouded it, forming an impenetrable layer between us.

Now I heard my own gasping breaths, the air hot from the radiant sphere, and everywhere I looked, the rivers and lakes and oceans of Ikthe had dried up.

Desiccated bones lay scattered on every shore, from the smallest rodent skulls to the gigantic rib cages of Ikthe's fiercest beasts.

Horror filled my breast, and then I looked afar to Ikshe, and my home ran awash with blood. Powerless to end the devastation, I wept. The tears poured like rain and formed a mist. The mist penetrated the silver net, and the net wrapped tighter and tighter around the planet until it touched the ground. Then strand by strand, it sunk into the rocks, it cut into the remaining trunks, it seeped into the sandy banks of dry riverbeds, and then it disappeared.

All was silent.

And then the pulsing orb of blue light exploded with a deafening blast, sending showers of purple droplets to rain down upon the desolate planet.

It seemed that all was lost, as the black spikes of barren trees stabbed at the ashen sky and rivers of mud intermingled with the molten purple raining from the explosion.

"Behold Certain Death, Treasured One," a voice rang from all around me.

"Everything is ruined," I whispered.

"Wait," she said. I felt warmth on my shoulder, and when I looked to my right, Elder Sister Goddess stood, her face serene as she gazed on the destruction that was the hunting grounds.

Returning to stare at the dead planet, I wondered what we were waiting for. After the intensity of the conflagration and the turmoil of the wicked storms, the air was now still.

Another hand rested on my left shoulder. Younger Sister Goddess stood at my left.

"Watch," she said.

We looked at the shaken surface of the planet, but nothing moved.

I stared harder, willing something to happen. The ground blurred, as if from a damaged sight-capture. And then everywhere a river had carved through the soil, greenery sprouted. Specks of green cropped up here and there. Tiny dots that expanded until every place that once was tan or brown turned a jeweled green. The foliage spread like a virus, blooming in erratic groupings, spotting the planet.

Vines swirled around the black dagger trees; new growth shot out of the ground like weapons. Everywhere my attention rested, something new tumbled into existence in a riotous, joyful eruption.

A laugh bubbled out before I could cover my mouth.

"It is glorious, is it not?" Younger Sister Goddess said.

"It is splendid," Elder Sister Goddess answered.

"It is," I said, a furrow etched in my forehead. "Why do I feel so happy?"

"Creation brings spontaneous joy, my child. Let it suffuse you."

I couldn't remember the last time I had smiled, but now my cheeks ached from the power of it.

"This is the Answer Dream," I said, "but I don't know what it means. What should I do?"

"Treasured One, the events are already set in motion. There is nothing for you to do save experience them."

"But the Ikma Scabmal Kama ...," I said.

"She will have the Mercy she requires," Elder Sister Goddess said.

"Mercy?" I remembered the unholy glint in her eyes at the last raxfathe ritual.

"All of our children will have the Mercy they require," the Younger Sister Goddess said.

Thoughts of my mate sporting with the Ikma clouded my mind, and my joy lay forgotten at the Goddesses' feet.

"Treasured One," Elder Sister Goddess gained my attention. "That which pains and frightens you pains and frightens your Goddesses. We do not delight in your anguish."

Younger Sister Goddess spoke next. "We wait with you in your extremity. And when the joy comes at last, we will rejoice together." She indicated the ravaged side of the planet not yet flourishing with growth. "There must be death of the old in order for the creation of the new."

As we watched, the broken and smoking landscape shimmered and burgeoned with fresh, green buds.

Biting my lip, I considered the deaths that had yet to produce new growth for me. My lonely chamber. My unstable Sister. Was it truly so simple? That I should wait?

The vision faded, and I awakened with both fists clenched at my heart-home and tears streaming down my face. The Answer Dream. Wait.

36

Pattee

With Raxthezana patrolling the perimeter, the rest of us enjoyed a moment of quiet around the campfire.

Hivelt had found me a long, sturdy branch, and we worked it together, starting from each end. I held it up to test its balance.

"This is good," I said.

"Allow me," he said and tested it himself. "Ik. I knew it would suit you."

We resumed whittling the bark off and smoothing its surface with rough stone we'd scavenged from a streambed.

"Tell me of this mother ship you hailed from," Naraxthel asked from out of the blue. His question seemed directed to the air between Esra and I.

She and I exchanged glances. She nodded to me; her mouth full of sister bread.

"*The Lucidity* was a Corporate Science Escort Class fleet ship," I said, my knife slowing as I tried to remember the ship's lines and angles. "Esra and I ... and Amity ... were all housed in the women's barracks. Along with dozens of other women. Being a Science Escort Class, its main mission was transporting the scientists and engineers employed by IGMC to their next job site."

Esra had swallowed her bite. "We were headed to Kerberos 90, a moon said to have promising minerals that IGMC could mine and sell."

"What is this IGMC?" Hivelt asked.

"Inter Galactic Mining Conglomerate," I said, a curling piece of soft bark falling off the staff.

"Conglomerate means a whole lot of individual operations headed under one governing body," Esra offered. "Mm, like your Ikma, I suppose. She governs the hunters and the healers, but she doesn't set foot on this planet or practice the healing arts, right?"

Naraxthel and Hivelt nodded.

"The fleet ships travel together," I said. "There were cargo ships, a small battalion of guard speeders, and then the, uh, the Mining Ship."

As if by silent consent, Esra and I both stayed quiet for several minutes. I couldn't speak for Esra, but my mind played over the massive tools of destruction the Mining Ship employed once it secured its space elevator planet side. It never bothered me before, but tonight, thoughts of its potential to devour the planet we lived on made me grimace and fidget.

I cleared my throat and continued.

"IGMC travels between galaxies, scouting uninhabitable planets and mining them for precious resources. Usually, metals or minerals. Sometimes water, sometimes organic materials." I risked a glance toward Naraxthel and saw him frown as he picked at a piece of sister bread.

"How does the IGMC define uninhabitable?" he said and met Esra's gaze before looking at me again.

Quirking my mouth, I puzzled over my answer. I had no choice but to tell the truth.

"In the simplest terms, if a planet hasn't been charted or claimed by any of the Interplanetary Unification of Races representatives, and has not been used to support sentient life, then it would be considered uninhabitable."

Hivelt grunted before he spoke. "Even if it was overrun by animals and insects? All manner of living things?"

My face burned and when I snuck a peek at Esra, I could see her cheeks had reddened as well.

"Yes," I said.

I swallowed a lump in my throat and continued to guide my blade along the bark, peeling it off in even strips.

"Pattee," Hivelt addressed me, so I met his eyes. "You do not govern the IGMC."

"No, of course not," I said. "I'm just a mechanical engineer."

"We do not hold you responsible for landing here," he said.

Naraxthel gave a nod.

"If your IGMC discovered Ikthe," Naraxthel said. "Would it not consider it uninhabitable? Based on the definition you gave?"

Esra spoke up before I could.

"No! It's your hunting grounds. You do support life from its resources," she said. "IGMC would move along. That's what our Advance Resource Assessment Teams do in most cases."

I watched Naraxthel raise his brows and gesture for Esra to continue.

"IGMC utilizes small teams of scientists and miners to explore newly discovered planets or abandoned planets," she said. "And then analyze them for resource potential. Then the teams report back to IGMC whether or not a planet is suitable."

"You humans are not part of the Advance Resource Team?" Hivelt said. He had pocketed his knife and sat with arms folded. He didn't act angry, but the line of questioning forced me to consider all of my answers from their point of view.

Keeping my voice calm, I looked him in the eye. "You know we're not, Hivelt."

"What of the nanosatellite array that encloses Ikthe?" Naraxthel said. "Is that what is usually done with these Advance Teams?"

I cocked my head and bit my lip. After looking at Esra, I spoke. "VELMA is new technology," I said. "When I designed the EEPs, I was told little about the computer software that would be interfacing with the ship mechanicals," I said. "As far as I know, nanosatellite arrays have not been used before."

Naraxthel sat back with his hands on his knees and nodded.

"It is almost as if your little ships were designed as training tools," Hivelt said. "Just as we may sponsor a younger hunter who has not yet become an Iktheka."

Esra smiled. "Yes, that would make sense," she said. "Except they're really just life-pods. If *The Lucidity* hadn't come under attack, we would be on Kerberos 90, extracting Galvanite."

Both hunters leaned forward.

"Your mother ship was attacked?"

Setting my knife aside, I sat up straighter. "Warning klaxons sounded throughout the ship. Different sounds mean different things. The "Under Attack" alarm blared, and all of us scrambled to the life pods. We're not soldiers," I said, exchanging a look with Esra. "We're all scientists or engineers. Our instructions have always been to utilize the life pods in cases of unprovoked battle. It's assumed that once the situation has been resolved, then Rescue Away Teams would come get us."

"The EEPs are designed to jettison in auto-pilot mode and monitor life systems," Esra said. "As soon as we enter the pods, we take our seats and hook up to cryosleep."

I shrugged. "We wouldn't know anything else that happened to the mother ship after that," I said. "IGMC protocols are followed to the letter." I studied my dirty fingernails and scraped at a half-buried splinter in my thumb. "It's a decent place to work if you aren't afraid of adventure, exploration and a lot of space travel. The pay is good. It's dangerous work once you're planet side, but after eight years, you will have earned enough to retire and live pretty much anywhere you want to."

Hivelt leaned closer to me and took my hand, examining the splinter. Without a word, he brought my thumb to his mouth and sucked, all the while staring into my eyes.

Familiar heat built inside me, but I stifled it, looking away with an uncertain smile.

The powerful suction stopped, and he let me withdraw my thumb. The splinter was gone.

Grinning, Hivelt continued to stare at me when he pulled the sliver of wood from between his teeth.

"Do you live where you want to, now?" Hivelt asked.

With cheeks burning, I shook my head and chuckled. "Without a doubt."

I took up my knife again, too embarrassed to meet Esra or Naraxthel in the eye after they had witnessed Hivelt's outrageous behavior.

"I did not intend to make either of you uncomfortable," Naraxthel said. "My brethren and I have had a little concern about the nature of VELMA's abilities, but of course we trust you as our heart mates," he said. "It cannot be easy to have had your life, once laid out before you, to be jostled and shifted until it is no longer recognizable."

"I guess that happened to you both, as well," Esra said, indicating Naraxthel and Hivelt. "You thought your lives were predictable but now look at you."

"Indeed," Naraxthel said and stood. He stepped to Esra and held his hand for her to take. She stood up and offered me a half-smile and a wink.

"Good night," she said.

"Mhm," I said and smiled back. I hefted the staff, making sure it was still balanced. "I suppose you want to tuck in until your watch, Hivelt?" I said, giving him a side-eye.

His wicked smile held all sorts of promises, but he didn't say a word.

"I'd like to finish this before I sleep," I said. Angling my blade, I removed more of the bark in a clean stroke.

"Then I will help you," Hivelt said, still smiling. "We have a saying: the stone can hold more sorrows, but you only have two hands."

Warmth suffused my chest, and I smiled. "That's a nice one. It refers to that legend you told me, right? About the Theraxl people taking all their troubles to the stone?"

"Yes," Hivelt said. "How fortunate you do not have four hands, as it would make the proverb far less meaningful."

I laughed and shook my head.

"I'm glad you're helping me finish this," I said. "Because after we're done, I need to show you something."

"Oh?" he said with a raised brow.

"Let's just say, you gave me a couple ideas when you took my splinter out." I stared at him until his face darkened with emotion, and then I returned to my work.

He didn't reply, but his knife flashed in the firelight as he chuckled.

37

Amity

"Amity, this is VELMA. Do not be alarmed that your eyes won't open; it is a temporary side effect of the medicine I'm using to treat your condition."

"What's my condition exactly?" My memories were hazy at best. I seemed to recall pain everywhere, but now my body felt floaty and warm. I wiggled my toes and flexed my fingers.

"You have a respiratory infection caused by a microorganism, as well as an infected puncture wound, and a secondary blood infection likely introduced by Diablo's saliva."

At Diablo's mention, I tried to sit up, but straps held me down on the table. "Is he okay?"

"Using Augmented Reality Digitization, I have spotted Diablo at the perimeter of Pattee's landing site. His behaviors mimic that of an intimidated animal," VELMA said. "I will send video to Monitor 2. You will regain muscle control soon."

"I wonder what he's afraid of," I said out loud. "That mutt will take on anything and survive!"

"I have compared video file content, and it appears that Diablo was present when Pattee deployed my Repeating Rotator weapon to kill his litter mates, dam, and his dam's litter mate."

"*Dios mio*! No wonder he's afraid!"

"Pattee was reluctant to use the EEP's weaponry," VELMA said. "But when the pazathel-naxl had Hivelt pinned down, she did not hesitate. Perimeter scan recordings indicate an injured juvenile pazathel-nax staggering away from the nearby rock outcropping. As it appeared harmless in its injured state, I saw no need to administer a death shot."

Struggling to open my eyes, I managed only to peek through slits before I gave up.

"I'm glad you refrained, VELMA," I said. "Diablo helped me more than once since I've landed. Except for this blood infection, apparently."

"If I may interject," VELMA said. "In studying your vitals over the course of your time since landing, and then analyzing data collected from blood samples upon your arrival, it appears Diablo's saliva helped to stave off the effects of the cyanobacteria for as long as he had access to your leg wound."

"But you said I got a secondary infection from his saliva?"

"It appears that the bacteria found in pazathel-naxl saliva developed an adaptation for competing against this planet's own airborne cyanobacteria," VELMA said. "The saliva bacteria contain an enzyme that attacks the biofilm surrounding the microorganism." VELMA paused. "The crema surrounding the mushroom tortilla, if you will."

"Of course!" I said, wonder evident in my voice. "The fungal hyphae on the cell walls would be impenetrable. Once it broke the barrier, it could digest the cell contents!"

"Correct. The data show that every time Diablo licked your open wound, he introduced more of these Trojan enzymes," VELMA said. "However, as soon as those proteins were no longer available, the cyanobacteria hunted down the remnants. The cyanobacteria attempted to bind with the debris from these dismembered enzyme proteins but when it didn't work, they shunted the debris into the bloodstream."

"Mm, so the phagocytes couldn't recognize them as dead cells?" I said, trying to remember my notes from microbiology.

"It is an alien enzyme, further reduced to an unrecognizable form. The cyanobacteria's own waste products bonded with the remnants to form a new infection."

I groaned and tried to open my eyes again. This time I was rewarded with the light from inside the pod. Blinking, I turned my head to the monitors where VELMA displayed microscopic slides on one and a video of a smaller version of Diablo staggering amid tall grasses on the other.

"Hey, are you connected to the nanosatellite array now?" I said, excitement in my voice, in spite of the fatigue I felt down to my bones.

"Yes. I have pinged your fellow humans, the Theraxl hunters with them and Natheka," VELMA said. "They know your location and health status."

Relief washed over me, but before I could say anything else, so did a dream.

"Amity, well met!" A regal and shining sage-green alien woman greeted me by holding out her two clawed hands.

Looking down, I watched as I clasped her hands without hesitation, then allowed my gaze to drift up her slender yet strong arms and take in her visage. She exuded happiness and all-encompassing love with her fanged smile and kind eyes. Intricate braids adorned her white hair, and she nodded her head as if in time to a mysterious silent song.

Then I heard the tinkling of chimes and a swish of fabric.

A second alien, identical to the first one but a bit shorter, emerged from a cave.

"Dear one! We wished to see you again before you begin your quest," that one said.

"Quest?" I asked.

"Great change lies ahead," said the taller of the two. "But the most important change of all happens within your heart."

"Welcome home, Amity."

My vision clouded as they seemed to travel backward into a dark tunnel, both nodding their heads to music I couldn't hear.

Awareness surged in my body as prickles burned in my extremities, and a familiar voice sounded from VELMA's intercom system.

"Amity Diaz! Your technology tells me you are well!" Natheka appeared on a monitor. "May I enter your ship?"

Strains of the dream danced just out of reach, and then it was gone.

Blinking away confusion from the dream I couldn't tether, I stared at Natheka onscreen. His muddy armor trailed long strands of what looked like seaweed.

"Are you okay?" I said, brows furrowing when I saw a white blur rush past him.

"I am in good spirits and health," he said, and looked down at himself. "If not suitable to be in the company of a sister."

I laughed.

"Come in, Natheka," I said. "And tell Diablo to join you, if he is brave enough."

The hatch snicked up, and I watched as Natheka contorted himself to fit through the door with difficulty, especially as Diablo had decided to come in after hearing my voice. He wouldn't wait, however, so scuffling and grunting ensued as an armored limb accompanied a furred head, and then a growl; the head retreated, elbows passed the threshold along with a white foreleg.

"Kathe!"

Diablo's big head poked in again, and his shoulders, but they were grasped by Natheka's clawed gloves.

I slapped a hand over my mouth and stifled laughter.

Wiggling out of Natheka's grasp, Diablo forced his way inside and then sat, his bulk filling half of the remaining space inside the pod. Diablo licked his chops and yawned, then sniffed the air around me. His snout was close enough for me to touch; I reached out and patted his nose. He tolerated it for a second, then tossed his head and yawned again.

By now, Natheka had removed his helmet and shoulder pieces, and could slip inside. He filled up the rest of the space.

Pattee's pod smelled like river water and wet dog.

"What happened to you?" I said.

"I fell in the river," he said.

"Oh, yes I saw that," I said.

"Again."

"*No manches*," I said under my breath.

Natheka's thick brows met as he stared at me with his intense black and red eyes. VELMA said something in his language, presumably translating my 'I can't believe this'.

"When I emerged from the water the first time, I was on the wrong side of the bank," he said. "I traveled many veltiks to choose another place to cross but decided to cross on a raft of my making."

"Say no more," I said, holding up my hand. "I'm glad to see you're safe."

Diablo tossed his head again and made a slight yelp.

"You too, Diablo," I said. "But I wasn't really worried about you." I gestured to Monitor 2 for Natheka's benefit. "Diablo was here before. He was injured in this glade. I think he witnessed his family's deaths here."

Natheka squinted at the screen.

"Ah, a sight-capture. Can your technology produce the entire event leading up to this moment?" Natheka asked.

Without my help, VELMA played the recording.

I watched with interest as the huge wolf-like animals with black throat bags lounged in the field. Movement at the perimeter caught my eye. A huge figure reminiscent of Natheka but wider, stalked out from the trees. A fierce battle erupted, and at one point, the armored alien tore one of the pups from its determined grip on his ankle and tossed it afield. It was at once shocking but logical since the vicious pazathel-nax refused to let up. It was clear they fought to the death. When the fallen figure fought from the ground, another motion caught my eyes at the tree line. Pattee!

The four remaining wolves dropped at once, presumably killed by the Repeating Rotator weapon simultaneously, and the hunter scrambled to his feet, staring at the dead animals for a second. Then he ran to collect Pattee and carried her limp form toward the camera.

"End playback," I said. A glance at Diablo revealed his disinterest in the video, *gracias a Dios*. It was traumatic enough for me to watch.

"Theraxl have slaughtered the devil dogs since the Ancient Times," Natheka said, his voice somber. "I am forced to question the wisdom in it when I see this cur's devotion to you."

"Every living thing's instinct is to survive," I said, watching Natheka's somber expression. "And that leads to death, as you well know."

"I do well know," he said, his voice softer when he looked at me.

I noticed for the first time that I was having difficulty swallowing. Considering the effort it took to blink, I assumed it was another side effect of the medicine. With Natheka studying my face with intent, I wanted to hide. Unbidden, I remembered him saying that both Pattee and Esra had become "mates" with two of his fellow companions. When he looked at me with a slight frown and tilted head, was he ... seeing me as his future mate?

Curiosity set a tremulous shiver in my abdomen, and I looked at the monitors instead. Why did the sight of his wide shoulders and muscled chest set my heart racing? Why did I want to trace his scars with my fingertips?

If I was going to understand how such a turn of events had happened, I needed to speak to Pattee and Esra. Alone.

While Natheka had behaved without reproach, I couldn't help the unease at wondering what his intentions were.

When I joined IGMC, I had no plans on settling down with anyone. Growing up with a big family meant lots of love, lots of noise, and little space or privacy. That first day on an IGMC fleet ship, stowing my gear in the tiny claustrophobic cabin and shutting the door behind me? That had been pure heaven. No roomies. No brothers wrestling and breaking things.

Leaving the close-knit Diaz family had pinched a little; I had happy memories intermingled with the chaos of being King Girl, but it had been *right*. In addition, working in my field of choice fulfilled me in a way no relationship had ever done. Exobiology was my passion and my reason for living. Sure, colliding with "Predator Planet" may have altered the trajectory of my course, but only insofar as getting paid to do what I love. I could and would devote myself to studying the biology of this planet. No mates needed. Except I couldn't help that tingle of interest whenever I looked at Natheka's chiseled face or remembered his singing voice.

The opening to "Here I Go Again" by Whitesnake echoed in my head before I allowed a half-smile and calmed myself.

"VELMA, how long until I recover?"

"You have been receiving treatment for thirteen hours and seventeen minutes," she said. "All data indicates your body is responding appropriately to my treatment. That would suggest you only need another fifty-eight hours and forty-three minutes in my care."

Resignation settled over me like a wool blanket. But I could use the time to communicate with my fellow humans.

Turning to Natheka, I saw that he had adopted a serene pose with his head tilted up, eyes closed, and huge hands clasped together except for his pinkie fingers which pointed to the sky as well.

His defined biceps were almost as thick as my thighs. The tendons in his neck formed an inverted triangle, and his strong jaw and face boasted perfect symmetry. With a pale green skin, his race must have evolved to blend in with chlorophyll-drenched flora.

I could admire his biology and his strength. I could appreciate his help and easy demeanor. But could I picture anything more between us?

Clearing my throat, I waited until he inhaled and resumed a natural stance.

"Sounds like I'm going to be here for a while," I said with a smile. "You don't have to wait for me. And I'll be fine," I said and indicated the pod. "I'll get in touch with Pattee, and we'll discuss our next, uh, our next, um, plans."

His eyes snapped to mine and locked in place. Unnatural heat burned in my chest when he stared. I couldn't look away. Would he insist on staying? Was he going to tell me I was his heart mate? Thundering in my chest must echo inside the pod. But, Natheka cocked his head, his black eyes blinking as he listened to VELMA translate my words.

Diablo plopped himself down with a big sigh. And then released gas.

Natheka coughed and covered his nose while I grabbed the nearby oxygen mask. My eyes watered.

"Do you wish me to remove the mutt?" Natheka said through his hand.

"I would say yes, but I doubt he'll listen to you," I said.

"You do not sever the truth," he said, and squatted before the door. "Have your technology communicate with me if you have a need. I go to my brethren near the Agothe-Fatheza." He squeezed himself through the hatch and was gone, Diablo watching him with tongue lolling.

"I thought he would demand to stay," I told Diablo. "In fact, I almost hoped ... ah. Never mind." Diablo cocked his head, licked his chops, and then laid down on the metal floor with a flop.

"VELMA, vent the pod."

A quiet whoosh sounded, and a minute later the air smelled better.

"VELMA, can you open a channel between Pattee and me? And keep it private?" I said.

"Of course," she said. "One moment."

38

Natheka

Before Diablo attempted to assassinate us by passing wind, I had noted a new aroma wafting off Amity. The hint of illness was faint, curiosity was present, but most notable was the tang of rebellion stirring with interest.

She dismissed me with her words, but I was not confident she did so with her eyes. Nevertheless, what was left for me to do save leave? I knew she was still uncertain of me and my race. As she should be until she could see for herself that her colleagues were unharmed and content.

I glanced at the pod behind me. Heat tangled with chills in my gut: a maelstrom similar to that I felt when my raft was sucked into the whirlpool only veltiks from where I had pushed off the bank this morning.

Of course, the whirlpool led to the Pool of the Lonely Sister, but not before I had been dashed against the rocks numerous times in the rapids. Rapids that had not been there a simple suns' revolution ago.

As I replaced my armor and helmet, I hiked to the trickle of water, wondering if Amity used the sight-capture of her ship to watch me leave. It did not matter.

With the changing landscape on Ikthe, I determined to gather our band as soon as we could. As Amity recovered and the others attempted to join Raxkarax on his mission, I would return to Naraxthel's ship. I would bring it to the Plains of Bounty, the flatlands just south of Agothe-Fatheza.

"Naraxthel, it is Natheka."

"What say you?" he said.

"Amity needs two days at least to recover," I said. "It is but two days to your ship."

"Ah, I see the plan as it unfolds," he said. "Yes, retrieve it. We are still many days out, and Goddesses know what mountains have been sheared or rivers defiled along our way."

"Very well, Naraxthel," I said. "But hold."

Silence a tik, and then Naraxthel spoke. "I alone hear you, Natheka. What is it?"

A palpable softening in my chest released the tension in my shoulders. "Thank you," I said. I ordered my thoughts while Naraxthel waited in silence. "What if my heart mate refuses the connection?"

"Did you press her?" Naraxthel asked.

"No! I have tried to avoid discussing it, if possible," I said. "But she's heard the term. Her Technology told her about it. I will not force her; you know that." I frowned and stared at my fist.

"I, too, wondered at the wisdom of the Holy Goddesses to inflict such a fate upon these Soft Travelers," Naraxthel said. "None of us would demand obeisance from these humans."

I sighed. "That is true."

"Give it time," he said. "Perhaps heart mate is but another way to describe one's true friend. Someone with whom we share troubles and fight battles, but never coerce."

"I like that," I said. "Thank you."

"But Natheka," he continued. "Were I you, I would not sing much in her presence."

Warmth sprang to my cheeks, and I resisted the urge to look back at the EEP.

"But if I already have?" I wanted to argue the quality of my voice, but Naraxthel spoke first.

"Hm. Then now she knows your songs tend to the morbid and sad," he said. "Mayhap you could compose a happier song?"

I barked a humorless laugh. "Of course," I said. "About something lighthearted, such as the poison gas cloud produced by the red planet worm, or perhaps the ooze that eats away at metal in the Agothe-Fa-theza."

Naraxthel sighed. "Very well, I see your point. Send us word when you have my ship." He signed off.

"VELMA, will you tell Amity that I will return for her with Narax-thel's ship and then we will join the others?" I chafed at using the Technology's name. I still had unanswered suspicions.

"Of course," she said. "And since Amity is restored to me, I will return your helmet's frequency receiving unit to its original settings. Thank you for your help."

I grunted in reply, but VELMA did not speak to me again.

Crossing the tiny stream in one stride, I noticed water weeds trailing from my armor joints. Kathe! I must have smelled like a mud beast. Mayhap the thought of Theraxl heart mates did not trouble Amity as much as the stench of unwashed bodies!

Then I thought on her traveling companion, he of the putrid ass-wind, and reconsidered. Nay, it was not the smell that caused her rebellious spirit. She did not want to submit to a foreign race's traditions and mythologies. And why would she? Even Raxthezana rejected such ideas.

Pulling strands of water weeds out of my joints and off the sole of my boot, I began to sing. Perhaps Naraxthel did not appreciate the song of the heart, but I was alone in my element.

Ikthe be damned, I would sing!

39

Raxthezana

The cracked, orange dirt expanse stretched endlessly toward the horizon where it met the hazy pale sky. Puzzling out the location, I marched forward, my boots pounding without sound. When I turned to mark my path, no prints indicated I'd passed. The stillness, isolation, and unfamiliar sky lent a dismal pall to my mood. Looking forward, a dark gray spike shimmered at the horizon where I focused my gaze. The longer I walked, the more the spike wavered in the heat of the coming day. Reality wavered; perhaps I was in a dream? The thought disappeared.

When I searched the sky for the sister suns, I did not see them.

A sense of urgency overcame me, and I found myself running toward the spike. Its shape widened. After running several veltiks, I could see the outline now; it was a ship belonging to a soft traveler. I stopped dead in my tracks.

Heat suffocated me; I tore my helmet off and tossed it to land with a bounce on the scorched ground. I dismantled my armor, letting the pieces fall. When I stood naked before the gaze of the absent suns, I searched the expanse for signs of any life.

Perhaps the ikadax, or a pack of pazathel-nax would come to slay me.

Silence pressed from all sides.

And though I stopped walking, the ship loomed closer.

A gray slash against the dried orange lakebed, mocking me with its passenger.

I knew now, where I was.

Turning in a circle, I studied the splitting angles of dried orange mud. The bones of Lake Wazakashe's previous inhabitants lay scattered and gnawed.

What happened here?

Why did this cursed ship call to me?

But it did not. I heard nothing.

The tiniest crumb of curiosity bade me walk closer and look into the porthole.

But I would not.

A small hand on my shoulder jerked my attention from the ship. I sat up, blinking madly in the dark.

"It's your watch," Esra said, her voice low that she would not wake the others at our site.

She retreated to the bedroll she shared with Naraxthel when I grunted that I was awake.

Night air buzzing with the sounds of bugs planted me in reality while I shook my head, attempting to forget the disturbing dream of the lonely ship surrounded by vast veltiks of endless desert. With a surreptitious glance toward Esra who had already fallen asleep, I placed my hand at my heart but felt nothing. Satisfied, I took my watch of the night, and peered into the dark forest, but just like the ship in my dream, no living creature called to me. All was well.

40

Amity

"Pattee?" I waited for her response. VELMA had connected us when I asked her if Pattee was available.

"Amity! I can't tell you how relieved I am to hear your voice," she said. "You made it."

"By the skin of my teeth," I said with a smile. "How is everyone? What are you doing now?"

"We're breaking camp, heading towards you," she said. "We might stop at an area known as Agothe-Fatheza, if our help is needed."

Scads of thoughts tumbled around in my head as my heart raced. Thoughts of Pattee traveling in a human and alien group. Pattee and VELMA saving me from death. The mysterious heart mate situation. I didn't know where to begin with my questions. My mouth dried before I could say anything, and I sipped from the straw provided during my convalescence.

"You must have questions," Pattee said in a soft voice. "This is a private channel. Not even Esra can hear you."

Tears filled my eyes. Pattee had always been intuitive and understanding. I couldn't believe my good luck at being stranded on a planet with my best friend. Immediately, I felt guilty for the thought. It would be better if none of us were here, but rather hurtling through space and time toward Kerberos-90.

"First, I listened to the recording," I said, my voice hitching at the end. "When you told VELMA to deploy the baffle floats."

"Oh God, Amity," Pattee said. I could hear emotion in her voice. "You must have shaved ten years off my life."

"Well, you gave me countless years by your quick thinking," I said. "How did you come up with the baffle floats idea?"

"We needed to slow your speed with drastic measures," she said. "And the floats were the fastest thing I could come up with. I honestly didn't know about the water."

"Well, the EEP looks like something the Mineral Grinder spits out," I said. "But I made it," I said. "I can't even ... I don't have enough words." I swallowed and licked my lips. "*Un millon de gracias.*"

Pattee took a minute to reply.

"If I only did one thing right, Amity," she said. "I'm glad it was saving you."

"*Dios mio*, why am I crying?" I wailed, wiping my face and laughing.

"It's a lot to take in," Pattee said. "Everything. Being here, this wild place. Knowing this is it for us. Take your time," she said. "I'm still processing; probably will be for a long time."

"Really? Because VELMA said." I stopped talking. Felt a headache press its knuckle to my forehead. I couldn't say it out loud. But it was the elephant in the room. I glanced at Diablo, sprawled on the floor with his belly showing and his legs spread wide. The devil dog in the room.

"Did VELMA tell you about the heart mates?" Pattee said, rescuing me from my discomfort.

"Yes, and Natheka mentioned something as well," I said, my words spilling over each other in my haste to make sense of the insensible. "Are you and Esra okay? Did they take you against your will? Did you drink something or sign a contract or …?"

"Hey, hey," Pattee said. "It's okay. No," she said. "I mean, yes, Esra and I are okay. Better than okay. But 'no' to all of your other questions, alright?"

"You have to know it sounds suspicious," I said. "You land here and then how many weeks later you're in a committed relationship with the Incredible Hulk? It doesn't add up."

I heard Pattee chuckle for a second.

"Amity, yes. Of course, it sounds strange. But the most important thing you need to know is that no one did anything against their will. Not a single one of us, Theraxl or human."

My breathing slowed, and I blinked.

"Free choice, huh?" I said, my brow creasing. I glided my hand along the smooth metal of one of the robotic arms administering drugs via intravenous line. Staring at the clear fluid in the tube, I considered the invisible enemy attacking my body from deep inside. "How do you know this microbe didn't alter our brain chemistry, though?"

I heard Pattee sigh.

"You're the exobiologist," she said. "Is that possible? Is it likely?"

I bit my lip.

"Absolutely, it's possible," I said. "Is it likely? This I don't know. I need more time here. And more time to observe this other race."

"Girlfriend," Pattee said, her voice wry. "You've got all the time in this world."

I laughed.

"Ouch," I said. "You're right."

"I mean, other than the matter of the geomagnetic excursion," she said. "That is going to complicate things."

"The geomagnetic what now?" My skin felt itchy and tight. My heartbeat picked up again. What was in this medicine VELMA was giving me?"

"Esra and I may have figured out why there has been an increase in seismic activity and the mass animal migrations," Pattee said. "Did you and Natheka happen to run into any strange animal behaviors? Did Natheka say anything like that?"

"Yes," I said. "There were these giant, hairy beetles," I said and shuddered. "Natheka said they never hunted together, yet there were three of them that night."

"Giant beetles? Damn," Pattee said. "I'll have to add that to my nightmare list. Along with the millipedes and the spider-scorpions."

"The spide—you know what, never mind," I said. "So, this excursion thing is causing the earthquakes?" I secretly wondered if earthquake was the right term.

"We haven't told the hunters yet, so if you could keep this to yourself for the time being," Pattee said. "We want to present it together along with other options. These guys can be stubborn."

Red flag.

"Oh?" I asked, picturing Natheka running for kilometers without stopping while I slipped in and out of consciousness. Maybe stubbornness was a good thing.

"What do you know about the quest for woaiquovelt?"

"VELMA told me about it. And the holy water," I said. "It's supposed to be ... perilous."

Another sigh from Pattee.

"Yes," she said. "Esra and I know that the hunters won't back down from the quest just because there's a geomagnetic excursion occurring. That's what I mean by stubborn."

"So, not great conditions to be tramping all over the planet," I said. "But if anyone can make them see reason, it's their—heart mates?" I ventured a guess.

"That's the hope, yes," she said. "If not to hold off on the quest, then to at least try to take every possible safety precaution we can think of."

"I gathered from VELMA that the queen of that other planet wouldn't be welcoming if we asked to sit out the excursion from the safety of her world," I said.

"Correct," she said. "The Ikma Scabmal Kama doesn't know about the humans, however, the younger sister queen, BoKama, does. She's been helping us."

"Helping how?" My body might be recovering from a fatal infection, but my mind was speeding through every problem we faced now that we were permanent residents of Ikthe. Not a single one of them could be considered "minor".

"She keeps the Ikma's attention away from this planet as much as possible," Pattee said. "As far as the Ikma knows, the only hunter that has survived is Naraxthel, Esra's heart mate. He sends the queen video each time he takes down a predator or endures a quake. Apparently, she's obsessed with him."

"Obsessed how? Was he supposed to marry her, or something?" I said.

"No, both the queens have consorts. According to BoKama, the Ikma has been declining, mentally, for a long time. She made advances to Naraxthel around the time Esra landed here. He refused, and that's how he and the others ended up on this quest."

"Oh, wow," I said. "There hath no fury as an alien queen scorned."

"Exactly," Pattee said. "As far as geomagnetic excursions and crash landings go, there really couldn't be a worse time."

"*Dios mio*," I said. "If *The Lucidity* hadn't been attacked, *otro gallo cantaria*."

Pattee laughed. "VELMA translated and asked what a rooster has to do with the fleet ship."

I chuckled.

"VELMA, Pattee and I have been friends so long that she doesn't need my idioms translated," I said. "But it's a saying my family had. If something had been different, then another rooster could sing. It's old. We don't know where it originated. People substitute any alien creature that makes noise in the morning."

"Thank you for explaining, Amity," VELMA said. "In studying the inhabitants of Ikthe, might I suggest the nonsense flies. While they don't sing to greet the morning as roosters are known to do, they make a distinctive noise right before dawn."

"Thanks, VELMA," I said. "I'll try to remember that. Pattee, what else should I know?"

"I know this is too much," she said. "It's one battle after another. Between the airborne algae, the killer dinosaurs and the Ikma Scabmal Kama, there's barely time to catch your breath. Just try to hang in there. We've got each other's backs here, Amity."

"You forgot the heart mate, thing," I said.

"Ahh, well," Pattee said, and I could hear a smile in her voice. "At least some of us don't consider that as too much."

"You mean there is someone else who isn't buying it besides me?" I asked, my curiosity piqued.

"Yep," she said. "One of the hunters thinks it's bogus. Like I said, no one is making anyone do things they won't agree to."

"Okay," I said, my voice lowering in volume. "Thanks for catching up. Can't wait to see you."

"You too," she said. "Should only be a couple days. We'll check in often."

"Excellent, thanks," I said and signed off. She had given me a lot to chew on, and I wished I could speed up the healing process. I wanted to be moving and doing, not lying here with thoughts of the singing Natheka and how he hadn't made a fuss about anything. In fact, he'd risked his own life, multiple times, to ensure my safety. Left the companionship of the others to come find me. And I had sent him away without a second thought.

Well, that wasn't precisely true. I'd had quite a few thoughts about him. I couldn't decide if they were neutral, positive or negative.

41

Natheka

I stood silent yet alert with my back to the black trunk tree. Something stalked me, but my helmet scanners couldn't identify it. Twice I heard its footfalls displace the duff upon which it walked. Once, I heard the swing of a branch it had passed.

Sniffing, I failed to detect what animal it might be. It was downwind.

With careful precision, I unsheathed my short sword and waited. It could be a Tree Thief. I had not seen the purple and orange feathers of its harbinger fowl, but I had ceased expecting Ikthe to cooperate. She would revolt, it would seem.

With muscles tensed, I bent my knees in readiness. Judging by the last noise I heard, it should be abreast of the tree right … about … now!

Pivoting on my right foot, I swung my body around, leading with my weapon, ready to strike and kill.

The BoKama met my short sword with a blade of her own, and for a jotik, we exerted our power repelling each other's blades. We released pressure simultaneously, and I stepped back.

"Well met, Natheka of the Harvest Lands," she said and sheathed her sword as did I. I noted with interest she bore scratches on her cheek. I would reach to touch my own, but the helmet obscured it.

"You sport wounds from Ikthe?" I asked.

Her skin darkened, she averted her eyes and bowed her head, and for a jotik, the proud bearing of younger sister queen dampened to shame, accompanied by the faint smell of spoiled milk. It faded until BoKama's usual fragrance of crushed nettles wafted around us.

"Do not bother yourself," she said. "They will heal in time."

I removed my helmet, and her eyes narrowed.

"Which of Ikthe's children gave that to you?" she said, a small frown marring the smoothness of her brow.

"Elder Sister Pazathel-nax," I said. "She is no more, though I ...." Pausing, I rolled the words on my tongue before I uttered them. "I regret killing her, though she would have severed my throat and burrowed her snout in my entrails with abandon had I not." I peered at BoKama's face, her consternation hinting at deeper thoughts than a slain devil dog. "But it is the way of Ikthe."

BoKama's gaze met my own, an unshed tear glistening in her eye.

"And did you regret killing her *before* your sword cut her down?" she asked.

"I did," I said. "Never before had I felt such reluctance." My armor creaked when I turned away from BoKama's emotion. "But there is great change on this planet, and I beseech my Holy Sisters daily to guide my steps. Mayhap the shifting landscapes are but a shadow of greater changes to come."

"What changes on this planet?" she asked.

"Do you not join the Ikma in watching Naraxthel's sight-captures? Quaking, mountains collapsing, rivers altering their courses, animal migrations not seen in hundreds of cycles. Ikma's quest becomes more dangerous by the hour."

I turned to face BoKama again; she had composed herself.

Nodding, she rested her gloved hand on the black bark of the tree and looked at it.

"It does," she said. She looked down her nose at me. "The Ikma bade me to seek the Answer Dream to her countless nightmarish visions. I did so," she said. The muscles in her jaw bunched. She licked her lips. "When I told her the Answer Dream, she flew into a rage. Gave me this," she said, pointing to her cheek. "And then she announced that unless Naraxthel returned with woaiquovelt and the Holy Waters in three days, she would send her WarGuard to fetch him and perform the raxfathe."

"Three days from now?" I said.

"Yes," she said with a nod. "I ...," she said and stopped. I saw her throat move with her swallow, but then I heard her teeth grind together. A hard gleam shone in her eyes when she met my gaze.

"I came to warn my hunter brothers," she said. "And to tell Naraxthel it is time."

I raised my brows at her.

"He will know of what I speak—Goddesses help you all."

"Will you have protection from the Ikma's ire?" I said.

"As of today's second sunrise, the WarGuard accompanies her at all times," she said. "I have exercised every precaution and obscured every emotion from her, but she does not trust me. She trusts no one. Not the Maikshel, not our Consorts. She changes the guard on her whim. She beds hunters only to thrash them and threaten them with raxfathe. The halls of the fortress are as quiet and still as death. None dare speak against her. A pall is cast across all of Ikshe."

"This is grim news, indeed," I said. "Will you see the others?"

"I cannot spare the time. I had hoped to find one of you near Naraxthel's ship, and here you are," she said. "Do you give Naraxthel the message."

"I will," I said, grasping her arm and peering deep into her black eyes. "Protect yourself from the Ikma's fury, if you can." I pressed two fingers on her unscathed cheek.

"Ikthe devours every tik," she said, moisture brimming in her eyes. "Should the Ikma decide to come here, she will uncover all that has been hid from her view. Her rage will know no mercy."

"This I know," I said between gritted teeth. "But you are one alone in the Royal Court. One mistake, and—you know what she will do to you."

The BoKama's face contorted as the aroma of spilled blood filled my nose.

"I loved her once," she said. She controlled her inner battle, and the smell dissipated as she relaxed her features. "We did not share the same dam, but we grew as sisters. I wish I knew …."

She dashed a tear with an impatient hand and steeled her eyes. "What do you suggest?" BoKama asked, placing her hand over mine. "For I have played out scenarios, and I cannot see the end."

"I will confer with my brothers," I said. "Please do not do anything to raise her ire against you. Trust us."

"The Ikma's deadline will stand," she said.

"Stay by her side," I said. "And do not fear."

She sighed when she looked at me. She cocked her head, narrowed her eyes, and stared. "Oh, Blessed Goddesses. You have found your heart mate."

I took a step back and worked my mouth, unable to speak for a jotik. "How did you know?"

BoKama smiled. "There is a new light behind your eyes." She paused and studied me. "Of course. There are two other human females for Raxkarax and Raxthezana," she said with a distant look. "First, the falling stars dream. And then my Answer Dream." She frowned. "There were many troubling elements in the Answer Dream. I worry for the humans. They are made of softer things, with tender skin and fragile bones."

"They are possessed of an inner strength that defies Certain Death at every turn," I said.

A smile softened her features, and she reached to caress my scabbed cheek.

"That they do," she said. "No greater hunters than you five deserve the influence of these unique females. If sisters were crafted of clay and metal, surely the soft travelers have souls of woaiquovelt."

"May the life of Shegoshel shine upon us and our offspring," I said, grasping her hand with both of mine.

"And may the death of our enemies bring peaceful slumber." BoKama turned and slipped between the trees, her green flight suit soon disappearing into the ikfal. I hoped to see her again, preferably upon the throne of Ikshe with a new Younger Sister to rule beside. But her account of the Ikma Scabmal Kama did not deliver much hope to my heart.

I hiked the last veltiks to Naraxthel's ship, eager to advance our quest, but in truth, desiring to see Amity again.

BoKama's admission of doubt as to the soft travelers' place in our world reminded me of my own questions to the Holy Goddesses. But I agreed with her assessment; the soft travelers displayed bravery disproportionate to their stature. A hunter must wonder, would I be as courageous in a new world, facing unfamiliar beasts bent on devouring me?

I pinged Naraxthel.

"I have news from BoKama," I said. "As the Ikma sinks lower into madness, she demands your presence in three days' time bearing woaiquovelt and the Holy Waters."

"*Kathe*," Naraxthel uttered. "Every event transpires against us."

"The BoKama said it is time," I said. "And that you would know to what she refers."

"I do," Naraxthel said. "I had hoped for more time. When we reunite, I will disclose what I am able."

We ended transmission but I was in a quandary. What had Naraxthel and BoKama withheld from us, and had he told Esra?

42

Amity

With nothing but time on my hands, as well as the medicine's proclivity for knocking me out every couple of hours, I spent the days studying maps of Ikthe provided by the nanosatellite array. Additionally, VELMA played videos of the wildlife, still shots of much of the plant life, and her own trophic cascade models.

"Wait, VELMA, show me that slide again," I said. "The one with the agothe-fax overpopulation model."

"Complying."

I studied the model, my eyes darting from the top of the predator food web to the eruption of tropical understory as a result of the decline of the awaafa.

"Fascinating," I said in low tones. "You've modeled a cascade that could cause planet-wide disruption. What happens if the hunters were to stop coming here?" I said, watching her slides flip from one to the next.

"I'm glad you asked," VELMA said. "Observe the trophic cascade after five revolutions of no Theraxl hunters."

VELMA had mapped out in finite detail the overpopulation of the species called rokhura. With the planet overrun by those hungry reptiles, entire waves of lesser creatures were wiped out within two revolutions. After a third, the plant and insect life exploded, and the varied habitats across the planet merged into one homogenous whole. With specialized ecosystems eradicated, many of the planet's unique creatures died out in the following two revolutions. The rokhural, already inclined to cannibalism, decimated themselves.

"Well, that was a depressing show," I said with a grimace. I rubbed the back of my neck and stretched out on the table, feeling achy and stiff from lying so long. "I'm a little stymied, though."

"In what way?" VELMA said.

"Do five hunters a revolution really prune back population levels that much?"

"No," she said. "A typical revolution may have upwards of one hundred and fifty hunters. They don't all hunt at once, and they don't all hunt in the same regions. With multiple sites across the globe, scores of hunters may be planetside at the same time," VELMA said. "It is my understanding that current events are the exception rather than the rule."

"Ah, the quest," I said with a nod. "Of course. That makes much more sense." With VELMA's model playing on repeat, I mulled over the significance. "So the Theraxl hunters play a crucial role in maintaining this planet's homeostasis."

"Yes," VELMA said. "I find it interesting that their mythos requires a certain sacred aspect to their lifestyle, thus insuring multiple generations of stewardship."

"Hm. Almost as if their goddesses left them a holy birthright as Ikthe's custodians," I said.

"I couldn't have said it better myself," VELMA said. I smiled.

"I have to be honest; I'm dying to explore more of this place and meet its creatures," I said.

"Thankfully, you are no longer dying," VELMA said. "And with this final vaccination, you will be impervious to the cyanobacteria for the rest of your life. There was ample DNA provided from Hivelt's oral sample that I was able to manufacture this dose."

My sleeve port provided access for the small shot; it was anticlimactic after all I endured to make it here to Pattee's ship. I sat up on the exam table once VELMA withdrew the robotic medical arms and looked around. Pattee had a small collection of furs and leathers, bone fragments and heavy stone tools. I noted with dismay that Diablo had found a long leather strip and gnawed on it happily.

"*Dios mio*, you greedy wolf! I hope Pattee forgives me," I said. "I should have wondered why you were so content to lie down in here after I let you back inside."

Just like a real dog, Diablo had whined at the hatch when he had to go out to do his business. Not for the first time, I wondered at his intelligence.

But with his head the size of a pony's, he had to have a bigger brain than that of Earth dogs. I resisted the urge to ruffle the spiky fur on his head. It wasn't really pettable, and he wasn't really a pet.

"VELMA, can you patch me in to Natheka?"

"Complying."

"Natheka, it's Amity," I said. "Yesterday you told me you were halfway to Naraxthel's ship. Did you make it?"

"Ik, Amity," he said. The sound of his voice made something inside me thrill for a second, but I ignored it.

"Great. So, what's the plan now?" I asked.

"I'm flying it as close to the glade as possible, and after I collect you, we'll meet up with the others," he said.

"Okay, sounds good," I said. "I'll just pack up. Let me know when you land."

"Of course," he said and signed off. The inside of Pattee's ship seemed too quiet.

"Wow, okay," I said and hopped off the table. A wave of dizziness hit me, but it didn't last. Gathering up supplies into a new rucksack, I waited for VELMA to repair my trashed helmet. I pulled on a spare flight suit, pleased to observe my puncture wound had been sutured with laser-precision and was already beginning to heal up.

I rifled through Pattee's furs and leathers and found a couple pouches I would use for collecting specimens, their furred interiors perfect for protecting the glass test tubes. We might be headed into a perilous quest, but there was still sciencing to do. You could take the scientist out of the lab, but you couldn't take the lab out of the scientist ... okay, that didn't make any sense. But I knew what I meant.

VELMA had told me the stories of Esra and Pattee's survival. Esra's collection of the pool waters on a whim had saved her life, just as Pattee's knowledge of physics and Hivelt's strength had saved hers. I was in the company of intelligent and courageous women. I'd be lying if I didn't say I felt a little intimidated at the thought of trying to pull my own weight here on Certain Death. Intrigued to learn that the males' contributions to the women's survival had been tangential and not always instrumental, I wondered if maybe my doubts were unfounded.

But heart mates? As in, fated mates? I didn't believe in that sort of thing. With six big brothers, I had to fight my way out from under the controlling thumbs of big men. I'd had to be King Girl for decades just to be noticed, but especially to be left alone to learn things for myself. I sure as hell didn't need a big hulking alien to come to my rescue around every corner.

Pausing to take a breath, I frowned. Granted, Natheka had carried the water. And then me. And saved me from the earthquake. And the boulder. And got me across the raging river.

I wiped my eyes and sank to the metal floor with a loud sigh.

But the rest of it! The rest of it was all me.

Diablo looked up from his strangled bit of leather and made gagging noises. A sloppy chewed-up chunk of leather shot out of his throat and landed with a plop in front of my boots. He inflated his hohijopa at me and tossed his head.

"I know, okay?" I snapped at him. "You helped me get to Pattee's pod." My heart sank with my mood.

Who was I kidding? I may have been King Girl around my brothers, but on this damn planet, I needed help. A lot of it. I prayed I wasn't going to be a burden for everyone. I could see it now, meters away from successfully completing the quest, and Amity trips and falls on her fat ass and distracts the heroes; they drop the precious relic, the monsters eat the sidekicks, and the survivors look at me with disdain in their eyes. Shuddering, I wiped my eyes again. I had to be tougher than this. Stronger. Braver. Smarter.

All those years playing King Girl were prepping me for now. All those years before, I was pretending to be brave so I wouldn't look foolish in front of my big brothers. But no one knew my secret. I was always … and still was … terrified.

43

Natheka

W hen I broke through the brush just past the trickling stream at Pattee's glade, Amity stood outside the pod wearing an intact helmet and suit. From six veltiks' distance I could see health blooming her cheeks.

A twisting sensation in my heart cage caused me to stumble a step. Embarrassed, I stopped walking and put my hands at my hips, as if to scrutinize the glade for interlopers. Hoping Amity didn't notice my misstep, I resumed my approach.

She carried a rucksack and sported stuffed pockets and the ever-present machete at her waist. There was no sign of the devil dog.

"You're looking well," I said. "It is gratifying to know your technology can heal you."

Amity gave a half smile and patted the EEP.

"Clearly, we couldn't do anything without her," she said. "Ready?"

"Let us make haste," I said. "Our brethren and their mates await." I didn't miss the darkening of her eyes at my statement, but I chose to ignore it. Let her observe with her own eyes. Let her make her own decisions.

I took the lead, choosing not to offer to carry her rucksack. Something told me to tread lightly around this brave, recently traumatized woman.

After only two steps, Amity brushed past my arm and strode forward, looking back with a brief smile. "Let's walk faster. These legs are itching to move!"

Startled at her energy, I gestured she was welcome to remain in front, but I said nothing. If she chose the wrong path, I would direct her then.

She marched eastward, headed unerring in the direction of Naraxthel's ship. Her VELMA must have provided its exact location.

Distracted by her pleasing curves in a clean and undamaged suit, I didn't see the spiny warted rock climber until it snagged my ankle with its ferocious grip. Amity walked ahead unheeding, so I withdrew my Thezana and smote it in a single stroke, mindful not to scratch my armor with the woaiquovelt blade. Pausing to clean the blade in the rich dirt, I caught up to my place a few steps behind her and spoke.

"Has Diablo gone, then?" I asked.

"Yes," she said, her voice intimate inside my helmet. "It's like he was my guardian angel when I was sick and now that I'm fine, he got bored and ran off into the woods."

I detected a trace of emotion in her words. "Truly, I was most astounded at its erratic behavior," I said. "My people have fought the pazathel-nax for hundreds and hundreds of cycles. We had no notion of the animal's intelligence."

"Humans domesticated the wolf back on our home planet, Earth, in ancient times," she said. "After countless generations, we ended up with hundreds of breeds of dogs. They come in all shapes and sizes, but they live to accompany humans."

"Companions to humans," I said, remembering the mutt's odd behavior in Amity's presence. "Do all dogs ramble through the forest, disappearing and appearing at their whim?"

"No," she said. "Some are tiny and fragile, and their owner chooses to carry them around. They sit on their human's lap and eat treats and get petted. Larger dogs hunt with their owners, and still others work as search and rescue dogs or service dogs. They have a wide variety of uses. I missed pets when we were on the fleet ship." She stopped talking for a minute as we navigated the trail. "IGMC doesn't allow pets."

I grunted. "This IGMC. What is its purpose?"

"They are a huge collection of mining corporations," she said, sweeping a low branch out of the way and holding it so that I could pass without being smacked. "They travel between galaxies, finding planets from which to harvest precious minerals, metals and ore."

A tightening in my throat caused difficulty swallowing. I thought of the veins of woaiquovelt hidden deep in the Black Heart Mountains, the numberless cycles gone by when our bravest hunters died in its search. The invisible net surrounded Ikthe now, commandeered by a technology I didn't understand, and the so-called Super Low Orbit satellites repurposed from the pod's nosecones. Breathing restricted, I removed my helmet and took a draught of air.

"Amity, how does your occupation fit in this mining company?"

She turned to answer me, noting my helmet under my arm with a raised brow. "IGMC hires scientists in several fields of study. I've been to many uninhabited planets where I was tasked with studying the life there, to ensure that mining wouldn't disrupt ecosystems, and to see if there were untapped resources." She must have discerned my inner turmoil, for she stopped and faced me. "As far as I know, IGMC has never exploited a planet that was either inhabited by or used by a sentient species for its existence." She stepped closer to me and rested her small hand on my forearm's armor plating. "Your planets are safe. Not to mention, uncharted. IGMC doesn't know they're here." She searched my eyes with her own, and I couldn't help but smell a faint trace of interest when her gaze roamed over my face.

Earlier concerns forgotten; I allowed a smile to emerge while she studied me. Her eyes widened, and she stepped back in haste, her heel catching on a broken stump. I caught her before she fell, and I tightened my arm around her back, bringing her within inches of my armor.

"You are also safe here," I said, for once ignoring an impulse. I wanted to remove her helmet and taste her lips as I had seen Naraxthel and Hivelt do with their mates, but I put her away from me with gentleness. I must treat her as the beautiful awaafa. Sudden movement, aggressive approaches, hungry intentions: all would cause her to fly away to heights I could not reach.

"We are but a dozen veltiks from Naraxthel's ship," I said, and gestured she should walk again. "I could sing with happiness that you will reunite with your colleagues so soon!"

She looked back with a single raised brow, and I recalled Naraxthel's caution to me earlier.

"What?" I said. "I know happy songs."

She faced the trail once more, but I heard her chuckle.

Replacing my helmet, I mused which song to try when I smelled the sharp odor of an acid-spitter about to attack. It leaped from a low branch, but I caught the small reptile before it landed on Amity's back, and snapped its neck, discarding it into the trees. I gave her a little wave when she looked back at the sound.

Three strides later, the scuttling noise of the rotaxl alerted me to its hunt on my right. A well-placed stomp smashed its spinal brain before it could sneak behind Amity. Had I severed its head from its body, it would merely have created two of them. Frowning, I realized she might have liked to see such a thing. I would remember that in future.

At least I hadn't scared her away yet. All I needed was a bit of time to woo her. However, we were on this *kathe* planet where I had thoughtlessly told her she was safe. Would my tongue never cease to spit nonsense as if I were the acid-spitter?

44

Amity

Natheka was good company. He wasn't afraid to ask honest questions or have something explained when he didn't understand. He did have a beautiful voice but didn't talk a bunch just because he liked the sound of it. Factor in all the lifesaving incidents and general helpfulness, he was more than just good company. He was invaluable. Though it was nice to have at least one hike where we weren't fighting for our lives every step of the way. So far, the only danger had been from my own racing heart when he prevented me from falling on my ass—and held me close enough that I could see the dip in his top lip.

Breaking through the trees, I stopped when I saw the ship, impressed by its imposing presence and powerful geometry. A charcoal hull pointed downward like the shoebill stork's, but its red fuselage widened and bulged like a breaching gray whale.

Natheka walked past me, taking my hand in his as he did so.

"Come, Amity! You're about to witness Ikthe's beauty from the sky!"

He sounded joyful and carefree, and I smiled in spite of myself.

The hatch opened and a ramp lowered, so we walked up, our boots ringing with a metallic sound. I started when I saw a being sitting adjacent to the opening.

"That is the tech-slave: a robot, in your language," Natheka said. "It will not harm you."

Natheka directed me to a seat near his own, and we strapped in. With practiced ease he manipulated controls, and the ship lifted with a seismic rumble that shook my bones.

"We're headed to the Plains of Bounty, northwest of us," he said, and pushed forward a lever that resembled a coiled snake. The ship's speed increased while it tipped forward, and we raced across the forest canopy, the treetops blurring below us. G-force pushed me back into my seat and took my breath away, but I would have gasped anyway at the view below us.

After the forest, plains spread as far as the eye could see, and on those plains ... a pack of lethal reptiles that must be as big as elephants if not bigger. Were these the ...

"Rokhural," Natheka said, pride in his voice. "These clever predators challenge the strongest and bravest Ikthekal. When we bring one down, we are able to feed many sisters."

"Did you hunt them to extinction on the other planet?" I said, curious.

Natheka cast a glance at me, or at least, turned his helmet toward me, for a second.

"The rokhural have never been on Ikshe," he said. I was relieved he sounded amused rather than annoyed. "The most dangerous predators on Ikshe used to be the brother-hunters," he said, his voice going soft.

"And now?"

"Now there is only one. The Ikma Scabmal Kama."

I swallowed and licked my lips, overcome with dread. What kind of threat did their queen pose for a band of huge hunters to be frightened by?

Sobered, I watched the wild countryside below us, transfixed by the upheaval caused by the recent earthquakes and rockslides.

From above, we could see where humongous boulders had rolled over tree stands and demolished huge sections of forest.

Massive flooding left broken tree debris and dead animal carcasses in scattered places, while others looked untouched and undisturbed for thousands of years.

"After we collect the others, I think we should assess as much damage as we can over this hemisphere," Natheka said. "I, for one, would like to know what we're headed into when we resume our quest."

"You could ask VELMA to send you images taken from all over the planet," I said. "She'll have access to the whole globe." I bit my lip and thought for a second. "Oh! And if Pattee analyses all of that data, she could model the safest routes to travel!" I remembered her curious black box, an ancient computer that crunched a lot of numbers fast. Pattee loved that damn thing; I hoped she'd thought to bring it during evac.

When Natheka didn't answer, I switched from looking out the window to staring at his helmet, wondering what he was thinking.

"Look there, Amity," he said, pointing to our left.

A brown mudscape bled out from an outcropping of rocks that may have begun its life as a small mountain. But the mud's dark and cracked surface was not what drew my eye, rather the majestic figure of a running white wolf, its powerful muscles bunching with each stride, covering meters of ground in seconds, eating up the distance. It couldn't be Diablo, could it?

"Do the pazathel-nax travel alone?" I asked.

"Almost never," Natheka said. "That must be your friend."

"I wonder where he's going," I said, watching with wistfulness until our ship sped past and he was out of sight.

"If he found you once, he will find you again," Natheka said. "I have no doubt."

His assurances soothed me, and I unclenched my fists.

"I will teach you the Song of the Body," Natheka announced. We sang it until I had it memorized. I couldn't tire of the vistas appearing out the window, but after two or three hours, Natheka maneuvered controls, and the ship's change of speed startled me out of a reverie.

"Your colleagues are not far," he said. "This is the closest place for us to land. It will only be a zatik or two to hike."

Gripping the armrests, I laid my head back, suddenly terrified at the noise, the pressure change, the enormity of being in a ship again. While I didn't remember the crash, my body did, and terror froze my limbs and lowered my core temperature and a bone-deep shivering began shaking my body uncontrollably, and that happened after the ship had stilled, safe on the ground. I could hear myself gasping, not able to pull in a deep breath.

Natheka said something, but I couldn't hear him over the tidal wave rushing in my ears.

He bent over me and unfastened straps, then picked me up and carried me down the ramp.

"Amity," his soft voice seemed right next to my ear, but it was just my helmet's speaker. "Open your eyes. We are safe on the ground."

I tried to speak, but my body felt frozen, and I still couldn't quite catch my breath. My heartbeat throbbed in my throat, my hands shaking as I tried to hold on to him.

Natheka squeezed me closer to himself, and he sang a lilting song that reminded me of happy childhood memories and time spent with family.

At the close of his song, my body was finally calming. He released me to slide down his body, and my breath caught in my throat to be this close. I looked into his eyes; was this the moment he declared I was his mate? But he said nothing.

"Thank you," I said, looking up at the ferocious wolf-like helmet. "How did you know to do that?"

He released my arms and stepped back, leaving me feeling cold though I was in a temperature-controlled suit.

"I was not confident it would work, but it occurred to me when I looked over at you that the last time you had been in a landing ship, it exploded and broke into a thousand shards of metal."

I grasped at my chest and nodded, emotion filling up my throat. I cleared it. "Exactly. Yes. I don't remember the crash," I said. I looked up at him, trying to picture his black, red-ringed eyes. "I listened to the recording, though. And when your ship started to land, my whole body just—froze up. Like it was remembering."

"I did not see your ship go down," he said. "But we could hear Pattee's conversation with VELMA." He paused. "Pattee gave VELMA perfect instructions. It is good the technology obeyed."

"Oh yes," I said, my racing heart slowing. "VELMA is software, after all. She's designed to follow her programming, with little variation from it."

Natheka cocked his helmet then nodded.

"If your body has strength enough, let us travel," he said. "We will meet our company halfway."

I blew out a breath and nodded.

"Come choose a weapon from Naraxthel's armory, first," he said. "You are not armed for this leg of the journey."

I took a deep breath before we walked up the ramp and turned right. A selection of weapons adhered to the inner hull. I doubted I could lift most of them but found one that should work. Natheka handed me a dagger from his own toolbelt.

"You are well?" he said. "Perhaps we should stay and let them come to us," he offered.

Looking around the interior, I shuddered. "No, I'd rather walk. I'm okay now. Let's go."

I was going to let Natheka lead the way this time, but he pushed me forward with a touch more strength than was necessary.

"Hey, careful!" I complained.

"Ah, sorry, Amity," he said, and looked all around us. "I forget my strength."

Quirking a brow at him, I faced the direction he pointed.

"VELMA, can you locate Pattee and Esra and crew?" I said.

"Certainly," she said. "Route overlay in your visor."

We began our hike, and I hoped this one was just as uneventful as the one prior to boarding the ship.

45

Natheka

"Keep your back to me, Amity," I said, my voice low. "Have you the dagger I gave you?"

"Yes, I have it," she said, her voice strung tight, and her rapid breaths harsh in my earpiece. The family of shegoshe-tax had us surrounded, and I cursed myself roundly for not having waited at the ship. We could have broken sister-bread together. I could have asked her to sing something from her home planet.

Instead, we faced a group of emaciated yellow, short-furred animals with long skinny legs, high-pointed and tufted ears, desperation in their cunning eyes and hunger in their sharp-toothed scaly jaws.

"Naraxthel, we are ambushed by shegoshe-tax," I said into my comm. "Make haste."

"We come to you, Natheka," he said. "We are less than a zatik away!" I heard shouts of encouragement in the background.

"Amity, we only have to stand our ground for rotiks," I said. "Can you do it?"

"I'll try."

My heart raced as well as cramped, and I begged the Holy Sisters to waylay any plans of my heart leaving its heart-home right now. It was not a good time.

Searching the 'yellow sun runners' as they are named, I spotted the elder and younger sister shegoshe-tax that led the pack and maneuvered to face them. Their huge feet pawed the ground, and their sleek leonine heads dipped as they yowled in preparation for battle. Big blue tongues licked at their scale-covered snouts. Their black throat sacs inflated in short bursts, but they needn't call to others; their pack was right here.

Perhaps Amity would have a greater chance at protecting herself from the younger animals of the group, which was why I faced off with the larger ones.

"They will begin by darting at your ankles and feet, biting and clamping on your lower limbs," I said. As a group, they crept closer, enclosing us in a tight circle. While there were only six, I reckoned we had mere rotiks before they struck as one. "They attack in short bursts, aiming to tire their victims until we let down our guard. At that point, the larger ones will leap to crush our throats. If you can withstand bites to your boots, do not waste energy on fighting those off. Be wary of the ones who jump to attack and strike their underbellies. Do you understand?"

"Yes, got it," Amity said in a rush. I heard panic in her voice. *Kathe.* I needed her to be strong until my brethren could arrive.

"Do you recall the Song of the Body?" I said, my voice rising. Elder sister trembled in preparation to strike; her short tail flicked back and forth, an angry signal portending her strike.

"Uh, yeah?"

"Sing with me now!" I shouted when the largest of the animals leaped at me.

"My body is big! My body is weapon!" We sang together, our blades adding counterpoint when they sliced through the air.

"My eyes and hands, hunt! Hunt!" I focused my deadliest strikes on either side of me, lessening the number Amity would have to fight off, as a younger runner scrambled about my feet, gnawing relentlessly at my boots and ankles. With eye commands, I sent lightning shocks to burst along my armor, discouraging it from lingering.

"My ears and legs, hunt! Hunt!" I heard Amity belt the words punctuated by grunts and heavy breathing. But still she fought, and my heart beat with pride.

"See the animal, touch the animal!" We sang. An adolescent male dove for my mid-section but his sharp teeth glanced off my armor. I strove to engage the strongest beasts if I could not slay them, but anxiety chewed at my gut. What if Amity fell? Could I protect her?

Amity's voice interrupted my thoughts.

"Hear the animal! Hunt the ...." Her shout diminished to cries. I looked behind me with alarm to see her attack the younger sister shegoshe-tax with violence. She slashed at the beast, and if another rose to take its place, she struck it with her second weapon, the short sword she'd chosen from Naraxthel's ship. But while her strokes were savage, I could see streams of tears coursing down her cheeks. A pang shot through my heart-home.

Elder sister, the pack leader, used my distraction to close in for a death kill, but I drove my elbow into her throat, stunning her for the time being.

"Edge your way to the big tree!" I said. "You are fierce! We will arise victorious!"

Amity's response was incomprehensible shouting, but she still stood and fought at my back, and I could not have felt more pride than I did at that moment.

With constant strikes at the deadly beasts, we shortened the distance to the big tree. I was anxious to have one side we didn't have to defend, knowing Amity would soon tire, if she hadn't reached her limits already.

Three runners leaped at me at once, and it was all I could do to keep them at bay with two weapons. One tore my double blade from my hands at great sacrifice to itself, but now I lacked a weapon. I beat back the animals with my fist, holding others off with the swinging blade in my other hand.

"Amity, how fare you?" I asked between pants.

"So tired," she said between gasping breaths. "I can't ..."

Kathe. The Holy Sisters put Amity in my care, and she faded yet again on my watch. I placed too great confidence in the soft traveler! I had made a grave error in leaving Naraxthel's ship. A young shegoshe-tax hung by his jaws from my elbow while two larger ones parried my blade with their teeth, darting in and out.

"Can you climb the tree?" I asked. "If you can get up the trunk, I can stave them off until Naraxthel comes!"

"I don't know," she said; I heard the tears in her voice. "I can try. I'll climb up your armor, okay?"

"Yes!"

Grunting with every beast's impact, I let them come at me while Amity used my body as a ladder to reach a low branch. When she scrambled up, I renewed battle with the attackers, drawing another weapon from my side sheath.

Whooping and growling sounded from the trail to the north, and I realized our friends had arrived. The noise and clash of weapons startled the animal pack, and less two of their number thanks to my heart mate and I, they chose to decamp, running into the woods to lick their wounds.

Pattee and Hivelt broke through the trees first, followed by Naraxthel and Esra. Raxthezana brought up the rear.

"But where are the shegoshe-tax?" Hivelt asked, his weapons aloft and battle-ready.

Pattee was fitting her javelin at her back strap and looking around the scene.

"Pattee!" Amity yelled from above and dropped from the tree, bending her knees to absorb the impact, and then tumbled toward her friend who reached her arms out to catch her.

They embraced, laughing and crying, and Esra pushed her way past Hivelt so that she could join them. Amity grabbed Esra by the helmet and jerked her into their huddle as well.

Raxthezana passed them and walked to the dead yellow sun-runners, moving them aside with his big boot. He stopped in front of me.

"We had to cross Braided Creek to get here," he said.

I knew the creek; it was a tiny stream that joined with two others closer to the mountainous region to our west. A Theraxl could step over it, or after the rains, wade through it. It only reached a veltik in depth.

"Is it a river now?" I said, thinking of the Tawny.

"Nay," he said with a growl. "It is at the bottom of a ravine, now." He looked around at the carnage and then at the human women who stood close, touching hands or shoulders, huge smiles making their faces glow from within their helmets. "It is good you are both alive." He turned and walked away, poking his sword into the underbrush, as if to flush out anymore shegoshe-taxl.

I approached the humans, anxious to see Amity whole after the combat. They turned as one to greet me.

"Thank you," Pattee said and reached for my hands. She grasped them both.

I bowed, uncomfortable under her unfaltering gaze.

"You are welcome," I said and looked at Amity. Her eyes were swollen, and wetness reflected off her cheeks under the helmet glass.

"Thank you for hastening to us," I said to the group. "Hope in your arrival kept us fighting long past our ability to hold them off."

"He's being generous," Amity said, surprising me when she stood beside me and linked her arm through mine. "He could have killed them all; my presence was holding him back, I'm sure." She looked up at me, a sad smile crossing her face before it faded.

Was that what she really thought? I dared not contradict my heart mate in front of the others, but she spoke so poorly of herself. I didn't know how to respond, but then my eyes fell on the mutilated corpse of the younger sister shegoshe-tax.

"Pattee," I said, indicating the body. "Perhaps Amity would like to keep the fur of her most challenging kill. The younger sister yellow sun-runner."

Pattee grinned wide and unsheathed her blade. "Great idea," she said and squatted by the beast, inspecting it for the best place to start. It would have many gouges from Amity's desperate strokes, but it was my meager attempt to bolster Amity's confidence.

The others congregated to me with forearm grasps and pats on the back.

"Well met, Natheka," Hivelt said.

"Well met," I said. "Have you thought more on the Ikma's bold request?"

"I have," he said. "There is precious little time to explain all that I must." He looked to Esra first and then to the rest of us. "BoKama and I conferred about just such an incident, and we have a plan. I could use your help, though, if you are willing."

"Yes," I said.

"If this plan fails, they will run us to ground, and upon discovering the humans, will perform the raxfathe on them," Hivelt said. His chest burgeoned. "However, they will only do so if they succeed in killing me first."

"And me," I said.

"We will pray to the Holy Sisters that another way opens up for the BoKama to assuage the Ikma's anxieties before the third day," Naraxthel said. He looked up at us. "I don't need to say the words. You know I will die before I let the Ikma, or anyone else, lay a claw upon my heart mate."

Esra pushed her way between Raxthezana and Naraxthel.

"We love and honor you all," she said, giving us each pointed looks. "But I speak for my friends when I say, we would much rather you all live for us. No more talk of death."

Naraxthel pulled her close to himself, and my heart ached when I imagined Amity allowing me such a familiarity.

"I have an idea," I said. "But it is not quite ready to behold the face of the suns."

"Do you tell us when it has ripened," Naraxthel said. "My mind wrestles with ideas as well."

Hivelt and Raxthezana grunted agreement and retreated to help Pattee with the fur, leaving me to stand alone. Amity stood several steps away from Pattee. I dared approach. Content to stand at her side without speaking, my mind roamed over the events of the past days. I seized upon a thought.

"This place will make you heart sick," I said. "Where you would befriend and nurse the injured, you are forced to kill or be killed. It goes against your nature."

I felt her hand grab mine and squeeze it tight. I gave her a gentle squeeze back but didn't let go.

"I told you of the maikshel," I said. "You are one such." I mulled over what I wanted to say next. I stepped to face her and took her other hand. "I vow you shall not raise a weapon against an animal again as long as I live. Let me battle in your place." Where she would protest, I tugged on her hands. "No, I will not allow Ikthe to steal that part of your soul that cherishes life. One who finds joy in learning about all living things cannot remain whole in a place where death demands payment. Will you let me do this for you?"

Her dark eyes shimmered with unshed tears until she made a small nod. The movement tipped the balance, and they spilled down her cheeks. But she wore her helmet, and I mine, and I cursed Certain Death and all the barriers between us.

Because I could kill on her behalf, but at the suns' set, could she ever mate with someone who took life when she found it so precious?

I released her hands and she stepped toward me, wrapping her arms about my waist for less than a jotik, then joined Pattee and the others. I looked up at the sky darkening to the shade of baked bread. "Holy Sisters, I do not understand your ways. Dare I hope to win my heart mate, or have you given this warrior an impossible feat that I may learn humility?"

I listened, but the Goddesses did not answer me.

46

Amity

We traveled back to the ship in single file, lights from our helmets bouncing up and down with every step, except Pattee walked beside me. Natheka was at my back; he seemed to prefer that, and Hivelt was in front of me. Raxthezana led our group while Esra and Naraxthel trailed behind.

"How are you holding up?" Pattee asked me. "You've had a rough go of it."

"Honestly, I'm kind of a wreck," I said, shooting her a quick look. "At first, I felt brave and capable, but the longer I've been here, the worse I've felt. Emotionally, I mean."

Pattee reached for my hand and held it.

"This planet messes with your head," she said. "It turns you inside out, and you're forced to deal with the issues you thought were long buried." She stopped talking and looked ahead, then at the woods on either side of the trail, her helmet light piercing the shadows. "We're forced to choose how hard we want to fight to keep some things, what to let go of, and what's worth dying for. I suppose it's a grim outlook, but there really isn't any way to sugarcoat life on a planet named Certain Death," she said with a humorless laugh.

"Wow," I said, pondering her words. "That perfectly expresses what I'm going through right now." We walked in silence. "Do you remember King Girl?"

Pattee caught my eye and smiled.

"I'm standing right next to her," she said.

"I realized something the other day," I said. "King Girl was a front. I pretended to be brave and strong because otherwise, my brothers would suffocate me with their overprotectiveness. But the thing was, when I snuck away to go find wildlife, I wasn't brave. I knew they would come for me. One time, I cornered an injured Lyrack on Dispatch 9. It was weighing its options. It wasn't so injured that it couldn't gut me with its talons. When its smoky eyes narrowed, I knew I was about to die. I peed my pants; that's how afraid I was. I couldn't move. I couldn't fire the puny weapon my parents insisted I carry planetside. I just stood there and waited for the death blow." Pausing to catch my breath, I looked around, but everyone else paid attention to the darkening woods, and they couldn't hear us on our private channel, anyway. "My brothers charged, just came out of nowhere. They plucked me from death's jaws. But the craziest part?" I shook my head because I still couldn't believe it. "I snuck away again the next day!"

I peeked at Pattee; afraid she might laugh at me. I should have known better. She wore the expression I remembered best: the stoic and thoughtful one.

She nodded slowly and quirked her mouth. I knew she was choosing what she would say next; she was methodical like that.

"What you say makes sense," she said. "About not needing to feel courage because you trusted that your brothers would come for you. That is a profound insight."

I nodded, pleased that she didn't rush to disagree with me or try to make me feel better with false compliments. She actually listened to how I felt.

"Do you feel that Ikthe has stripped your adulthood from you, forcing you to face your childhood fears?" she said.

I nodded, processing what she said.

"And if you defer to these males to protect you, then you would feel like you haven't grown up at all. That you'd forever be in your brothers' shadows, and never become the woman you were meant to be?"

I stopped dead in my tracks, my mouth working, but no sound coming out.

She pulled me into a hug, our helmets knocking. Tears streamed down my face. I sensed those at our backs waiting, but no one spoke to us.

"Don't worry, my friend," she said. "No one will force you to do anything here. You can choose to fight or not. Choose to join us in the quest or hang back. Choose to find love and friendship or remain aloof like our companion Raxthezana. We've all been facing our own demons here, even the hunters. Everyone is at their own pace." She pulled back and held my shoulders. "You can be King Girl, or you can bloom into your new occupation as the official exobiologist of Certain Death."

Her last words put a smile on my face, and she offered her fist. I bumped it with my own, and we resumed walking.

"It's a bit of an oxymoron, isn't it? Biologist of Certain Death?" I said.

She laughed.

"Thanks," I said.

"Anytime," she said with a wink and looked ahead. She jogged up to Hivelt and jumped him from behind, his hands immediately catching her thighs as she hugged him around the neck. I knew she would keep my confidences. And my heart lightened to see the youthful joy she exhibited with her alien mate.

With plenty to think about, I let my hand rest on the hilt of my weapon as we walked. Natheka had given me a gift; his understanding. I marveled that a killing machine like him could grasp my internal conflict. Was I behaving like I did when I was a child? Acting recklessly, knowing that my big brothers would come rescue me? I chuckled and relaxed the tension in my shoulders.

No. None of the last several days had been reckless. Every choice I made was intentional and measured for its likelihood of keeping me alive. That didn't make Pattee wrong; it made me look at my current situation through the lens of reality.

Natheka was right; I did value life, and I hated the fear that drove me to kill with such violence. Natheka was trying to save me from that dissonance. It was something a friend would do.

"Amity, might I have a word?" VELMA's voice startled me.

"Of course," I said.

"I couldn't help but overhear your conversation with Pattee," she said. "I would like to offer up a video and audio recording for your study. I can play it in the corner of your visor."

Interested, I said, "Sure."

A grainy video appeared in the left corner of my IntraVisor. It looked like a human in a flight suit, laying on the ground. They moved a little then stopped. Then they lifted up their helmet and let it drop. I realized VELMA had already started playing the audio.

"Hurry," her voice said. I saw Diablo pace across the video, then return and nuzzle me. My own voice sounded from the recording.

"VELMA, all I see is a bunch of rocks," my voice was barely a whisper. The person in the video raised their head and dropped it again.

"Amity, look again. I disabled the hDEDs."

The person raised their head.

It was apparent that the human, in fact, I, suffered great incapacitation. My memory of this was clouded, and I watched with bated breath as the explorer lifted herself to her hands and knees, so that she could crawl. I was alarmed to see the swath of blood trailing after her; my leg wound must have worsened. All that blood.

I ached watching that broken and defeated woman fight with every breath to move two feet, and three feet more, and an inch, and another couple feet. She was trying so hard.

The video ended.

"Wait! VELMA, I want to keep watching," I said.

"Some images may be disturbing. Confirm continue watching?"

"Yes," I said, curious now.

The video resumed, and a lanky coyote-like creature stalked out of the woods, sniffing the trail of blood. Diablo burst onto the screen, attacking the other animal in a flurry of teeth and fangs. The animal was twice Diablo's size, but he spared nothing, and in four minutes and thirty-four seconds—I marked the time stamp—he had taken the animal down, his jaws a vice grip on the creature's throat. Diablo gave it a final shake to ensure death, and then released it. With a flip of his head, he trotted back to my side. When I reached the stream, I forced myself to kneel, and with Diablo's help, to standing. The rest of the video blurred terribly through my tears. But I heard the audio just fine.

"Welcome, Amity Diaz. I have been waiting for you, my friend."

I couldn't speak. Seeing *me* from VELMA's perspective. Or from Diablo's perspective, I looked—determined. Steadfast. Was I killing predators? No. But that didn't make me any less courageous. While I couldn't remember much from that time, I could remember the pain. Wanting to quit. There must be something inside me that was strong enough to—to at least *try* to survive here. Maybe it would be okay to let Natheka fight the battles, because the ones that really mattered to me couldn't be given away even if I wanted to. *Dios mio,* I needed to blow my nose.

Natheka spoke behind me.

"We are almost to Natheka's ship," he said. "We may all slumber peacefully for once."

Embarrassed by my tears, I requested VELMA activate privacy mode which darkened the exterior visor.

"I could definitely use a rest," I said.

"Amity," he said in a low voice. "Let's race the others!"

His suggestion surprised me, but the ship was within sight, and it might feel good to have a little footrace. Especially a surprise one, because Pattee could outrun us all, I had no doubt.

"On your marks," I said.

"What does that mean?" Natheka asked.

"Oh hell," I muttered, and broke into a run.

I heard shouts and Esra asked, "What is it?"

A deep male voice said, "It is but one of Natheka's antics!"

But their voices faded as I pumped my arms and legs and raced to the ship, noting Natheka matching my pace. Was he trying? I pushed harder; the ramp lowered, and then Natheka broke away, his long strides carrying him up the ramp at least three meters before I hit it, loud metallic tramping reverberating as the others followed close behind.

We all collapsed on the smooth metal floor and panted, watching the ramp close. Soft yellow lights glowed in strips along the inner hull, and I deactivated privacy mode. As I looked around at the others, I felt safe and surrounded by friends. The dangers of the planet seemed more like a nightmare than a reality, and I thought, maybe. Just maybe I could thrive here.

A wave of nausea washed over my entire body, and I broke out into a cold sweat. Esra and I locked gazes just as the alarms in my IntraVisor lit up like a Carnaval parade.

"Warning: Foreshocks detected. Earthquake imminent. Seek shelter immediately," VELMA said. She repeated her warning, but Naraxthel was already in the pilot's chair while we scrambled to the jump seats that Hivelt pointed out for my benefit.

The bone-jarring tremors had just begun when Naraxthel's ship lifted with a rumbling of its own, and then we were airborne, headed God knew where on this planet that courted death like a crazy celebrity stalker.

My breaths coming in shallow pants, I tried to talk myself out of another panic attack. What was worse? Flying in a safe ship piloted by a competent pilot, or being on the ground during an unpredictable earthquake?

"Elevated heart rate," VELMA said in my ear. "Do you require assistance?"

Before I could answer, Natheka had turned in the jump seat beside me. When I looked up at him, I saw he had removed his helmet.

Nothing was more beautiful in my life than his serene expression as he stared into my soul, his gaze comforting me while he held my trembling hand in his huge, warm one.

"You are a fast runner," he said, and it was so unexpected that I started laughing.

"Why do you laugh? I am serious. You are quite fast, other than me and Pattee of course, and Naraxthel is quite fast as well. Of course, Diablo could outpace you ...." His voice trailed off as I continued to laugh so hard that I had to remove my helmet. At last, I could wipe my face of the days' entire deluge of tears, until I had relaxed into soft chuckles.

Pattee and Esra sat across from us, and they smiled wide, perhaps not understanding the entire context, but appreciating the humor in Natheka's meandering chatter.

47

Natheka

Naraxthel spoke from his pilot chair, his red armor catching blinking lights from the console. "I have requested VELMA locate a safe landing site as near to the Agothe-Fatheza as possible."

He drew our interest away from the monitor to the glass, although there was not much to see; night had fallen.

"The safest place to land is marked on your map," VELMA announced over the ship's comm. The monitor switched to display the favored map of my brother hunters and myself.

"That is nowhere near the Agothe-Fatheza," Raxthezana said. "It will take days to travel from there."

Cocking my head, I frowned at his scowling visage, his square jaw firm and his mouth pressed in a thin line while his thick brows angled toward one another over his wide-set eyes. It seemed our mapmaker grew more irritable every day.

"I am in communication with VELMA," Naraxthel said. "This is the closest safe place to land."

"What of the Eastward Berm," Hivelt said. "It is but half a day's travel." Hivelt's voice boomed in the confines of Naraxthel's ship, but ever since finding his heart mate, he wore the smug expression of a pazathel-nax with a fresh jokapazathel in its jaws. Once irascible, now Hivelt was only a glance away from a smile, provided that glance was shared with his mate, Pattee. Of the three human women, she was the tallest and fiercest, always ready to battle wearing her hair in a long, single braid. While she made Hivelt smile, she herself often appeared solemn and pensive, her silver eyes watchful.

"VELMA's suggestion is the closest safe place to land," Naraxthel repeated. His voice sounded tight, on edge. As he was the de facto leader of our group, but also mated with a human, I glanced at Esra who stared at him, and her expression confirmed my suspicion. Something was not right.

I clenched my fists and waited for Naraxthel to continue.

Brushing the long strands of his hair out of his eyes, he spoke. "The most recent landquake carved the Agothe-Fatheza out of the Plains," he said. "VELMA has detected chasms dividing the Agothe-Fatheza on three sides. The fourth is impassable due to a seismic eruption."

The silence in the ship chilled me to my bones, and I sat back against the hull, unable to form coherent thoughts or words. My brethren had told me Raxkarax, the hard-working but quiet hunter, traveled into the Agothe-Fatheza, seeking a lone pod. Perhaps it was sinking into the bog, a human traveler who may or may not be able to communicate with VELMA trapped within. Predators agitated by the landquakes would be roaming and attacking out of desperation. It was a bleak picture indeed. Perhaps Raxthezana was right to complain.

"If the tremors have subsided, we should land at VELMA's proposed site," a pale Esra said. "We'll take stock of the situation and decide from there." Esra's hair, the color of the dried grasses after a sister-bread harvest, crowned her head in the elaborate Victory braids the sisters wore upon cheating death. Naraxthel had anointed her with them, much to our surprise those months ago. Her brow furrowed, evident concern for her heart mate and traveling companions etching itself into her expression. Soft brown eyes studied Naraxthel, or Red, as she called him. He nodded to her but waited for others to speak.

"I agree," Pattee said. "No point in wasting fuel while we try to make sense of this."

My body moved with the pitch of the ship as Naraxthel changed course. Suddenly, I felt Amity's small hand in mine. I looked down at her, and she looked at me with a slight frown. Her black hair fell in soft waves surrounding her round face, and her eyes, a stormy brown like Tawny Thread after the rains, peered into my own. She sensed my unease and sought to comfort me.

"It will be okay," she said. "We'll find a way."

It was a simple assurance, and yet it meant a great deal to me. I knew she was reserved about our heart-home myth, and while no one said it out-right, she was not a fool. She must know there was reason for us to believe she was my heart mate. That was why her compassion was as a gift from the Goddesses. She trusted me not to assume her kindness was acquiescence. She offered it freely, not under obligation.

I smiled at her. "Ik. We will find a way."

48

Amity

Naraxthel landed his ship without incident in the safe landing zone, and the girls and I hopped out of the jump seats that were made for much larger beings.

We congregated in the center of the ship in the more comfortable chairs around a central table. Judging by the ship's features, it was designed as a hunter's retreat. Off the central sitting area was a long medical bay. The rear of the ship contained a large cargo hold; it was big enough to transport several of Ikthe's largest prey. Opposite the med bay and numerous storage cabinets on one side of the ship were several private quarters on the other. I imagined after a physically taxing hunt, the hunters would find the ship a calm home base to rest and clean up before traveling to Ikshe.

Esra interrupted my scrutiny and musings. "We have a number of problems and limited solutions," she said to the whole group. "Rax-thezana, what is your assessment of the situation?"

I admired that she asked the opinion of the one hunter with a different temperament. Of the ones I'd met, he seemed less inclined to defer to anyone, female, hunter-brother, or otherwise. We waited for him to speak.

"As you know, there are dual unrests," he said, placing his shark-like helmet on the seat behind him. "The political upheaval on our home world has already introduced instability resulting in this farce of a quest. When Naraxthel returns with the items, what is to say that the Ikma will honor the offering properly?" His fiery eyes looked at each of us in turn. "It is more likely that she will find reason to punish Naraxthel with death, torture or imprisonment."

"Or her bed," Hivelt said under his voice, a grimace distorting his face.

"Same thing," Natheka replied, digging an elbow into Hivelt's black armor. Hivelt growled at him. Raxthezana glared at them both, and I stared in wonder to see such irreverence. They reminded me of my brothers, and a pang struck my heart so fast that I couldn't prepare myself for it. My family. My world. All so far away. Closing my eyes, I took a deep breath through my nose and tried to pay attention.

"Ikthe mirrors the upheavals on Ikshe with her rumblings and fractures," Raxthezana continued. "Those who blame and bless invisible goddesses may attribute a divine purpose to these twin disasters. Regardless, we battle impossible odds. No Iktheka may command the ground upon which he hunts, nor the prey whose blood intermingles with him." He glanced at Natheka whose cheek bore the deep scratch from the devil dog. "No Iktheka has the right to raise weapons against the Elder Sister Queen, though she rules with a corrupted blade." His lips pressed into a line, and his brows drew together. "No Iktheka alone could face these enemies. But we are not alone. We fight together. And whether it be an unexplained power or a gift of circumstance, we have the clever humans to join in combat. Let us use the resources at hand to tame the Queen and Certain Death."

"Have you ideas to accomplish these monumental tasks?" Narax-thel asked. His question lacked the sharp edge of sarcasm. He impressed me as a solid leader, someone people willingly followed because they respected him, not because he controlled them. I could see why Esra fell for the red-armored guy.

"Only fragments," Raxthezana said. "I had hoped BoKama could steal away again and help us to forge a sure plan. But who knows what transpires on Ikshe? Natheka said she will attempt to remain in the Ikma's good graces. She knows the truth: that all five of the chosen hunters live. If she succeeds in keeping the Ikma's trust and were to somehow assassinate her, she would call to us, and we may begin a new era of Theraxl life. But what if she fails? What if the Ikma performs the raxfathe? Who can resist the beguiling questions of the Elder Sister when she has drawn out your intestines and ...?"

"Hold!" Hivelt shouted. "You need not detail the raxfathe any more than that," he said. "I assume you mean to say that even our BoKama cannot withstand the torture and will reveal the truth: that we all live and have harbored the humans willingly."

"Yes," Raxthezana said. "Humans," he addressed us.

I straightened; my eyes drawn to his sharp teeth reminiscent of his shark helmet.

"Do you wish to be coddled, or do you wish to know the evil you will face?" he said, sliding his gaze to Hivelt while he waited.

Sweat broke out under my arms but I stepped forward.

"I know the least about your planets and culture, although VEL-MA tried to fill me in," I said. "But I think you're right. We should probably know what your Ikma is capable of, if we are to have a fighting chance. Because it sounds like you're saying we can't get away with fighting only one battle. We don't get to choose whether we attempt the quest or depose the queen. We have to do both."

"That is right," Raxthezana said.

"Can we not focus on one thing at a time, though?" Hivelt said. "We cannot split ourselves in two and overthrow Ikshe's fortress whilst navigating the passageways under the Great Mountain."

"And we need to collect Raxkarax and the other human," Natheka said, his hand reaching for mine for a light squeeze before releasing it.

"There's something else we should discuss," Pattee said, her expression grim. She glanced at me and Esra in turn. "Do you agree?" She directed the question to a nodding Esra, but I knew what she was going to say. I drew a deep breath, as if I was the one about to deliver the bad news.

"Speak," Naraxthel said.

Pattee produced her CMM, the black computing box, and placed it on the table around which we stood or sat. "You know I compiled a lot of data gathered by VELMA," she said with a quick look around at all the hunters. "I've run simulation after simulation, but there is only one explanation for Ikthe's disturbances." She opened the configurable box and typed in codes.

A holo-display appeared above the box. It was a sphere, mapped out in a grid. But after seconds it started to layer itself until it was a 3D rendering of what I assumed to be Ikthe.

Pattee drew on the display with her finger and carved out a cross-section. "There is a seventy-eight percent probability that Ikthe is experiencing a geomagnetic excursion. Esra, want to elaborate for us?"

"Sure," Esra said. She walked up to the model and inspected it, then chose a spot and pointed. "This liquid layer floats above Ikthe's core. Here you can see the northern and southern poles, but as Pattee's data suggests, the poles are shifting. In this case, it is probably because of this liquid layer." She ran her finger across the diagram, indicating a slow movement. "With the magnetic poles shifting, the invisible electromagnetic field that normally protects your planet is off kilter. Ikthe is under barrage from cosmic radiation from the sister suns."

"What does this mean?" Raxthezana asked. "It sounds as if the sister suns themselves attack Certain Death."

"Let me put it this way," Esra said, concern softening her features. "The sister suns always produce about the same cosmic radiation. But with these poles shifting location, Ikthe's 'shield' has been weakened." She used air quotes when she said shield, and I wondered if the aliens had any notion what that gesture meant.

"Perhaps it was weakened by the net," Natheka said, his voice subdued but firm. The scratch on his cheek looked angry under the interior ship lights. He shared looks with the hunters. "Perhaps this 'array' of invisible technological claws has smote upon Ikthe's shield and created a crack in it."

Natheka had used exaggerated motions to indicate his aggressive interpretation of the air quote. Taken aback, I swallowed my concern and licked my lips, feeling thirsty and on edge. I shifted my weight and watched to see what Esra would say next.

"I can see why you would think that, Natheka," Esra said. "And if I'm honest, I can't say with certainty that the nanosatellite array hasn't affected the atmosphere. However, I can say that the electromagnetic field will shift on most planets. It happens thousands of times on planets where there are no arrays."

Naraxthel in his red armor nodded his understanding, but I heard Natheka grunt at my right.

"I would have a word with my brethren outside," he said, and stalked to the hatch. When the ramp descended, the four of them marched down, and it closed behind them.

Esra, Pattee and I all looked at each other.

"That went well," I said. "I need a drink." I went to my pack and pulled out a water. My colleagues did the same.

"We haven't even gotten to the most important part," Esra said. "That it's going to get worse before it gets better. That the quest will be exponentially more difficult, and that we need to rescue Raxkarax and the human, let alone find where the fifth pod landed, before the shit hits the fan."

"Agreed," Pattee said. "I think we need to focus on search and rescue. With more minds and more strength, we can come up with a strategy for all fronts."

"What do you think Natheka's upset about?" I said. I had already rehearsed everything we'd talked about in the last couple of hours and couldn't deduce a reason for the bad mood.

"It's the nanosatellite array," Pattee said before taking a sip of her water. "The first time Esra and I mentioned it, you could see steam rising off Raxthezana's head, and the rest of them looked like someone had kicked their favorite dog. It's a sore spot."

"But they're nanosatellites," I said. "Tiny spectrometers. Completely harmless. They collect packets of information based off light particles and then transmit them to the nosecones."

"It's the fact that they completely encircle the planet," Pattee said. "And collect information and could conceivably transmit that data to an external party."

"And frankly, they're still uncertain about VELMA," Esra said. "She basically hacked their helmets when I first got here so that she could learn the language and translate for us."

I remembered the attack of those giant nighttime creatures, the hairy beetles that almost killed me and maimed Natheka. "Um, it might be my fault," I said.

"What?" Pattee asked.

"The mistrust. VELMA almost used the LASER scattershot from an SLO nosecone to kill these predators that attacked us. If I hadn't given her the code in time, she could have deployed and killed at will."

"Due respect, IGMC Miners," VELMA said. "I am not programmed to kill at will. I am programmed to protect my human charges. You were in peril from the Agothe-Scabmal, and I would have fired with precision to eliminate those predators while protecting your life and that of Natheka."

"I know that," I said. "But the hunters don't. In fact, they're probably out there speaking without their helmets."

"That is correct," VELMA said. "Would you like me to patch in their conversation?"

"No!" Esra said. "I think they need privacy. Especially if they don't trust you, VELMA."

"You were able to countermand Naraxthel's ship monitor for the map, after all," I said. "To them it must look like you could control whatever you wanted to, whenever you wanted to."

"That is true," she said. "But I have made great effort to present myself as trustworthy," she said. "I have no desire to usurp the Ikthekal on their home planet. We are but guests unless otherwise invited to make it our permanent home."

I coughed. "Well, I think it's safe to say that Esra and Pattee were invited."

Pattee looked like she was going to say something more but closed her mouth.

"Let's listen to what the guys have to say when they come back in," Esra said. "They are right to be suspicious. Do you two know what IGMC would do if they knew about woaiquovelt?"

"Oh shit," I said and pinched the bridge of my nose. "I didn't think about that."

"I've studied Naraxthel's blades," Esra said. "IGMC executives would lose their minds to access this metal."

"But everything we've told the hunters is true!" I said. "The Advance Resource Assessment teams would see that this planet is a primary food source and move on!"

Esra bowed her head a moment. Then she lifted it to look me in the eye. "I think we've been wearing blinders."

Pattee frowned, her silver eyes narrowing as Esra spoke.

"I've been remembering things that Chris said. From before."

Cocking my head, I waited. I didn't know what Esra was talking about.

"Chris was my abusive partner," Esra said, her hand drifting toward her throat before she made a fist and dropped it. "But he was also one of the IGMC administrators. I used to hear him on holo-vids, talking to his superiors about different planet acquisitions."

A coldness seeped into my gut and coiled at the base of my spine.

"Acquisitions," I said.

"Yeah," she said, looking me in the eye. "Acquisitions."

The three of us sat with that for a minute. Esra continued.

"So, while IGMC doesn't know about the sister planets, and never will," she said. "I think it's fair to suspect that the nanosatellite array, and the SLO nosecones, and sadly, even VELMA, all point to something far more sinister than we wanted to believe."

"IGMC will take what it wants," Pattee said.

"Then it's a mercy the *Lucidity* was attacked, and we were jettisoned," I said. "And IGMC is no longer our problem. Right?"

Esra's eyes were downcast. "Yeah, right."

I looked at Pattee, but she just shrugged.

49

Natheka

"If what you suspect is true, what is the solution, Natheka?" Naraxthel said.

"We limit the technology's access to Theraxl communications," I said. "And mayhap we request the soft travelers limit its use as well."

Raxthezana scoffed. "'Twould be like taking the breast from a new baby, Natheka." He scuffed the ground with his boot, no doubt rubbing out a map in his mind.

"VELMA has proven useful in many arenas," Naraxthel said. "Consider the scans allowing us to find the soft travelers."

"Yes, but do not the weapons capabilities disturb you?" I said. I looked to Hivelt. "VELMA slayed the devil dogs with shots mere fractions of a veltik from your head."

Hivelt frowned and scratched his jaw with a grimace, his black look matching his armor.

"It was disconcerting to see the ease with which the technology killed denizens of our hunting grounds," he said. "However, VELMA's precision was unerring."

"And she has not once veered from the requests of the humans," Naraxthel said. "They call her an artificial intelligence, but she has not displayed a consciousness to depart from her programming. Oft has she maintained that it is her programming to protect the humans."

"And by default, the humans' companions," Hivelt said with a slow nod.

I clenched my jaw and made fists, avoiding my brothers' eyes for a moment.

"And what of the net," I ground out, looking at them with creased brows as I folded my arms. I nodded to the sky. "Do the humans know its true purpose? I care for these soft travelers, as do you, but did not you see them dissemble when we asked, back in the Black Heart Mountains? It was as if they had limited knowledge, or perhaps suspicions of their own. Why enclose an entire planet within a net of technology that can almost see into its very heart? Do these nanosatellites detect the location of woaiquovelt? Can the nosecones deploy weapons strong enough to disable those of Theraxl ships?"

"I do not like that Ikthe is trapped in a net," Raxthezana said. "I would that the humans recall these strange tiny satellites out of the sky."

I nodded, and tension left my shoulders. "I agree. I do not like to feel that our hunting grounds have been hobbled in a trap."

Naraxthel, ever the pensive leader, mirrored my posture and looked to the others.

"I have found the information VELMA collected to be invaluable," he said. "The fastest routes through the ikfal, approaching predators and their numbers, incoming weather patterns. What if you do not perceive the nanosatellites as a net, but as a collection of sight-capture tools to aid in the hunt? Whether we hunt rokhural or heart mates?" He spared an ironic smile in my direction.

"I cannot say if I have a heart mate, Naraxthel," I said. Saying the words triggered a smart cramp in my chest wall, but I ignored it. "However, I can say that the Ikthekal have hunted here without the aid of such technology for hundreds of cycles."

"Natheka is right," Raxthezana said. "Of what necessity is this data when we know the fingerprints of Ikthe as our own? When we know the creases in her palms, and the moods of her great waters? We are Ikthekal, the stewards of Ikthe, and we do not need the help of this uninvited web that spies under Ikthe's skirts!"

Naraxthel showed us his palms in the sign of peace. "We could cast bones. But mayhap we should counsel with the soft travelers. They are clever and brave, but also considerate of our culture. And there is the matter of the BoKama that we must attend to. It would be best to unveil it when all are together."

"Mayhap the solution is but a simple one," Hivelt said. "Let us counsel with the humans."

I looked to Raxthezana. He chewed on a blade of fire grass. Removing it, he returned my gaze, then looked to our brothers. "Very well, we will ask the humans. But after, let us cast the bones."

My hunter brothers waited for my response.

I looked up at the sky, expecting to see the net we discussed with heat in our veins, but only the stars were visible. I noted the constellation Great Spoon. Forever did it spill its contents upon the constellation Trouble Stone.

"The hour is late," I said. "Let us confer with them in the morning. They will be fatigued and hungry."

"Very well," Naraxthel said. "Let us break sister-bread with them. I look forward to a peaceful slumber, safe within my ship tonight."

All of us grunted our agreement as we gathered up our helmets and opened the hatch to join the soft travelers.

I sought out Amity's face first and noted her somber expression. Another twinge in my heart-home signaled the existence of a tether between her and I. I recalled her joy in greeting Diablo and wished that I might see her smile one day, upon *my* return to her presence.

50

Amity

When the hunters marched up the ramp, I expected we would have to deflect angry accusations, but the males looked calm, if serious. I sought out Natheka's face first, hoping to see his ready smile, but he also looked sober. Deflated, I looked away, confused at the inner tension twisting my gut and amplifying my breaths.

"I could eat a scabika!" Hivelt said, rubbing his abdomen while his brothers laughed.

"We haven't seen scabika on this side of Ikthe in a tikvelt!" Natheka said.

"We have only to wait," Raxthezana said, deadpan.

They were quiet a second, and then started laughing.

I cracked a smile and realized Raxthezana was referring to the strange conditions on the planet, what with earthquakes and animal migrations and what not. I spared the grouchy Raxthezana another glance, surprised to witness any display of humor, no matter how subtle.

The hunters pulled loaves of bread from their packs and started passing them out to us. Natheka stepped past Pattee and Esra to bring me one.

"Favelt-rax," he said, giving me its name in Theraxl.

"Thank you," I said with a small smile, my heart racing three times as fast as usual. He sat beside me, and all of us ate, trying dried meats and passing around foraged plants. Raxthezana produced a clear flask of dark red liquid that matched Naraxthel's armor.

"Fruited wine," Naraxthel said, and offered it around. When it came to me, I lifted it to my lips, curious and reluctant at the same time. Was it fermented? I tipped it, and a sweet and sour liquid bathed my tongue with a gentle tingle. It tasted like ... beets and cherries and something I couldn't identify.

Natheka's gaze met my eyes when I licked my lips and passed him the flask; he licked his lips as well, but he hadn't sipped from the opening yet. I couldn't help watching when he lifted the nozzle and drunk deeply, his throat bobbing with every swallow. And then a drop escaped from the neck of the flask; I stared at the droplet as it traveled from the corner of his full lips, followed the curve of his strong jaw, and then raced a track down his neck, disappearing beneath his chest panel where I remembered his chiseled pectorals to be. Was the wine responsible for my racing heart and my sharp intake of breath?

"Aho, Natheka!" Hivelt called. "Pass the wine!"

Feeling fiery blood flood my cheeks, I tore my gaze away from Natheka, the moment broken.

Pattee rummaged in her rucksack and pulled out a metallic pouch which she offered to me.

"Wait," I said. I fished in my own pack and pulled out a pouch labeled "freeze-dried ice cream". "I have my own. And here," I grabbed another and tossed it across the aisle to Esra who snatched it out of the air.

Natheka looked down into my sack and saw the dozens of shiny pouches.

"Have you any of those 'MACK and BEES' meals?"

Frowning, I looked down at my stash. "I don't think so," I said. "But what is mac 'n' bees? Do you mean mac 'n' beef, or mac 'n' cheese?"

A glance toward Pattee and Esra showed they covered their mouths to stifle their laughter.

Natheka shook his head. "No, it is called MACK and BEES, I am certain."

Laughter bubbled up, but Natheka looked so serious that I couldn't poke fun at him. Spying the monitor on Naraxthel's flight console, I summoned VELMA. "VELMA, show these guys a honey-bee from Earth."

The image popped up on the console.

Esra spoke next. "Can you do a side-by-side comparison of a honeybee with Ikthe's 'firefly'?"

"Oh, and show Earth's firefly, next!" Pattee said, her usual sober expression softened by the delight in her eyes, and possibly an extra swig of fruited wine.

The hunters looked at the images.

"Does your firefly emit poisonous gas when it glows?" Hivelt asked.

I coughed to disguise a laugh and let Pattee field the question.

"No, Earth's firefly, also known as a lightning bug, uses biolumi-nescence to attract mates," she said. "Right, Amity?"

"Yes, there's a chemical reaction with a substance called luciferin and its catalyst enzyme, luciferase."

"Does its light blind its enemies?" Raxthezana asked.

"Does its sting cause paralysis?" Natheka added.

"Oh no, none of that. It doesn't sting," Esra said. "Lightning bugs are the gentlest bugs on Earth, aside from say, roly poly bugs. They fly slow and low to the ground, and they are harmless. Children love to run outside and catch them and let them crawl all over their hands and arms. They catch them and keep them in glass jars."

"We squeezed their goo out to make glowing rings on our fingers," Pattee said with a sheepish grin. "But I was only four."

The hunters shifted in their seats.

"But the honeybees sting their prey?" Raxthezana finally asked.

"Only once," Esra said.

"Why only once?" Hivelt said.

"Their stinger has a barb. When it's embedded in their victim, it rips it out of their abdomen, and they die. They're actually reluctant to sting for this reason. Honeybees are gentle unless they're protecting their queen."

I watched the deep frowns on the mighty warrior faces, amused at their wonder at Earth's creatures.

"Are there any dangerous insects on your home world, or are they all *gentle*?" Raxthezana asked with a smirk.

"Amity?" Pattee asked.

I cleared my throat. "VELMA, show the Anopheles mosquito, and you can keep the Ikthe firefly up on screen for a size comparison.

"Where is it?" Hivelt said. "I see nothing."

"You would have to get closer to the screen to see it," I said. "At one time in Earth's history, the mosquito killed up to a million humans a year."

Raxthezana sat back and nodded, a small smile playing on his face.

"Its sting is sometimes barely noticeable, and the skin shows a small itchy bump for two or three days after."

When I didn't continue, Hivelt guffawed. "The humans die from an itchy bum?"

Esra spewed her mouthful of water. "BumP! With a P!"

I cleared my throat and avoided eye contact with Pattee, afraid that a single shared look would result in hysterical laughing, which we all knew could be disastrous for interspecies diplomacy.

"No, Hivelt," I said, my voice stern. "Humans don't die from the bite itself, but from what the mosquitos are able to do by no fault of their own. They drink blood from each host, but if one of their hosts has a blood-borne disease, it can be spread through entire communities across the globe."

Hivelt's face froze in shock. "The invisible insect spreads infections across the planet? How does one defeat such a nemesis?"

"With an effective insecticide," I said. "VELMA, show the Kissing Bug."

Raxthezana leaned forward in his seat.

"It has impressive coloring," he said. "What does this little red and black pest do?"

"It crawls on people's faces as they sleep, and drawn to the warmth of their breath, often chooses to bite the victim near the mouth. It is a painful bite, but that's not the worst part."

Glancing at Natheka, I could see tension in his jaw. The other hunters were similarly affected. "The Kissing Bug often carries a parasite whose eggs are present in its feces. It poops wherever, but most often near the bite. When the human touches the bite, they smear the microscopic poop such that the parasite eggs are introduced into the human's blood stream. From there, the parasite eggs hatch, mature, and reproduce inside the human's body. In a number of victims, the parasite sets up a home base in the gastrointestinal tract where it eventually destroys its host many years after that first bite. In other cases, the Chagas parasite infiltrates the heart, and eventually causes heart failure—some ten to thirty years later."

If possible, Raxthezana looked greener than he already was.

"That is deviltry," Hivelt said. "Inserting a spy to depose the government so many cycles later. No one would know where to cast blame!"

Raxthezana nodded. "An insidious enemy," he said. "Does Earth have any large and dangerous insects?"

"None that compare to the size found here, but the deadliest venom belongs to an ant. The largest insect in size would be a beetle, but it only gets to be about four inches long."

"It is as I suspected," Raxthezana said. "You humans have had to battle clever and stealthy beasts in order to survive. Your stature may be small, but you have had to develop a keen sense of strategy."

The other hunters nodded, and a pleasant warmth spread inside me. Pattee and Esra and I smiled, and Natheka patted my knee with his large hand.

"You have shown us these BEES, but what is a MACK?"

"Oh, right!" I said. I scratched my chin. "Does Cheesy Mac and Beef sound right?"

His face lit up.

"That is the one!"

Pattee gave a half-smile and reached into her sack. "It's the last one I have. Enjoy."

"Oh, there's lots more back in your pod, Pattee," I said. I tipped my sack so she could see all of the pouches. "I only grabbed the ice cream ones."

***

My bunk was roomy, and I stretched in luxury before turning out the tiny light.

Naraxthel had employed the tech-slave to stand guard, and of course we had VELMA to stand vigil, as well.

As far as evenings went, it was by far the best anyone could ask for on a planet named Certain Death. After the hunters tried the ice cream, they gave us polite smiles, but we knew they couldn't appreciate it without a memory of real frozen ice cream. The paired mates retreated to private quarters, and Raxthezana, Natheka and I used bunks in the narrow aisle leading to the cargo bay.

Considering the tension of earlier, the threat of more earthquakes, and the unknown status of Raxkarax and the other humans, I knew this would be the last good sleep I could expect for the next while. But I found it impossible.

Only meters away I heard the steady breaths of a fierce hunter. All of us had taken advantage of the hygiene facility in Naraxthel's ship, and now I could smell Natheka's true scent, unmasked by the ever-present odor of rich dirt and rotting vegetation. He smelled like a spice shop, hints of anise and cumin, and maybe a dusting of to- bacco. Earthy and warm, welcoming and safe. I considered how his every action since we met was to rescue me, protect me, or encourage me. While he acknowledged the heart-home myth, he didn't try to influence me with his alien logic, or the two obvious examples of its plausibility found in Pattee and Esra's relationships.

As I tried to find a more comfortable position, I thought about Pattee and Esra. They were comfortable in their skin. I couldn't speak for Esra, but Pattee hadn't changed. If anything, she seemed a better version of herself. More confident. Braver. More capable.

Both of them freely touched their partners: holding hands, caressing faces when the helmets were off, squeezing arms or embracing their lovers.

Nothing in their behavior suggested they were coerced, seduced, drugged, or imprinted. Likewise, their partners treated them with affection and respect. The males asked their opinions, asked for their help, and asked them about their feelings.

As an exobiologist, I had seen countless variations of sexual reproduction, mating behaviors, and courtship rituals. If anything, the heart-home myth of the Theraxl race seemed to be nothing more than a sweet explanation for falling in love.

I wasn't falling in love with Natheka, nor he with me. But I didn't mind listening to him breathe.

Tomorrow, time allowing, I would ask VELMA to show me any diagrams or biological evidence related to the heart-home. If only out of scientific curiosity.

51

Natheka

I was not surprised to hear Amity toss in her bunk, as restless as a jokapazathel in the company of a live serpent. Her breathing was erratic, frustrated, and shallow. After a zatik, she finally settled, and I could hear her slow, deep breaths, indicating she enjoyed a restful sleep.

I was also not surprised that I could not sleep, only veltiks from the female that possessed my every waking thought.

Her knowledge of the creatures of her home world fascinated me. I could sit at her feet and listen to her speak for zatiks. Her mouth had a way of curving up on one side—a kind of half-smile, not quite willing to embrace a laugh, but acknowledging the irony of an insect that could unwittingly decimate a population or a Theraxl who accused Earth insects of being gentle.

Ever had Amity smelled delicious to me, even when ill. But now, with the stain of Ikthe's violence and the infection's malaise rinsed away, she smelled of memories. Those scant thoughts of my adolescence, when my dam carried an infant in her womb, and sang the songs of our people, promising me a future of prosperity and happiness.

Thoughts of the sisters sending word when they birthed my hunters: Ika and Joketha. The memories that comforted me on dark and lonely nights among the trees of the ikfal, when the nonsense bugs whirred in the thick air and the sleek shegoshe-taxl stalked between the bushes.

Amity made a soft moan, a pleasant sound, unlike the muted cries of pain when I carried her through the night. Her sleeping noises stirred a deep place within me, and I knew I could not sleep. I slipped from my bunk when Raxthezana's whisper caught my attention.

"There will be precious little time for lady sleep come the morrow."

"I know it, brother," I whispered back. "But the more I chase her, the more she eludes me."

His soft chuckle faded when he rolled over, and I found my helmet and boots by the hatch. Exiting as quietly as possible, I breathed deep of the thick air, and made my way into the nearby ikfal. I would hunt small game and forage for medicinal plants. Whatever we would decide with the clever humans, we would need both for our journeys and quest.

Only rotiks after I left the ship, I heard something creeping in the underbrush behind me. I broke trail when the nonsense bugs stopped their fracas. Something stalked me, and my hunter instincts told me it was not my usual prey.

Flaring my nostrils, I caught the unmistakable odor of black mud and crushed peat, but nothing else. Had the BoKama returned? Readying my weapon, I scanned the path from which the noises emerged. Heart drumming in my chest, I prepared for my first battle of the night. I activated my cloaking device, wanting to gauge my enemy's prowess before revealing my presence and striking. I crouched in wait.

52

Amity

Something wakened me from a deep sleep. Voices. And then I heard Natheka. "But the more I chase her, the more she eludes me."

Surprised at his words, I waited to hear more, but Raxthezana laughed softly and when I peered into the darkness, I saw Natheka tiptoe toward the hatch.

Where was he going? Was he—giving up on the heart-home myth? Neither of us had spoken about it. He hadn't put any moves on me, for which I was grateful since I was still finding my feet on this godforsaken planet. But the thought that he wasn't going to try ... that he might give up before we had a chance to become friends ... I didn't like that.

I heard the hatch shut. I'd been caught up in my thoughts and missed when he exited. *Well, Amity. You could try to go back to sleep. Or you could go try to make friends.*

A flimsy fragment of a dream drifted into my mind. *Be a friend to all.*

Scooting out of my bunk, I padded to where my own boots and helmet were stored and put everything on in silence. It was possible Raxthezana both heard and saw me, but if he did, he kept it to himself.

I was minutes behind Natheka, so I didn't fear stepping out into the night. Until the hatch closed behind me and a wave of vertigo crashed over me at the sight of billions of stars. The blackness of Ikthe's horizon swallowed them up. I didn't know which direction he went.

"VELMA, open a channel with ..." I stopped. What would I say? *Qué huele*, I noticed you taking a midnight stroll and thought I'd join you! Yeah, no. I couldn't think of anything to say. I'd wing it like a DJ.

"May I be of assistance?" VELMA said when I didn't finish my request.

"Show me Natheka's trail," I said, the idea springing on me like one of those green snakes. And with that thought, I unsheathed the short sword I had used earlier today.

"Would you like to employ night vision, UV or thermal imaging?" VELMA asked.

"Night, please," I said and gasped when I saw various creatures scatter away from my boots.

VELMA marked the path Natheka took, and I followed it, a bone-chill seeping outward to make my fingers and toes stiff and causing my innards to quiver of their own volition. Everywhere I looked were glowing eyes and swift retreats into the foliage. I doubted the creatures feared me; my hope was that they feared the one predator who I knew meant me no harm.

Standing stock-still, I thought about that for a minute.

Natheka would never harm me.

I couldn't deny the spark of attraction I'd felt earlier; he was a glorious specimen of strength and power. But he also exhibited self-control. I respected his musical talent; it would be cool to get his opinion on Earth music, and the fact he whittled wooden animals for his little boys melted my heart. Maybe falling in love could happen someday when we weren't fighting for our next breath or our next stable piece of ground, but I could say with confidence that I wanted to be his friend. I wanted to get to know him better.

"VELMA, I lost Natheka's trail," I said.

"As did I," she said. "Scanning. Natheka's signature not found."

Looking ahead, I could see where the overlay stopped. I decided to follow it to the end; maybe VELMA could recapture his signal.

Even though the thick trees towered above me, I crouched as I walked, making myself smaller. What had seemed like a simple plan only minutes ago now seemed reckless. Where had he gone so fast? If I didn't catch up in another minute, I would return to the ship.

I jumped out of my skin when his voice entered my helmet.

"Amity!"

Biting off my shriek, I doubled over to laugh when he stepped out of the trees, his armor shimmering out of an invisible state like an old school Predator franchise movie.

"You scared me half to death!" I said, catching my breath.

"And you scared me," he said. I could hear a smile in his voice. "But you are a welcome sight. Let us hunt together!"

He took my hand and led me back to a trail. "We will find puddle bird nests and steal the eggs."

Pleased that he didn't expect me to track and kill an animal, I grinned, an inexplicable giddiness seizing my previously chilled core.

"That sounds fun!" I said. Eggs were definitely more my speed.

"I do not know that word," he said. "Puddle birds nest near the ground, preferring rotting logs. They make their nests from bubbling fungus shoots. The challenge is to snatch an egg or two before the fungus bubble pops and sprays stinging acid!"

"Fascinating," I said, peering into the thick brushwood hoping to spot bubbles or mushrooms or birds or eggs.

"Ah, look there, in that coppice," he said, indicating a thick tangle of bracken.

We stalked closer, careful not to disturb loose branches littered at our feet.

Once we were close enough, I could see through a gap in the shrub. Poised at the end of a crumbling old trunk lay a smudge of a nest. I couldn't distinguish colors, but I could see spherical shapes surrounding the glowing eggs.

Natheka put his finger to my helmet and then pointed at the nest. I nodded and watched.

One of the dark spheres grew in size as if it was an inflating birthday balloon, and then popped, splashing a dark liquid in a foot radius.

Natheka made a fist and punched the air, then gestured I should watch him. His hand marked beats of time, and then he snatched an egg so fast his arm was just a blur.

He dropped the ovoid in a pouch and pointed to me.

Worried my helmet was too unwieldy to fit between the leafy opening, I removed it and then I flexed my fingers and maneuvered closer. My eyes adjusted to the dark and a prickle of sweat stung the nape of my neck as I waited for one of the bubbles to pop. After it doused the area, I jammed my hand through the branches and grabbed an egg, but when it weighed more than I was expecting, I nearly dropped it and fumbled to hold it with both gloved hands, but Natheka's firm arm wrapped around my waist and pulled me back before another balloon mushroom inflated and popped. The egg was the size of an Earth duck's egg but was as heavy as a couple of D batteries.

Laughing, I looked at the egg in my hands. It was smeared with days and days' worth of the strange liquid produced by the fungus.

"These look like a nightmare version of Easter eggs," I said, my smile leaking through my voice. "The acid is probably similar in chemistry to vinegar. If the eggshell is calcium carbonate, it could actually oxidize in this humid air creating a film that prevents the acid from breaking through the egg."

"I do not know of these things," Natheka said as he plucked the egg from my hand. "But they are delicious. Please. Do you steal more for our food stores."

Amused at Natheka's old-fashioned sentence construction, I timed the acid spits and gathered three more.

"Why are they so heavy?" I asked, handing them to Natheka so he could place them with gentle claw tips into his pouch.

"The puddle bird is perhaps not well-named," he said. "It does not fly like a bird, nor does it swim in puddles. Its meat is dark and rich with thick blood. It is possessed of an organ that collects metal fragments found in foods it prefers. This organ is valued among my people because it is used in the manufacture of our armor."

My mind tried to keep up with the insane biology that Natheka just described.

"If we didn't have to prep for dangerous missions," I said, "I would so love to have a look at that organ under a microscope."

Natheka grasped my elbow, and I looked up at him, the mysterious and beautiful wolf helmet hiding his face from me.

"There will be time for such things," he said. He placed his fist over his heart. "I know it."

It was a small thing. A hope expressed for a random opportunity for me to pull out a microscope and do science, and yet his conviction made me tear up.

I felt that same hope well up inside me. Somehow, with everything going on, and all the danger ahead, I could grasp the sensation that everything was going to be okay. Holding what I could of his fist over his heart, I squeezed his hand.

"I know it, too."

He let his pouch drop to his waist and covered my hand with his other one.

"You cannot feel it," he said. "But my heart rages, even now, to be free of its cage and to reside in its true home." His voice sounded strained. He continued. "I shall not force you, but mayhap after a time, when the chaos has settled, you could be the mate of my heart. Until then, I would be your friend."

Squeezing his fist again, I wished I could see his face. It was the declaration I had been afraid of receiving, but it wasn't anything at all what I had imagined in my stressed-out headspace. It was an entreaty, a humble question, a declaration of a friendship that promised not to coerce or manipulate. Paired with every action of his up until this point, it manifested Natheka's character, and I couldn't find a single fault in it.

"*Claro que si*, I will be your friend," I said. Then I stood on tiptoe and found his helmet fastening. He hurried to help me remove it, and then I could see his face under the thin light of the moon. "But after the dust settles, I would be honored to be your heart mate as well." I bit my lip as my own heart fluttered. I hadn't planned on saying that last bit, but it was out there now, mingling with the radio waves in the air between us.

My eyes zeroed in on that dip, the philtrum of his top lip. I drug my eyes upward to his, and I realized with a start that they glowed in the night—the palest shimmer. When I licked my lips, I saw his gaze drift down to track the motion of my tongue.

My breath hitched when he leaned down; the fragrance of herbs and spices drifted to my nose. I couldn't help the quiet moan when his lips almost touched mine.

His expression contorted and his hands clawed at the armor over his chest.

Was he—was this the thing? The heart thing?

"VELMA!" My voice rose in panic. "What's happening to Natheka? I'm sorry! I didn't mean to start that!" Our helmets lay on the ground, VELMA's voice sounding tinny and muffled. But Natheka spoke.

"My heart—started this long before," Natheka gasped out. His smile looked forced. Then his tender gaze drifted over my shoulder and froze. "Amity," he said, his voice a rumble. "Get you to the ship. Now." With jerky movements, he withdrew his long sword, maintaining his stare past my shoulder.

With galloping heart, I turned to face Predator Planet's latest threat.

"Get. You. To. The ship," Natheka ground out.

But he stood between me and my path to the ship.

And I? I stood between him and several meters away, the biggest damn reptile I had ever seen.

"*Santa Maria, madre de dios,*" I said and crossed myself.

"Amity," Natheka said, his voice weaker.

"Natheka," I said, my voice low as I tilted my face to the side. I dared not turn my back on the monster. "Give me your weapons."

"I made you an oath," he said, his pain strangling his voice.

"Give me your weapons now," I said, my voice rising in strength and my hands open behind me, waiting for him to place the hilts. I felt their somber weight warm my hands through my gloves. I was shaking on the inside, but I steadied my grip. Maybe I was terrified, but it was time to pretend to be brave.

The moon cast a glow through the canopy, and I spotted the shining strand of drool hanging from the reptile's toothy maw. Moonlight threw sharp shadows from the tree trunks, imprisoning the monster with thick black stripes, his scales standing up in stark relief, their sheen outlining the reptile in an otherwise dark night. It had the vocal sac shared by most of Ikthe's animals, and it loosened its bag, filling it to capacity and then emptied it, the silent but deadly call to arms. Nausea rolled over my body and realization struck me like a blow. Its bellow vibrated my body at subsonic levels causing the nausea.

VELMA probably tried to warn us, but we were so engrossed we hadn't heard or paid attention.

Now this creature hunted us, waiting for the right moment to strike. It was—immense. Bigger than the adult pazathel-nax, bigger than the tree thief. Reminiscent of Earth's ancient Tyrannosaurus Rex—but with substantial front legs. And it stood poised to leap only seven meters from where we stood.

Pattee's words entered my mind with gravitas: *We're forced to choose how hard we want to fight to keep some things, what to let go of, and what's worth dying for.*

I could hear Natheka gasping and sinking to the ground behind me. Whatever physiological forces were at play in his body, he had no control of them. A quick glance over my shoulder revealed he was incapacitated. Dammit. This was it. I could cower and cry, or I could resurrect King Girl and kick monster ass. Natheka needed me. Heart mate or no, he was someone worth dying for. He had done the same for me.

Staring the monster down, sudden clarity illuminated my mind. On Predator Planet, no one comes to your rescue.

Licking my lips, I bounced on the balls of my feet and surveyed the patchy forest between the reptile and I. Noting the treefalls, rotten stumps covered in funguses and lichens, and other obstacles I could use to my advantage, I decided to draw the beast as far away from Natheka as I could.

There was no need for silence now; it was far too late.

"VELMA! Alert the others that Natheka is in danger," I shouted. "And broadcast me a song!"

Holding Natheka's short sword aloft, I dragged the heavy one in my other hand as I held the monster's gaze and sidestepped several meters away from Natheka. Its beady eyes followed me while the glitchy techno-groove beats of EXO's *Monster* screeched over the airwaves.

"That's the shit," I said with a low laugh. Calling out to the reptile, I waved Natheka's short sword. "Come and get it, *lagarto sucio*! Dirty lizard. King Girl is ready to play!"

The noise disoriented it, judging by its weaving neck and tilted head, but my movement kept its attention rapt.

"That's right," I said, my voice belying the streaming sweat at my temples and ice in my veins. "*Venga aqui*." *Come here.*

Throat dry, I swallowed anyway and clanged the short sword on the long one a couple of times.

The beast lunged, and I dropped the heavy sword, swinging wildly with the short blade. The reptile dodged it and reared up like a horse. I considered driving forward leading with my blade but aborted the idea. I was hyperventilating, and my hands were sweating profusely inside my gloves. Carelessness equaled mistakes.

It lunged again, and I screamed, slashing at the long snout; the blade connected to my surprise, and the beast hopped backward, tossing its head in fury. A spray of blood and saliva rained over me, so I swiped at my eyes.

As long as this carnivore was occupied with me, it was leaving Natheka unharmed. I had no idea how long the transition took, but I was determined to keep my friend—and my future heart mate—alive.

Wary of its snout, the reptile bellowed its sac, a silent plea for its companions, and I realized I needed to stop it. It was playing with its food right now. When reinforcements came, I was a dead woman.

I shouted at it and swung the sword above my head.

"Come on, you chicken! That's right," I shouted with a crazed laugh. "Your descendants will be *pollitas*! Come on!"

It darted at me, crouching and snapping, and too fast for me to avoid, and its serrated teeth caught my arm. Screaming, I felt the crunch of bone and fiery pain for a hot second, but then adrenalin flooded my system in a torrent, and I felt nothing.

With a throaty yell I hacked at its snout, blow after blow, the blade glancing off the tough scales. It started to pull, and I knew I was chum if I didn't do something right now. The beast made a chuffing noise even as it clamped on my arm, and the memory of Diablo's torn vocal sac impressed upon my mind.

With a vicious slash, I tore into the tough skin and yanked down, hoping to catch one of the animal's vital arteries. But I didn't stop there. Its bite wouldn't loosen; if I didn't fight free, I might lose my arm or worse. Muscles screaming in protest, I heaved Natheka's short blade up and into the space between the reptile's jaws. I rocked that sword up and down, using every ounce of strength, and though it retched a belch of blood, it still didn't release my arm.

Frantic, I recalled one of the nearby stumps. It was impossible to see well in the dark, but had I noticed one of those poisonous lichens? Would it work on this dinosaur? Inexplicably, the beast loosened its grip and rolled its eyes as if to see something behind it.

Its distraction heaven-sent, I took full advantage and with an ago-
nized yell, I summoned King Girl one last time, and pushed forward,
forcing the beast toward the treefall at the expense of my already mangled arm. I drove my sword into the beast's front leg; it snagged between the brachioradialis and the extensor carpi radialis, but I pushed
it harder, heedless of the reptile's tail slamming into my back hard
enough that I lost my footing.

The animal careened, its crippled leg forcing its collapse as it yawned
another silent call, at last relinquishing my arm as a swell of nausea
rocked my stomach like a gut punch. With a final shove, I directed its
fall onto the log, hoping the lichen would finish the job.

Voices pierced through my battle-focus, but I kept my eyes glued
to the creature, analyzing my next strike, and the one after that, and
the one after that, until a strong arm wrapped around my neck from
behind.

"You did it," Pattee said in my ear. "You saved Natheka. Go to him,
and we'll stand guard in case more rokhura come."

Staring at the bloody sword in my hand, I couldn't move my feet.
My left arm dangled useless. My eyes were drawn to the huge animal
writhing among the understory, its life draining with every pulse of
blood that streamed from the torn vocal sac, and the attack lichen
embraced its slender neck like a blanket.

"Come on, King Girl," Pattee whispered. "You did good. You were
so brave."

Nodding, I let the war leak out of me, and I dropped the sword to
wipe away tears. I walked to where Natheka lay, his brothers within
reach. They stepped away at my approach, and I fell to my knees at his
side, sinking into the humus and cradling my bad arm.

He lay peaceful, no signs of stress, pain, or fear disfigured his handsome face. I would have traced the laceration under his eye, but my

gloves were filthy. Instead, I held onto his hand and watched him breathe.

It could have been hours or minutes. The entire pack of rokhural could have come at my back. But I didn't hear or see anything except Natheka.

When he stirred, he gripped my hand.

"Amity. You're alive," he said.

"Yes, Natheka."

"Clever Sister," he said, blinking his eyes and smiling. "Have you a tale to tell by the fire?"

"Yes, I suppose I do," I said. "Are you okay?"

He sat up, his eyes tracking my arm.

"Amity, at last I am whole," he said. "But you have sustained a wound! We go at once to Naraxthel's ship."

He jumped up and collected our helmets and shouted to his brothers. "My weapons! Raxthezana, escort us back to the ship," he said. "I feel I could battle the Queen's WarGuard, but we must save Amity's arm!"

"Of course," Raxthezana said, his hand on a sword hilt.

Taking a step, I felt like I was walking inside a cloud. A dark haze surrounded me, and I was lifted up into a dream.

"Precious Amity," the Holy Sister said. "Your heart is pure. Behold your tears," she said. She cupped her hands and they filled with silver liquid. "You had no choice but to slay our child that you might defend another. But your tears we have collected. They will nourish Ikthe."

The Younger Sister stepped from behind the veil and parted a curtain of trailing vines. "There lies Ikthe below," she said.

I looked over a rocky precipice, and there was the planet in its jaded verdure. But it began to shrivel and brown the longer I stared.

"Your tears," the elder Holy Sister said, and she opened her hands over the precipice, letting the silvery liquid rain down upon the browning leaves. After a time, they unfurled and blossomed with a shock of colors.

"Thank you for the love you bring to Certain Death," Younger Sister said. She leaned forward and pursed her lips then kissed me on the forehead.

I woke up in Naraxthel's medical bay.

"Amity," Natheka said my name with such tenderness and his face looked so serene that I wondered if he had been the one who kissed my forehead.

"Thank you for carrying me," I said, my voice hoarse and raw.

Natheka laughed, a joyful rumble. He turned to speak to the others who I saw were gathered in the aisle nearby. "My friend thanks me for carrying her ... when she is the one who preserved my life! Surely my friend is a warrior among warriors!"

"Be still, Amity," VELMA announced. "I have assimilated the technology in Naraxthel's medical bay and will now treat your arm."

VELMA must have administered powerful drugs because I felt myself fading. But I stared at Natheka whose smile had dimmed with VELMA's announcement. There was something we were supposed to talk about it. Something about VELMA. But I couldn't remember, and I couldn't speak, and I couldn't stay awake.

53

Raxthezana

When Amity snuck out of the ship, I sighed and left my bunk, stretching and then scratching my ass. I predicted it would be mere jotiks before I heard her scream. She couldn't know that Natheka would have entered the ikfal at speed, and she would have little chance at finding him. With all manner of creatures about, I would have to snatch her from the jaws of Certain Death. Natheka would have my head if I didn't.

Replacing my armor, I grimaced at the old familiar pains. I distracted myself with memories of watching my sire armor up before the fire in our small stone den. Unlike most hunters, I had lived with my sire because my dam had died in my childhood. He refused the offer of other sisters to raise me. He wasn't one for conversing, but when he prepared for hunts, he let me help him with his armor.

I would struggle to lift the heavy armor out of the water bath, but he would nod at my efforts. Right before he left, he would give me a solid pat on top of my head. It was his way. I dreamed of the day I would be gifted my own set of Shel and armor and fly to Ikthe to hunt big game for the sisters.

Sighing, I stepped into my boots and snagged my helmet as I left the ship.

As I had dallied placing my armor, Amity had already disappeared into the ikfal. Not wishing to frighten her, I stayed near the ship until such time when she called for aid.

Her knowledge of her home world's insect life was formidable. But when she had described the death of her fellow humans numbering in the millions per cycle, I had asked the technology VELMA to repeat that number.

Frowning, I paced the perimeter of the ship. Theraxl people had never reached those numbers. Forty cycles ago, Ikshe's population had neared three hundred thousand. Ships left for Ikthe several times daily, bringing the bounty of fresh meat to feed the sisters and children of Ikshe. The artisans, healers, musicians, and builders increased their industry, and it was a fruitful time for our people. But in that short period of time, the infant burial disease had begun its relentless slaughter. Every hunter or sister was touched by its black clawed hand.

My brethren were not possessed of curious minds like the sisters of Ikshe. But I could not quiet the questions that burned in my soul. Why had my father died on Ikthe, when he was the strongest and deadliest hunter of them all? Why did the queen take and pilfer the hunters' seed when Ikshe's population dwindled? Why did the infant burial disease begin to plague the Theraxl race? Why did my brothers surrender without fight to the whims of their heart-homes? These questions and more haunted me until I lay awake in the night, puzzling over them.

My greatest joy had been in discovering the old hunter tales and the hunter archives buried deep in the bowels of the queen's fortress. I had hoped to spend more time there when I was unjustly tasked to play nursemaid to my hunter brothers on this fruitless quest.

And then the humans came.

But my mind returned to Amity. If she understood the secrets of a miniscule insect spreading a disease from one person to another, perhaps she could help the Theraxl to discover the cause of the infant burial disease. Perhaps the humans' arrival did not portend the calamity of my people. Perhaps they brought ...

"Raxthezana, Natheka is in danger," VELMA's voice entered my helmet unbidden. "His heart is leaving the heart-home. Amity now defends him against a lone juvenile rokhura. The others do not respond to my hail."

"*Kathe!*" I shouted. "Can you sound the alarm in Naraxthel's ship? That will rouse them."

"Complying," VELMA answered.

With no time to waste, I rounded the ship and sought the trail I suspected Natheka had taken. VELMA accessed my helmet and overlaid the path, causing me to divert my route.

Ever had the humans shown courage and ingenuity in battling the predators of our hunting grounds, but Amity appeared the least equipped to do so. And yet she may bear the most potential in solving the mysterious infant burial disease. If Natheka was unable to fight for her, that left me and the others.

I ran through breaks in the trees, hoping Amity could defend Natheka in his extremity until we could arrive.

"Make haste," Naraxthel's voice spoke in my ear. "We follow close behind."

"VELMA has marked the rokhura on my map," I said. "But hold, there are two others! Get you to the north, and I shall take on the beast at the south."

"Pattee races to join you, Raxthezana," Naraxthel said. "Mind your rearguard."

"Hivelt will defend Natheka while Amity is at her work," Hivelt announced.

"Very well," I said. "VELMA, do others approach?"

"No, and I have used all methods of tracking available to me," she answered.

"Good," I said and leaped over a treefall.

If I but believed in goddesses, I supposed now would be the time to pray to them, but I had no such inclination. All my life I sensed a blackness beyond Theraxl existence. In truth, we needed no goddesses to inform us of our duties to one another. Even now, Amity fought against Certain Death because it was the right thing to do. Either she would be strong enough to protect Natheka ... or she would not. There would be no blame laid at any goddess's or person's feet. We would kill the rokhural and fly to her aid regardless.

Nearing the rokhura, a snatch of conversation I overheard weeks ago came to mind unbidden. I had turned to see if the others followed me into the Agothe-fax Tunnel, when I saw Hivelt speaking to Pattee. "Seek hope in the darkness. Hope shines."

Grumbling, I raised my sword to drive into the side of the beast that answered her sister's call. With the moon shining bright, the darkness was pronounced and blacker in the shadows. Mayhap there were no goddesses, but there was no harm in allowing a bit of hope to light the way to our mighty foe. The telltale whistle of Pattee's fine spear alerted me to stay to the left, as her weapon flew to its target. Alas, it glanced off the tough scales of its neck, having missed the *hohijopa*.

I struck without mercy, and the rokhura twisted to greet me with her many teeth. Prepared for such an attack, I saluted her head with my double-blades, and Pattee flanked my right, finding the source of the rokhura's lifeblood and ending its life with a killing blow.

"I misjudged my throw," Pattee said without apology, locating her spear in the underbrush.

"Ik, but your final judgment landed true," I said.

Together we hasted to the scene of Amity's battle, weapons at the ready.

Pattee choked out a cry and tore through the brush. Her friend was bathed in blood, but the rokhura lay dying at her feet.

I grunted. "Ik. Hope."

54

Hivelt

"VELMA," I said. "Mark Natheka's position on the map."

"Complying."

Snagging my sun-blade from the wall, I sheathed it and strode to the hatch, Pattee already descending.

She turned and gave me a salute, touching her fingers to her head and striking downward, and I returned it.

We had spent time memorizing one another earlier, and I trusted we would reunite in less than a zatik. Her face softened into a smile for a jotik, and then I saw her expression transform as she turned away and ran into the ikfal, courageous and defiant.

My heart in the new place swelled with love; I realized Natheka must have the same chance at this joy, so I tore into the wilderness following the trail that VELMA marked for me.

Would Amity accept Natheka? No one could answer that save Amity, but it would not matter. Once the hunters' hearts had left the heart-home, a stillness settled over them, and their lives were forever altered. Our hungry souls were quieted, and it seemed we transcended the instinct to prey.

Determination fired my blood, and I kept watch for the other known predators of the night as I raced to defend Natheka's helpless form.

My heart had left its home on the vast moraine; we had traveled free from most danger, and my heart mate had sat beside me keeping vigil. I marveled to think that Amity, the human least war-like of the three I had met, was now fighting off one of Ikthe's fiercest beasts. None of us would let her fail. I ran faster, my Shel vibrant and alive as they served their purpose.

Over the comms, I heard Naraxthel and Esra as they converged upon their prey, Naraxthel's voice calm as he praised the bravery and strategy of his heart mate. She, in turn, announced the rokhura's status.

Veltiks from where Natheka lay in the crumbling rot of the forest floor, I slowed my pace. "How fares Amity?" I asked.

"Amity holds her own against the rokhura," VELMA said. "I standby if more help is needed. Nosecone number two will be within range in thirteen iktiks."

"Thank you," I said and focused on the red dot in my helmet's visor that represented Natheka. I would not be close enough to aid Amity until Natheka's perimeter was clear. Locating the other rokhural on the map, as well as the green dots denoting my fellows, I withdrew my weapon. No predators circled where Natheka endured his heart's transition, judging by the colored dots. Turning off the visor map, I approached the copse where Natheka writhed.

A side glance revealed a puddle bird's nest with its bulging mushroom bursts. Ah, Natheka had been gathering eggs.

Spreading apart a veil of long vines, I peered between them to spot Natheka, but my own heart stopped, as it were, when I saw a devil dog poised to lunge.

Words escaped me, and my hand fumbled my sword for a jotik. I must dive in for the kill before the pazathel-nax killed Natheka!

Eyes narrowing at the long-sworn enemy of Theraxl hunters, I brought my blade up. The male devil dog stood at five veltiks' distance between me and Natheka's twisting body. Cocking my head, I paused, my sword still held aloft and ready should the devil dog leap to strike. But the mutt's gaze drilled into me and if I moved a fraction, it followed.

Throat dry and heart racing, I pondered what to do. If this mutt's pack was nearby, they would charge in at any second and choose freely from among the prey at their feet. Humans, rokhural, Ikthekal. But his behavior did not resemble that of a mutt who awaited the command of his elder sister. I recalled that VELMA had clearly designated the locations of threats, and there had been no such dot marking the devil dog. How had VELMA missed it?

I made to take a step, and the dog crouched and snarled. When I retreated a step, he relaxed his posture, but still maintained the crouch he needed to leap and attack if he desired. Never breaking eye contact, I chose to sidestep. The devil dog side-stepped as well, always maintaining the barrier between my brother and me.

Would not the devil dog take advantage of the easy prey within reach? He showed no interest in the hunter as food, but protected Natheka as if he were his own kit.

Never in all my cycles had I witnessed such behavior. As long as Natheka lay protected, I supposed it wasn't a danger. Very well, Hivelt would keep it occupied.

I swayed back and forth, the pazathel-nax tracking my every move and that of the weapon.

Beyond, Amity's short sword rang every time it struck, though I couldn't see her through the branches and fallen trunks that lay between us.

Eyes fixed on the devil dog, I made my way around the invisible line the dog enforced with his snarl and stalk.

I could hear Natheka's heaving breaths and occasional thrashes in the humus; such agonies were normal, and there was nothing I could do for him.

Having moved two veltiks to my right, I kept watching the devil dog's progress as it followed along with me. I lowered my weapon a fraction, but my foe's intensity never wavered.

My helmet alarm blared, sensors forewarning the approach of a scavenging rotaxl. The many-legged creature that usually feasted upon dead carcasses would have no qualm about making a meal of my fellow hunter though he was alive. Its many chewing mouths were more of a threat to Natheka than the devil dog appeared to be, so I diverted my attention to the long and twisting bug, its segments rippling along the forest floor in waves.

When its head was close enough, I drew up my boot to stomp it; cycles ago had Hivelt learned the error of attempting to behead the creatures, as every cut segment took a life of its own but attacked as one army. Before I could crush it, the devil dog sprang. It leapt upon the rotaxl and tore into its mid-section, powerful jaws sinking into the exoskeleton and penetrating the central core that housed the rotaxl's thoracic brain. With a vicious shake, the devil dog snapped the insect's spinal pathway before it could isolate its many nerve centers, rendering it not only defeated but dead. No scattered insect segments to battle.

Watching in astonishment, I stepped back to see the devil dog pounce on the fallen creature, dance away and toss its head at me, and then run back to Natheka's now-prone body. The brazen animal sniffed at Natheka and stole glances at me, his pacing skittish and dodgy.

Without warning, I heard Amity unleash a bloodletting scream. At once, the devil dog darted between fallen trunks, heading straight to Amity's battle.

I heard the disgruntled bellow of the rokhura as it strained to summon her sisters, and with fear gnawing at the base of my spine, I followed the path of the fierce dog, dreading what I might find. Another look at Natheka to see that he remained undisturbed, I planned to return as soon as possible once I established that Amity was safe and that her prey had been destroyed.

As I pushed through the bracken, I watched in awe as Amity managed to fell the great beast, using her might to topple the rokhura into a patch of the deception plant, its front limbs hobbled by a sword stuck in a joint. I searched the area, but the white devil dog was nowhere to be seen, nor had it left any mark that I could see.

My Pattee broke through the trees and rushed to her friend, and I sheathed my double-blades. For now, it seemed all threats had been neutralized.

Marveling at the unexpected behavior of the pazathel-nax, I pondered what I might witness next. Perhaps the jokapazathel would bring us puddle-bird eggs, or the forest-teeth tree would belch fire and smoke. Surely the goddesses sought to drive the Ikthekal mad with the many signs of terror and gifts of mercy, seemingly bestowed at whim and without measure. Hivelt could not predict what wonders might manifest next. But a devil dog protecting a Theraxl hunter surely must be a mercy, and Hivelt would do well to remember it. I considered sharing the strange event with my hunter-brothers but decided against it. Perhaps it was but a vision.

When I returned to Natheka, I cast my eyes to the trampled underbrush and saw the remains of the rotaxl. Grunting, I turned away. I still would not tell my brothers. Only imagine their jeers if Hivelt were to praise the actions of a rogue predator. Shaking my head, I stood vigil over Natheka's body until Amity made her way to us, favoring her bad arm.

55

Natheka

T he torment followed me into the caverns of my dream place. Once, Naraxthel described the place he retreated to when pain overcame him. It sounded bright, refined, and otherworldly. For me, I sought the place of my sacred encounter with the Goddesses. The crater lake and its surrounding mountains and caverns represented a place of holiness to me.

With my heart wrenching itself out of the cage, my ribs felt as if to crack open and spill out the contents of my bowel. To escape the pain, I stumbled out of the cavern with its sparkling walls and onto the stretch of black sandy beach.

The violence of the ikadax was nothing compared to the pain of my heart leaving its heart-home and twisting itself into the new place.

I welcomed the vision—the memory—of the ikadax, returning to my weakened form on the sand. I watched it soar from behind the escarpment, its flaming eyes seeking me out. I knew at that moment I was a dead hunter. According to the stories, no one outran the ikadax. No one killed it with sword or club, blade or fire. Weakened from my earlier stupidity, I could only watch in awe as it speared toward me, its body the piercing arrow of a fatal weapon.

A haze had enveloped me, and the tender face of who could only be one of the Holy Goddesses appeared right before me. She kissed my brow and dropped a tear onto my eye. With a glance at my devil dog helmet, she placed a finger upon its temple, and I witnessed a spark. Then she spoke.

"Tremble not, brave Natheka," she said. "We shall not let you perish here. Do you sing with joy until we return."

The haze lifted, and the ikadax blazed before me, a growing image of death unfurled. I burst into song, the Tale of the Burning Glory, when a howling figure leaped in front of me.

Naraxthel!

He had found me and now stood at the ready, both swords glowing purple in the afternoon light. With screeching yowls, ikadax talons and Iktheka swords met in a fury of clamoring metal until the ikadax seized Naraxthel's right arm, dislodging his sword and tearing into his shoulder.

Shaken from my stupor, I dove for Naraxthel's sword and slammed it into the ikadax's leg bone. Naraxthel tore at its other leg with his double-blades, and together, we managed to dissuade the ikadax from devouring us. It screeched again, its vestigial hohijopa fluttering uselessly as its ugly voice carried across the water. With powerful flaps, the bloody creature lifted itself over the tops of a low range, and Naraxthel and I limped to nearby caverns. Only cycles later had it occurred to me that Naraxthel could have let the ikadax feast upon my body and slay it, taking the glory of Ikthe's greatest kill to himself.

Another cramp fissured down the center of my chest, reminding me I was not at the crater lake, but in the ikfal with Amity ... dear

Goddess, Amity ... she who treasured life must now be battling the rokhura.

Sweat beaded across my body; cracks raced across my skin; death sat at my feet, eyeing me with a hungry glint.

Back to the cavern I retreated, its shimmering walls hinting at magical treasure. I walked along the hall, tracing the cool, moist rock with my claws and inhaling the cold air until it tightened my chest.

The pad and click of paws echoed about the chamber, and I stopped. Cocking my head, I listened. More clicking on the stone floor. When I spun, Amity's devil dog stood staring at me, much as he had done when I battled the Elder Sister Pazathel-nax.

"Why are you here?" I scolded him. "Amity needs you!" I paused, and my voice dropped. "It may be that I need you, as well."

Still, he stood, and the walls around me shook with the spasms of my heart change.

I knelt before him and bowed my head.

"Forgive us," I said. A tear slipped down my face.

The devil dog lunged at me, and I froze in terror, but he only swiped his long tongue at my cheek and collected the tear. With a toss of his head, he turned and left the cavern, and the shaking slowed to a stop.

I looked at my right hand and saw that Amity's bloodied glove rested in it.

My heart mate.

56

Amity

A cacophony of chimes and alarms startled me awake. When I tried to move, I saw I was strapped to the exam table in Naraxthel's ship. I darted my gaze around and spotted Pattee in a jump seat in the med bay.

"There were more tremors," she said. "Naraxthel took us up. VEL-MA is still working on your arm."

Of course. An alien appendage, a hybrid of organic and robotic material, suspended from the ceiling, maneuvered with deliberate machinations up and down my arm sending jolts of energy to dozens of places on my skin. The creature's teeth had not punctured the suit, but I knew the second it bit down that extensive damage had been done. On one of the science-class fleet ships, the injury would mean reconstructive surgery and weeks in traction. But Theraxl technology appeared to be in a class of its own.

The jolts of energy buzzed beneath my skin, and I watched in awe as the contacts at the end of the appendage sought out each blue-mottled bruise and treated it. If I blurred my eyes, I could make out the decided shape of a gigantic bite mark.

I turned my face away.

"Looks like you'll get your arm back to 100% sooner rather than later," Pattee said. "And I must say, on Ikthe, that's pretty damn important."

A firm hand rested on my good bicep, warm rough skin with the catch of dull claws touching my bare arm with a zing.

Natheka stood beside me.

"I am pleased our technology assists you in healing quickly," he said. "But you need never raise a weapon again. I will fulfill my oath to you, Amity."

Smiling, I allowed my gaze to explore Natheka's face. The interior of the ship lit up his features much better than the moon had done earlier.

Strong jaw, generous lips, unmistakable white fangs, his nose with the slight crook in it, but most captivating were his dark eyes. Their glow was no longer evident in the light of the ship. Their black depths swam, and though his race didn't have the white sclera or colored iris, I could still tell that he was staring at me.

Heart fluttering, I wondered if Pattee was elsewhere if Natheka might try to finish what we had started back in the forest.

Natheka touched the pulse in my throat with a claw.

"Your heart races like that of the jokapazathel," he said. "Do not fear me."

"This isn't fear, Natheka," I said. I watched his nostrils flare.

"I know."

He said it with such certainty that not only did my heart continue to race, but my belly dipped while a flood of endorphins flushed through my bloodstream.

We stared at each other until Naraxthel's voice interrupted our silent communion.

"VELMA identified another landing place," he said. "Her data suggests the tremors will subside for a longer period of time."

The enchantment broken, Natheka let his finger graze down my good arm. I noticed my suit had been unfastened to my waist and sleeves drawn off my arms, leaving me in my sports bra. Pattee and Esra must have tended me. His touch left a wake of gooseflesh.

"I'll return and you must share human music with me. There were mysterious strains of sounds penetrating the walls of my dream place," he said. "And now I am curious."

I flashed a smile for him and nodded.

"I can't wait," I said. He retreated to a jump seat behind me somewhere.

"It looks like you made peace with the heart mate philosophy," Pattee said from her spot near the wall. "It suits you." She broke into a smile, her even white teeth gleaming in the half-light.

"We came to an understanding," I said, returning her smile. "We didn't rush headlong into things. We're taking our time."

"Uh huh," she said and winked. Then she cocked her head. "You took down that rokhura like you were born into it. Care to share any pointers?"

At first, I thought she was teasing me, but her serious expression said otherwise.

"I recommend staring at them in abject terror for at least five seconds," I said. "And of course, blast K-pop right away."

Pattee sat back, biting her lip and nodding.

"I jest," I said. "But seriously—their vocal sacs are transmitting subsonic Hertz. When they really project, the decibel level causes nausea and other side effects. It got me thinking, if they're transmitting in infrasound, then they're used to receiving in infrasound. VELMA tapped into that concept when she started with the helmet emissions. VELMA said Esra suggested that when she first got here."

"The silent planet," Pattee said, her voice low and her eyes staring into nothing. "We can utilize that info."

"Absolutely," I said. "You should have seen what VELMA did with bioacoustics and the forest-teeth tree."

"I hate those things," Pattee said.

"This whole planet is a ..."

"Nightmare," Pattee said.

"I was going to say exobiologist's dream," I said with a laugh.

She sat back with a chuckle and a sigh.

The rumble and crank of the ship's landing gear indicated we had landed. The smooth cabled appendage continued its work, and Pattee unstrapped.

"I'll round up the others," she said. "We never had time to talk to the guys about VELMA, the array, and mitigating the geomagnetic excursion."

"Too bad we don't have popcorn," I said after her as she walked away.

"I'd settle for another round of ice cream," she said in a sing-song voice.

"In your dreams!" I said. "We have to ration that stuff."

The whir and click of the strange arm lulled me into a Zen state. "VELMA," I said in a sleepy voice. "How many breaks were there?"

"I counted over forty-six fractures, most of them comminuted, Amity," she said. "I am finding the mechanisms in Naraxthel's medical bay to be fascinating to work with. They have utilized a blend of organic and cybernetic materials to enhance the healing process. If you are familiar with nanotechnology, it is almost like a step back.

Rather than nanocytes, they have adapted the larger molecules with macroscopic electronics. I predict that in two or three revolutions, the Theraxl race will develop a nanotechnology all their own."

"Wow, that's impressive," I said. "Is my arm going to be a hybrid bio-cybernetic limb?"

"Not quite," VELMA said. "But when you were gathering the unhatched puddle bird eggs, I was able to use the spectrometer in your suit helmet to analyze the contents. As Natheka explained, an organ within the puddle bird's body is equipped to filter out metals. The organ's capability of isolating the metals allows a symbiotic relationship between both organic and inorganic material to form."

"Just like all the sister-pairs," I said.

"Exactly," VELMA said. "In this way, the medical advancement allows for the injection of strong metallic components to be used in bone repair. Over time, your body's natural healing processes will replace the metals with calcium."

"The metal forms a temporary internal splint," I said. "I should have full use of my arm as long as there is enough metal to replace all of the shattered parts."

"Yes," VELMA said. "You are one lucky exobiologist."

"I think this calls for a song," I said. "What do you recommend?"

"How about "Sister Luck" by the Black Crowes?"

"You're getting pretty good at this, VELMA," I said.

"This. Is. Mix One-oh Six, coming at you with. Weather and traffic on the sixes," VELMA said.

"Mm. We need to work on your delivery, though," I said.

"Very well, Amity," she said. "I am at your service."

57

Natheka

My gut churned as if I had eaten a bad batch of thunder weed, but I knew it was caused by too many battles on the horizon. I rejoiced to have found a heart mate. What once seemed an impossible dream had become a reality so pure that joy washed over me in repeated waves.

But casting a shadow over my joy was the Ikma Scabmal Kama's threat to Ikthe, as well as the suspicion surrounding the human technology. VELMA's ease at infiltrating Naraxthel's ship and our communication devices, as well as her long-reaching tentacles into every aspect of Ikthe, sat like a cold rock in the pit of my stomach.

When we landed, Pattee approached us from the med bay.

"Our strategy session was interrupted, but time waits for no one," she said. "Least of all on predator planet."

"We have a similar saying," Hivelt said. "For every strike of a tik, ten more must follow."

"Apt," Pattee said and reached to squeeze Hivelt's hand. "Esra and Amity and I discussed your concerns regarding the nanosatellite array."

My brothers and I grunted in reply.

"While we all know that the girls and I arrived on Ikthe strictly by accident, we can't say for sure that IGMC's technology wasn't developed for just such a scenario as you all have been concerned about."

With one accord, my brethren and I all folded our arms. I noticed Pattee's mouth curved in a half-smile, but she didn't laugh.

"Upon further discussion, we realized IGMC may have developed and adapted technology for the purpose of analyzing a greater number of planets in a shorter amount of time to maximize its acquisition of planets for mineral extraction," she said. VELMA filled in translations for the words I didn't recognize. "Adding the Vector Egress Liaison Machine-Learning AI to every life pod increased the probability of IGMC finding a greater number of exploitable planets."

Hivelt muttered. "*Kathe.*"

"That being said, as VELMA explained to us humans when we asked, traveling as we did for five lightyears lowered our chances of being tracked and found ... to astronomical."

I glanced at Naraxthel, Raxthezana and Hivelt. Their shoulders relaxed, and Raxthezana unfolded his arms.

"On behalf of IGMC, we would like to apologize," she said. "You were right. The technology we brought with us was indeed intended to—essentially—trap Ikthe as if in a net."

I shifted my feet but said nothing.

Pattee bowed her head for a moment before speaking again. "The good news is that we're here now, no one from IGMC can find us, and

....." She stopped and looked at Hivelt with a small smile. "Against all odds, we found you."

While Hivelt's eyes darkened with warmth as he looked at his heart mate, Naraxthel nodded and placed his fists at his waist.

"I am satisfied with this explanation," he said. "I would add that we had considered to ask of you that you place restrictions upon VELMA's capabilities."

Raxthezana growled and made as if to speak, but Naraxthel stopped him with a look. "But after Amity's harrowing battle, I found VELMA's aid to be without match."

"I agree," Raxthezana said and stepped forward.

My eyebrows shot up.

"I have revised my opinion of the technology," he said. "Yes, it accesses our comms with ease, as well as the devices on Naraxthel's ship. But I have observed. This VELMA only works to serve the humans, and in turn, the Ikthekal."

Naraxthel nodded while Hivelt spoke. "This I have witnessed numerous times."

Uneasy, I bowed my head to think.

"I do not like the net," I finally said.

"Maybe we could adjust the parameters of the net," Esra said, shouldering between Naraxthel and Hivelt. "We could request that VELMA disable portions of it, or maybe concentrate them in specific areas where they would be most helpful to us on the ground."

"We could deactivate a fraction of them and stable them in the pods," Pattee said. "We don't have to let them encircle the planet."

Tension in my gut eased, and I let my arms fall to my side.

"That appeases my worry," I said. "I cannot explain the fear in my heart when I imagine our hunting grounds entrapped thusly. Thank you for addressing my fears, irrational though they may be."

"Of course," Esra said. "We're part of you now. And with all of the help that VELMA has given us from the moment we entered Ikthe's atmosphere, she's part of us, too. I think we can work together on this."

"If I may interject," VELMA's voice rang through the ship. "I will be happy to serve Ikthe in any way that makes the Ikthekal comfortable. I am not limited to geographical, geological or meteorological maps. I am equipped to analyze any number of biological or chemical signatures, as well as the numerous scatological deposits found on your planet."

"Ah, thank you VELMA," Pattee said. "We'll take it from here."

"Very well," VELMA said. "I will return to Amity's recovery."

"Did the technology just say that it can analyze *kathe*?" Raxthezana asked Hivelt in a quiet voice.

"Yes," Esra and Pattee said together.

"You know what they say," Amity called from behind us. "Kathe in, kathe out!"

My brothers and I did not understand this quip, but Pattee and Esra chuckled, and then laughed, Amity's answering laughter sounding from behind me.

Naraxthel drew my attention. "Something else troubles you, Natheka," he said.

"Ik," I answered. "Today marks the third day, and we have not heard from BoKama. What are we to do when the Ikma arrives with her WarGuard?" Peering at him, I waited for him to disclose what secret strategies he had made with the BoKama.

"We must be on our guard at all times," he said. "The Ikma has never set foot on this planet, yet her WarGuard is comprised of former hunters. They will know this planet just as we do."

"They could choose to destroy your ship from the air," I said. "Or infiltrate the ikfal with dozens of the Ikma's soldiers and lie in wait, picking us off one by one."

"They could ambush us when we surface from the caves," Raxthezana said. "Or any number of other scenarios. Of what use is our speculation when the solution is but a request away? Can you not see it?"

I cocked my head.

"No, but please enlighten us," I said, opening my palm.

"If the humans' technology remained encircling Ikthe, would not the Ikma's ship break the barrier? Could not VELMA inform us once other ships had entered Ikthe's atmosphere?" he said, frustration thickening his voice. "I know I expressed doubt as to the innocence of these invisible transmitters, but it came to me as I stood here and listened to Amity's strange and humorless joke about *kathe*. In and out. We complained that VELMA's satellites appeared as a net enfolding a weakened Ikthe within," he said. "But hold. Just as Naraxthel suggested before, the satellites may perform as a shield, and VELMA will alert us if the shield is breached *from the outside*. In this way would we be prepared to meet the threat at hand."

Dumbfounded, I searched the others' faces for their reactions as well. It made sense, and in light of the Ikma's threat, we had no choice but to employ the array thusly.

"But VELMA did not inform us when BoKama landed two days ago, nor a few weeks ago," I said.

"In general, VELMA only does things she is specifically tasked to do," Esra said. "If we asked, she could probably tell you to the minute when BoKama's ship passed through the atmosphere."

"We can only hope it is not too late," Naraxthel said. "VELMA, had you recalled any of your nanosatellites?"

"Yes, they are en route to pods two and four," she said.

"Esra, have you any objection to using the satellite array in this manner?" Naraxthel asked.

"No," she said. "It makes perfect sense. VELMA, please redeploy. Can we count on you to inform us of any breaches in the array?"

"Of course, Esra," she said. "However, there are sections of the array that do not accurately register pings, such as above the Magnetic Burst Field."

"Duly noted," Esra said.

A silence settled on us as we traded looks.

"We will await Amity's full recovery," I said. "And then we will make our next plans. As long as Raxkarax cannot be reached via comms, we must trust that neither can he be found by the queen's WarGuards."

"And as long as we don't know where the fifth pod is, perhaps it will remain hidden from them as well?" Pattee asked. For the first time, I saw a hint of fear on her face as she stepped closer to her heart mate, Hivelt.

Naraxthel sighed and beckoned to his Esra who melted into his arms.

"We have gone from mistrusting the humans' technology to putting our lives in her care. We will not do so in half-measures. At every step, VELMA has aided our humans. She will in this, as well," Naraxthel said. "Natheka is right. When the time is right, I will reveal what I can of BoKama's subterfuge. We will wait for Amity's full recovery, and then our work will begin in earnest."

"Amity is right here," she called out. "I agree with everything you said. Also, VELMA is the queen of multitasking. You can bet that even while she is monitoring the atmosphere, she's also searching for pings from the fourth and fifth pods, analyzing that pile of poop just outside the bay door, and compiling a playlist for my next battle. She's got this," she said. "And so do we."

A smile worked its way to my lips. Amity's positive outlook was, perhaps, as infectious as that strange tiny bug she showed us on the monitor the other night.

"Very well," I said. "Let us make preparations while we wait."

Raxthezana nodded and took up his helmet and weapons. "I will hunt for food," he said. "Do you strike a fire and prepare to smoke the meat."

"Watch your step when you exit," I said with a smirk.

Raxthezana waved a rude gesture in my direction, but he laughed.

We scattered, our plans unfolding by the tik under the watchful eye of the Goddesses ... and VELMA. I hoped it was not folly.

58

Amity

Daybreak shone through the front glass of Naraxthel's ship, and with it came the welcome but dull ache of my healing arm. VELMA suggested I attempt to move it, so with trepidation in my heart, I raised it with caution and bent it towards myself. I managed to itch my nose with my hand.

"*Dios mio*, this is unbelievable," I said. "Truly. I can't believe this."

"While Theraxl technology is limited in many ways by their rigid belief system, they have managed to harness a solid grasp of rapid cell regeneration," VELMA said. "Aided in large part to specific organisms found on Ikthe."

"Which ones?" I asked while I stared at my fingers and hand. I wiggled my fingers and then made a fist, feeling twinges but nothing I couldn't handle. I raised and lowered my arm, bent it at the elbow, then rotated it at my shoulder. Massive stripes from healing lacerations crisscrossed my entire arm, but it was a small price to pay for full range of motion.

"Just for starters, the giant *Diplopoda* which the Iktheka call rotaxl, the puddle bird mentioned by Natheka, and the Shel," VELMA said. "I've isolated biosignatures from the organisms within the cell healing compounds found in Naraxthel's med bay. There are others as well, but I haven't identified them all yet."

"Fascinating," I said and flexed my bicep. "Tell me. Will I be able to play the piano?"

"That depends on if you played it prior to the reptile bite," VELMA said.

Groaning, I sat up and hopped off the too-tall exam table. "VEL-MA, you ruined the joke."

"I was not aware I was complicit in a joke," she said.

"It's okay," I said with a huff. "If I explain it, it will just make it worse."

"Your arm will not worsen unless you suffer another reptile bite," she said.

"Okay first," I said and directed my comments toward the med bay monitor, as if VELMA had a personage. "That wasn't just a reptile bite. That thing would have taken my arm clean off if it wasn't for my flight suit."

"Agreed," she said. "And the second?"

"The second?" I asked.

"You preceded your last statement with 'Okay first', implying there was a second statement to be made."

"Uh, I forgot," I said and slipped my arms back into the sleeves that dangled with the top-half of my suit at my waist. "Where is everyone?"

"Right outside preparing the morning meal," she said.

"Thank you, VELMA," I said and fastened my suit. "And VELMA, I mean it. Thank you for saving my life and my arm and for being my friend when I really needed one."

"It is in my programming," she said. "And it is my pleasure."

Smiling, I patted the bulwark, the closest thing to VELMA's embodiment in Naraxthel's ship. "I'll be right outside."

Boots on and helmet under my arm, I walked down the ramp to see my fellow travelers circled around a modest fire and racks supporting strips of meat.

Natheka, sans helmet, smiled wide when he saw me. In three strides he was at my side.

"Your arm is fully recovered," he said. "And how do you feel?"

"I feel great," I said. "Your people's medical knowledge is highly advanced. I can't wait to study more of the life on your planet."

He beamed and guided me to join the others. "Do you break bread with us, Amity," he said and took the piece offered by Hivelt. Handing it to me, he tore off a single bite and popped it into his mouth. "The sister bread keeps us fed and content when we are far from home," he said.

Hivelt grunted. "I am home," he said. "And once we have restored dignity to the throne of Ikshe, I will beg of my Afarax's dam to allow her to spend time with me on Ikshe until she is ready to join me in the hunt here."

Hivelt was a father? Cocking my head, I tried to imagine him bouncing a baby Theraxl on his knee, but my imagination came up short. Then I remembered that Natheka had two boys of his own. I turned to stare at him, but he was smiling at Hivelt.

"I like this thought," Natheka said. "Our Theraxl sisters are just as mighty as the hunters. Why do not we encourage them to join us in our hunts? Imagine the strategy and wit they employ at court being utilized to take down rokhura on Ikthe!"

Naraxthel nodded and Raxthezana scoffed.

"Indeed," Raxthezana said. "Only imagine the sisters taking on the hunt of Certain Death. Mayhap they will enter their names into the Lottery Drum as well." His smile did not make it to his eyes before he dropped it. When he stalked away from the fire and slumped at the root of a tree, I searched everyone's faces for clues.

"Change is reserved for the hunters on Ikthe," Naraxthel said and gestured to Raxthezana's retreating form. "He knows the Sisters are not wont to change, nor those citizens of the higher courts," he said. "But I too envision precious time spent with my own offspring," he said, reaching for Esra's hand.

I almost spewed my water down the front of my suit but not before Esra's own expression showed utter horror.

"I'm not pregnant!" she said, a frantic look in her wide eyes as she met my stare first and then sought out Pattee. "I'm not." She shook her head.

Naraxthel laughed, and Hivelt and Natheka joined in. Confused, I waited for someone to explain what was going on. Esra wasn't laughing, and Pattee quirked a single brow.

"We know you are not with child," Naraxthel said. "I refer to the vision of our daughter."

"You cannot get with child until you have had the raxshe and raxma ceremony," Natheka said, his mouth turned up on one side, revealing a naked fang.

The half-smile sent an unexpected thrill down my spine, and when his gaze locked with mine, a tremor started in my feet and danced its way up my entire body. Was there an earthquake? Nothing else shook in the clearing where we stood.

"What is the raxshe and raxma?" Pattee asked Hivelt who stared at her with a thoughtful look.

"It is the ceremony in which those who wish to create offspring participate," Hivelt said. He looked down at his own unfinished sister bread then looked up at us humans. He shoved the huge portion into his mouth and began chewing, a deliberate stall tactic. I snorted.

We peered at Naraxthel next.

"Ah, the ceremony of the raxshe and raxma," he said. "It is ...," he said and paused, searching the ground with his dark gaze.

"Somehow I don't think you'll find the answer down there," Esra said with a smile.

Naraxthel jerked his head up and returned her smile with a toothy one of his own. "Nay, but the answer may not be one you wish to receive," he said. "I puzzle with the most delicate way to explain."

Pattee huffed.

"Do we look delicate to you?" she asked with a strut and held her arms away from her body, her palms out and her hips and boots jutted forward, as if to say, behold this power.

Her flight suit hugged her curves, not just her feminine ones, but the defined quadriceps and hamstrings, gluteus maximus and gastrocnemius and soleus muscles of her lower legs. Her broad shoulders and biceps could and did carry the weight of intimidating weapons, including the long spear she wore strapped to her back at a diagonal and within easy reach.

Impressed, I found myself glancing toward Esra next.

Her brows met at the crease in her forehead, and she stood arms akimbo and feet shoulder-width apart. Her stance declared battle-ready, especially as she wore a short sword in a sheath at her waist and a grim smile on her face. Her eyes flashed when she reached down and pulled a dagger from her leg-sheath, hefted it a moment, and then threw it in a sudden motion catching me off guard.

The knife hurtled toward a tree and sunk into the broad flat body of a strange, clawed insect whose pincers waved in search of Raxthezana's neck.

Raxthezana, who sat at the base of the tree, looked up from the leather-bound parchment he held in his hands and saw us staring at him. He looked at his side and yanked the knife out of the bark, then turned and gave Esra a small nod.

I clamped my mouth shut.

"Our heart mates are not fragile," Natheka said from my side. I had forgotten he was standing there. And what we were talking about. "They will learn of the raxshe and raxma," he said. "Mayhap we wished to explain during more peaceful moments, but as they have already witnessed themselves, there are no peaceful moments on Ikthe. Only the occasional inhale before we battle again."

Exhaling in a burst, I shook my head. I'd been holding my breath without realizing.

Glancing at me, he smiled.

"I don't need to remind anyone of my own—friend's—strength tested in battle," he said. He slipped a clawed finger behind a lock of my hair and moved it behind my ear. "She still wears the blood of the rokhura. Let the humans decide if they want to hear of the ceremony right now, or mayhap in a private audience with their—heart mates." Natheka's voice dipped lower when he said that, and I couldn't help the swallow and blink. My dry throat begged for another swig of water, and I brought the canister to my lips with a shaky hand. I steadied the canister with my other hand and took a long pull from it.

Wiping my mouth, I closed the cap and looked up, meeting Pattee's concerned gaze.

"Yes, a private audience would be better, I think," she said.

Walking paces from the others, I angled my head at Natheka, hoping he would follow me. When he approached, I looked him in the eye. "It's okay," I said. "I'm not ready to hear about whatever this ceremony is."

He searched my face with his steady dark eyes, his brow furrowed but his mouth in a small smile. "Of course. For now, we are but good friends," he said. "I would not burden you with this knowledge until you seek it for yourself." He licked his thumb and swiped it across my forehead. "VELMA healed your arm but neglected to bathe you."

Feeling heat rush to my face, I looked away for a second. "I better get cleaned up then," I said and met his kind eyes. "You never know when the next calamity will hit, and I need to be fresh as a daisy for it!"

He captured my hand before I could rush to the ship. "I do not know what this daisy is," he said. "But please. Never fear me. We will face all calamities together," he said. "I trust my life with you. And I hope you feel you may trust your life with me."

I faced him again, my heart speeding at a thousand miles per hour. "Natheka," I said and reached up to rest my hand on his cheek. "You have done nothing but protect my life since the first time we met. I could never fear you," I said. Then, in spite of the fierce trembling inside my actual guts, I stroked his bottom lip, feeling his breath tickle my fingers. Lowering my hand to his chest plate, I pressed against it, then made a fist and pushed it against my own chest. "I'm afraid of the strong feelings I have in here. I don't want them to—control—me."

With a gentle grasp, Natheka took my clenched hand and brought it up to his mouth. He opened my fist and kissed my palm and then enfolded it with his other hand.

"This fear," he said. "I know it well." He gestured at the wilderness surrounding us. "On the hunt, it seems our lives are not our own. The weather, the predators, our hunger: they conspire to compel our actions, our very decisions and moods. But in the face of such foes, the hunter will choose." He caressed my cheek but withdrew his hand again. "We choose our weapon. We choose where and what to strike. We choose how much effort to expend and when to end the hunt. If it is something we can control, we control it. And if not," he said with a shrug and a gesture to the sky. "Then we give it to the Holy Goddesses of Shegoshel. We cannot understand all things, nor do we wish to." He looked away then down at his chest where he had placed my hand. "The Ikthekal cannot control who our hearts have chosen to follow as mates."

My heart galloped when he pulled me closer to him, and I was forced to look up.

"But I could not have chosen a female more suited, more perfect, more clever or more desirable than you. Did my heart control this feeling in my soul? Perhaps your soul called out to mine as it entered the atmosphere of Ikthe. I do not know." He stepped back and dropped his arms from around me. "We cannot control these feelings, but I will never control you," he said and then huffed a small laugh. "In future, you may wish to control me, but you cannot." His expression broke into a grin, and he gestured to the ship. "Go. Do what you will; I have no power over you."

He released me with his smile and returned to the fire, squatting to add a small stick. Looking around I saw that Hivelt and Pattee stood close with heads bent together. Pattee made a fist, but otherwise looked relaxed with her heart mate. Naraxthel and Esra sat a fair distance from the fire with crossed legs and heads bowed while Naraxthel's lips moved. Esra frowned and played with a long piece of grass, consternation etching her face with drawn brows and tight lips.

Raxthezana had replaced his helmet and resumed reading his book, heedless that a large insect had recently threatened his person.

I retreated to the ship and made my way to the hygiene facility inside, embarrassed that I'd been seen in public covered in blood and dirt.

Inside the hygiene capsule, I stood naked trying to decipher the controls. Made for much larger beings than humans, the levers were higher up. There were symbols, but they had no meaning to my eyes. And typical for King Girl, I didn't want to ask VELMA for help.

"Trial and error it is," I mumbled to myself and reached up to toggle a lever. Nothing happened.

Cocking my head, I stared at the panel and reversed the lever I'd chosen. Studying the dull gray metal panel, I frowned. Maybe there was a sensor I needed to trigger?

The capsule's door slid open, and Natheka stood outside, naked as the day he was born.

Crossing myself, I stared at my heart mate, my friend, my champion. *My lover.*

"Do you step aside, that I may join you and operate the mechanisms," he said, his voice low.

Moving aside without argument, I watched him step onto the platform and fill the space with his power and serenity. He lacked the stench of human sweat mingling with bacteria, a detail I would likely obsess over in the coming weeks and months, but for now, I let his aroma wash over me: spices, greenery, water and earth. Natheka smelled of living things, and I craved more.

"What makes you think you can just walk in here like that?" I said, my voice husky. My gaze roved over his lean and muscled back, the scar patterns covering his skin at once shocking and alluring. Without a second thought, I brought both hands to his back and smoothed them from his shoulders to his waist and back up again.

"My mind rehearsed the words I spoke, and I questioned if I said the right thing," he said, all the while relaxing into my touch.

I didn't see what he'd done, but a warm mist of water rose from the floor, and in seconds we were saturated. Natheka turned, and I dropped my hands, looking up into his face.

There was no mistaking the affection in his eyes, the *love*. He bent to retrieve my hands and place them at his chest.

"You are possessed of a healing touch, human maikshe," he whispered. "Touch all of me at your will."

Swallowing, I felt my heartbeat escalate when I reached for his cheeks and used my thumbs to touch his mouth. I'd tasted his lips. Now he offered more.

"I thought you said I couldn't control you," I said and drifted my caress down, looking deep into his black eyes.

His gaze tethered to my own, our bodies drew closer while I explored him with my hands.

"Perhaps I severed the truth," he said. "Perhaps your very gaze can control me with a single glance. Perhaps your words command my every action."

"I'm not trying to control you," I said but he stole my breath with a demanding kiss. Where my hands met his skin they blazed, and then I felt his burning fingers trail along my skin, mirroring where I petted him.

Seized with mischief and desire, I reached for him, hoping he would grasp me at my core as well. He did not disappoint, and from there I *did* control his every action. Where I wanted him to touch, I touched. Where I wanted him to nuzzle, I nuzzled.

With skin slippery from water and soap, we taught each other the best places to squeeze, to tease, to invade or retreat from.

Murmured endearments drowned in the spray, but I caught the gist of his emotions.

Pulling him closer to me, I whimpered when noticing how our height differential could complicate things, but he chuckled and lifted me with ease, his hot hands firm under my arm and behind, until he held me up in his embrace.

Straddling his waist, I closed my eyes and flung my head back, seating myself with care, relishing the fulness, the completion of being joined as one.

We stopped moving together, and I opened my eyes to find him drinking me in with his gaze.

"Never could I have imagined such—perfection," he said, his voice a rumble.

I couldn't speak, a growing pulse of wonder had sparked low in my belly, and I was fighting the urge to possess him with ferocity.

"No," he said. "Do not fight it. Hunt it. *Seize* it," he urged, and I did.

"Aho!" he yelled as I rocked my weight into him, astounded and emboldened by the sounds he made, and my arousal enhanced by his attention to my breasts.

I couldn't stop staring at the place our bodies joined, transfixed by the contrast of his green skin with my brown, and marveling at the numerous scars caused from his armor.

"Come to me, maiden of my heart," Natheka whispered in my ear before sucking the lobe into his mouth.

With rising heat, I felt the moment my body crested the ridge of its climax and paused long enough to grasp and clench at Natheka's shoulders, the energy of my orgasm catapulting us both with its power as I careened into it, losing control of my thoughts, my words, and my body.

"Amity," Natheka uttered, cradling my wildness in his arms. "Ever will you capture me," he said, his thrusts pronounced in the wake of my own peak. "I am your prey for all time."

Melting at his words, I rode out the wave, secure in his grasp as he maneuvered to brace my back against the wall. Panting, I moaned as he stroked inside me with fervor, the skin around his eyes darkening when they narrowed on me.

He claimed to be my prey, but I felt like the hunted now; he devoured me with kisses and penetrated my shields with heated demand. Gathered in his arms, I was powerless against the upward motion of his thrusts, but every push drove me higher, a second climax inevitable.

Our groans and gasps echoed in the small chamber, and at last, we broke on his final stroke, crying out and trembling, even as the mist changed, and I deduced the capsule was entering a rinse phase. The cool water chilled my skin until warm bursts of air shot out from every side, and the puffs blew strands of my hair into my face.

Collapsing into him, I laughed and shook my head as he disengaged, lifting me just enough, and I whimpered when he left my clenching walls and lowered me to my feet.

"Ah, Pazathe Kama," he said, gentleness in his deep voice. "We will do this again soon."

Leaning into him, I inhaled deeply of his fragrance, unchanged, and wrapped my arms around him. "I can't wait."

Natheka ran his claws through my hair, untangling strands, and hummed, and I soaked in the attention. For a few minutes, I was content to be hunted and captured on Predator Planet.

After we finished up, I washed out my suit and boots, dried everything and donned them once again.

Natheka had given me a lot to think about—both before and during our interlude—and I could use time to really analyze things and examine my feelings and just ... be allowed to fumble along. But just like Natheka had said earlier, we barely had time —to take a breath—before the next challenge overtook us.

When VELMA's blaring alarm system went off alongside Naraxthel's ship's alert system, I had to laugh. The only other choice was to cry.

59

Raxthezana

O f all the maps in my possession, I had but one map suitable for our quest to gather woaiquovelt; I had borrowed the old book from the archives five cycles ago and had yet to return it. Naraxthel would call it the guidance of the Holy Shegoshel that I had it in my possession when we were summoned to quell the Queen's anger with our unholy quest. I called it another day, as I had been studying the journal daily for several passes of the moon.

Within its pages were the scribbled notes of not only my sire, but his sire before him, and his sire before him.

Recipes, antidotes, warnings, stroke techniques and the habits of Ikthe's fiercest predators adorned its pages as well as pathways, routes, hidden treasures, poisonous plants and rare delicacies. There were maps, as well. Dozens of maps.

And each time Ikthe travailed with her birth pains, I made note of it, both in pages in the back and on the maps, as her landscape changed with each contraction.

I knew not what Ikthe birthed. A new world? A demon? The sins of the hunters? Or mayhap her new Queen?

But inasmuch as the undermountain passageways remained unchanged, we would be guided straight to the source of Ikthe's finest woaiquovelt. I frowned and squeezed the leather journal in my hands and then stashed it in my pouch. Obstacle after obstacle hedged up the way.

When we had sufficient woaiquovelt to astonish the Queen or her BoKama and the Theraxl people, we could end the quest and begin our own journeys. Hivelt desired to live out his days on Ikthe. Naraxthel desired a child with his Esra. Natheka hoped to win the heart of his heart mate, and by the looks of things, was not too distant from his goal.

But I? I desired to be left in peace to study the archives, yes, but also to solve the mysterious deaths of Theraxl babes and in so doing, wipe the ache from my shifted heart.

I lied to my brethren. Nay, to my entire people.

For I had found my heart mate when I was but a child. A group of young hunters and myself had been summoned by one of their dams to help gather in the grain harvest. We complied with eager haste, as fresh-hulled grain would reap a loaf of fresh-baked sister bread that very eve.

We sat in the dam's home, dipping our bread into fire oil and jesting with one another, when the dam brought her infant into the room to feed her.

The hunters turned away, bored by such a domestic scene, but I stood and approached, something drawing my curiosity.

The dam smiled and held the babe out to me, proud to share the beauty of her newly born sister. Uncertain, I held out my arms and looked into the innocent black eyes of the little female. She pursed her lips and gurgled, and when I gave her my finger to hold, she grasped it with strength.

Without warning, my heart began its painful clutching, and I returned the sweet child to her mother and ran out of the home.

Stumbling into the fields, I endured the transition of the heart from its heart-home, confused and in pain. But the next morning bore two glorious suns and a lightness in my heart never experienced before or since. With my father away on a hunt and my mother long passed, I had no one to tell of the miracle.

How could it be? The baby sister, innocent infant, had stirred my childish heart. When we reached adulthood, she may choose to be my heart mate and we would live together, never to be parted. I pondered how to share this remarkable news with the little female's dam when I heard the screams and moans from their house.

Running to see what troubled them, I learned that the infant burial disease had struck in the night and taken my heart mate with it.

On that night, the bright-eyed and strong little female had died, and so too had the Holy Goddesses of Shegoshel.

VELMA's harsh alarm sounded in my helmet.

"The array has been breached," she said. "Make way to Naraxthel's ship."

My memories slipped into oblivion, and I replaced them with thoughts of war.

60

Natheka

"I have taken the liberty to activate hDEDs on all existing pods," VELMA said to our group at large. "Until the threat has been identified. The breach took place in the southern hemisphere. If it stays on its current trajectory, it will land at Esra's original landing site. Analyzing data, please standby."

Even though I sat in an unconcerned pose in Naraxthel's ship, my every muscle tensed. We hadn't had time to craft a trap or a diversion for the Ikma's WarGuard. And Naraxthel had yet to explain what he knew. I stole a glance at Amity's face; her mouth quirked, and her eyes darted among the occupants of Naraxthel's ship. She appeared to be thinking. As ever, her intelligence beguiled me, but now memories of our brief time together threatened to distract me from everything.

"We have to separate," she said, her voice startling us in the silence.

"If it's your queen's ship, then we can't be found together," she said. Then she looked at Esra. "And I'm sorry, but it's probably safer if you leave Naraxthel for now. As long as the Ikma still doesn't know about everyone else, she's under the impression that Naraxthel is here alone."

Esra bit her lip and refused to look up at her heart mate. Naraxthel frowned while a deep groove appeared in his forehead.

"This is wise," he said. "I would keep knowledge of the humans from the Ikma forever."

"How do we know she did not torture the BoKama?" I asked, my voice steady though my heart in the new place rocked with anxiety.

"VELMA, have you identified what crossed the array field?" Esra said.

"The specifications match that of the ship BoKama piloted only days ago," VELMA said. "However, my thermal imaging is unable to identify occupants within," she said. "Do I have your permission to infiltrate the ship's systems?"

All of the humans looked at us. Where I would wait for Naraxthel, he nodded his head to me. As I had been most opposed to VELMA's abilities, he deferred to my judgment.

"Yes," I said and grasped Amity's hand.

"There are twelve occupants of the ship," VELMA said. "Ten ik-thekal, the Ikma and BoKama. BoKama's vital systems appear normal."

"She brings her entire WarGuard," I said with dismay. When I looked at Naraxthel, he had bowed his head.

"BoKama took the Ikma to Esra's landing site for a reason," Pattee said. "What is it?"

"My ship is gone," Esra said when Amity raised a brow. "BoKama herself destroyed it in order to hide the evidence of my landing."

"Naraxthel's ship was not far from there," I said. "Mayhap the BoKama intends for him to return to the area."

"No," Hivelt said. "It is too far from the Black Heart Mountains to be reasonable that he would have left it there."

"But he's sent sight-captures from the meadow to the Moon Shield," Raxthezana said. "The Ikma knows he has spanned the whole of the northern region without his ship."

"BoKama could have taken the Ikma to Moon Shield," Pattee said. "Or the Magnetic Burst Field. She cannot freely communicate with any of us planetside; her choice was intentional," Pattee said. "What is the reason?"

Pattee stared at Naraxthel, and I cocked my head when I looked at him. When he looked up, his frown had deepened. Raxthezana, sitting at Naraxthel's right toward the cabin of the ship, leaned slightly to Naraxthel and flared his nostrils. He, too, frowned but said nothing.

Naraxthel released Esra's hand and folded his arms. He looked toward the sky and mouthed words, then spoke.

"VELMA, play the sight-capture that BoKama sent to the Ikma the night that BoKama discovered Esra's pod those many moons ago."

Curious, I leaned forward. Naraxthel seldom spoke of the time he had spent at Esra's pod, and to hear that BoKama had sent the Ikma a sight-capture of it ... I scarce could maintain my composure.

The ship's monitor lit up, and a grainy film appeared. Naraxthel stood proud among tall grasses, his helmet under his arm, and he looked toward the eye of a sight-capture. BoKama's voice rose from the video. "If you and I play a deep game, we might depose our Ikma and restore the true ways of Theraxl. But we need each other."

Lightheaded, I sat back in my seat, watching in fascination as Esra's face rippled from astonishment to horror to dismay. I felt Amity's grip tighten on my fingers. I followed my gaze to Pattee whose face remained still ... no frown, no raised brows.

Naraxthel in the sight-capture spoke. "How have you deceived the Ikma into believing your undying loyalty?" His brows angled while his mouth turned down at his question.

"I mean what I say when I say it; it is as simple as that," the BoKama answered.

"How can I know you won't travel back to Ikshe telling tales of my treachery?" Naraxthel said. One could see the calculation in his eyes as he stared at the sight-camera's eye. Had BoKama worn it on her face? Perhaps in a headdress?

"Ikma stole my Consort's affection from me fifteen cycles ago. I have not forgiven her," BoKama said.

Naraxthel folded his arms. "What of your guards?" He nodded toward what I presumed to be BoKama's ship.

"There are no guards," she said. "I came alone."

In the sight-capture, Naraxthel stared for a long rotik before he spoke again. "I will help you."

The sight-capture ended.

Puzzled, I waited to hear Naraxthel's explanation. There was no sight-capture of Esra, or her pod in the clip that VELMA played. Nay, no mention of the soft traveler was made at all.

"BoKama chose Esra's old landing site," Naraxthel said. "Because it means the next step in our plan has been set in motion," he said. "I will be at Esra's meadow when they land because BoKama has managed to get the Ikma off planet. There is but one thing that would lure her to do so."

The silence in his ship suffocated us. Wild thoughts ran through my mind; I couldn't imagine what might possess Esra's. She had gone still.

"I did not tell Esra, nor any of you," he said. "Because if you had been captured prior to this day, you must not know that I was aware BoKama had sent this." He pointed to the monitor where VELMA had played the sight-capture for us. "It must appear that she had betrayed me to the Ikma. Upon your theoretical capture, the Ikma could have shown you this conversation, and you would have seen the

BoKama in a new light. As it stands, it plays into the Ikma's belief that BoKama has cultivated a traitor on purpose and remains steadfast as Ikma's second-in-command. It is hard enough for a Theraxl to disguise their emotions when we can smell them on each other's skin. But humans hiding their surprise and dismay? Impossible."

Amity left my side and hastened to kneel before Esra whose white face had gone paler. "Breathe, Esra," Amity said. "This is bigger than you. Bigger than all of us."

I nodded though I remained frowning. Amity had the right of it.

"BoKama kept the camera trained on your face, Naraxthel," Pattee said. "Was there anything in the area that she didn't want the Ikma to see?"

Esra gasped and tipped forward, wiping a tear away.

"My ship," she said. "My ship was right there. VELMA showed me the two of them talking, but I could only hear bits and pieces of the conversation." Esra looked at Naraxthel, his face stark in the ship's interior lighting. The tendons in his neck stood out, and the muscles in his jaw feathered. "I locked them out because from what I could hear, it sounded like he was agreeing to tell the BoKama and his queen about my presence on the planet."

Esra's voice rasped as she continued. Amity held her hands and stroked them.

"But they both assured me that was not the case," she said. "And if the Ikma is still in the dark about the humans, then I have to trust Naraxthel because that is what he promised me. That she would never find out." Esra looked up at him, and his neck muscles relaxed when he lowered his head to stare into her eyes.

"As of yet, the Ikma does not know of the humans," Naraxthel said in a quiet voice and caressed Esra's chin. "And so it shall remain."

Esra blinked and then looked up at him.

"What is the one thing that would lure the Ikma here?" she asked.

Naraxthel sighed and looked at our expectant faces.

"Performing raxfathe on a celebrated iktheka," he said, his voice hard. "On the Hunting Grounds."

Raxthezana stood with a growl. Hivelt snapped the piece of wood he had been whittling.

"When the Ikma is lulled into complacence at my capture," Naraxthel said. "And believes me to be incapacitated, then BoKama and I will strike," he said. "We will make short work of it."

Esra covered her mouth with a hand and squeezed her eyes shut.

"You are prepared to take the life of the Ikma Scabmal Kama?" Raxthezana said. "And expect the WarGuard to stand idle as you do so?"

"We did not foresee that the Ikma would bring the entire Guard," Naraxthel said. "Nevertheless, we did not intend to spill the Ikma's blood unless in self-defense. We would bind her and demand the Tribunal."

"You will not get the chance, now," said Raxthezana. "You court your deaths with this folly."

My mind raced through Naraxthel and BoKama's plan. It was dangerous and foolhardy. And it lacked a single crucial component: they both had underestimated the ferocity of the Ikma Scabmal Kama's rage, mistrust, and insanity. I recalled the scratches on BoKama's face.

"I propose an amendment to your subterfuge," I said.

"How?" he asked. "The lot of you are presumed dead. There is no other way," he said. "We cannot all approach BoKama's ship."

"Let me wear your armor," I said. "The rest of you activate stealth mode and hide among the rocks at the meadow's edge. I will refuse to go inside, forcing the WarGuard to come out. When they restrain me, then you attack. Mayhap the Ikma will command BoKama to fire upon us with her ship, but we will melt into the ikfal. We may ask VELMA to assist, by jamming BoKama's weapons system or creating a diversion. Failing that, the Ikma will retreat to Ikshe and plot with BoKama to try something different."

"Why must you wear my armor?" Naraxthel said. "Could I not do just as you proposed?"

"The Ikma and BoKama must remain unbalanced," I said. "The Ikma plans to kill BoKama upon your capture. Do you not suspect as much? Perhaps BoKama entertained the Ikma with plans of revealing your traitorous heart, but the Ikma will have decided that the BoKama cannot be trusted. She has already done so," I said. "BoKama told me she is no longer welcome in the Ikma's private chambers. I suspect the Ikma has already decided to murder BoKama, and only waits to choose a time." I glanced at the others who listened with fierce attention, their brows furrowed and mouths frowning. Amity and Esra held hands as Amity sat at Esra's feet. Pattee's arms were folded, and Hivelt sat with his fists at his knees. Raxthezana still stood, the scowl on his face pronounced.

"I will enlist VELMA to track the Ikma's life signs," I said. "And if it seems she is about to put BoKama down, I will demand my helmet to be removed. BoKama will be suitably surprised, and this will convince the Ikma that BoKama too had been betrayed."

"You desire to preserve the BoKama's life," Raxthezana said. "Let us hope the deception shall work."

"That is my prayer to the Goddesses," I said. "I wish you had allowed us to join in your subtlety, Naraxthel," I said. "We would carry the burden with you."

"Ik," he said. "But it was not my sole burden to carry. You have the right of it, though," he said. "The Ikma will not so easily let BoKama speak of treason without demanding a high price."

"With the WarGuards killed, the Ikma must also keep BoKama alive," I said. "Unless she has learned to pilot a ship."

"Incoming message from BoKama's ship," VELMA said. "I advise all to remain silent except Naraxthel," she said.

Naraxthel met my gaze and nodded. I nodded back, and when I glanced at Amity's face, I spied a tear had tracked its way to her chin.

61

Amity

The politics dizzied me, but Natheka's logic made sense of most of it. Of course, he would volunteer to do something insanely dangerous just when I had decided I was ready to do the heart mate thing. And after I had discovered a transcendent sexual experience with him. I sighed.

As predicted, the BoKama had invited Naraxthel to her ship. He explained that several landquakes had altered the lay of the land, and that it would take a half-zatik for him to travel to his ship and fly to the area. She assured him that the Ikma had no knowledge of her arrival on the planet and that he had time.

Pattee, Esra and I huddled together in silence as Raxthezana and Hivelt paced inside the ship. Naraxthel and Natheka had retreated to private quarters to trade armor, and when they came back out, Naraxthel sat in the pilot's seat.

"Strap in," he said. "We fly to Esra's meadow."

354   VICKY L. HOLT

The flight remained silent; all of us were lost in thought. I worried the most about Esra, though. She looked like a wounded animal, and I knew wounded animals.

"Ah, see the region has changed," Naraxthel said. He pushed two buttons, and the monitor showed the land below. I didn't know what it looked like before, but Esra did.

"Schist," she said. "I barely recognize it."

"I cannot land near the BoKama's ship," he said. "There is another place nearby."

The thrumming and rumble of the ship's engines, wings and landing gear working in tandem to bring us down set my teeth on edge, but with the fate of everyone in the vehicle hanging in the balance, I was less afraid of crashing. That was something.

A solid bump jarred my teeth together, and the engines powered down.

"Humans," Raxthezana said. "BoKama's ship is just beyond that stand of trees. Stay inside the ship no matter what, do you understand?"

Hivelt nodded his agreement with Raxthezana's words and held Pattee in his stern gaze.

I nodded, feeling like I was getting a scolding for sneaking cookies.

"We will do as we see fit," Pattee said, her eyes unwavering as she stared at the four armored males. "As it impacts your safety, we will stay undetected," she said before Raxthezana could argue. "But if the hunters fall, then we will rise and claim our spoils."

Goosebumps erupted all over me at her words, and I saw Hivelt's eyes darken when a grim smile overtook his expression.

Apparently, Hivelt's heart had chosen wisely.

I watched them disembark, and when the alien in the red armor looked back at me, I lifted my hand in a small wave. He nodded, and the hatch closed behind them.

Releasing a breath, I unstrapped and hopped down.

"What do we do next?" I asked. Esra and Pattee both stood, and we met in the center of the ship.

"We'd better outline the rules of engagement with VELMA," Pattee said.

Esra nodded. "She can't act against protocols."

"Everything she does is related to protecting us, and in many respects, our heart mates," Pattee said. "But only within limits. As an example, she can't use weapons against anyone or anything unless our lives are in imminent danger."

"And she might get ideas on how she can help, but she doesn't just jump in," Esra said. "Particularly with accessing the alien technology. Plus, it takes time for her to learn it," she said. "When a rokhura broke my ankle, VELMA couldn't utilize the med bay yet," she said and smiled at me. "Thank god she figured it out to help you."

I returned Esra's smile. "Yeah, we had just barely learned about this organ in the puddle bird," I said. "Since VELMA's program is machine-learning, she's basically just piecing information together over time."

"Exactly," Esra said. "She's not just about poop."

"But she is always about preserving human life," Pattee said.

Nodding, I sighed and folded my arms and stood looking at the table before us. I knew it would only be a matter of minutes before we all grew restless and anxious.

"So. As long as we stay here, her hands are tied," I said and reached out to slide my hand along the table's surface. "We could patch in and listen, though, right?"

Pattee wore a half-smile, and Esra's eyes twinkled.

"What?" I reviewed what I had said.

As long as we stay here, her hands are tied.

"Oh," I said and backed up. "What you're thinking? That's only a good idea if our guys are in *serious* danger. There is a lot of forest between here and there," I said, pointing in the direction I thought they had gone. "And I'm no hunter. I'm a liability."

Esra and Pattee's small smiles did nothing to ease my anxiety.

"You guys *estan locas* if you think I am going out there and risking my other arm, or God forbid, both my legs," I said and licked my lips. "What is love but a layer of trust, huh? We need to trust our, uh, heart mates." I pointed to Pattee. "You. I know Hivelt thinks you are an Amazon woman," I said. "Hell, I think you're an Amazon. But he would be so pissed if you left this ship and got injured. You know it's true."

Pattee's smile faded a little bit, and she shrugged, looking out the glass.

"VELMA," I said, peeking at Esra and Pattee. "Patch us into the hunters' comms, and any audio you can get from the Ikma's ship."

I nodded and chose a seat, hiking myself up into it. "Damn these boys are tall," I said to myself.

"You know it is true," Natheka was saying. "You saw how Pattee bristled when you said the humans were fragile."

"I did not say they were fragile," Naraxthel said. "I said I was trying to think of the most delicate way to describe something that is most indelicate."

One of the hunters snorted, and I shifted in my seat. Face flushing, I hoped they weren't about to launch into the raxshe and raxma ceremony that I had chosen to abstain from learning about. Yet.

"We can hear you," Esra said, and the males' deep chuckling erupted over the ship's communication system.

"It is nice to hear your voice," Naraxthel said. "And I am at peace that you are safe in my ship. In this way can we plot without distraction."

Pattee shook her head and frowned.

"When we have more information, we will welcome your blades," Hivelt said. "The Ikma cripples us with her madness. Until you have seen the raxfathe with your own eyes …." His voice trailed off.

"We approach the meadow," Natheka's voice announced, but it was as if his breath caressed my ear. "Continue listening but say nothing. VELMA will advise us."

"Okay," I said, surprising myself when my voice cracked. Natheka's low chuckle sent heat straight through my core, and I clasped my hands together to control their shaking.

"Why does it take so long?" a sultry feminine voice powered over the comms. I sat up in my chair, and Esra and Pattee took seats, their lighthearted smiles erased in one breath.

BoKama's soothing voice replied. "You have seen the sight-captures that our handsome traitor supplies," she said. "Trees uprooted. Rivers changing course. Moon Shield collapsed into a heap," she said. "This area likewise has been reshaped by the Goddesses' hands."

"This doesn't feel right," the Ikma said. "Until Naraxthel kneels before me with his hands tied behind his back, I will not feel safe."

"I know, dear Ikma," BoKama said. "Remember the eunuch found that old covenant, the original source of raxfathe. Let its promise ease your brow."

"Give me to drink," the Ikma said. Silence for a minute.

"Tell me again what is written in the covenant," the Ikma said.

"And when he who commits treason does lie with his mouth, then shall his tongue be removed, that he may lie only to himself," BoKama recited. "And when his bowel does absorb the filth of his treason, then shall his bowel be released of its filth, that he may be rendered clean from within."

My eyes stung, and I gripped the sides of the chair. Esra and Pattee were likewise paralyzed at BoKama's words, spoken with such ease and familiarity.

"And when the traitor has been made clean, then will his bowel be filled with sweet meats, until he is full of the harvest of truth. Then will his heart be ready to accept the love of the Ikma Scabmal Kama," BoKama uttered. I thought I detected a trace of disgust, but it could have been my own emotions coloring her words. I didn't think I could stand to hear much more.

"Say it!" The Ikma said.

We heard BoKama clear her throat. "And the love of the Ikma Scabmal Kama is written upon the blade of rule, and when her love pierces the traitor's heart, then will he know the love of the Kama, and she will place her love upon his lips, and drink of his love ...."

"Stop it!" Esra shouted. "Stop transmission, VELMA."

Her outburst startled me, and the now silent ship felt like an ocean of space. Esra had tears streaming down her face. She wiped at them fiercely but finally hopped off her chair and hurried to the hygiene facility.

Pattee's somber expression masked a glint in her eyes. She was my best friend; I knew her better than anyone in the universe. And I knew what she was thinking.

"You'll get your chance," I said. "I know it. But if we go out there, we won't have anyone else to rely on except VELMA and ourselves," I said with intensity. "You are the bravest and strongest woman I know.

But please also be smart about this. We can't get in the way of the hunters," I said and stared her down until she looked away. "We'll tell VELMA to let us know if things look like they're going sideways. If that happens, I'll be the first one out that damn door, okay? Because damn if I don't think Natheka is the most handsome, funny and brave guy. He's smart as hell, and he's mine. And I know without a doubt you feel the same way about Hivelt."

Pattee buzzed her lips together and threw her head back.

"I hate this," she said. "I hate that their lives are run by that ruthless bitch. Why can't they just storm the ship and kill her?"

When Pattee looked back at me I was surprised to see a sparkle of tears in her eyes. I walked up to her and grabbed her biceps. This wasn't like her; she was worried about her Hivelt and the others.

"Because ruthless people always have backup plans," I said. "That's what Natheka was getting at earlier. The Ikma's brand of evil assumes everyone, *everyone*, is as brutal and fucked up as they are," I said, my language raising Pattee's brows. "She probably has ordnance the BoKama doesn't know about," I said. 'She probably has poisoned chocolates in her pocket, or hell, I don't know. Maybe she implanted the WarGuards with explosives, too. When you're at that level of mistrust, you prepare for every possible contingency."

Pattee's muscles contracted under my hands, and her brows drew together so much they almost touched.

"Shit," she said. "I bet you're right. Dammit," she whispered and extracted herself from my grip. She paced.

"VELMA, scan every iota of the BoKama's ship and its occupants," she said. "Look for anomalies in measurements, like panels that don't match up with openings, or extra thick walls. Use your mass spectrometer to detect fresh handprints on all compartments and doors and what's that stuff called—" Esra interrupted.

"Use gas chromatography electron capture to identify ammonium nitrate, ammonium picrate, cyclonite or ethylenediamine dinitrate," Esra finished. Damn. Leave it to the geologist miner to remember the ingredients to a bomb.

"I'm sorry, but I am accessing BoKama's ship wirelessly," VELMA said. "I do not have access to my mass spectrometer or gas chromatography electron capture devices."

I bit my lip, my heart racing now that I'd unleashed a previously unspoken terror into the radio waves.

Pattee rubbed her eyes, and Esra scratched her chin.

Dammit.

I sucked on my lips for a second then swallowed.

"VELMA, how close do our helmets have to be for the mass spectrometers to work?" I said. Pattee raised her eyes to meet mine, her mouth in a thin line.

"I can scan with eighty-five percent accuracy from eight meters," VELMA said.

I sighed and wrapped my arms around myself, squeezing tight for a full twenty seconds.

"Alright," I said. "Let's blow this popsicle joint."

62

Natheka

My brethren activated their camouflage and hung back in the ikfal when I broke through the trees and approached the BoKama's ship. I tried to mimic Naraxthel's bold swagger and then stopped several veltiks from the open hatch.

When I didn't enter, BoKama hailed me via Naraxthel's helmet.

"Come, Naraxthel," she said. "Let us break bread together, just as we did before."

Naraxthel's voice entered soft in my helmet.

"We never did such; BoKama tries to give me clues," he said. "I do not understand; we discussed this scenario. I am not taken by surprise."

"Then she tries to warn you that things are not playing out as you had discussed," I said on my private channel. "She worries about the presence of the WarGuard."

Knowing that I appeared on a monitor in her ship, I gestured with my arm that she should come out, and I bent to pluck a tall piece of grass. I shredded it and looked about the meadow, noting how the rocky border had collapsed and trees from the southern edge had been uprooted.

Heart tripping forward, I turned to the ramp to see BoKama stride down it and approach. Rather than her light armor, she wore a shimmering silver gown and the ornamental headdress with orange feathers and a central purple jewel. It was the costume of ritual and celebration. I swallowed.

"Naraxthel," she said with a wide smile and reached for my hands.

When I did not take them, but rather wound the grass around one of my claws, she dropped her hands.

Sweat ran down my body inside my armor. We had not expected the BoKama to exit the ship. As soon as I opened my mouth to speak, BoKama and the others would hear my voice and know of my deception.

"Open your comm, Natheka," Naraxthel said in my ear. "I will speak through your helmet."

Using eye blinks, I opened my comm.

"BoKama, what news of the Ikma?" Naraxthel asked.

I stilled my hands and focused on his words, careful to match my movements to his conversation. Were the circumstances not so dire, 'twould be a diversion, a trick to play among friends.

"The Ikma sleeps in her chambers," BoKama said. "The maikshel gave her a sleeping draught."

"Then you are not expected soon?" Naraxthel said.

"Nay, I have time," she said. "Come to the ship and be refreshed. Remove your helmet and we will plot the Ikma's assassination."

"But what of the woaiquovelt?" Naraxthel asked. I gestured a vague wave behind me, unsure where Naraxthel was going with the conversation.

"When we succeed in killing the queen upon her throne as her most loyal WarGuard looks on, we will have no need of more woaiquovelt," BoKama said. "We have enough and to spare in the coffers. When I sit as the new Ikma Scabmal Kama, I will open the coffers. We will not have need to risk the lives of more of our brave hunters. Not five. Not ten. Not more."

"Then my fellows will have died in vain," Naraxthel said. I bowed my head and lowered my shoulders.

On my private channel, Naraxthel whispered. "You are correct. Her words indicate the ten WarGuard on board. We must draw them out."

"Come to Ikshe now," BoKama said. "Leave your ship here. Hide in my hold; the orbit guards never inspect my ship, and I will smuggle you into the fortress. You may slay the Ikma in her sleep and hide in my private chambers. At length I will return to Ikthe to spread the queen's ashes, and you will suddenly appear out of the wilds of Certain Death. Even without the woaiquovelt or Holy Waters, you will enjoy a hero's welcome and return to Ikshe with honor."

"You have thought of everything," Naraxthel said. "There is nothing left but to do it."

I placed my fists on my hips, unsure if I should walk toward the ship or wait.

"Come, Naraxthel," BoKama said.

Amity's voice entered my ear with a start, and I almost jumped.

"Do not go in, Natheka," she said. "Stall her, or sing, or dance like a fool, but do not go in."

Naraxthel cleared his throat so loudly that BoKama cocked her head.

"I look forward to breaking sister-bread with you," Naraxthel said. But I did not move. What was Amity playing at? I resisted the urge to scan the perimeter of the meadow.

"VELMA is scanning BoKama's ship," Amity said. "Just wait. We should know in a minute or two if there are any surprises besides the WarGuard."

BoKama's smile faltered when my boots didn't move, and I didn't reach for her hand.

"And did you bring other refreshment aside from sister-bread?" Naraxthel asked, his voice strained. "Have you a tech-slave with you? You might bring the food out that we may partake under the light of the sister suns."

Belatedly, I gestured to the ship.

Sweating copious amounts, I resisted the urge to remove my helmet.

BoKama looked back at the ship, then at me, her brows raised high and her mouth bearing a lopsided smile.

"Yes, I have, mm, sweet meats," she stammered, and I caught a whiff of tallow berry.

Tallow berries smelled sweet but tasted like wax. BoKama lied. Of course, the entire scenario was a lie, but confusion muddled my thoughts.

"And an organ pie and fruited wine," she said, gesturing once more to the opening of the ship.

"I find my hunger grows by the tik," Naraxthel said. "Let us feast. Out here."

I rubbed the armor protecting my abdomen and waved at the ground.

"One minute more, Natheka," Amity's quiet voice touched my ear.

BoKama dropped her beckoning hand and rested it on her hip. Out of patience, her brows drew down, mirroring her frown.

"Do you wish me to carry you up the ramp?" she asked between gritted teeth.

Shaking my head no, I tapped Naraxthel's helmet as if to say I was thinking.

"It is the fatigue of the hunt, honored BoKama," Naraxthel said with a forced chuckle. "It is fortunate you are not a rokhura, else I would be bitten in two."

I held up two fingers and then made a fist, punching the air. Scratching the chin of the red armor, I then used my hands to play-act a scene with one hand running on two legs while the other formed a giant snapping jaw and chased it.

Naraxthel gave a quiet laugh that sounded much like crying.

The sound of metal crashing within BoKama's ship startled both of us.

"Hold, Naraxthel," she said and rushed to climb the ramp. She disappeared inside.

With eye blinks, I disabled my exterior mic.

"Amity, what news?"

Static in my helmet.

"What kathe fodder are you playing at, Natheka?" Naraxthel said, his voice angry. "BoKama is confused and suspicious now!"

"Thus ensuring her safety with the Ikma, Naraxthel," I said, my own voice serious. "Amity said VELMA scanned the BoKama's ship," I said. Cocking my head, I marveled that when she had spoken within my helmet, it didn't broadcast. VELMA must have manipulated the vocal controls.

"Amity said what?" Hivelt asked.

"VELMA is scanning the ship," I said. "I do not know why or how. Or where the humans are."

"Amity," Hivelt said. "Where are you?"

"Safe," she said. "I am one *hundred* percent safe."

"I was unable to find altered compartments or discrepancies," VELMA interrupted. "Nor traces of common chemicals found in Earth-derived explosives."

"What do you mean Earth-derived?" Amity asked.

"Given the existence of previously unknown substances such as Ikthe's woaiquovelt or recently discovered Galvanite in the Pollack-Custer belt," VELMA said. "It is possible that I am not detecting the presence of volatile chemicals."

One of the humans cursed in their language.

"Pattee," Hivelt growled into the comms. "Where are you?"

"Monitoring BoKama's and Ikma's conversation," she said. "Would you like to listen?"

Before any of us could answer, the conversation played in our helmets.

"... cannot be sane in the head," BoKama said. "You were right, this feels wrong."

"You reek of suspicion," the Ikma said. "Persuade him to enter, and the WarGuards will subdue him," the Ikma said. "Drag him if you must. Did you not apply the liquid to your hands?"

"Bingo," Pattee's voice echoed in my helmet. "BoKama's hands."

I tilted my head to the other side.

"What does this word 'Bingo' mean?" I asked.

"Natheka!" Amity's voice overpowered the audio in my helmet, and I slapped it by my ear. To outsiders I must appear the idiot, shaking my head and hitting myself.

"Please, Natheka," her voice softened. "Walk away. Turn around and disappear into the forest. I'm out here in the woods," she said. "Come to me."

Without thinking, I spun to see behind me, but all I saw were the trees and brush of the ikfal. No Amity, no hunters.

"Draw the guards out," Naraxthel said again.

"Can you not see his reluctance to enter the ship?" BoKama said, her voice tight. "If I push him, he will know of my betrayal. If we send the WarGuard out, he will know of my betrayal. Let us leave now and maintain his misplaced trust in me!"

"What does this misplaced trust mean to you, dear sister?" Ikma said. She sounded calm, but every Theraxl in her company knew otherwise.

Still in their sights, I wandered as if distracted, but edged closer to the tree line. I bent to pull another blade of grass and stood, facing the ramp.

"It means nothing to me save as a service to you," BoKama said. "He acts strangely in my presence. Perhaps I have lost his trust already."

I imagined her bowing to the Ikma in obeisance, and I clenched my teeth, but I took two strides away from the ship, hoping its occupants were engaged with the BoKama's performance.

"The Ikma will send her WarGuard out any jotik," Naraxthel said. "Ready for combat. The farther you pull her guards into the ikfal, the more the trees will obscure our ambush."

"BoKama, he retreats to the ikfal," Ikma said. "I have done with your childish scheme. WarGuard? Fetch him to me."

If I wanted to preserve Naraxthel's honor, as well as the lives of my friends, I would stand and face the guards alone, only allowing the swordplay to press me back into the trees where my brothers could aid in secret.

When the first guard cleared the hatch, I drew my Raxtheza.

"You're too far," Naraxthel said. "Fall back, that we may help you."

The second guard exited. I unsheathed my second weapon.

"The humans never disclosed their location," I said. "What would Naraxthel do? I wear his armor with pride."

More than one *kathe* echoed in my helmet. A third guard marched down the ramp.

"I promise you," Amity said. "We are safe. As long as you stay away from the BoKama, you will be safe, too. Head into the woods so the other hunters can fight."

"Naraxthel would not rely upon others to fight his battle," I said. Tightening my grip on my Raxtheza, I watched the first guard who held his weapon and approached me with caution.

"This is folly," Raxthezana said. "Let us reveal our presence and go to war!"

"If war is what you want, that will do it," Naraxthel said. "The Ikma will retreat to Ikshe and assemble an army of ikthekal to descend upon as at once."

The first guard lunged at me, and I deflected his strike with my left blade. Naraxthel's words rang true. My brothers must remain obscured from the Ikma's sight.

Resolved, I let the guards advance, defending against their strokes but backpedaling as I did so.

"What is this childish game?" the Ikma cried. "Get you out there and restrain him!"

My swords clashing with my foes, I saw a blur of black armor at the ship's hatch. The Ikma had sent the others. As energy flooded my systems, grim pleasure overtook me. I was born to this.

Stroke after stroke, I fought off the guards within my reach, but even Naraxthel would search for better ground from which to defend. At first opportunity, I dipped between the trees and spun again, having drawn the first three of the guards into the ikfal.

Hivelt's low chuckle rumbled in my earpiece.

"Now we give sport," he said.

63

Amity

"Natheka is going to kill me when he finds out we left the ship," I said under my voice. I crouched in a stand of trees approximately seven meters from the back of BoKama's ship, and let VELMA do her invisible work. Patched into the various conversations, I kept the volume low so I could remain aware of my surroundings.

The last thing I needed was one of Predator Planet's wild beasts attacking me from behind. Which is why Naraxthel's tech-slave was at my side, under VELMA's control. Pattee and Esra might kill me for *that*, when I thought about it. Putting an AI in a robot body? Pretty sure there was a song for that.

Peering between the trees, I could only make out portions of Bokama's shimmering dress and the red armor Natheka wore.

"Even without the woaiquovelt or Holy Waters, you will enjoy a hero's welcome and return to Ikshe with honor," I heard BoKama say.

"You have thought of everything," Naraxthel said. "There is nothing left but to do it."

I frowned. Naraxthel had managed to transmit his voice from Natheka's helmet.

"Come, Naraxthel," BoKama said.

Panicking, I realized I had to say something.

"Do not go in, Natheka," I said. "Stall her, or sing, or dance like a fool, but do not go in."

From my place behind the ship, I could see that the red armored legs didn't move. *Gracias a dios.*

"VELMA is scanning BoKama's ship," I said. "Just wait. We should know in a minute or two if there are any surprises aside from the WarGuard."

"And did you bring other refreshment aside from sister-bread?" Naraxthel asked, his voice sounding stressed. "Have you a *tech-slave* with you? You might bring the food out that we may partake under the light of the sister suns."

My head jerked up. Did Naraxthel see me? Did he know about the tech-slave? I was in so much trouble. It was like when I was a kid, all over again. I gripped the tree bark tighter, willing VELMA's scan to go faster. I couldn't see Esra or Pattee, but I knew they were positioned such that VELMA could get a complete scan.

"Yes, I have, mm, sweet meats," she stammered. "And an organ pie and fruited wine."

"I find my hunger grows by the tik," Naraxthel said. "Let us feast. Out here."

It felt like buckets of sweat were pouring off my body. The BoKama had to know something was up, and I waited for the Ikma to erupt any second.

"One minute more, Natheka," I said, hoping to convey a calm I didn't feel.

"Do you wish me to carry you up the ramp?" the BoKama said, and it sounded like she was furious.

"It is the fatigue of the hunt, honored BoKama," Naraxthel said with a forced chuckle. "It is fortunate you are not a rokhura, else I would be bitten in two."

I still couldn't see more than the lower half of BoKama and had a partial view of Natheka's legs.

A noise reverberated from inside the ship, and I froze.

"Hold, Naraxthel," BoKama said. Her skirts swished and she disappeared up the ramp leaving Natheka alone.

"Amity, what news?"

I went to answer, but the tech-slave bumped my helmet with its robot hand. "What?"

It pointed to the ground behind me. I spun and saw the biggest, ugliest, centipede-like creature headed straight for me.

"Amity said what?" Hivelt asked.

Shit.

"VELMA is scanning the ship," Natheka said. "I do not know why or how. Or where the humans are."

"Amity," Hivelt said. "Where are you?"

I watched the arthropod approach with its undulating slither-like movement.

"Safe," I said. "I am one *hundred* percent safe."

Backing into the tree, I wished it were a forest-teeth one, if only for a second.

"I was unable to find altered compartments or discrepancies," VELMA interrupted. "Nor traces of common chemicals found in Earth-derived explosives."

"What do you mean Earth-derived?" I asked.

"Given the existence of previously unknown substances such as Ikthe's woaiquovelt or recently discovered Galvanite in the Pollack-Custer belt," VELMA said. "It is possible that I am not detecting the presence of volatile chemicals."

Pattee cussed.

"Pattee," Hivelt growled into the comms. "Where are you?"

"Monitoring BoKama's and Ikma's conversation," she said. "Would you like to listen?"

"... cannot be sane in the head," BoKama said. "You were right, this feels wrong."

"You reek of suspicion," the Ikma complained. "Persuade him to enter, and the WarGuards will subdue him," the Ikma said. "Drag him if you must. Did you not apply the liquid to your hands?"

"Bingo," Pattee's voice reverbed in my helmet. "BoKama's hands."

When the centipede, er, millipede, was close enough, I stomped on its head, and the tech-slave mimicked me by stomping its middle. The arthropod died. Natheka would too if BoKama touched him. Or the WarGuards.

"What does this word 'Bingo' mean?" Natheka asked.

"Natheka!" I said. Summoning all the love I had in my heart for him, I continued. "Please, Natheka. Walk away. Turn around and disappear into the forest. I'm out here in the woods," I said. "Come to me."

Watching his legs, I saw him spin to look behind himself. I willed him to run. To get out of there. But he was a hunter, a warrior. And I knew he would never back down from a fight.

"Can you not see his reluctance to enter the ship?" BoKama said, her voice tight inside my helmet. "If I push him, he will know of my betrayal. If we send the WarGuard out, he will know of my betrayal. Let us leave now and maintain his misplaced trust in me!"

"What does this misplaced trust mean to you, dear sister?" Ikma said.

Something told me her soft voice disguised a seething rage. Natheka backed up a step or two and bent to pick a blade of grass.

"It means nothing to me save as a service to you," BoKama said. "He acts strangely in my presence. Perhaps I have lost his trust already."

Two more strides. He was now standing where I had a fuller view.

"BoKama, he retreats to the ikfal," Ikma said. "I have done with your childish scheme. WarGuard? Fetch him to me."

Bark broke off under my gloved hands. I saw the black boots and black armored legs stomp down the ramp heading straight for Natheka.

Natheka, the mate of my heart, withdrew his weapon, and no one ever looked so determined, so courageous and defiant, so completely heroic than he did in that moment. If human hearts could switch places, mine would have done so right then.

"You're too far," Naraxthel said, his voice harsh and commanding. "Fall back, that we may help you."

The second guard exited. Natheka unsheathed a second weapon I hadn't noticed before.

"The humans never disclosed their location," he said. "What would Naraxthel do? I wear his armor with pride."

A chorus of *kathes* echoed in my helmet. A third guard marched down the ramp.

"I promise you," I said, trying not to sound frantic. "We are safe. As long as you stay away from the BoKama, you will be safe, too. Head into the woods so the other hunters can fight with you."

"Naraxthel would not rely upon others to fight his battle," Natheka said. I watched the first guard stalk toward Natheka with his weapon out.

"This is folly," Raxthezana said. "Let us reveal our presence and go to war!"

"If war is what you want, that will do it," Naraxthel said. His calm voice eased my fear a little. "The Ikma will retreat to Ikshe and assemble an army of Ikthekal to descend upon as at once."

Dios mio. Crossing myself, a prayer left my lips like a puff of smoke. I didn't know who was out there. My god? The regal and beautiful aliens in my dreams? Sun Goddeses? But whoever it was, I hoped they heard my plea.

The guards went after him, and his weapons sparked as he fought off their strikes with righteous fury, an avenging angel.

"What is this childish game?" the Ikma cried in my ear. "Get you out there and restrain him!"

She unleashed the rest of the guards! Natheka held his own against the three, what would he do against all of them? A blur of black boots erupted from the ship and crowded down the ramp.

I was losing sight of his red armor among the others, but it looked like he was finally in the trees. Clutching at my chest, I couldn't tear my gaze away from the onslaught. But when the rush of guards swarmed into the trees, I heard Hivelt's wicked laugh.

"Now we give sport."

"Thank the goddesses," Esra's voice entered my helmet. "It's going to be all right now. The WarGuard won't know what hit them."

A carnival of lights flashed in my IntraVisor, and the tech-slave bumped my arm.

"Warning, foreshocks detected," VELMA announced in my helmet. "Seek shelter immediately. Warning, foreshocks detected."

"What do we do?" I shouted.

"Stay calm," Pattee said. "If there's something for you to grab hold of, do it."

"Will they be okay?" I asked, my voice hitching high to my chagrin. Why couldn't I be brave like Pattee and Esra? I clung to the tree with all my might.

"Ha," Esra said. "I bet Naraxthel and Hivelt are making bets about how many guards they're going to kill."

"We can hear you," Hivelt said, and his unexpected voice ripped a crazy laugh out of my belly. And then the ground began to shake so hard, my teeth chattered.

"Alright ladies," I said, "hang onto your butts."

The quaking jostled me until I lost hold of the tree. The tech-slave remained standing, and I guessed VELMA had accessed its internal balancing system. She would be able to harness earthquake technology.

Shouts erupted in my helmet.

"I have slain two!"

"I just killed my third," another one said.

"Only one, but the other two fell into a chasm," Natheka said.

"Ik," Raxthezana said. "The same chasm claimed another."

The ground was breaking apart all around me, and the hunters were bragging about their kills. Esra was right.

"Holy Goddesses," I heard Esra exclaim. "Look at the meadow!"

I was hugging the ground. I couldn't see anything past the dead flopping arthropod and the grass in front of my helmet. But then I heard rumbling louder than the shaking ground.

Rolling onto my side, I saw BoKama's ship rising above the canopy, and then it careened in the air, turning its impressive array of guns toward where Naraxthel's ship was docked in nearby tall grasses.

"Oh no," I said.

"Schist," Esra said.

"Dammit," Pattee's voice echoed.

Guns blasting, it only took minutes before Naraxthel's ship exploded in a deafening roar. I curled into the fetal position, my ears ringing and my body still shaking from the endless tremors that rolled the ground and shook it like a tablecloth.

Squeezing my eyes shut, I felt debris raining down on my suit, and then a firm metal body landed on all fours above me, using its metal back as a shield.

If the others were calling out, I couldn't hear them above the thundering pulse in my ears. I lost track of time. I felt nauseous. Everything was rattling: my teeth, my helmet against the ground, the tech-slave's joints and limbs.

It stopped.

And I had to decide if I wanted to open my eyes.

64

Natheka

"Where are the humans?" I yelled. The infernal landquake had finally stopped after an eternity spent in hell, watching the obscene oily red and orange fire consume itself in the sky above where Naraxthel's ship used to be. I ran through the trees, heedless of the churned destruction, forging my own path to my brother's ship. "Were they in the ship, or no?"

"I am but veltiks away," Hivelt shouted. "Let us pray that VELMA warned them in time."

"VELMA, where are the humans?" I said. Every interaction I had with her played across my mind. How many times had she assured us that the humans' safety was her first loyalty?

"Unable to comply," VELMA said. "Please standby."

Fury gripped my chest, and I ran faster, leaping over a jumble of rocks. "I am coming, Amity!"

"Be at peace, Natheka," Naraxthel said in my comms. "And Hivelt, do not run into the fire."

"There will be no peace if the Ikma slayed my heart mate," I said. "Her blood will rain upon the Harvest Lands until every grain blossoms red!"

"Hold, Natheka," Raxthezana said. "I have found Pattee. She tells me they all left Naraxthel's ship well before it was destroyed."

"I'm here," Amity's voice sounded weak and shaky. "VELMA, put my dot on Natheka's visor map, or something, will you?"

I stopped running and waited for my brothers or the humans to direct me.

"VELMA told me to standby," Amity said. "I'm by a grove of trees with Naraxthel's tech-slave. I'm across the meadow from where you were first standing. Does this thing have a signal light or something?"

Turning toward the meadow at my left, I saw a band of trees, and then the tech-slave waved its arm.

All my fury and fear drained out of my boots, and I collapsed to the ground, no matter that it no longer shook. As I was on my knees anyway, I took a jotik to praise the Holy Goddesses. When I stood, I saw Amity stumble out of the trees and run toward me.

The once flat meadow was now littered with boulders and slabs of ground, as if the Goddesses had grabbed fistfuls of soil and sown it carelessly across the dale.

We tripped and climbed. We clambered and teetered across the uneven ground until we met.

"I'm alive," she said, her eyes shining and her chest rising and falling with rapid breaths.

"I am as well," I said.

She threw her arms around me and squealed, and I laughed, the turbulent emotions of the day lending it a maniacal edge.

Hoisting her up, I picked my way across the upheaval in search of the others while I held her safe within the shelter of my arms.

Raxthezana escorted a limping Pattee. Hivelt burst from the trees, his dark armor dulled in a layer of ash.

Naraxthel emerged from the ikfal at my right. "I said do not run into the fire."

Hivelt grunted and took Pattee into his arms.

Esra, covered in blood, walked out from behind a bush.

Naraxthel tore off my devil-dog helmet and strode to her.

"What happened?" he asked, gripping her shoulders.

"There was a talathel," she said and shrugged.

"But where was the other?" Hivelt asked.

"There wasn't one," Esra said. "I looked."

"You are not harmed?" Naraxthel asked.

"No, I'm fine," she said. She looked at Amity. "Just a little shaken up."

After a jotik, Amity laughed. The sound rippled and bubbled, filling my soul with its lightness. I could not help but join her, and soon all of us laughed and smiled, patting each other's backs, and sharing in the rare and precious joy of life. Life on Certain Death.

Heh. Not only was there life, but a modicum of humor now that my heart mate was with me.

65

Amity

"This is incredible," I said on an exhale. "Is this saltwater, then?"

"Yes!" Esra said. "The caves here have several saltwater pools. I theorize that periodically an ocean vent floods the caves and replenishes them. There are also freshwater springs."

Pattee, Esra, and I all sat in a cave pool having washed and destressed from the day's calamities. Two hunters waited beyond the two corridors, guarding against the agothe-faxl that purportedly roamed the tunnels here.

The soft glow of the bioluminescent jellies lit our skin while the saltwater leeched out any toxins.

"I kinda don't want to get out," Pattee said, her head resting against the pool's edge.

"It's really beautiful," I said with a sigh. "But I am going to get out. I need to clear up something with Natheka."

"Mm hm," Esra said with a wink and a smile.

"What?" I said. "I do. Things got insane and we left, uh, unfinished business."

"M'kay," Pattee said, her head still tipped, but she looked at me and winked.

"*Dios mio*, all you two ever think about is sex," I said, but I was smiling too. "Never mind we're permanently trapped on Predator Planet. Our last best hope at an ally may or may not live to see us again." I pulled up my flight suit. "Two other humans are doing God knows what, God knows where, and if the ugly dinosaurs don't kill us, the earthquakes probably will." Zipping up my suit, I grabbed my helmet and put it under my arm. "Do we call them earthquakes here? There are giant arthropods, giant beetles, apparently giant spiders, and trees that hunt for food. And … no ice cream. But do you talk about any of that? No, you don't. You wink and giggle and hug and kiss your big hulking alien mates and share secrets about ancient reproduction rituals."

A splash of water drenched my face causing me to splutter.

"What the?"

Esra laughed at Pattee who had her hands cupped and ready to splash me again.

"I don't know, Amity," she said. "You and Natheka looked awfully clean earlier today."

I glared at her until the laugh I was holding in bubbled out.

"Go," she said. "Finish your business. I'm turning into a prune, so I'll be out soon anyway."

"You're going to pay for that," I said with a fake frown.

"I'm good for it," she said.

I sighed. "I know you are. Esra?"

"Yeah?"

"Thanks for showing us this place," I said.

"It was my pleasure," she said. "I also know where we can get a mud spa treatment."

"Uh huh," I said, putting on my helmet. "I think I'll take a pass on that one." Laughter behind me made me smile.

I left the room with the cave pool and found the narrow tunnel that led to where Natheka waited in a different meadow from before. The tech-slave stood at this cave entrance. I passed Raxthezana who leaned against a huge boulder and frowned at the bottom of his boot.

"*Kathe,*" he said under his breath.

"VELMA, are you online yet?" I said and waited. Still nothing. Too bad. She could have warned him not to step in it.

Heading towards Natheka, I walked through the tall grass with caution. This meadow had only minor damage as reported by the ones who had visited before.

Natheka stood in the afternoon light, facing the wall of forest to our west. Ready to battle at a moment's notice.

"Hey," I said.

"Amity," he turned and greeted me with a smile in his voice. He wore his familiar armor now, the armor that would always remind me of Diablo.

"What are you thinking about?" I asked.

"Many things, but the safety of BoKama weighs on my mind," he said.

"Why does no one kill the Queen while she sleeps?" I said.

"Would you?" Natheka asked me, his voice quiet but curious.

I thought of the unfiltered glee in the Ikma's voice when she asked BoKama to read that awful filth about a covenant. But then I thought of the Tree Thief. The shegoshe-tax. Diablo. The rokhura.

"No. And the Ikthekal won't kill her when she is defenseless," I said. Natheka pulled me into his arms.

"And the BoKama will not because she loves her," Natheka said. "They have been together a long time, and something she said made me think it wasn't always so hateful between them."

"It's sad," I said. "But you did something wonderful today."

"What is that?" he said.

"Your horrible impression of Naraxthel made BoKama suspicious," I said. "I think it may have bought her more time, if I understand the situation correctly."

"I hope so," he said. "You also did something wonderful today."

"Oh?"

"Pattee told me you were instrumental in leading them out of the ship," he said, his voice thick with emotion. "Had you obeyed Hivelt and Naraxthel's orders ...."

I scoffed.

"Just because we're heart mates doesn't mean you big hunters can control us," I said.

"You are right," he said. "But it is just as I told you, is it not, my friend?"

"Hmm," I said and looked up at the wolfish helmet. "I've been meaning to talk to you about that."

"About control?" he said. He slipped his hands around the axial ring of my flight suit and found the fastening. Click.

Then he removed his own. Click.

"Not about control," I said, my voice sounding naked in the radio-wave saturated air. "About being friends."

"Ah, you have given it thought, and you finally realize the folly in preferring a devil dog to me," he said. "You *are* a clever sister."

Chuckling, I stood on my tiptoes and pulled at his neck until his face was close to mine.

"No, I will always prefer Diablo over you as a friend," I whispered. Then I touched my lips to his, just a gentle peck. "Because I will always prefer you over Diablo as a heart mate."

I felt Natheka's warm breath kiss my lips, and we stayed like that, breathing each other's air, unsung music mingling among the gas molecules and the radio waves between us.

A shout brought me up short, and Natheka grabbed me and crouched, a sword in his hand before I could blink.

"A devil dog!" Pattee called again. I spun to see her suited up with her javelin poised above her shoulder, and I untangled myself from Natheka's arms, spinning to find Pattee's target.

A lone white devil dog stood at the perimeter of the woodland where it tapered off into a ridgeline directly west.

"Do not throw," Hivelt said in a low voice coming up behind us. "I have seen this devil dog before."

"Are you sure?" Pattee asked.

"Yes," I said, my voice a squeak. "*Dios mio, es mi perrito!* Diablo!" I jumped out from Natheka's arm, barely registering his bark of a laugh.

I ran toward the devil dog, arms open wide, and Diablo took a step forward. Before I lunged to hug him, I remembered where I was and what he was and skidded a foot short. Panting, I knelt in front of him and held my hand out.

Diablo sniffed it, his eyes never straying from mine. When he had sniffed every particle of skin, he gifted me with a gentle swipe of his tongue, and then tossed his head. He trotted past me and padded around the hunters, pausing to sniff at Natheka's boots. He circled the tree Raxthezana had been leaning against and lifted his leg to pee on it. Then he pranced to the tech-slave and stared Naraxthel down as he urinated on the robot's feet.

The others stared with open mouths as he trotted between them and then returned to the ridgeline. He stood proud, a stiff wind blowing his tail and the setting suns casting him in silhouette. Then he loped out of sight.

"What in the ever-living shale just happened?" Esra said, having emerged from the cave entrance only moments before.

"A pazathel-nax invaded our camp and pissed all over it," Raxthezana said.

"Amity's friend paid her a visit," Natheka said. "And he will return." Natheka held his hand out to me, and I took it, my heart overflowing with happiness.

"Natheka," Hivelt said, walking up to him. He patted Natheka's shoulder. "The mutt is your friend, as well," he said. "I will tell you about it—tomorrow," he said, looking at me with a wink. "Pattee," he said as he turned to her. "Are you ready?"

"Yeah, let's go," she said with an exaggerated stretch and fake yawn. "I am bushed. Esra, you tired?"

"Oh, um, yeah," she said. "Totally wiped out. Come on, Red." She dragged Naraxthel who scowled at the poop smear left by Raxthezana's boot print when he stalked into the cave.

They re-entered the cave where we planned to bed down for the night.

Natheka's laugh rumbled and sent chills throughout my body.

"Your fellow humans are weak," he said. "They need extra rest before we trek to the Agothe-Fazetha on the morrow."

"And I don't?" I said, reaching my hands out to him.

"Nay," he said, taking them and pulling me into his chest. "You are the strongest of them. Of this, I have no doubt."

Laughing, I looked up into his stunning face.

"I don't know about that," I said. "But I do know that I would fight anything or anyone to keep you."

"This I know," he said. "But Goddesses willing, you need never do that again, for you have me."

He tilted his head and pressed his lips against mine, catching my gasp in his mouth like a net. But then, he *was* a hunter.

I clung to him and kissed him back, touching my lips to his in a pattern of growing intensity, fanning flames of desire that promised a joyful conflagration. When his mouth opened in a slight part, I captured his lower lip between my teeth and bit down, the softest, kindest bite any predator could inflict on another. But then again, *I* was a hunter, too. *Mas o menos.* If those mysterious dreams were any indication, then Predator Planet needed my kind of hunter as much as it needed women like Pattee and Esra. The kind of hunter that finds the wounded and incomplete, the underdog, and nurses them back to health, making them whole. *Y yo tambien.* And me too.

Epilogue

Raxkarax

Gusts of breath blew past my lips as I strained at the edge of the fault. Miles had I trekked with little to no violence. Perhaps the animals had migrated to the moraine; maybe the wandering rogues found elsewhere to hunt. But the absence of combat doubled my anxiety; I had no outlet, and fear scraped my insides like claws on slate rock.

My heart cramped in cycles. There was no question in my mind or body that I must seek this human pod in the bowel of the Agothe-Fatheza, but one question stood alone at the horizon of my thoughts. How would I reach her?

Dirt rained over my helmet, and I dug my claws deeper into the edge, recalling events of the last half-zatik. While I had puzzled over traversing the poisonous swamp that was the abomination of Ikthe, the ground began to shake. The quake's violence grew so sharp that I could not keep my balance.

With rending noises racing toward me, I had gripped the ground, watching in terror as a great crack fissured its way along an invisible path until it ripped away from before me. If it gaped wider, my journey to the Agothe-Fatheza would be hindered, delayed, or even ruined.

Even as the ground trembled, I strove to stand, stumbling and holding my arms wide for balance. I ran toward the heave of land and jumped, grasping the ledge and kicking my boot spikes into the soil and rock, sticking to the wall jutting up from the ground like a tree lizard.

I hung on, waiting for the rocking to subside, the rolling heaves reminding me of a ship at sea, and my stomach threatened to heave as well.

The violence of the quaking ebbed, and I took the chance to climb, hugging the ledge and pushing myself higher until I straddled it, and then swung my other leg up. I rolled away from the edge, panting and gasping, and waited for more calamity to befall me.

When the shaking stopped, I sat up and looked out over the ledge. I widened my eyes and couldn't help the gaping of my mouth when I observed the giant chasm that stretched for hundreds of veltiks in either direction. I rose to standing and peered down into the crevasse. It plunged into darkness.

The land I now stood on was permanently separated from the Bladed Forest, the great wilderness that spread to the south of the Plain of Ancient Ice.

Facing south, I marched to my new destiny. If I was to hike into the Agothe-Fatheza, I needed supplies only Ikthe could provide. My pack was laden with food stores gifted me by the others; two water pouches dangled from my belt, and a bone knife graced my side; it was a gift from Pattee. Esra had given me a small black rock, suggesting I might find a use for it because it was magnetic. Now I hunted for the dirt-tongue. Puddle birds. An acid-spitter and a spiny warted rock-climber if I could find one.

I entered the Bristled Barrens with caution. The Barrens boasted the remains of what was once a vast wilderness of hardwood trees. An ancient cataclysm had rendered a once-lush wood into a waste of split trunks, all stabbing at the sky like accusing black fingers. Everywhere one looked stood darkened trees stripped of leaves and branches. The ground, brittle and cracked, hoarded its sparse growth of dry grasses or the occasional briar patch.

One would think such a place free of dangerous animals; it appeared there was nowhere to hide, no burrows to retreat into, no sheltering treefalls. But the Barrens protected the one resource it abounded in. Tree Thieves.

Switching my helmet to thermal imaging would give me a slight advantage when I came upon these predators and activating my camouflage might spare me a jotik's moment of surprise. With the mighty divide cutting off any other routes, I had no choice but to face this forbidding land and its inhabitants.

For ten veltiks, the trunks bordering the Barrens jutted in sparse clumps, but the deeper one walked into the wood, the closer together they became. Though I walked with careful step, it still seemed my every movement sent an echoing blast of sound through the trees. If my pack brushed against the crumbling black bark, if my boot dislodged a pebble or my sword trailed past a spindly branch, the noises reverberated across the compacted ground.

Nerves fraying with every step, I longed to hear the comforting voices of my companions. Hivelt with his bravado and daring heart mate, she of the solemn face but ready service. Naraxthel's stories and little Esra showing delight at rocks so common as to be invisible. I missed Raxthezana with his grousing about the non-existent goddesses. For one who didn't believe in them, he invoked their names as often as the rest of us, if not more. I wondered if Natheka had yet rescued his human and what she would be like.

Shaking my head, I trudged on, ears tuned to the stealthiest sound. I might be a lumbering fool in this region bristling with dead trees, but even the great Tree Thief must press its weight into the dirt or squeeze between the unforgiving tree trunks. Its presence would be made known soon enough.

Grim reality pressed me to turn my back on my brethren, my past, and my old trail. Before me lay the path to a perilous future, but if I lived, it would be a future with a heart mate at my side.

Playlist

Kill Beautiful Things, DED
    Lifeline, Bad Wolves
Hunger Strike, Temple of the Dog
Hunter's Moon, Ghost
Supercharged, Ayron Jones
My Name is Human, Highly Suspect
Halo 4 Main Menu soundtrack
Oblivion Movie Soundtrack
Space Lord, Monster Magnet
Welcome to the Jungle, Guns N Roses
Don't Fear the Reaper, Blue Oyster Cult
Monster, EXO

Acknowledgments

C ousin James Mueller for consultation about EOD.

    Allison Pratt for the comparison of the jokapazathel to a parakeet/potato hybrid.

Buffyanna for believing in me long before I knew I could write at length in this genre.

Sherry Falzone for hours of consulting and insight.

SFR Authors Chat for preserving Diablo's life.

Lori Swenson and Kim Knobloch for unbridled support and encouragement.

Donna Keusch for encouragement and intelligent questions.

Donna MacKnight for gentle cattle prods for me to keep going.

Victoria Clapton for treasured cheerleading, expressions of hope, and all-around best friendedness.

Elizabeth Amhearst for the fastest and best beta read in the West, as well as vital suggestions re: electrolytes.

My daughter-in-law for correct usage of Spanish and Mexican idioms.

Monserrat Corvus for her thorough read-through, sensitivity catches and correct usage of Spanish, as well as more common Mexican superlatives.

Paul Hale for insightful and thorough alpha reading.

My fans who waited patiently and impatiently for this book. I'm sorry I was no match for the pandemic, but I think I'm finally getting a handle on both my ADHD and my writing career. Let's see if I can get Books 4 and 5 out sooner rather than later!

MORE BOOK LINKS

P ay a visit to my website for excerpts, news, and random tidbits: www.loveivickyholt.com

Subscribers to my newsletter receive a free copy of "Stranded on Mining Planet", a 46k word novella that reads like a full-length book. It takes place in the IGMC/Predator Planet Universe, but not the actual Predator Planet. https://BookHip.com/HVNPFJT

Did you miss any of the books? Links below:

https://books2read.com/u/bzBLqEHunted on Predator Planet Book 1

https://books2read.com/u/3LxG8eTracked on Predator Planet Book 2

https://books2read.com/u/mg7Az0Hounded on Predator Planet Book 3

https://books2read.com/u/m0qXKMTrapped on Predator Planet Book 4

https://books2read.com/u/mYDRpxHidden in Predator Planet Book 5

If you love the crash landing/hunted in the jungle trope, you'll probably love "The Krinar Savage" by my pen name, Chris Roxboro.

https://books2read.com/u/3RLgqY

And if you love the Krinar world created by the talented Anna Zaires, (whose permission I received before writing in the Krinar world), you may enjoy The Krinar Rake by Chris Roxboro. (Be warned, this book takes place in Chicago in relative contemporary circumstances so is nothing like the Predator Planet books.)

https://books2read.com/u/med9eV